SEAN LESTER DURHAM

15 Hours

Believing the impossible, is just the beginnin**g**.

This book is a work of fiction. Names, Characters, places, and incidents are the product of the author's imagination or are used fictitiously. Any resemblance to actual events, locales, or persons, living or dead, is coincidental.

Content

ALSO BY SEAN LESTER DURHAM

Welcome Home Thomas Burcher

—

Six Steps

—

9 Days

—

Page Intentionally Left Blank

<u>Chapter One</u>

L ooking down at the shopping cart, which was piled to the top, I was legitimately confused. I'd no idea this much stuff was necessary for a birthday party for a three-year-old girl. I shook my head in disbelief.

"Why are you looking at the cart like that, hun?" Sabrina chuckled.

"Do we really need all of this?" I replied, slightly annoyed.

"She's turning three, sweetie, not getting her own apartment."

Sabrina snickered softly and turned back around to face the shelf that held the paper plates and napkins.

"Honey, I calculated everything to the letter and trust me, what we have here probably won't even be enough." I doubted the sincerity of that statement, but my wife had this real annoying habit of being right about these things.

I never was. Ever.

"Well, can we hurry it up at least?"

I murmured, glancing down at my watch.

"I still have to grab her present from the pet store and it's getting late."

"You were supposed to do that yesterday, weren't you?" Sabrina quickly replied.

I was certain she already knew the answer to her question.

"Yes sweetie I was, but I got so caught up on getting ready for this Tokyo trip. Let's not forget that I'm the one that wanted to get her the kitchen set, but you're the one insisting we get her this puppy."

"Well," replied Sabrina, "she's been crying about this puppy for the past year, and I think it's ok if she finally gets one, don't you? They said, and even you've said at times, that these German Shepherds are the best kind of dogs for small kids. They're protective, and I figured that alone would help seal the deal with you."

Before I could open my mouth to respond, Sabrina's face was already a half inch away from mine.

"Besides," she grinned. "It'll give her something to focus on when we need our time together, right? At least until we're comfortable enough to put her in daycare or school, whichever one comes first."

I couldn't help but to smile. She was good. She knew what to say and when to say it.

"Of course, sweetie," I replied behind my smile. "But do you really believe a puppy will keep her attention for as long as we need it to?"

Chuckling shyly, Sabrina turned her attention back to the shelves.

With three girls; ages sixteen, twelve and now three, I'd gone through my fair share of girl's birthday parties over the years. I was completely familiar with the "process." I was practically an expert at this point. I cherished these moments. I was leaving early in the am for a weeklong business trip to Tokyo, and not seeing my girls during that time, made moments like these much more special and important.

Leaving the family for overseas business trips was never an easy thing to do—bitter-sweet indeed. It's been this way since my promotion. A promotion that now required me to travel overseas at least once a month. A promotion that solidified my title—the Chief Architecture Manager for *Havock and Company Architecture*.

I spent years designing small projects, but now I was responsible for making sure projects, seemingly huge projects, started and finished by the strict deadlines set.

Havock and Company had grown and expanded over the years, gradually transitioning into legitimate projects on virtually every continent. It was an important position, but it kept me away from my family and frankly, at times, it has kept me away from the world. Work was first, it was essential, but my being in this position, was due to relentless, persistent and dedicated hard work over the years, along with a bit of extreme and unfortunate luck.

When my two oldest daughters were four and one, I was a couple of years out of college, working a dead-end job, struggling to pay bills. I decided to not stop, to continue diligently working towards what I wanted, what I needed, until I got it. It's essentially what we did to get to a position we strategically aimed for. I'm proud of that, but over the years, it's become difficult to ignore the distance I sometimes felt coming in between my family and I

A better way of life wasn't the only motivation for my fierce determination and hunger. The fact that I almost lost both Sabrina and Natalie, played a lot into me changing my entire perspective on family and life in general.

Sabrina's pregnancy with Natalie didn't go full term. It was a kidney infection that nearly cost them their lives right after Natalie was born. It was something that damaged my faith in the world and ultimately, restored it again. Now here I was, another year, another party. It was more fun than I imagined it would be. The smile on Natalie's face made it all worth it. She enjoyed it, and I enjoyed the fact that she enjoyed it.

We named her birthday present "Bucky." Natalie instantly fell in love with him. Once again, my wife had nailed it. Watching Natalie play with Bucky was one of those moments in which I'd cherish forever. It would always remain in the deepest parts of my subconscious where those memories resided. As I found myself lost in my daughter's jubilation and indescribable happiness, I would occasionally glance over and catch my wife staring at me, grinning, with the "*I told you so*" look.

We gazed upon the brightly lit face of our three-year-old daughter, who had instantly fallen in love with this animal, the one that I argued against for the past few weeks. It was situations like these in which being wrong never felt so wonderful. I took a step back as the kids played, ate, and danced to the music with Sabrina. I closed my eyes for a moment, and just like that, the kids and the noise were gone.

Laying firmly on my back, on top of my bed falling asleep—the day had worn me ragged. I heard Sabrina downstairs vacuuming. I honestly tried forcing myself to get up and go down and help her finish what was left of the cleaning, but I figured I'd close my eyes for just a second. I was tired, so tired. I found myself drifting off to sleep, just for a few seconds before going down and helping her. I peeked over at the clock; *9:17 pm.* My eyes got heavier as I soon drifted off to sleep. Wasn't long before I slowly opened my eyes, the clock read; *4:23 am.* My eyes felt as heavy as bricks. I couldn't believe I'd actually slept this long. My flight was scheduled to leave at 6:00 am, so I was essentially already cutting it closer than I'd planned.

I quickly hopped out of bed, but not before leaning over to kiss Sabrina who was deep asleep. I made my way into each of my daughter's room and kissed them each on their foreheads, something I did every time I left in the mornings. During regular work weeks, they would already be up, and we would all essentially leave at the same times, but when I had early flights, I would catch them sleeping peacefully, like this morning. I had to move Bucky out of the way in order to get to Natalie. It had only been one night, but he had already decided that the twenty-dollar doggy bed apparently wasn't good enough for him. Natalie's bed was perfect enough for him. I gazed down at her and smiled. I thought about how much joy, happiness, and overall fulfillment she and my other girls brought to my life. They all had special characteristics. Each were one of a kind. But Natalie was not only different, she was special, extremely wise and unimaginably caring. She was more of her mother than me—they all were.

The drive to Orlando International Airport was about twenty-five minutes from my home in Altamonte Springs, Florida, but it always felt a much shorter drive than that. Altamonte Springs was home, going on ten years now. *Havock and Company* operated primarily out of Manhattan, but they conducted business all around the world so there really wasn't a need for me to be in the same location as the company itself. I did a lot of work from home and of course, traveled accordingly when needed.

Sabrina, my wife, was a Sioux Chef at a relatively upscale restaurant in downtown Orlando. She was passionate about cooking and that, I admired about her. Nevertheless, when I left on business trips, which was quite a bit, I was always concerned about the burden she carried in maintaining the house. I wasn't oblivious to what she was doing and how she was handling it. It was undoubtedly tough. She would always tell me that when it was time for me to slow down and be at home more, God would see to it and make it happen. Deep down, I felt I was the one not supporting *her* enough at home and the only person that could change that was me. I was looking to right that wrong as quick as possible.

The early morning, pre-dawn drives to the airport always allotted me the much-needed quiet time alone to deeply ponder on my life. My mind was relatively clouded for the most part. It was clouded with my day-to-day activities, work, and focus on being what I needed to be for my family. There wasn't any more room for anything else. My career would always be the first thing I found myself pondering on. *"Funny"* would be the first word that comes to mind when attempting to describe the life changing, unconventional, and slightly unbelievable way I found myself in my professional position to begin with. But there was hardly anything amusing about it.

Nearly fifteen years ago, and I remember as if it was yesterday—one of those days I would never forget, for as long as I live, due to the direct and immediate impact it had on my life.

I was driving from Columbia, South Carolina, back to Florida from a business trip, after having just joined the company that fall. I was fresh out of grad school and was thrown right into the fire— the real world. The business trip was a complete failure. Had it not been for the unfortunate and tragic events that followed, I probably wouldn't have lasted as long as I have with the company. The shocking radio broadcasts broke through the car like an armored truck through a barricade.

"The Tragedy in the Sky," is what they were calling it. To call it "tragic" would be an understatement of sizable proportions.

On November 19th, 2000, four 757s coming in from four different major commercial airports across the United States, all carrying a total of four hundred and fifty passengers, collided into one another in midair over the Dallas metropolitan area. The tragic events of that day saw my company lose its Vice-President and seven other high-profile members. This set-in motion, a wave that caused ripples to trickle all the way down to me. The very next week, I was promoted to one of the high-profile positions previously held by one of the unfortunate souls on one of the doomed flights. It all shook me to the core.

Not only did I suffer from imposter syndrome for quite some time afterwards, I had a very difficult time dealing with it considering it hit so close to home. But that day not only changed my path in life, it changed my outlook on the world, life, death, everything. Nothing has changed since that day.

Here I was, fifteen years later, about two positions away from being President of the company myself, but the empty feeling I had buried deep within me had a lot to do with the fact that as much as I loved my family, I wasn't home being a father, a husband, nearly as much as I needed to be. It bothered me immensely. This was a part of my life that was broken and no matter how much I pretended that it wasn't, it was.

As always, when traveling for business, the closer I got to the airport, the more nervous I got. I was still quite afraid of flying, but this flight was one of those I would probably suffer more from boredom than fright. Fifteen hours from here to Tokyo. I wasn't looking forward to it or the jet lag. The walk down the half mile terminal toward my gate was very exhausting, but boarding was surprisingly quick this time.

I boarded the plane, found my seat, retrieved my iPod from my carry-on and wasted no time plugging the instrumental and soundtrack tunes into my ear, as I laid my head against the window. I closed my eyes and felt myself gradually beginning to relax as I was still exhausted from the day before. It wasn't long at all before I was airborne, headed for Tokyo as I left everything behind.

Chapter Two

The Counsel of Father Miyake

Two days had passed since arriving in Japan. Two days of nothing but meetings, and the usual attempts at stalling by contractors. I figured they'd discover who they were dealing with before I left, like always.

These business trips were always eye openers, and provided me with tons of insight, but they always ended the way I needed them to, for the most part.

The vibration on my hip startled me slightly. It was the phone. I quickly retrieved the phone from my hip and noticed that I had about twelve missed calls – all from Sabrina. I nervously dialed Sabrina's number, as I gradually made my way out of the room and into the hallway for a bit of privacy.

"Sabrina?"

"Steve—I've been calling and calling........"

"I know sweetie. I've been in meetings all morning and had my phone on silent. What's going on?"

In all my years of marriage, Sabrina had never sounded so distraught, so defeated, and so blatantly dark. I instantly knew something was wrong. Hearing my wife break down over the phone, immediately ripped everything from within me. I knew right away that I wouldn't be able to handle what she needed to tell me. A part of me wanted to simply pull the phone away from my ear, as if that would save me from the inevitable.

"Baby what's wrong?! What's going on?!"
I heard Sabrina voice starting to recede away from the phone as her cries rang out in the background.

"Sabrina?!"

"Steve? Can you hear me?"
Immediately hearing my mother-in-law's voice didn't help my heart. It only added to my sudden fears that whatever it was, my wife didn't have the strength to tell me.

"Ma!! What's going on?"

"Steve... "
My heart pounded uncontrollably at this point, and I was running out of air. She paused.
I was growing nervously impatient at this point.

"Ma, just tell me. Just...whatever it is, just tell me."
I could hear my mother-in-law on the other end taking a deep breath, and I knew it was a struggle for her to let go of whatever it was that she was holding on to. I knew it

wasn't anything good, as my eyes began to fill with tears, just out of fear alone.

"There's been an accident. It's Natalie....."

"Oh God! My baby, where's my baby Ma?"

"Steve, listen to me, just......listen. The puppy, it fell into the pool, and Natalie jumped in to save him, she.... " My mother-in-law paused once more as she began to break down, but I could hear her fighting through the pain, through her breakdown, to tell me what she needed to tell me. She was struggling, mightily.

"Steve, she jumped into the pool to save the puppy, and she saved him Steve. She saved him, but she didn't make it. Our baby is gone. I'm so sorry." My eyes widened and my heart began to race as I listened to what my mother-in-law was telling me. Hearing her breakdown over the phone cause my legs to give way as I stumbled backwards into the door. My co-workers immediately began filtering into the hallway upon hearing the noise of my dead weight falling against the door. They were looking at me confused while helping me up to my feet.

"Are you ok, Steve?"

My co-workers appeared very frightened and concerned, the frightened look on my face probably didn't help matters. As soon as I was helped to my feet, I immediately sprinted full speed out of the building, moving rapidly toward the parking lot where my car was located.

"I'm coming home now Ma," I yelled into the phone.

"Ma, I'm coming home now!"

I ended the call and hopped into the car. I immediately started the engine and raced towards my hotel. I refused to believe what I just heard. I couldn't accept it. I wouldn't accept it. Eventually, I knew I had to wake up from this nightmare—an extreme case of denial I found myself submerged in.

"WAKE UP STEVE!!" I cried out.

I smacked myself across my face, as I frantically raced down the highway. A nightmare, that's all this was. There was no way that this was happening.

"WAKE UP!!" I screamed.

I was going about seventy miles per hour on the highway, dodging in and out of traffic. At this point, I was gone, mentally. I wasn't even sure if I was driving or flying. Nothing else existed outside of my world at this moment. I was nowhere *and* everywhere at the same time. It was essentially as if I was outside of myself.

"Pleeeeease God, No!" I yelled as I shook my head.

"NO!"

For what felt like an eternity, my eyes were closed as I

raced down the highway. I suddenly felt my heart begin to race faster, dangerously fast. It felt like someone was beating a bass drum in my chest, non-stop. It started to become very difficult to breath. I finally opened my eyes. The cars around me started to become blurry. I didn't see the back of the car I was rapidly approaching, but I didn't see much of anything at this point. My eyes were focused directly ahead, but my mind was not in the same place as my body. I managed to snap out of my mini daydream, but it was already too late. I slammed into the back of a car. The impact was fierce. I felt every bit of it, as my head instantly bounced off the steering wheel. I immediately felt myself starting to black out but wasn't completely unconscious. Not yet. I could feel myself slumped helplessly over the steering wheel as I heard the horn blaring loudly. I took one short breath after another and found it difficult and slightly painful to breath. I didn't know what dying felt like, but figured this was as close to it, as I struggled mightily to keep my eyes open. I fought, but it was to no avail. I heard the people around me attempting to open the door to assist me. I never saw them, I only heard them, but their voices sounded far away. My chest burned as my lungs struggled to circulate sufficient oxygen. I no longer had the energy to fight the state of unconsciousness that quickly overwhelmed me as I closed my eyes.

My eyes slowly opened. The pain in my chest felt faint, but it was there. I felt extremely dizzy, but immediately realized that I was lying in a bed, gazing up at a white ceiling. The last thing I remembered was crashing on the highway. It didn't take long to gather myself and my thoughts. It didn't take long for me to remember the pain, the phone call from Sabrina and my mother-in-law. The tears immediately began to fall, as I vividly replayed the conversation in my head.

"How are you feeling son?"

The voice derived from my right. I turned my head towards the voice and standing there was a man. He appeared to be a man of the cloth—a priest. The collar the priest was wearing, along with the Bible he was carrying—dead giveaway. He appeared to be a young priest, probably in his early forties at the most.

"I uh....."

I stammered and paused as I attempted to answer his question but couldn't find the right words to do so. I gazed back up at the ceiling as I shook my head. The pain was still there, and it was real.

"Who are you?" I replied.

The priest immediately bowed and extended his hand, apparently expecting a handshake in return.

"My name is Father Haru Miyake."
I stared at the man's hand, and didn't realize until he pulled it back, that I hadn't returned the gesture. I don't think I ignored it purposely, my mind just wasn't in the room. Father Miyake took a step back and smiled, genuinely.

"Your company contacted me through the embassy a few hours ago. They sent me here to make sure you were ok."

"And to see if I've completely lost it, huh?"

"Well, though your mental state is very important, they seemed genuinely concerned about your well-being. They sounded extremely genuinely heartbroken on the phone when I spoke with them. I too want to extend my condolences for your loss."
Father Miyake gazed deep into my eyes as he spoke.

"Your name is Steve? Can I call you Steve?"

"I don't care." I quickly replied.
Father Miyake continued to speak, but I immediately and unconsciously tuned him out. I didn't hear much of anything he was saying. I nodded my head as I saw his mouth moving but didn't hear the words. I didn't respond right away, as it was very difficult for me to say anything at

this point. Deep down, I didn't want to do anything except cry until I had nothing left, until I fell dead. I simply couldn't even look at Father Miyake.

I gradually glared up towards the ceiling, but immediately closed my eyes while Father Miyake continued to speak. I felt the tears slowly began to fall down my face.

"No, Father, I refuse to believe it. Why?!!" I cried out while shaking my head in denial.

 I immediately fell back on to the bed and began crying. My sudden outburst startled the priest somewhat, but he quickly gathered himself. I buried my face in my hands. Father Miyake stopped talking, slowly stood up and walked gingerly towards the window. He slowly turned toward me and began walking in my direction.

"I cannot imagine the pain that you're dealing with right now, but just know that God... "

"Please.... Just don't. Save it."

I interrupted the priest as I glared at him, angrily.

"God, isn't here, nor has he ever been here. Don't waste your time here with that."

 I angrily wiped my eyes and face and took a deep breath, forcing myself to calm down, in order to converse appropriately with Father Miyake. I truly wanted, needed to hear what he had to say. I knew he had a rebuttal— they always did.

Father Miyake glanced at me with a look that suggested he understood. He nodded his head at everything I was saying. I was certain he didn't agree with it, but I knew he likely understood my pain and frustration at this point, or he was at least trying to.

"Why Father? Why was she taken from me? Why did your God take my daughter?!!

Father Miyake slowly walked closer to me, and gently placed his hand on my shoulder.

"Son, you look at it as God "taking" your daughter, but she is his daughter as well. You were simply caring for her until he called her home."
I shook my head, stubbornly, as the tears fell freely.

"I refuse to believe that, Father. I can't accept that. She was my baby. Why would God give me something so irreplaceable, so full of life, so engaging, and just take it all away from me?"

Father Miyake gently smiled at me as he gazed deep into my eyes.

"Steve, your natural human and earthly eye shows you what you want to see, and rarely does it show you what you need to see. And that's ok. We're all deceived at times here on earth by what we see and what we think we know. You truly must walk by faith, and not by sight. The universe is bigger than your daughter, bigger than you and I, but this life is all that we've known, since we've crawled around as babies. This life, the way we exist, is the only thing we know. We're used to this and only this, nothing else. When the universe—which has been ordained and given permission by God, to take and give as it pleases, calls us to begin that other journey, a journey we all eventually have to go on one day, we naturally, logically, and understandably get scared. We're scared because of the fear of the unknown."

There was a long pause as Father Miyake took a moment to gauge my reaction to what he just shared with me.

"Steve, did any of your daughters cry when you first dropped them off at daycare for the first time?"

The question initially came across as slightly rhetorical, so I didn't respond right away, as the memories of me dropping each of my daughters off for the first time suddenly popped into my head.

"Yes." I softly replied.

"That's because they were afraid." he whispered. "Afraid of the unknown. They were being separated from everything they'd ever known since birth. We are no different when it comes to life and death. We look at death, and sometimes the unexplainable things in life, in such a negative light but in reality, we should embrace it.

We should embrace life, death and all that comes with it. Embrace the journey, because make no mistake about it my son, there is a journey, and Natalie is on her's right now. People are afraid of what they don't understand, and it's hard to understand this. It's hard to use faith during the times we really need to."

I tilted my head back frustratingly, as I closed my eyes while listening to Father Miyake. I was hearing him. What he was sharing with me, was surprisingly comforting on the surface, as I understood the logic in it, but it did nothing to numb the sharp pain deep within. It comforted me to a certain extent, but there was still a stinging and piercing feeling in my heart right now. A feeling that no medicine or priest could possibly cure or heal.

"Mr. Trawick? How are we feeling?"
The Doctor's voice suddenly rang out, startling me as he walked into the room. I never looked his way.

"I'm fine Doc," I replied, as I gazed aimlessly out of the window. "When can I leave? I really need to go home now. My family needs me."
The Doctor wasted no time as he nodded his head.

"Well you suffered a severe anxiety or panic attack while driving—which of course, caused the crash. The crash didn't cause any significant injuries aside from bruising, and a minor head injury, but your lungs were impacted by the attack. They struggled to circulate air adequately during the three to four minutes before passing out. That caused minor strain on your lungs, nothing major. I do, however, want to monitor your lungs and breathing over the next twenty-four to forty-eight hours, and then you can go home."

I immediately shook my head slowly in disagreement.

"I feel fine Doc, considering the circumstances. I need to go home and be with my family right now."

The Dr. paused, smiled and stood up, preparing to leave.

"I know Mr. Trawick, and I promise you, I'll get you out of here soon as possible so you can get home. I just want to make sure you're ok."

He leaned in closer, as he checked my vitals.

"It's imperative we make sure your lungs can handle a long flight back in an airplane after suffering the attack you did."

The doctor nodded his head in my direction as to seal the discussion, turned, and quickly walked out of the room.

I turned towards Father Miyake.

"Father, before I woke up and saw you standing next to me, I had a dream. I dreamed that Natalie was sitting on my lap and looked into my eyes with a really innocent look, and she said to me...."

Pausing mid-sentence, I caught myself becoming emotional.

"She was sitting on my lap and looked me in my face, it was so real, really vivid– she says; *"its ok daddy, he'll take care of it after you lose power."*
I was confused, and I was certain that my face conveyed that sentiment.

"What could that possibly mean? That has to mean something, doesn't it father?"

Father Miyake turned toward the window and smiled– deep in thought, clearly pondering on my question. I began staring out of the window with him as I waited for his response. I knew deep down, Father Miyake probably knew I wanted this dream and everything else my mind now perceived to be closely "related" to what I was dealing with, to mean something, anything to help it all make sense. I was looking for anything of substance to grab hold to at this point. I unrealistically wanted Father Miyake to have all the answers. I knew he didn't. With a gentle smile across his face, Father Miyake stood up and gingerly walked towards the window. He stood in front of the window, looking out over the city, with his hands in his pockets.

"A few years ago," he finally replied. "I had a vivid dream that has stuck with me ever since. I dreamt that I was inside a hospital one moment, and the next, a group of kids were carrying my body out of what appeared to be rubble. To this day, I assumed that rubble was the hospital, in some sort of disaster. If I told you that I knew what that dream meant, I'd be lying to you. That dream happened almost two years ago, and to this day, it truly has no significant meaning to me or my life. But the universe is so vast and immense that my dream may have meaning for someone else's life. That dream could've been someone else's dream, possibly one of those kids that was carrying me. It's a possibility that one of them could've dreamed that they were with a group of kids and for some strange reason they had to carry a priest through the rubble."

I was taken aback at how open-minded Father Miyake was coming across. I'd never heard a priest speak the way he spoke. I believed my face must've held the same expression or slight shock that I was feeling as he smiled and continued.

"I'm a priest, a man of God, Steven but I've never confined my beliefs, my thinking, to a box. It's kind of the main reason the hospital requests me so often to come in here and provide grief counseling. People tend to shy away from religion and its consistent, judgmental sentiments. As far as your dream, I haven't the slightest idea as to what it means. I have come to the realization that it most likely, and I do use the phrase "most likely" loosely, means that at some point, in an existence somewhere in time, that dream was more than a dream. We don't know what it means my son, and we may never know. It requires faith, strong iron clad faith, as a key component necessary to take part of this journey. The journey we take through God's creation called the universe."

He was undoubtedly reading my face, looking for any noticeable expression or response from me.

"I feel so powerless." I whispered, as I shook my head and closed my eyes. "I feel as though I don't have any strength left. I can't begin to know how to be there for my family when I return home. I don't know how I can be strong enough when I'm not even strong enough to hold my own head up right now, much less my entire family's. I just feel like I have no say in what happens in my life or my family's lives, and frankly father, that scares me."

Father Miyake smiled. His smile was genuine. I could tell he truly enjoyed what he did, and truly loved counseling.

"Steve, the last thing you should feel is powerless. Half of the time, we're so caught up in our day to day lives that we don't even realize the life, the power, we have within ourselves, with our tongues and with our thoughts. But sometimes it takes us stepping out on faith in order to realize the power and ability we have. We won't know unless we open ourselves up and began speaking life into the universe to affect the things around us that appear to be incapable of being moved or changed. There are times, as humans, when we're opened to receiving any and everything the universe has for us. Usually, these times are when our minds are completely opened for whatever reasons, albeit good or difficult, but opened, nonetheless. It is then, we have the ability to change everything, anything, but it requires stepping out of the norm and into faith. There are no mistakes in this life. I truly believe it all happens for a reason—everything. You just have to be able to understand what that reason is and determine how that reason affects you going forward. "

I knew deep down in my mind, deep down in my currently withered soul, there wasn't a legitimate reason for my daughter to no longer be here right now. At least not to me it wasn't, and no one would convince me otherwise.

Not this man, not even God himself. In a way, what Father Miyake was saying made sense, but I chuckled at the notion that this was all planned. As Father Miyake spoke, I was started to become afraid, afraid of the fact that I was beginning to *somewhat* accept what he was saying, and that started to bother me.

"When things like this happen Father, is this your God working in "mysterious ways"? Because I for one don't understand it at all."

Father Miyake grinned gingerly as he again gazed out of the window at the steadily darkening sky as evening approached.

"God doesn't work in mysterious ways, Steve. We simply haven't the cognitive understanding and brain capacity to realize that the ways we deem "mysterious" are actually normal, all things considered. There is no such thing as "mysterious ways." There is only what you see and know, and what you're supposed to be seeing and knowing. We are a long way from seeing and knowing what we're supposed to because of our worldly ways as humans. Our minds are currently too.....busy. Too cluttered."

I tried not to smile, but the way he spoke, amused me, just slightly. We stared at each other in silence for about five seconds before he smiled. Speaking with him provided me with a bit of comfort I hadn't expect to feel this quickly.

"Father, you seem like a fine man, but has anyone ever tell you that you should work on communication? You speak in riddles."

His smile widened as he accepted my critique.

"I get that a lot," he chuckled. "But I know when the time comes, you'll not only understand what I'm saying, but you'll wonder why you didn't understand it sooner. Do you know the *Serenity Prayer*?"

"I don't." I quickly replied.

"Here, repeat after me," he uttered.

"God grant me the serenity to accept the things I cannot change, the courage to change the things I can, and the wisdom to know the difference."

After briefly hesitating, I repeated after him. I ended up repeating it about five times before I truly understood what I was truly saying. Father Miyake and I spent the next forty-four hours discussing life, death, and everything in between. I was hurting, and there wasn't much that I was trying to understand at this point outside of trying to utilize logic to explain Natalie's death. Father Miyake helped me get a better understanding. He helped me get a better grasp of the journey I was a part of, at the moment, despite my refusal to truly accept it. The pain firmly planted in my soul wasn't going anywhere, but at this point, it was no longer about me. It was about my family, and the immensely emotional challenges that awaited me when I returned home. But the pain had been somewhat alleviated now, primarily because of the counsel of Father Miyake. I'm not the most religious man, never have been. I hadn't paid much attention, if any, to anything outside of my immediate family and life. The only thing that existed in my mind was my family and my career. Nothing else mattered that much to me, but for a moment, for a brief moment, Father Miyake helped changed my perspective on a few things, and was able to at least get me to begin to understand.

I wasn't sure if it was the medication or the sharp emotional pain running through the deep parts of my soul, but it was as if my mind was shifting and changing, the more we spoke. The pain was still intense, and I had a feeling it would be that way for quite some time.

<u>Chapter Three</u>

Agent Jason Barrington

<u>Hour One</u>

I walked aimlessly around the Tokyo airport in a daze. I followed the meandering route through the terminal to my gate, as I prepared to board my flight. I wasn't really sure what was happening to me, but I was beginning to feel inexplicably stranger by the hour. The counseling with Father Miyake eased my spirit, and if anything, it forced me to slightly change my thinking on some things that I normally wouldn't be open to changing. I wasn't exactly sure what I'd experienced in my counsel with Father Miyake, but I was fairly certain that without his counsel, the past forty-eight hours could've gone much differently.

Nothing looked the same at this point. The sky looked different, the air smelled differently, and everybody looked different. I didn't know what it was, but my sense of awareness was suddenly sharpened, heightened and felt slightly transformed. My mind seemed to be suddenly operating with a fresh sense of clarity, a sense of openness that it never had at any point in my life. It truly felt as if the extreme grief deep within me had essentially turned something on or off within me, within my body and I had no idea why.

As I stood in the middle of the airport, I calmly gazed around. The sights, sounds, people, and the smell of the airport, all seemed so vividly present, as if I was receiving it all, everything. Whatever this was, it felt as though it was more *me* than my surroundings. Maybe this was how I was supposed to feel all the time and maybe it wasn't. It didn't take much for me to understand that my entire life, my immediate world, had been so shutoff to the universe, to everything that wasn't important to me, because I didn't allow anything in. I had closed myself, my mind, off to everything around me for such a long time that I wouldn't be surprised if I'd completely missed everything from everywhere that I was supposed to be receiving, because of it. But today, right now, it, whatever "it" was that I was missing, seemed to have found its way into my world.

I knew it wasn't a coincidence that this sudden feeling coincided with my current overwhelming grief. The day I heard about my daughter's death, my entire world shifted, something within me switched on or off, I have no idea which.

My flight was scheduled to leave Tokyo at five pm, which meant it was about six am back home. I boarded the plane, an unusually non-crowded flight for this kind of business flight.

Fifteen hours was the total flight time from Japan to Florida. Altamonte Springs, Florida was where my family and I called home for the past decade. A very quiet and peaceful suburban town, but a small town, which meant they were all likely currently in mourning over Natalie's death along with my family, at this moment. I didn't quite notice the rest of the passengers as they boarded the plane. It wasn't intentional. I constantly found myself daydreaming about Natalie.

As I made my way through my aisle, I noticed a little girl three rows behind mine, it was Natalie. I gave a quick double take, it wasn't her. My mind, undoubtedly playing tricks on me. It was indeed a girl, but not Natalie. Sitting down in my seat, I took a deep breath and slowly exhaled.

"Ok Steve, you can do this." I whispered to myself.

"Hate flying?" a voice deriving from my left asked softly behind a chuckle.

I quickly turned towards the voice. A grey bearded man, with a blue beanie on his head. He had a laptop opened in front of him on the seat tray. I was at the window seat, and he occupied the aisle seat. I had unknowingly passed him on my way to my window seat, and I hadn't even noticed him. That's how out of it I was,

I suppose.

"Umm, I guess you can say that." I replied through a forced grin.

The man nodded as he chuckled slightly. He seemed very polite, yet I really wasn't in the mood to talk to anyone right now, as Father Miyake had snatched all the conversation I had left in me for a while. I however, didn't want to be unnecessarily rude. I turned my head towards the window and begin gazing out.

One minute I was staring at the still lifeless ground of the Japanese airport, and the next—the clouds, as the plane began flying above them. I was so spaced out that I didn't actually remember taking off. But here I was, above the clouds, and my mind still back on the ground, on my family back home, and what unfortunately awaited me when I eventually got there.

I didn't know if I was truly ready for the pain that awaited me, but I could honestly say that I was probably more apt to deal with it at this point, than I was just forty-eight hours prior, thanks to the nearly two-day counsel with Father Miyake. The doctor prescribed me some medication to help me relax and to sleep during the flight. I saw no need to waste any time as I reached into my carry on to retrieve it. I shook my head, slightly confused and baffled. What I was feeling in my bag was unfamiliar to me. I gripped the cold, hard object and removed it from my bag.

"What in the world is this?" I whispered to myself. I turned the device around to view the front. I immediately discovered a note stuck to the front screen:

"Steve,

I realize that what little of your faith in life, humanity, God, and all things unseen, has been shaken, if not totally destroyed because of your unimaginable loss, and that's completely understandable. If you are the man that I believe you to be, your mind is now as opened as it has ever been, and all I ask is that you keep an open mind on everything that surrounds you. Inside this Nook is a 13-chapter story that I would like for you to read before you land. After you land, call me once you are home and had time to spend time with your family. Let me know your thoughts on this story. Once again, my sincerest condolences to you and your family. God bless -

- Father Miyake"

I stared at the note in utter confusion and surprise. It took me about three minutes, but I was eventually able to locate and press the power button on the device. Once the device powered up, I began trying to maneuver through the device, but I was unfamiliar with how it worked. I struggled mightily, like a monkey in front of a computer. I gazed around to see if anyone saw me comically struggling with the device, but everyone was either relaxing or engaged in their own electronics. Using my finger, I pressed every link and "button" on the device trying to find out what it was that Father Miyake wanted me to read.

"Is that some sort of an electronic book?" The voice uttered next to me.

"I'm sorry, what's that?" I quickly replied as I peered up at the man.

The man immediately pointed at the device in my hand.

"Is that an electronic book you have there?"

I didn't immediately respond. Instead, I examined the device like I was a scientist examining a glowing rock that just fell from space, before I ultimately began to shake my head.

"Well, yeah. Yes, it is," I finally responded as I finally spotted the word "*Nook*" on the back of the device.

"It's not mine though, that's why I look so confused. A friend of mine apparently put it in my bag without my knowledge."

I figured it was only appropriate that I at least tried to engage with the man sitting next to me. We did have about fourteen and a half hours remaining in the flight, and I figured I couldn't sit next to him this long without engaging in somewhat meaningful conversation.

"What you working on over there?" I asked the man motioning my head towards the man's laptop. The man quickly focused his attention on his laptop

"It's a write up for a film. I'm a film consultant. It's the reason for my trip to Japan." he replied behind a genuine grin.

"So you were consulting for a movie while you were over here?" I asked curiously.

He quickly nodded.

"Yep, a friend of mine is a movie producer and needed my *expertise*," he said jokingly. "I'm a retired physician so it comes in handy."

I extended my hand out towards the man.

"Steve Trawick."

The man extended his hand back.

"Dr. Bradley Thomas. Retired."

"What kind of work do you do Steve?"

I looked at him somewhat emotionlessly and forced a smile on my face.

"Uh....well, I'm an Architectural Manager for an architecture firm."

"Oh yeah? Like office buildings and such?"
"Well yeah, but not only office buildings, we design churches, stadiums, hospitals. We do it all."
"Oh? Interesting indeed." he replied.
Bradley seemed very intrigued by what I was saying. He immediately reminded me of Sabrina's uncle; genuinely sweet and asked a lot of questions.

"Were you in Japan on business?" Bradley asked.

"Yeah I was. I'm returning home now, the business trip was supposed to last until Friday, but had to cut it short early - family emergency."

I most certainly didn't want to go into the details about the emergency with Bradley at this point. But the way he looked at me, I was certain that the expression on my face didn't do a good job of hiding the pain. He picked up on it right away.

"Ah I see," Bradley uttered as he slowly nodded his head.

Bradley easily picked up the somberness behind what I was saying, and it immediately sparked an awkward silence.

"So yeah, I'm trying to see what's in this thing to read." I stated, looking down at the Nook.
It was my attempt to break the awkward silence.

"I don't know how to work one of these things. Me personally, I'm more of an old fashion, turn the page kind of reader."

"I'm with you, my friend." Bradley exclaimed as he grinned. "I read quite a bit, always have. Let me know what you're reading, there's a good chance I probably already read it."

I nodded, grinned, and turned my attention back to the Nook. I saw an icon where I believed a story should be. But instead, it was simply a blank white icon, the only icon that appeared on the screen. I didn't see anything else. I continued to look diligently. After I was unable to find any other story, I finally pressed the blank icon to reveal what appeared to be, a title-less story.

Title-less Story – Chapter One

"Pull over, I feel sick." Jason yelled to Julio, who was behind the wheel of the van.

"What?" Julio sharply replied.

"Dude, pull this shit over! I think I'm going to be sick." Jason yelled once more.

Hector quickly turned around laughing.

"Ha! Told you to stay away from that dip, dude."

"There's a little gas station coming up, I saw the sign a mile back. Pull over there." Jason heard Malvieo instruct from the passenger seat.

The van soon pulled over in front of what looked to be a small convenience store/gas station. They were about forty miles outside of the city, and they were surrounded by nothing but trees and rural land. Jason quickly hopped out of the van and ran directly towards the garbage can. The group thought it was funny as they saw Jason comically sprinting to get out of the van.

"Don't shit yourself, dude." Jason heard Rubio yell as he quickly exited the van causing an uproar of laughter from the group. Jason quickly ran over to the first trash can he saw, shoved his face in it and started throwing up, or at least they thought he was throwing up. Jason was putting on a wonderful acting job, dry heaving and such, but it was working. He sold it beautifully. After about thirty seconds, Jason lifted his head and held his stomach while grimacing.

"I'm going to run in here real quick and get some Pepto." Jason yelled to the group.

"Dude!! Hurry the hell up, we got to get this taken care of, ASAP!" Malvieo yelled back to him.

Jason nodded quickly and rushed into the store. Once inside, he immediately sprinted over to the clerk behind the counter.

"I need to use your phone!" Jason quietly barked at the clerk. The clerk pointed towards the door.

"There's a pay phone outside, around the side of the building."

Jason immediately shook his head before the clerk even finished talking.

"No, it's an emergency. Listen God dammit, I'm FBI working a case, and I can't use that pay phone. I have to use your phone, preferably your cell phone." Jason replied, while looking out of the door to see if anyone was coming.

"Ha, yeah whatever dude, I'm not letting you use my....."

The clerk didn't even get to finish before Jason quickly connected with a hook to the face - knocking him out cold. Jason remorsefully shook his head.

"Sorry." he whispered to the clerk as he leaped the counter and snatched the cell phone from the clerk's hip. Jason peeked outside to get a look at the crew in the van. They were busy talking and joking. He sprinted full speed towards the back of the store, into the bathroom, leaving the door ajar so he could peek out, as he immediately dialed his Special Agent in Charge.

Special Agent in Charge (SAC) Dave Watson—the leader of Jason's elite federal undercover unit. A former Military Intelligence officer who served in Desert Storm, along with several tours in South America, Africa, and Europe. A no-nonsense, straight shooter who did it by the book until the "book" got in his way from getting the job done. A twenty plus year veteran, Watson made a large number of high-profile arrests during his rise within the FBI as a Special Agent and Supervisory Special Agent, which justified his sudden rise in the ranks. Up for promotion as Section and Unit Chief three separate times, he turned down the potential promotions every time in order to remain the head of his elite undercover unit he adopted as his own. His team was highly effective and successful at what they did. Although, not many people knew what they did, including most inside the FBI. Their group, their cases, and everything involved with their team, was kept under strict and selective knowledge.

Outside of the Director and Section Chief, no one was aware of what Dave's team did, which was exactly the way it was designed, and the way Dave wanted it— too many leaks, too risky. He didn't trust anyone to run it the way he wanted it ran. He was guaranteed complete oversight of the team had he decided to take the promotions, but that wasn't enough for him. Dave was "hands-on" and "complete oversight" of his team as he sat behind a desk, just wasn't who he was. Dave was smooth in his delivery, and even smoother when taking care of business.

A marksman by hobby, he knew his guns like they were his kids. Which they essentially were, considering his only daughter didn't take too kindly to the type of work he did. They didn't have much of a relationship because of it.

He was very calm, moved extremely leisurely until it was time to really move and get things done. He epitomized the term "sleeping giant." It took a lot to awake him, but when he finally awoke, there was no one better at getting the job done.

The Director himself called Dave directly when he wanted info, which usually didn't sit well with the Section Chief. Dave and his team earned the trust of the Director over the years. The Director was very cognizant of the fact that Dave and his team got the things done that no one else could. The results and success rate for Dave's team spoke for themselves.

When Dave's team went after someone, they got them. Specializing in elite undercover and infiltration, utilizing both tact and advanced skills in weaponry and combat. His team managed to bring down thirteen high profile crime and drug networks/syndicates within a ten-year period in seven different states. The Director's latest request came during a late-night call to Dave;

"The President just chewed me out over this quiet, uncontested, yet confirmed noise the Cartel has been making within the U.S for the past two years. It looks like the Serrano Cartel has a major grip on a few major cities, and it's getting worse. Kidnapping, drugs, murder and even gun trafficking. The DEA has had their heads in this

for over a year now, and they aren't producing any results. The POTUS called me and asked me what we could do. The first thing that came to mind was you. I need you to get in on this as soon as possible. Can I count on you?"

That was the question Director Fields personally asked Special Agent in Charge, Dave Watson. Nine months later, Agent Jason Barrington or "Ramone," Dave's top undercover agent, suddenly found himself in a situation that appeared to be getting worse by the minute. Deeply infiltrated inside one of the main groups employed by the Serrano Cartel this side of the border, agent Barrington was losing his grip. This group, by any means, were responsible for the upkeep of the Serrano network within the United States, primarily the Western part of the United States.

Agent Barrington now found himself so deep within the group, he didn't know which way to begin climbing out of the hole he now found himself in.

The phone rang twice before Dave answered.

"Watson here....."

"This is Barrington....."

"Agent Barrington?!!" Dave replied behind a surprised tone. "Where the hell are you?!!"

"Go secure." Jason instructed.

"We're already secure agent Barrington. We lost you

when you.... "

"Sir I..." *Jason began, but immediately paused as he heard the front door of the store opening. He peeked out of the door and saw Julio entering the store, calling out to him.*

"Ramone!?" *Julio cried out.* "Yo, what the hell man? We got to go!!"

Peeking carefully out of the bathroom door, Jason saw Julio quickly making his way towards the back of the store looking down each aisle as he made his way past them. There simply wasn't any time to speak with Dave, to warn him what was about to happen. Julio quickly approached the door, causing Jason to panic, and quickly dropped the phone in the toilet, as there wasn't anywhere else to quickly hide it.

"Hey Ramone, you in here?!! The hell you doing in here?" *he asked while opening the door and peeking his head in. He immediately spotted Jason on the toilet, pants to his knees, holding his stomach – grimacing in pain.*

"Hey man!! What the hell?" *Jason yelled.*

"My bad man. I'm sorry. Boss says hurry the hell up." *Julio replied while quickly shutting the door. Jason peeked calmly out the bathroom door to make sure Julio didn't happen to stop by the front counter and notice* the clerk who was out cold. But, without so much as a glance in the direction of the front counter, Julio quickly made his way back outside to the van. Jason reached into the toilet and retrieved the phone.

The phone was destroyed, as was his attempt to warn Dave to let him know about the impending hit on the unsuspecting federal agent. He could do nothing but stare at the phone as he slowly shook his head. No one was aware of what was about to happen tonight and that was a problem, a big problem for him and the DEA agent that was being targeted by the group.

Hand-picked by Dave, Jason was deep within the FBI Counterintelligence Division when Dave convinced him that his talents and attributes would be best served within his undercover unit. Dave saw the cowboy instincts within Jason from afar - very instinctive and street smart. Five years out of the academy, he had already garnered a reputation of being somewhat of a silent assassin, and that was something Dave certainly could relate to.

He spent almost the past decade in the field, doing the dirty but vital work for the Counterintelligence Unit. Now doing the same for Dave's team. Coming out of the academy, Jason preferred and requested to be assigned somewhere in or near New Jersey—his home state. He was eventually stationed with Counter Terrorism Unit in the

Los Angeles area instead, before being reassigned to Dave's unit out of Lansing, Michigan. Being undercover for seven and a half months had undoubtedly taken its toll on Jason, and at this point, he wasn't sure if he had problems distinguishing what was real and what wasn't. He wasn't even entirely certain if he had the mental energy to even distinguish between the two. Watson's unit consisted of five highly trained agents. Each agent hand-picked by Dave himself. The team specialized in creative infiltration and undercover work, but they were also much more than that. They were basically a tight nit unit that essentially did whatever it took to get the job done. Sometimes, utilizing questionable and aggressive, but highly effective tactics and methods.

Dave had them training under a former high-level Military Intelligence colleague of his who was also a former Navy Seal. He provided elite advanced weapon and tactical training, training that most FBI agents didn't receive their entire careers. Dave wanted them overly prepared for any and all scenarios. By the second year, Dave noticed that Jason was naturally good at undercover work. He had gone undercover three times within two years. He boasted an impressive ninety five percent conviction rate from his undercover work.

The other team members: Agent Terry Brask, Agent Malcolm Willingham, Agent Zoe Terrell, and Agent Jim Burba, were also handpicked by Dave himself as Dave scrounged through every branch of law enforcement, military, or private security contractor service at his disposal—like a pro-scout rummaging through the college ranks looking for talent for his team. ** *Sitting quietly in the back of the van, Jason nervously found himself quickly slipping into a mini daydream. He thought only of his family. He thought how he may have already touched his wife for the last time, how he may have already held his sons for the last time. They were four and seven years of age prior to him leaving to go undercover. He had already missed one birthday, his oldest son Jackson's.*

When joining the FBI ten years ago, this wasn't exactly what he had in mind. Constantly leaving his family for weeks and months at a time, wasn't exactly the ideal situation, but apparently, he quickly became the best at what Dave needed him to do. Now here he was, deep undercover, right smack in the middle of one of the most dangerous Cartel affiliates gangs, this side of the border.

Jason knew that with this type of group, he literally couldn't be in anymore danger, if he doused himself with Jet fuel and struck a match. Though it wasn't that difficult to infiltrate the group, the hardest part was now maintaining his sanity, cover and humanity. He had witnessed some of the most barbaric tactics utilized by the group. Infiltrating the otherwise secret and extremely tight nit gang was as simple as creating a rap sheet a mile long, getting "arrested" and placed inside San Quentin Prison. It required taking a real beating or two from groups that deemed themselves enemies of the Serrano cartel, while displaying his toughness and grittiness during these beatings. He immediately garnered the curiosity and admiration of the top Serrano cartel affiliate leaders inside the prison. He was eventually approached by some of the low-level members, offering him an ultimatum that was beneficial to him in more ways than one - join or continuing enjoying the constant beatings from opposing gangs. Not only did he join, but he did enough during his three months inside to warrant a quick rise within the ranks and ultimately meeting with Malvieo, the low-level leader, once he was released.

Now, he found himself right in the middle of what appeared to be one of the most difficult situations he'd ever been in, during his tenure under Dave. Everything from the past seven months was now quickly coming to a head. Whatever was going to happen, it was going to happen tonight, he was certain of it. He understood that there wasn't really an easy way out of what he slowly

started to understand to be happening. Not only would he
not participate in the assassination of a DEA agent and his
family as their hit ordered, but there was no way he would
stand idly by and allow it to happen.

His attempt back at the store, to brief Dave on the
situation had failed, but Dave and the unit were already
aware of the "noise" surrounding a potential hit out on a
federal agent. But no one knew any of the specifics, no
one except Jason, yet his communication with Dave and
the unit was essentially cut off at this point. Jason was
positive everyone in the group was being monitored by the
cartel, so playing it careful, safe, and smart was what he
was thinking when he stopped the daily secret
communications with Dave and the unit.

The stunt in the store back there was as risky as
anything he'd done in the past few months, but he figured
it was worth it to at least try to warn Dave. It seems to all
be heading downhill fast and not being able to alert Dave
and his team of what was actually happening tonight, put
this extremely oblivious DEA agent and his family in
immediate and extreme danger. Jason began to feel as if
he was gradually losing what little control he had.

The agent–DEA Agent John Merriweather, had been
on the Serrano cartel's trail for the past year and
apparently had gotten closer than anyone before. There

was word out that Merriweather had turned a few of Serrano's underpaid and disloyal men, into confidential informants. There was also word out of the DEA that Serrano had also put a hit out on his own son, who was inside the United States making his own moves that were in direct opposition to Serrano's operation. This information, along with more damaging information that could potentially bring down the Serrano Cartel, was apparently the valuable Intel agent Merriweather was able to gather. It was the reason the Cartel considered agent Merriweather a "top priority" and a threat and Jason's group was the first group that was given the orders to take care of this "priority."

"We're about ten minutes out." Malvieo declared, "We're going to park about a half mile down the street from the house. We'll split into two groups. Marco will stay in the van with the engine running. Hector will patrol and secure the front and the right side of the house. Hector you will check out the scene and keep a lookout while we're inside taking care of business. You whistle if there's anything. Rubio will be on the side of the house tripping the alarm. Rubio, you will have five minutes to get it done. Me, Ramone, and Julio will go in through the back once you do. Again, no survivors, not even the dog.

The order is straight from the top, so just fucking get it done, no excuses, or it's all of our asses."

Malvieo was the self-proclaimed "leader" of the group. In reality, he was seemingly nothing more than a pawn that thought he was bigger and more important than he actually was. He was a lunatic with access to big guns, and apparently, he possessed the "qualities" and "traits" the Cartel needed to get things done on this side of the border. He never officially labeled himself the leader, but it was something that had become apparent these past seven months. Jason never asked or questioned it.

Malvieo killed a former member a few months back who questioned his leadership. He did it in front of everyone, but in Jason's mind, it was egregiously pathetic. The gun jammed on him three times. He then proceeded to put the gun aside and beat the poor bastard to death, but the guy instinctively fought back and damn near put a whooping on Malvieo. Jason thought it was funny, but probably more embarrassing to say the least. The idiot ended up having to have the man held down so that he can "finish" beating him. Malvieo broke his hand hitting him and had to muster up the strength to fight through the pain. He ended up shooting him with his uninjured hand, and yes, his left hand was apparently so weak the kick back from the gun forced the gun out of his hand. Jason remembered feeling bad for the poor bastard and even suggested they let him live. It was an attempted stall tactic on Jason's part as he had a pipe dream that he would be able to save the poor guy. He respected his fight and spirit but was unsuccessful. The guy was ultimately killed.

The gang was a small group of six: Jason, Julio, Hector, Malvieo, Marco, and Rubio. Rubio and Hector were actually American citizens of Mexican descent, while Malvieo, Marco, and Julio made it into the country through unconventional means. Malvieo was the "leader," but it was Julio who was actually the one that many feared, as he carried this dangerous and aggressively ruthless attitude around with him. Jason remembered witnessing him cutting someone's throat and then pulling the poor guy's tongue out through the neck. Julio was ruthless, yet playful and immature like a child. Jason sat in silence for the remainder of the ride contemplating and thinking about his family as well as agent Merriweather and his family. He was at a complete loss, thinking about what he could possibly do to prevent this night from heading down the direction it was headed, to prevent this inevitable blood bath he was walking into. It was all happening too fast.

The past seven months seemed to slowly crawl by with him being away from his family. But, on this night, this moment seemed to be happening entirely too fast. He wondered if it was all happening the way it was supposed to.

He slowly gazed up at the night stars out of the van window. Living in the city, it was very difficult to gaze up at the stars, something he did to help clear his mind since he was a young man. He wasn't certain why they had the effect they had on him, but they did. He was infatuated with them. The range of emotions he currently felt as he looked upon them suddenly began to overwhelm him. It caused him to think about things, life more clearly. He didn't know what it was, but he was suddenly experiencing a feeling he couldn't quite explain.

This feeling, this moment, felt kind of surreal, almost euphoric in a sense. It was as if his body and his mind were opening. Opening to what, he wasn't exactly sure, but essentially opening to everything. It was the strangest feeling, it didn't make much sense on the outside, but the more he thought about it, the more it began to slowly piece itself together in his mind. He welcomed it, as it seemed to carry an extreme sense of quiet yet refreshing and slightly unexplainable sense of limitless existence within it.

It was a strange feeling, one that he'd never felt before......

I slowly shifted by eyes away from the Nook, grinning slightly at what I'd just read. The words expressed in Jason's thoughts were quite similar to my own. Not sure what this character meant exactly, but it seemed as if he was "experiencing" the same unexplainable feeling of openness within his mind, as I.

I was quickly starting to, or at least I thought I was starting to understand why Father Miyake wanted me to read this story. It was a story he was probably familiar with. He possibly realized that this main character Jason, was probably somewhat surprisingly relatable to me and my current situation. I chuckled at the thought and appreciated Father Miyake's effort. Shaking my head, I grinned just slightly as I returned to the story.

Title-less Story – Chapter One—Continue

With a blank emotionless gaze, Jason continued to stare up at the stars. He suddenly realized that this night, could very well be his last here on this earth. It was a sickening feeling. He wasn't ready to go, he wasn't ready to die, but not being ready to go, just wasn't enough of a reason to not do what he felt he needed to do tonight. In this case, he didn't know what that was, but he knew what he couldn't do, and that was stand idly by while a fellow federal agent and his family were slaughtered.

Jason quickly caught himself smiling as he found himself lost in his surrealistic star gaze. Smiling at the thought of his sons and the moments he spent with them. He closed his eyes as he began to ask God for another chance to hold his family again, to be with them once again. He smiled as he began to think about how his sons, Jackson and Trey. He loved how they would loudly sing Israel Kamakawiwo'ole's "Over the Rainbow" to him to wake him up whenever they were lucky enough to catch him home asleep on the weekends.

*His wife taught them the words to the song.
She would sing it to them in an attempt to get them to fall
asleep faster and more peacefully at night. It essentially
worked every time. They fell in love with the song. It
practically became mandatory in order to get them to even
close their eyes once in the bed. She eventually bought
the CD for them, and now is forced to sing that song no
matter how tired she is at night. Something she looks
forward to every night. Jason appreciated the beauty
within the song, but it was made even more beautiful
when the boys sang it to wake him up. And no matter
how deep a sleep he was in, or how tired he was, when
they sang that song to him, he simply couldn't stay asleep,
as he'd wake up with a smile on his face every time.*

*"We're almost there." Malvieo barked.
The group immediately began checking their ammo. Jason
began checking his ammo as well, making sure he racked
the hammer to load a bullet into the chamber. He was
given a silencer equipped automatic weapon, an AR-15 -
something he had become very good at utilizing these past
seven months. Because of the training Dave would put
Jason and the team through; Jason was already familiar
with handling of pretty much all kinds of automatic rifles.
He only pretended to "learn" how to effectively use one
during the past seven months to keep suspicion down.*

Everyone else in the group had automatic weapons as well—all equipped with silencers. Jason gradually started to feel as though the odds were gradually stacking up against him. He suddenly and hesitantly began to realize that the only way he would even stand a chance at coming close to saving this man and his family tonight, would be to pull off some suicidal cowboy stunt, that would likely end with him losing his life. It was a tough to even think about, tough to swallow, but it was happening.

Jason knew that there weren't any "time outs" in this situation or in life in general. This wasn't a movie, no one to yell "cut." This was his life. This was also the life of an innocent man, a federal agent doing his job, and more importantly, his family, who had no idea what was going on, what this night would bring, and how it would essentially change all of their lives forever.

The van slowly turned down agent Merriweather's street. The neighborhood was a small suburban housing complex practically in the middle of nowhere. The houses were about ten feet apart from one another. The neighborhood was well illuminated in the front of the houses, but the back of the houses were perfect for covert movement. Jason looked at his watch, it read: 3:07 am. Having previously scouted the neighborhood, Malvieo already knew that after 2 AM, the neighborhood got eerily still and as quiet as a graveyard. No one came or went, walked a dog, got off work late, or even jogged between now and 4 am, making it the perfect time to complete the job.

"Remember, me, Ramone and Julio, will head inside and take out Merriweather and the family, you two;" Malvieo pointed at Rubio and Hector.

"You two will position yourselves at the front, and side of the house to keep watch. Rubio will join you Hector, once he finishes the alarm, understood?"

"Yes!!"

Malvieo's orders echoed through Jason's head. He knew he needed to quickly come up with a sufficient plan to counter Malvieo's orders but didn't know where to begin. He was really good at coming up with logical and valid plans within short time frames. Jason had come up with effective unscripted last-minute plans in crucial situations before, many times in his career but this, was not only "different," it was practically impossible without accepting the likelihood of some amount of casualties, likely, his own included.

His mind was as opened and as clear as it had ever been, but he was still nervous, which seemed to temporarily neutralize his creative thinking at this point. Hector turned towards Jason.

"You ready Ramone?"

Looking over at Hector and slowly grinned as he began to nod.

"Yep!"

The group quietly push closer toward the house which was about two blocks away from their parked van. The night was cool, but quiet, not even a dog barking in the distance. The stars adequately illuminated the streets, but not too much that it gave away their position.

The streetlights were dimly lit, just enough to effectively hide the group as they were all dressed in black. They stayed clear of the streets so that no one would be caught passing under a streetlight. They made their way through the bushes in the front yards of the houses.

They finally approached the house and stopped at the side where the thick bushes rested. The tall bushes provided perfect cover. The house was a two story, with no lights other than the front porch. The house appeared to be extremely quiet and if the multiple cars hadn't been parked out in the driveway, one would assume that no one was home. Jason knew he wouldn't be that lucky. He calmly gazed up at the stars and began shaking his head as he knew nothing good could possibly be written in the stars for him tonight. Rubio turned towards Malvieo as Malvieo motioned for Rubio and Hector to "go." Rubio immediately sprinted over to the side of the house to work on the alarm as Hector went around to his position. Julio and Malvieo quickly glanced at one another then peered at Jason.

"We wait for Rubio's signal, then we go." said Malvieo. Jason began looking around inconspicuously as Julio and Malvieo were focused heavily on what Rubio was engaged in. At this point, Jason began carefully surveying his surroundings, trying to figure out the best, most effective way to do whatever it was he was going to do. He still had no idea what it would be, but knew he was running out of time. Rubio carefully peeked from around the side of the house, motioning for Jason, Julio, and Malvieo to push towards the back door. The guys immediately began moving towards the back door, but Jason stayed back.

"I have to take a piss." Jason whispered.
Malvieo quickly glanced over at Jason

"Fucking hurry that shit up. Catch up when you're finished." Malvieo whispered as he and Julio headed towards the back door meeting up with Rubio. Once near the back door, Julio carefully and quietly removed the bulb from the back-porch light.

"We good to go?" Malvieo asked Rubio. Rubio quickly nodded his head.

Still pretending to urinate, Jason carefully glanced over his shoulder to see what his partners were up to. No one was focusing on him. They had already successfully opened the back door, lifted off its hinges and were headed inside. Jason patiently waited until they were all inside before making his move. Rubio and Hector were positioned at their guard posts, as Jason headed to flank around towards Hector's position. Jason's natural instincts and advanced training took over almost immediately.

Crouching down, Jason moved carefully—one foot in front of the other while keeping his head on a swivel. Hector held his silencer equipped MP5 on his waist as Jason took the advantage and quickly crept up behind him. By the time Hector knew what was happening, Jason had already firmly grabbed the MPK, leveled Marco with a swift roundhouse kick to the face and put two bullets in him, one in the head and one in the chest. He would take no chances tonight.

He understood that it was either kill or be killed at this point. He knew he needed to get inside the house as soon as possible without any more delay, and he wasted no time as he raised his weapon, took a deep breath and began pushing towards the back door. Jason strapped his automatic weapon around him like a gym bag and checked the ammo in the MPK he snatched from Hector;

it was fully loaded. The MK was much more compact and manageable than his AR15 right now, so it would be his weapon of choice. Jason aimed the MK, ready to fire with his finger on the trigger, and then carefully moved directly towards the corner of the house toward the back door. As soon as he hit the corner, Jason was immediately met with overwhelming gunfire from Marco. Marco's silencer was highly effective. Jason didn't even hear the gunshots, but he felt them as they whizzed by his head. Jason immediately noticed a brick BBQ pit about fifteen feet away. Immediately, he returned fire in Marco's direction as he quickly sprinted over to take cover, diving behind the pit. Successfully landing hard behind the pit, Jason noticed the lights on the second floor of the house turn on. He needed to act quickly.

He didn't expect to run into Marco, as Marco was supposed to be in the van waiting on them to finish the job. He had no idea why Marco had decided to join them, and it could only mean that his cover was likely blown at this point somehow, and Marco was needed for backup. It didn't matter anymore; he was all in at this point. Jason knew these guys were killers, merciless killers, but he had one advantage over all of them—tact and experience.

They were clueless as to how to tactfully utilize their positions and weapons to their advantage, something he had been trained on for the better part of the past eleven years. The advantage, if there ever was one, belong to him.

Jason laid gingerly and quietly on his side hanging out from behind the pit, and immediately noticed Marco posting up behind a tree. Marco looked to be reloading his weapon rather frantically and rapidly all while trying to signal Rubio to flank Jason from the other side of the pit. Jason noticed that Marco was painfully oblivious to just how exposed he was by not taking adequate cover and not being cognizant of his surroundings, Jason knew Marco was making a fatal mistake. Not wasting any time, Jason peeked around the other side of the pit. Immediately he noticed Rubio peeking from around the side of the house with his weapon. Jason steadied his aim at the location Rubio was peeking out from and waited for a clean shot. Not three seconds later, Rubio's head suddenly and quickly popped out from around the side of the house and was instantly met with a bullet from Jason's MK. Rubio was dead before he hit the ground.

Jason quickly focused his attention back toward Hector's location. Hector, still clearly unaware of his surroundings, and entirely too lax with his defense, turned his head frantically at every opportunity, waiting for Jason to make a move. Jason slowly wiped the sweat from his forehead, aimed the MK and pulled the trigger.

A head shot—he fired one single muffled shot, instantly dropping Hector to the ground. Hector was the youngest of the crew, and Jason actually took a liking to him, all things considered. But he couldn't take any chances tonight as he knew all of these guys would do anything tonight to prove themselves—killing Jason wouldn't be a problem for any of them. There would be no hesitation on their part, and neither would it be on his. There was no doubt at this point they knew what Jason was up to and probably already knew who he really was. However, it wasn't really important. His life, and the lives of the family inside the house, was more important at this point.

Jason carefully opened the back door leading with his weapon and sharp aim. He heard the screams and immediately saw Julio dragging what appeared to be a young girl down the steps by her hair. The girl's screams were blood curdling. Julio didn't see Jason and proceeded to throw the girl on the couch; apparently Julio had made his mind up to assault her.

Jason quickly aimed the MK directly at Julio.

"Julio, stop!"

Julio quickly turned around, gun in his hand, yanked the girl closer to him, and immediately pressed the gun against her head. He glared at Jason and smiled.

"Thought they would've killed you by now, el cochino." Julio barked behind a smug grin.

Screams echoed out from upstairs. Jason was now breathing heavy as he kept his aim on Julio. He glanced at the girl as she cried uncontrollably.

"Shut the hell up bitch!" Julio shouted at the girl. "What the fuck are you doing, amigo?" Julio asked with a bewildered look on his face.

"Huh? You trying to play hero?!! The hell you think you're doing, man? The hell do you work for? FBI, DEA? Who? Don't you know who you're fucking with?"

Julio bellowed behind a chilling laugh.

Jason stood with his gun aimed directly on Julio. He didn't speak, budge or flinch, at this point he was making it up as he went along. He certainly didn't want anything to happen to the girl, who he guess by now to be the daughter of agent Merriweather.

"Hey, let's see how tough you are," Julio whispered in a soft tone. "Put your shit down, and I'll put mine down.

"Fine." Jason replied sternly, willing to say anything to get the gun off the girl.

Gunshots and more screams came from upstairs. It sounded like two separate sets of gun fire, meaning agent Merriweather or his wife, were likely defending themselves.

"Let's do this like real men. Put your gun down, and let's handle this like men supposed to." Julio said, while pressing the MK harder into the head of the girl.

"Ok!!! Ok!" Jason uttered as he slowly lowered his aim. The girl was severely shaken as Julio pressed the gun harder into her temple.

"Alright Julio, Let's do this like men."
Jason tossed the MK on the floor.

"Now you drop yours."
Julio didn't waste any time. With his finger on the trigger, his smile widened as he began pulling the trigger back to likely finish the girl off, but Jason swiftly retrieved his semiautomatic weapon from his back holster, aimed it at Julio's head and fired one shot. Julio never saw what hit him. The bullet entered the front of Julio's head and exited the back as Julio's lifeless body hit the floor with a look of shock and surprise clinging to his face. Jason glanced up at the young girl who was crying and shaking. He reached out to her. She flinched. Jason looked at her and put his finger to his lips to quiet her down. Jason looked at her and put his finger to his lips to quiet her

down. Surprisingly, she looked at him and nodded her head to acknowledge.

"Can you drive?" he whispered to her.

She quickly nodded.

"Where are the keys to the cars?" whispered Jason, as more screams and noise derived from upstairs.

She slowly pointed towards the kitchen.

"Get in the car," Jason instructed her. "Drive down the road and call the police. Do that now."

"My parents!!?" the girl franticly whispered to Jason. Jason looked at the girl and wanted to give her something, anything of hope, but couldn't.

"You need to go now." he uttered sternly.

Without hesitating, she quickly sprinted towards the kitchen, out of sight. Jason gripped his MK and headed up the stairs, with the aim of the MK leading the way. Reaching the top step, he saw what appeared to be Agent Merriweather lying in a pool of blood in the hallway. He had a semiautomatic weapon gripped in his hand. Jason quietly checked his pulse; he was dead. Jason heard muffled crying coming from one of the far bedrooms down the hall. Tactfully and carefully, with his weapon aimed, he crouched and slowly pushed toward the sound of the crying, carefully checking every room along the way. They were all empty.

Aiming the MK, Jason finally made it to the room where the cries derived from. Once at the door, he spotted Malvieo stripping the clothes off a woman who Jason presumed to be Mrs. Merriweather. Jason didn't hesitate as Mrs. Merriweather eyes locked on him. Malvieo quickly turned to see who it was she was looking at.

"It's over!" Jason said, as he looked Malvieo directly in his eyes!

"You're right. It is over!!" Malvieo quickly replied, pulling Mrs. Merriweather closer to him and putting his gun to her head. "It's over for you and your family, you can believe that shit." Malvieo shouted.

"Move away from her!!" Jason barked with the gun aimed directly at Malvieo's head. Malvieo stared at Jason but didn't budge; didn't say a word. He simply began pulling the hammer back on the on his semiautomatic weapon.

"Don't! ....Don't do that!" yelled Jason as he shook his head.

"I will kill you Malvieo. Don't do it. This shit is over. Lay down your weapon."

Jason's aim was tight, and he was certain he could drop Malvieo, there wasn't a doubt, but at this point, he wanted to take no chances with Mrs. Merriweather's life. It was a stare down and no one was flinching. Sirens could now be heard in the distance, forcing a slight reaction out of Malvieo. He quickly glanced around franticly, checking his surroundings. He began backing up, pulling the weeping Mrs. Merriweather with him. Before Jason had time to react, Malvieo pushed Mrs. Merriweather into Jason and took an unexpected dive out of the window, headfirst.

Jason quickly turned towards Mrs. Merriweather.

"Call 9-11!" he yelled, as he quickly dove out of the window after Malvieo.

There was a roof beneath the window, so it wasn't a straight drop to the ground. Jason landed on the roof, on his shoulder, but didn't lose the grip of the weapon. He stood up on the roof and aimed his gun looking for any signs of Malvieo, there was none. Jason carefully jumped down to the ground and quickly rolled to his feet. He once again raised the MK to aim it. He knew Malvieo would probably make his way back to the van but didn't see him on the road headed that way. Suddenly hearing footsteps behind him, Jason quickly dropped, rolled, and aimed, but not before hearing gun shots. Jason had Malvieo in his aim and fired, but Malvieo had already gotten shots off. Jason returned fire and hit Malvieo in his chest. Malvieo instantly dropped to the ground clutching his chest!

Quickly racing over towards Malvieo with the MK aimed directly at his face. Jason kicked the gun away from his immediate area.

"You're dead," Malvieo uttered in-between coughs.

"Your family is probably already dead." he said as he began laughing. "As soon as you made that phone call to your team back at the store, it was picked up. The hell were you thinking?!! We were ordered to kill you right then, but I wanted to see just how stupid you were and how far you were going with it."

"Stupid decision by you," said Jason as he shook his head, "I've killed all of you."
Shaking his head Malvieo begin smiling.

"Got to admit though, it hurt just a little bit when I found out. I didn't see this coming from you, Ramone, or should I say, Agent Barrington? You should probably say goodbye to your family, my friend."

"Fuck you!" Jason barked. "You should've killed me when you were supposed to, or you wouldn't be dead right now. You don't know anything about my family."
The sounds of sirens could be heard as they got closer.

"Of course we do," replied Malvieo. "You think a nice family town house in Boyne City, Michigan is hard to find?" he asked behind sinister grin.

Jason immediately felt nauseous. His heart began to race, and his knees started to give way. He couldn't believe this was happening. It was as if someone had suddenly snatched the ground right from under him. Jason found himself getting emotional and nauseated over what he just heard but didn't want to give Malvieo the pleasure of seeing it. He stood up, aimed the gun at Malvieo's head, and fired two shots into Malvieo's head and chest. He watched as Malvieo quickly died. Jason immediately turned and sprinted down the road full speed, towards the van. Once he arrived, he tossed the rifle in the passenger seat and started up the van. He picked up the phone and immediately dialed Dave.

"Hello?" Dave's voiced echoed from the other end.

"Dave—my family! My family needs help now! Go help my family!!" Jason yelled into the phone while fighting back tears.

Jason lowered the phone and focused heavily on the steering wheel as he began driving away, towards home. "Home" was maybe six hundred or so miles away at the least, but that didn't matter at this point. Nothing could stop him from driving there at this moment. Jason didn't get but maybe a half a mile before he suddenly began to feel extremely dizzy and sleepy. He noticed a sharp pain on his right side. He reached down, felt his side, right under his ribs and saw the blood on his hand when he raised them to his eyes. He had been hit in the gut by Malvieo and didn't know it. Jason couldn't control the vehicle. He immediately reached for the phone as he began to slowly weep.

"This is agent Barrington, my family is in danger, help them, help them NOW!!!"

He barked the orders into the phone, not even certain if anyone was on the other end as everything started to become disoriented. Jason couldn't hold on to the phone anymore as his arm weakened. No longer able to hold consciousness, agent Barrington passed out, slumped over the steering wheel. The van, having not made it even a mile from agent Merriweather's street, veered off full speed into a ditch on the side of the road where agent Jason Barrington lay dying.

Title-less Story – Chapter One – The End

<u>Chapter Four</u>

Dave's Broken Promise

I didn't bother looking up from the Nook. I immediately proceeded to swipe the screen, to navigate to the next chapter—chapter two. There weren't many options on the screen that allowed me to turn the page. Nothing labeled "*next chapter.*" I wasn't sure what I needed to see or press in order to get to the second chapter, but I was certain whatever it was, I wasn't seeing it. The more I fiddled with the device, the dumber I started to feel.

"It shouldn't be this hard to get to the next chapter." I whispered to myself. I gradually began to lose patience. Nothing I pressed, touched, or swiped, did the trick. I found myself becoming increasingly annoyed.

"That look on your face," said Bradley as he smiled, "It's like you're reading something really intense over there."

His voice slightly startled me as I was so engaged in

the story. In my failing attempt to get to the next chapter, I had subconsciously tuned out the environment around me just that quickly.

"I uh—well, it's a pretty good story. Doesn't really have a title, but yeah, I seem to be having problems trying to navigate this thing."

Bradly nodded as he grinned.

"Yeah, I noticed you over there reading, and it seemed as if you were getting somewhat frustrated."

"Well, yeah it's actually a pretty intensely intriguing story." I replied. "This guy, the main character, Jason, is an FBI agent. The story starts with him undercover with some gang or group that is associated with one of the Cartels. His cover is blown, so they kill his family, but that's as far as I've gotten."

Bradley nodded as he listened intensely.

"Was his family protected while he was undercover?

Why wouldn't they protect his family?"

I quickly shrugged my shoulders.

"Well," I hesitantly replied. "I only read the first chapter but, I'm not really sure. I've always wondered about that though. When someone who works undercover work for the Government go deep undercover like that, wouldn't their family be subject to protection? Wouldn't it be risky to leave them out in the open without protection, considering how easy it is for one to have his or her cover compromised?"

Bradley slowly nodded his head and shrugged his shoulders.

"There's always something out there that's worth everything to someone." Bradley replied, "But I'm not entirely sure. If I was him, I would be upset that my family wasn't protected."

The discussion quickly had the feel of two old men discussing a news report. There was an immediate level of comfort I had in speaking with Bradley.

"I agree. This character–Jason, he should be livid with the bureau, Dave or whoever, for not protecting his family, and he should demand answers. It's what I would do if it was me.

"Exactly," Bradley replied. "So, it's an action story? Dave is another main character?"

I nodded my head.

"Dave is his boss, and it seems to have a lot of action in it thus far, but I don't know what type of story it is just yet. I can't seem to get to the next chapter. I don't think there is a second chapter. Or this thing is probably broken."

"Broken? Really?" Bradley flashed a genuinely perplexed look on his face.

"Let me have a look at it," he said, extending his hand towards the device and retrieving it from me. "I'm just as clueless when it comes to these things, but two heads are better than one I suppose."

With his index finger, Bradley swiped through the device twice and smiled. He oddly handled the device as if he had a blindfold on and someone was pumping instructions into his ear.

"Ah, here it is." he finally uttered through a soft grin.

"You found it?!!" I asked excitedly. I was slightly excited, but more disappointed in myself for not being able to find it myself.

"Well yeah," said Bradley, "All you had to do is swipe your finger to the left and the next chapter comes up. See....."

Holding the Nook up to demonstrate, Bradley swiped the screen back and forth as the pages quickly responded.

"Yeah, but I did that." I replied, shaking my head in frustration. "I swiped numerous times, to be honest, but whatever."

"No problem," said Bradley, "Let me know how the story turns out. You should be able to get a lot of reading done on this flight. I'm hoping I can get a lot of work done as well."

Bradley refocused his attention back to his laptop. It now seemed as though I was more electronically challenged than I initially thought. I was frustrated with the fact that I was certain I had swiped the device exactly how Bradley had demonstrated. I placed the Nook in my lap, shook my head in frustration, and jumped right into chapter two of this title-less story.

Title-less Story – Chapter Two

The faint beeping noise was consistent, yet its origin was unknown. The beeping itself had a familiarity to it. It reminded him of the fire alarm back home when the batteries were low. The beeps got closer and essentially louder as he slowly began to come to.

Jason struggled to open his eyes. They not only felt heavy, but really dry, as the beeping continued. He slowly opened his eyes and was immediately greeted by a white bare ceiling. He laid there in the bed, staring up at the ceiling—no motivation to move. Jason slowly turned his head towards the direction in which the noise derived from. His sight was still a bit blurry so he couldn't exactly see what was actually making the noise. His eyes eventually began to clear as he focused on the origin of the consistent beeping. He found it difficult to swallow as his throat was extremely dry.

Focusing his eyes on the machine to his left, he realized that this was the machine the noises derived from —a vital signs monitor. He noticed wires coming from the machine, and immediately followed them with his hand. He discovered that they stopped over his chest. An IV entered his left arm. He suddenly started to put it all together; he was in a hospital.

"What?"

He softly whispered to himself.

"Where am I?"

Jason allowed his head to carefully fall back down on the pillow and again found himself staring up at the ceiling. He slowly turned his head over toward the brightest part of the room, near the window. It wasn't a nice day. The sky was dark gray—the dark, gloomy gray, right before hell was unleashed. Rain gently began to hit the window, but it wasn't hard enough to generate a sound on the window. It didn't need to. It was a day befitting how he currently felt.

Everything gradually started to come back to him. It was sort of like when waking up in a different, unfamiliar location after being so used to waking up at home, and everything slowly starts to hit you. It took a minute, but everything started to gradually hit him all at once.

"Jason?" a voice to the left of him calmly called out to him— a familiar voice. Jason turned his head and was immediately greeted by Special Agent in Charge, Dave Watson and his team members, agents Terrell and Brask.

"Jason, can you hear me?" Dave asked.

"You have to bear with him as the medication will have his reaction time a bit delayed, but he can hear you." Jason heard a woman's voice whisper to his left. He turned and saw the nurse changing his IV.

"Water," Jason whispered. "Water."

The nurse already suspecting his throat was dry, had the glass of water and straw to his lips, practically before he could even finish his request. He immediately took a drink of the water until satisfied and turned his attention back to Dave and his fellow agents.

"Where am I? Where is my family?" Jason asked.

The agents attempted to inconspicuously glance at one another, but Jason noticed.

Dave motioned towards the other agents.

"Give us a minute. You too mam." he uttered as he nodded towards the nurse.

She nodded her head in acknowledgement, and quickly exited the room. Pulling up a chair closer to Jason's bed, Dave gingerly sat down and glanced at Jason with an emotionless and blank gaze. Dave began to nod his head, but he wasn't answering a question. It was as if he was subconsciously accepting what he needed to do and say. It was as if he was answering a question within himself, fighting this, or in some state of denial, and *suddenly came to the realization that this moment, right here, right now, was real. There was no way around what he needed to say, no easy way.*

"Do you remember anything that happened prior to you waking up here today?" he asked Jason with a curious look on his face. "Anything at all?"

His eyes appeared heavy, but Jason looked at Dave and slowly shook his head. He closed his eyes and continued to slowly shake his head.

"No, I don't."

Jason's opened his eyes and once again locked in on Dave's face. He wanted answers, and they weren't coming fast enough.

"You were admitted here over two weeks ago, suffering from two gunshot wounds and head trauma. Prior to that, you, agent Barrington, for the past seven plus months, had been deep under cover with a group affiliated with the Serrano Cartel, and two weeks ago your cover was blown."

"I do remember being undercover, vaguely," said Jason, "My cover was blown? How? Why?"

Dave sighed and closed his eyes as he realized it got harder with each question that came his way.

"Jason, you apparently blew your cover in an attempt to save DEA agent Drew Merriweather, who the group you

were undercover with, targeted for a hit. You and the group broke into his house, where you evidently attempted to thwart the assignation of agent Merriweather and his family."

Jason's eyes widened.

"Did I succeed?"

Dave silently looked at Jason for a moment as he was finding it increasingly difficult to respond with the necessary words.

"Your actions, agent Barrington, saved the lives of agent Merriweather's oldest daughter and wife, but agent Drew Merriweather was killed."

Jason closed his eyes and nodded his head to acknowledge what Dave was saying.

"Um," Dave whispered as he gazed down at the floor.

"I ....um," he paused. "There's more." he mumbled softly, this time looking Jason in his eye. Jason gazed back at Dave and though his short-term memory was shot, he didn't forget that Dave was a straightforward guy and didn't pull many punches. He was brutally honest all the time, and also knew that the only time he struggled to communicate like this, was when extremely difficult things needed to be said.

Jason slowly looked Dave in his eye and giggled facetiously as he closed his eyes and began shaking his head.

"Why is it so hard for you to spit it out, Dave?" Eyes closed, Jason shook his head as he heard Dave take another deep breath, his third since he started talking with Jason. Jason opened his eyes as tears slowly began to fall. "Dave, where's my family?"

Dave started to gaze around the room in an attempt to avoid looking into Jason's eyes, but Jason followed Dave's eyes with his head and eyes, giving him no way to escape.

"Hmm? Why aren't they here with me?" Jason asked while nodding his head. Tears continued to fall slowly from his weary eyes. Jason didn't know the answer, but at this point he expected and prepared for the worst.

"Look at me, Dave, look at me. Tell me why my family isn't here with me." Jason voice sharpened and got slightly louder.

Dave looked at Jason.

"Jason, after the Cartel made you, there was an immediate hit put out on your family. We don't know how your cover was blown. We suspect they may have been provided some Intel from the inside and they made you, sometime during the ride out to agent Drew's neighborhood. We intercepted their communications and was aware of the hit on your family, but it was already too late."

Jason began shaking his head stubbornly like a toddler refusing instructions.

"NO NO NO NO NO! David, what are you saying to me?!"

"Jason, I need you to hear what I'm.....what I'm trying to say to you."

Dave struggled in fighting back emotion of his own.

"You promised to protect them, Dave!" Jason quickly whispered. " You promised you'd protect my family! That was you, Dave! You said that! Why wasn't my family protected?"

Jason, who was gradually becoming more animated, and alert was no longer holding on to a calm demeanor. His adrenaline was pushing through the effects of the pain medicine pumping through his system. Dave reached out and placed his hand on Jason's shoulder. Jason immediately and aggressively shoved Dave's hand away.

"There was an explosion at your house the night of the incident. Your wife and Trey passed away instantly, but Jackson was in a coma because of the explosion."

"NOOOOOO!" Jason screamed. "Where is he?!! Where is my SON?!! I want to see him, Dave!!!"

Dave looked away from Jason as he attempted to gather himself.

"Jackson was in a coma for two weeks, and he passed two days ago. I'm so sorry."

Jason instantly yelled out as if he was in agonizing physical pain. It was as if he had just been shot multiple times again, but this time in the chest. Throwing himself back on the bed, Jason couldn't hold back any longer and let the tears and screams escape his shattered body and soul. "Why, Dave?!" Jason screamed. " Why didn't you protect my family?! Answer me, Dave!"

Jason found it; the sudden burst of adrenaline to sit up in the bed as he began snatching the IVs out of his arms and the wires off his body. Dave and the nurse weren't quick enough as Jason jumped from his hospital bed crying, sprinting out of the room, and quickly made his way down the hall full speed towards the steps. He jumped down the flights of steps - flight after flight. Dave, the nurses, and agents Terrell and Brask were doing their best to stay on his tail. They didn't want him to harm himself at this point, but his emotions and adrenaline was clearly allowing him to stay a step ahead. None of them were close enough or fast enough to stop him.

Jason finally landed on the first floor and sprinted for the first exit door. The rain was the heaviest, hardest rain he's ever felt in his life. He stopped, peered up at the sky, and allowed the rain to freely hit his face. His family, his reason for living, his everything, was gone. But for a minute, he found a bit of peace and tranquility just standing there, in a hospital gown, underneath dark gray skies and heavy rain with his face turned directly towards the sky. Jason couldn't fight back tears as everyone who was chasing him finally made it outside. They all simply stopped and gazed upon him in an attempt to figure out just what it was he was doing.

Jason turned slowly and looked at them. He slowly stretched his arms out as if he was holding a baby. He immediately began walking back and forth in the rain as he looked down into his arms and began speaking.

"Shhh!" he whispered, "Just come back to me. All of you, just come back to me. I'll protect you this time; I'll be there for you this time; I won't leave you this time." Everyone looked on with tears in their eyes at what they were witnessing. Dave couldn't bear to watch any more as the tears began to fall down his face as well. He couldn't help but to turn away.

"God dammit somebody help him. Get him out of the god damn rain!!" Dave yelled.

Jason paced back and forth about ten times but could no longer hold himself up as his legs and his consciousness suddenly gave way. He abruptly began falling to the ground like the power switch inside him was instantly shut off. Before he could hit the ground, Dave had already sprinted over, catching him, and held him as the rain continued to wash down over them.

Title-less Story – Chapter Two - The End.

<u>Chapter Five</u>

A Life Worth Taking

S lowly peering up from the Nook, I gazed directly out of the window. What I'd just read, affected me more than I should've allowed it.

The story was so vivid and gripping. I visualized every word. It was a story that not only grabbed you but forced everything else out of your subconscious. It was the only thing I could think about at the moment. It was intensely emotional, raw, and incredibly sad. I had no idea whether or not I should just put the story down or continue reading. I didn't want my emotions getting the best of me during this plane ride, but I wanted to continue reading the story. Looking down at the Nook again, I proceeded to navigate to chapter three of the *title-less story* I aptly titled "*Jason's Story*," but like the previous chapter, I was having difficulties navigating to the next chapter.

"The hell is wrong with this thing?" I whispered to myself as I swiped the screen the way Bradley had demonstrated for me.

I had a very difficult time believing this device was *this* difficult to operate. I glanced over at Bradley, who was focused heavily on his work. I was certainly too embarrassed to say anything to him about this again at this point. I figured I would have to figure it out on my own or simply give up. No matter where or how I swiped on this screen, what I pressed or touched, what I did, or how I held it, the story didn't have another chapter to navigate to. I now knew I wasn't crazy or stupid. I took a deep breath and let out a peeved sigh. I had grown increasingly tired of trying to do something that should be so simple. I sat the device down on top of my carry-on bag near my feet, peered out of the window, and began concentrating on the passing clouds we currently flew over. They were transitory while being effortlessly beautiful. It was hard not to get lost in them. They seemed so peaceful and delicate; it was as if they were pulling me in. As I gazed out into the afternoon sky, I found it increasingly difficult to not think about Natalie. I found it even more difficult to not see her face every time I closed my eyes. I knew it probably wasn't healthy for me, but it was happening. I needed a valid way to escape from that right now, and I was far from escaping it. I was beginning to feel somewhat trapped in this extremely cramped environment.

The story, *Jason's Story*, was certainly a lot to take in, and certainly had the potential for helping me escape.

As I stared out of the window into the passing scenery, I again started thinking about what I just read, about the raw and intense emotion within the story. I wasn't as much an avid reader now as I was in the past, so I wouldn't know if this story was a bestseller or not. I was out of touch on a lot of things, but whatever I was out of touch on electronically, my daughters usually were experts on. I adored that about them.

The story, what I'd read so far, was twisting and pulling at me. I suddenly and unconsciously began deeply contemplating on what I would do if in the shoes of this man, this character, "Jason." Namely, the part where he lost his entire family in one night. Couldn't help but to ponder on just how difficult it would be to cope and to maintain some kind of normalcy after going through something so tragic, so —utterly life shattering?

What I was facing personally, what I was feeling at this moment, was a feeling I wouldn't wish on anyone. It was unbearable pain. What I was dealing with, was tough beyond words, yet I found myself emerged in unfiltered pity for this character, Jason. No man could possibly understand the morbid yet slightly surreal feeling of wanting to be with a loved one that has passed. Unless, that man has experienced the sharp and deep pain associated with losing someone really close to them, they'll never understand it. I had seen it before, primarily on TV and movies, and heard about it, but never understood it. Never felt it. I now understood it. I now felt it.

I wasn't certain if I was actually feeling this way myself, or if I was simply speaking as to how I felt this character Jason should and would probably be feeling at this point— it was hard to tell the difference. I knew that if I was truly and unconsciously putting strength into thinking this way, it would be irresponsible and supremely unfair to my family, considering they needed me at my strongest during this tribulation, but there was no escaping the morbid thoughts that lingered in the back of my mind. It hurt so much. The pain was so unbearable within that I suddenly realized that the thought of killing myself to see my daughter again didn't sound as bad or morbid as it probably should have, and right now, I hated myself for feeling and thinking in such a way.

My family deserved better, but I couldn't promise them better because of the way the pain of Natalie's death consumed me. At least not right now I couldn't.

I reflected on this character, Jason, who was undoubtedly feeling the same or most likely, worse. Though I could only slightly relate to what this character was "going through," I figured Father Miyake wanted me to read this story, albeit an incomplete story, for a reason.

I'm sure Father Miyake believed I would be able to relate to the main character, Jason and what he was going through, but this was quite the tragic ordeal, to say the least, and "relating" to something like this was virtually impossible, even for me and all that I was currently enduring. The more I thought about this character and what he was dealing with, the more I came to the inescapable conclusion and realization that I wouldn't personally be strong enough to deal with it. I slowly started shaking my head at the disturbingly emotional thought of having to deal with what he was dealing with as tears began to fall.

For a brief moment, I felt foolish for allowing this story to move me this way, but I understood that I was being moved because I saw myself in Jason. I saw myself struggling to deal with the pain. Placing things within this context, it suddenly wasn't that hard to express the emotions befallen me at this moment.

"You finished the story already?" Bradley suddenly asked.

I was so caught up in my thoughts, my emotions, along with scenery on the other side of the air-plane window, that Bradley's voice startled me.

"Huh? Well....no. Not really."

I truly didn't want to tell him that I was having problems locating the next chapter again.

"How is it so far?" he asked.

I smiled. Since I was too embarrassed to tell him the issues I was having with the device, I figure it wouldn't hurt to talk with him about what I had read thus far, considering it was still fresh on my mind.

"Well, remember how it started off, right? The main character Jason is deep undercover? Well, he blows his cover to thwart an attempt on the life of a fellow federal DEA agent and finds out after he wakes up in the hospital that his family was killed in an explosion that same night. He also learns that his oldest son survives the attack."

"Oh no, that's rough but, a small light shine brightly upon him," Bradley responded. "At least someone survived, right?"

"Well, not quite," I quickly replied, as I somberly shook my head. "He actually loses his oldest son a few days before he wakes up. Just heartbreaking."

"Oh man, that's really difficult." Bradley immediately dropping the smile he had on his face.

"That's where I am at this point in the story." I said. "It's just real heavy stuff. I needed to take a break from it." Bradley nodded.

"Yeah of course," he said. "That's tough to even imagine. I couldn't even possibly imagine going through something like that and making it through."

I didn't respond as I really didn't feel all that comfortable sharing with him the ridiculous and unlikely notion that I had quite a bit in common with this character Jason— more than I cared to truly verbally admit at this point.

"It would be rather difficult, but I'm confident I would make it through." said Bradley, as he put his glasses back on his face and returned to his work on his laptop. I shook my head as Bradley's words sort of slightly perplexed me.

"Why do you say that?" I asked, confused. The question just seemingly floated off the top of my subconscious and into the atmosphere before I had a chance to really think about it. The question also seemed to catch him by surprise as he had already began typing on his laptop again.

"Come again?" Bradley asked looking over at me while removing his glasses. I sat up in my seat and slowly glanced down at the Nook.

"How do you know you would've made it through something like this? How can you be so confident?"

Smiling, Bradley leaned over closer towards me.

"Well, you don't ever know for certain," he calmly replied. "But I personally walk by faith, as most of you would call it. So, when I say that, it's because of the amount of strength I incorporate into everything that I believe. I have to believe that I'm strong enough mentally and spiritually to get through anything this universe lays in front of me. No matter how horrible or unfortunate it may seem."

"What about you?" Bradley continued, "How would you handle going through what this character has gone through?"

I didn't answer right away as I took a moment to gather my thoughts. "Faith," hearing that word again immediately annoyed me and I was unable to hide it. I could feel my head starting to shake as the word "no" just floated aimlessly around my subconscious upon hearing it

"I can assure you; everyone's faith isn't the same." I whispered as I leaned over towards Bradley. "It's easy for someone with faith as solid or committed as yours, to suggest that this man should simply *"try to get over it"* or *"try to get through it."* But that's something that's easier said than done, no? No one knows just how strong your faith is or how tough your strength is until you're tested, trust me I know— unfortunately."

With an inquisitive expression on his face, Bradley continued to nod, but seemed sort of taken aback by my words. My seemingly passionate response on '*faith*' caught him off guard a bit as he appeared to be processing my words. As I glanced at him out of my peripheral, it seemed as if what I just shared with him about faith slightly affected him as he appeared somewhat enlightened. He too took a moment to seemingly gather his thoughts. I had no idea what it was that I said, but it was as if he was hearing the concept of *subjective faith* for the first time. There was a bit of awkward silence as Bradley appeared to be contemplating deeply on what I'd shared with him.

"Well, what does he do? How does he handle it? Or have you not gotten that far?" Bradley finally responded.

"I'm not sure, I sighed. "I haven't actually gotten that far, but clearly this man has lost a great deal. He practically lost his entire family, everything that he lived for and his only reason for existing. I don't think he's going to simply "*make it through*" this. This is some tough shit to deal with, my friend. Honestly, I don't see how you could blame the guy if he wanted to give up or if he was thinking 'suicide' at this point. I just can't see anyone going through something like this, and not at least consider suicide, as morbid a thought as it is. Not saying it's what I would do, or agree with it, but this guy Jason, should undoubtedly be on the verge of giving up, due to the unbearable, unspeakable pain he's dealing with."

"You mean; take his own life?" Bradley asked with a slightly bewildered expression on his face.

"Well.....*suicide*, so yeah." I replied facetiously. My quick response filled the air saturated behind an obvious facetious tone as I smiled somewhat subtly at Bradley's display of apparent confusion.

"I don't disagree with that." said Bradley. "Me believing that this guy, this character, can actually get thorough what he's going through, is probably more '*wishful thinking*' on my part than anything. I know something like that is impossible to make it through without the emotional odds slowly beginning to stack up against you, mentally. But I also believe we are naturally and cosmically wired to be stronger than anything the universe throws at us, no matter what it is. I truly believe that. We just don't accept or utilize this "wiring" the way we were meant to."

I slowly nodded in response. I didn't necessarily agree with what Bradley was saying, but it made sense when I accepted it from within the vacuum in which he was delivering it. I didn't disagree with him on his sentiments, but I didn't completely agree with him on it. I just had a hard time accepting anything faith based 'reasoning' as any kind of logic surrounding my daughter no longer being here. At the moment, I needed more than that. As solid a guy as Bradley appeared to be, he was no different than Father Miyake—a soft spoken man who relied heavily on his faith, but whose opinions, feelings, and thoughts were no better or more accurate than mine.

I didn't have many answers right now. At this point, I didn't even know what the *questions* were, but I knew I still felt different. My body, mind, and my spirit, all felt different in a way that made it currently impossible to even define what "different" meant. It was a slightly euphoric feeling that I'd never felt before, ever. It wasn't as if I was high, but the feeling was somewhat similar, just without the substance. I was high quite a bit in college, this wasn't that. This was clearer, much clearer, much sharper and much more detailed and focused.

My entire state of existence felt almost transparent in a way. This was the surreal feeling you have when you're quietly witnessing a beautiful, breathtaking sunset or sunrise, from a top of a mountain, on a crystal-clear spring day—the refreshing and slightly cool air gently caressing your face. Now imagine while on top of this mountain, you glance out over the vast and immense area that lies just under that sunrise or sunset. That area, open, untapped, and unclogged—that's where my mind currently found itself.

I gazed at my hands in slight amazement, as if it was the first time seeing them. I slowly peered around the plane until my eyes eventually locked on Bradley, who had been looking at me this entire time and was way past concerned at this point.

"Are *you* ok?" he asked as he smiled slightly.

"You don't feel any different?" I asked curiously. I desperately wanted him to admit that he was so I would feel much better and much more relieved.
He seemed legitimately confused by the question.

"Different?" The confused expression on his face made me grin.

"Yeah—like, I don't know, slightly euphoric, almost a surreal feeling?" Bradley chuckled as he shook his head.

"No, I feel like my usual old self." he said behind a smile. "You feeling different? If so, it's probably the air at this point, no?"

It was possible that he was right, and maybe I wasn't crazy. But it was hard to shake or dismiss this feeling. It was almost as if someone had just opened the door, a door within my mind, and everything was coming in all at once, or at least that's what I believed I was feeling. I remember feeling this way in the airport, and even in the hospital. I distinctly remembered this feeling being somewhat magnified during the counsel with Father Miyake. I knew as much as I wanted it to be the altitude, it felt like something else.

"No, I'm fine." I uttered behind a forced smile. "But, to respond to what you were saying; I do agree with you that some of us are naturally stronger and built to deal with what this universe throws our way. I do think it's a very small percentage of the earth's population.

"In the case of Jason here," I motioned towards the Nook with my head, "I think we're dealing with someone that has given a lot of years to his career—to the bureau. I believe he has every right to feel betrayed. Just looking at it logically and not as someone simply reading a story, I believe he *should* be suicidal because of what he lost, and the immense pain that is now rooted firmly within his soul. It's not easy to live with this kind of pain. It's not easy to carry this...."

I took a moment to breathe as I battled the emotions within. I didn't want Bradley to see me at my most vulnerable. I didn't want him to know what I was fighting within. Bradley seemed to agree with me, as made clear by his constant head nodding.

"You have a point," he finally replied. "Just let me know how it turns out. If it's doing one thing, it's at least giving us something meaningful to discuss to help the transition go by much faster. That alone makes the story a winner in my book."

"Transition?" I responded curiously.

"This journey we currently find ourselves on." He responded through a smile.

The more he spoke, the weirder his verbiage seem. I nodded and smiled as he too smiled, placed his glasses back on his face, and gradually refocused his attention back on his laptop. Still, I needed help navigating to the next chapter of this story, if there even was one. At this point, I had nothing to lose by getting Bradley to help locate the next chapter again. I quickly reached for the Nook, so I could hand it over to Bradley for assistance, but while reaching for it, I immediately noticed the screen on the device was illuminated.

"Interesting." I whispered as I grabbed the Nook up off my lap and went directly to the story and tapped on its icon again.

Much to my amazement and shock, there was suddenly an icon for chapter three staring back at me. I was perplexed and felt slightly disgusted with myself for not seeing it earlier. I closed my eyes and shook my head as I slowly begin to smile. Whatever this device Father Miyake has left me with, it sure as hell didn't give a shit about my sanity or peace of mind at this point. It was playing with my emotions and mental state something terrible at this point. I glanced over at Bradley, who had refocused on his work. I relaxed a bit more in my seat, focused my attention back on the Nook and immediately fell into chapter three of *Jason's Story*.

Jason's Story—Chapter Three

There wasn't a house to return to. The place where he and his family called home, where the memories lingered. There literally wasn't a home to return to. The explosion ripped a hole into his entire existence. Rebuilding was an option given to him by the insurance company, but the Bureau determined that because of what happened that night, there was always the risk the Cartel wasn't finished. They didn't want to take any chances, so he was relocated to a house owned by the Bureau, in a town right outside of Lansing called Lake Odessa.

A new house, and what now suddenly appeared to be a new life—it all seemed to be happening so fast, yet it was all still so surreal. No one knew of his new location except the Director of the FBI, the Section Chief and Special Agent in Charge Dave Watson—his boss. Section Chief Keegan, was relocated to oversee the Lansing field office a few years ago and brought Dave and his team with him, forcing the entire team to relocate to the area. A move that didn't sit that well with the team, but Dave made the transition as smooth as possible, and promised the team it would be the last move for a while.

Losing his family was not only difficult to accept but, essentially impossible for Jason to wrap his entire existence around. He still refused to accept it, and believed at times, he was still stuck in a horrible, unforgiving nightmare. But, during the brief times when he actually had a grasp on reality, he knew it was real, but still accepting it, just didn't seem like a legitimate option for him at the moment. What remaining belongings that survived the blast, he brought with him to his new house, including his car. He covered everything that had the haunting faces of his family on them. There was quite a bit of clothing, pictures, toys, and other things that actually survived the blast, which he brought to the new place with him. With each day that passed, Jason found it increasingly difficult to accept the Bureau's explanation as to why his family wasn't better protected that night. He realized that it didn't help anything at this point to constantly dwell on it, but his deep anger towards the bureau, grew within him every day he sat alone in his new home, contemplating on everything that happened.

He wanted answers from the Bureau, from Dave, and from his Section Chief. He wanted answers as to why his family wasn't protected while he was deep undercover, putting his life on the line for the bureau. These were the questions that he found the strength to ask. Questions that no one could provide adequate or acceptable answers to.

He was placed on medical and personal leave—indefinitely and ordered to see a psychiatrist every week. Outside of that, there was nothing else. He really didn't have the strength to do anything else and didn't care to. Fellow agents, including his team members, called to check on him. He'd never answered. He would communicate via two-way pager with all that wanted to communicate with him; that was about it. When they stopped by, he never answered the door. He couldn't even find the strength to get out of bed to do so.

There wasn't much family around, as both his parents were dead, and his half-sister lived in Oregon. She begged him to let her come stay and take care of him, but he of course refused. He simply believed at this point, he wasn't any good to anyone, and realized that this feeling wasn't changing anytime soon. He didn't want to be an emotional burden on anyone.......

"Hey, can I ask you something?"

Bradley's voice suddenly interrupted my intense focus on the story.

"Yeah sure." I replied quickly, looking up from the story towards Bradley.

"Earlier when we were talking about "*faith*," and listening to you discuss what we're talking about in such a passionate tone, leads me to believe that there is something, probably a story behind that passion or disdain for "*faith*." Am I wrong?"

I slowly chuckled, as I glanced away from Bradley and began shaking my head.

"And if I'm out of line please let me know, but I only ask this respectfully." Bradley continued.

"I know, and it's fine," I replied. "I appreciate you asking, no matter what your reasoning's were."

I sighed and smiled. The smile was necessary to hide the pain. But obviously, I wasn't doing enough to hide it adequately.

"I'm assuming by now," I finally replied. "That it's obvious I'm dealing with something painful? It's been very difficult to hide at this point."

Bradley took his glasses off and placed them on top of his laptop and nodded his head.

"I spent half the time I've existed," Bradley replied. "In this universe, forcing other inhabitants of the same universe, to share with me their inner most secrets, primarily dealing with their health. I now have no interest in people's personal life or stories, and I'm never the one to proactively pry, as everyone has their own story, Steve, but yes, it's pretty evident that you're going through something— something pretty painful. It's none of my business but I..."

"I'm returning home to bury my three-year-old daughter." I calmly replied. Bradley looked at me, and I could see his eyes growing wider. He seemed to be looking past me or through me, almost as if he was blind in a way. It was an awkward silence as he continued to gaze at me. I interrupted him to save him the trouble of digging, and me the trouble of dancing around it.

"Oh man, I'm so sorry," he finally replied. "I'm so sorry, my condolences man."

"Thanks," I replied as I glanced out of the window at the passing sun and the clouds. A tear – I could feel one slowly making its way down my cheek, I immediately wiped it away.

I quickly turned back to face Bradley.

"So, that tone you hear—it's me dealing with internal struggles. It's me unconsciously responding to the priest that was counseling me in Japan about my daughter's death. He placed a lot of emphases on "*faith.*" It had nothing to do with anything you said. It's all me."

"Oh no," Bradley replied, "I hope I didn't insinuate that I was bothered or slighted by what you said? It was just a general and honest observation. Your daughter, I'm terribly sorry, Steve."

"Thanks again. She was.....um.... well, she was three years old and uh...."

I struggled to even get the words out at this point. But I figured if I was going to get him to understand, I would need to tell him everything, and talking about it at this point was as close to therapy I would get before I touched down back home.

"Wow, Steve I'm sorry, so sorry."
Bradley's words seemed immensely sincere as he appeared to fight diligently to contain his own emotions. He appeared to take the news harder than I imagined.

"She drowned," I quickly stated in attempt to continue the dialogue. "I'm not sure if you were going to ask how she died, but like you said, fifteen hours sitting next to each other, might as well have something to talk about." I said behind a slightly fictitious grin.

"Hey man, I'm sorry," said Bradley. "I can't even imagine."

"It's ok," I replied. "I'm dealing with it. I figure I'll discover how strong I really am by this time tomorrow after her funeral. She was beautiful. She.....effortlessly illuminated the room, and I don't know how, but this girl was so smart and wise for her age. She knew what to say and when to say it. She truly was a gift, a wonder."

Bradley continued to smile as I spoke of my late daughter.

I figured it was easy to see on my face, just how much I loved her and how proud of her I was. I wasn't looking at Bradley directly, but I could feel him staring at me out of my peripheral. I turned towards the window to prevent him from seeing my face, as it was impossible to hide my emotions at this point, so I didn't even bother trying. Talking about her and everything that made her a wonderful person, daughter, and human being. Talking about her right now and saying these things out loud made it worse and not better, like I expected it to.

"It's hard, I know it is," Bradley whispered. "And I'll ask God to strengthen you. If I could give you all of my strength right now I would."

I heard every word Bradley was saying, and I was grateful for his kind words, but I was starting to become too emotional.

"Hey, um, you said you were in Japan as a "film consultant?" I asked quickly turning back towards Bradley.

"Yep, that's right." Bradley quickly responded behind a grin. He was immediately aware that I was attempting to change the topic.
I nodded.

"What kind of consulting?"

"Well, I'm a retired healer and a friend of mine is a film producer. He's currently filming a movie over there. I haven't traveled much especially internationally in my lifetime, so I jumped at the opportunity to do this. It's been a wonderful experience, to be honest with you."

"That's awesome," I replied. "How long you been doing this?"

"Well, for quite some time now. I was doing it sparingly when I was a healer—quite the experience indeed. You'd be surprised at what I've learned while doing this. I've learned more about life in my time as a movie consultant than all my time preparing to be a healer, and the time I was actually practicing medicine."

"Wow! Really?" I was surprised to hear him say this.

He seemed to be very passionate, I could hear it in his voice.

"Yep, it's been rewarding. It was the perfect opportunity."

"I certainly understand," I replied. "What type of movie were you consulting on in Japan?" Bradley opened his mouth to answer Steve's question but was quickly distracted by something on his computer.

"Give me a few," he whispered, as he focused his attention on the screen and began typing.

I immediately shifted my focus back on the pristine evening scenery directly outside of my window. The clouds and the setting evening sun began to instantly move me as I stared off into the distant sunset over the Pacific. I still had trouble figuring out or trying to understand the way I was feeling right now. Maybe there wasn't even a word for it, but whatever it was, it wasn't going away. I was clueless as to what it was, but it was all over me. And the immensely sharp euphoric feeling that accompanied it, was even more difficult to explain. It was almost as if something, life, the universe—whatever, was finally discovering who I was or recognizing me for the first time through this unbearable pain.

It was as if my eyes were opening for the first time. My senses, for the first time were clearer, much sharper. It was as if I was simply allowing everything in. It didn't make sense to me, but that was the most surreal aspect about it—my warped and caged sense of "logic" and "sense" suddenly didn't mean much to me at this point. It was almost as if my way of thinking had been altered, and I was, in some weird way, looking at everything in a much different perspective. I had no idea why that was. I didn't understand the way I was feeling. I knew what I was personally going through, was the worst pain I've ever gone through in my life, emotional or physically. I knew I shouldn't be feeling like this, but I was. I closed my eyes, laid my head back, and began thinking about Natalie. I began to reflect on the times when she would be at her happiest just being around me. She would bring me gifts in the morning to my bed side to wake me up. *"Daddy, close your eyes,"* she would say, *"I got something for you— Ka-prise!!"* she would yell while handing me one of her dolls or stuffed bears as a *gift* from her. It's essentially how I started my day, pretty much every day, before going to work."

I wiped tears from my face and closed my eyes. I allowed whatever this was to fully engulf me as I knew it was something I couldn't outrun. Emotionally, I had no idea what I was flying home to, but I knew I had to find a way to dig deep and uncover some sort of strength for my family. I knew they weren't strong enough to deal with it without me—without my strength. As I glanced down, I realized that for a brief moment, I had forgotten I was holding the Nook, and had actually begun the third chapter. I glanced back over to Bradley who was working diligently on his laptop which was my cue to turn my attention back to the story.

<u>Jason's Story- Chapter Three—Continued</u>

Gazing at the stars always helped. It's something he did prior to the tragedy, but now it took on a whole new meaning and reason, as it helped him escape—somewhat. It couldn't, however, help him escape from his own mind, his own morbid thoughts as he found himself no longer wanting to be here. This life, right here, right now, he just didn't have the motivation, the energy, the will to be here, or to live anymore.

Gazing at the stars helped him escape from the place he no longer wanted to be, if only for a moment but it didn't help him escape from his existence. In the back of his mind, he realized thinking this way wasn't healthy, but he didn't care anymore. He slept about twenty hours out of the day and didn't eat much, if at all.

Since leaving the hospital, he probably lost about ten pounds in two weeks. He left a pre-recorded message for people to text him via two- way pager as he preferred to communicate that way at this time. He didn't want to hear anyone and certainly didn't want anyone to hear his dark, dead, and deeply depressed voice at this point. As part of his mandated bureau implemented trauma evaluation, he continued to see the psychiatrist once a week. It didn't help much at all primarily because, he didn't want it to help. Some days were slightly better than awful, and some nights were slightly worse than horrible, but overall, it had a feeling of a car slowly headed down the highway towards an open sink hole filled with fire and acid.

His mind was now his worst enemy as it played the most sinister tricks on him. His mind, since that night in the back of the van before everything happened, had seem to unfold itself, and now felt opened in such a way that seem to pull the world around him closer towards his mind—his subconscious. This night, the stars were out, and the sky was so clear that one could literally count them all. Jason found himself attempting to do just that. As he counted, deep down, he felt as if he was slowly giving up.

He wasn't exactly certain if he was quitting or not, but whatever this was, he knew he couldn't continue on this way. His mind was conflicted and gradually waging an intense and emotional battle within itself. The feeling was one of exaltation, yet it was indescribable, incredibly confusing, and conflicting for him as well.

As he gazed upward toward the stars, he began to count them—something he used to do as a child, and *sometimes as a man. As he started to count, Jason realized that with every star he "touched" as he pointed to them with his index finger, it was as if he was now seeing the stars clearly for the first time ever. It was as if just by looking and gazing upon them, he could tell which star was actually a star and which was a planet. He could seemingly tell which star was the youngest and brightest. This feeling that had fallen over him, was one that was not only difficult to explain and put into words, but one that allowed every type of thought to enter into his mind— unfiltered. He began to look past the stars and smiled.*

He looked past them and looked towards the heaven, towards God.

"You take my family away from me and now you make me crazy?"

Jason nodded his head as he spoke. He nodded in such a way as if he was waiting for a response to his question. He couldn't understand how and why he was feeling the way he was feeling, but he not only didn't understand it, he knew whatever it was, it was likely the first symptom or stages of a potential breakdown.

"Ha! Too good and too almighty to answer me, huh? Answer me, dammit! Is this what you brought me in this world for? Is It?"

His voice echoed across the quiet suburban neighborhood, as he yelled out to God. No longer holding anything back at this point, Jason allowed the pain and the hurt in his voice to resonate across the brisk, quiet night sky and continued to stare at the sky with a cold, emotionless blank stare, as if was looking upon the face of God herself. His mind was as clear and as opened as it had ever been at any point in his life, so it made it somewhat easy to figure out what God and the universe wanted out of him now— wasn't hard to see. So, he would oblige both. He slowly fell asleep that night atop the roof starring at the night stars. Knowing now what it was that he needed to do.

The cold, brisk Michigan countryside, early morning air, gradually woke Jason out of his sleep. He hadn't intended on falling asleep on the roof, but realized he was extremely exhausted and mentally drained. He smiled at the morning sun which was well on its way over the horizon. It was a new day, a different day—a better day. A day he decided would be the beginning of the rest of his life. He carefully showered, shaved, and brushed his teeth; his morning routine every day when he would get up with the family before heading off to work. He prepared himself a breakfast–pancakes, eggs, bacon, and ice-cold orange juice, just the way his wife made it for he and the boys every weekend, the way she knew they liked it.

Sitting at the table eating his breakfast, he slowly glanced around the table as he saw his family sitting in their respective places at the table back home, laughing, and enjoying their breakfast, the way they always did at home.

Jackson always talked the most at the table.

"Is it good daddy?" Jackson asked him with a big smile on his face.

"Yes son, it's very good." he responded while smiling and rubbing Jackson's hair.

But there was no one at the table with him.

Jackson wasn't there, his family wasn't there–no one was there with him. He was sitting at the table alone. Just he and his memories, memories that now haunted him like ghosts. Jason slowly finished his breakfast and washed the dishes.

"One of these days you guys will be big enough to wash the dishes." he said smiling, as he looked back at Jackson and Trey, who smiled back at their father. There was a suit that Tracy and the boys bought him for Father's Day last year. A tailored suit that he only wore once. Somehow, this suit survived the explosion with just minor damage. He retrieved the suit from the closet and memories of the day that he first received it, exited the closet with it. Jason dressed himself in his suit as he thought about the first time he put it on over a year ago, when he celebrated Father's Day at his favorite restaurant with Tracy and the boys.

Fixing his tie, he smiled as he reminisced about that day and how the boys enjoyed celebrating that day with him. The thought of them constantly saying "Happy Father's Day" repeatedly, all day was something he'd never forget.

He now felt confident, as a surreal and euphoric feeling overwhelmed him as he looked himself over in the mirror. He closed his eyes, and shook his head, like he was shaking off a bad headache in a feeble attempt at shaking away this feeling that had slowly consumed his world, his mind as of late. The feeling came from out of nowhere, but he didn't allow it to disrupt his happy moment. Looking himself in the mirror, he smiled—this was the happiest he'd been in quite some time. He stood there staring at himself and nodded his head.

"Ok, I can do this." he nervously whispered to himself. Standing outside of the kitchen door that led to the garage,

Jason reached for the keys. He was ready for this journey and looked forward to it. After staring at the door *leading to the garage for what felt like forever, he slowly reached for the knob and opened the door.*

His car, a late model sedan, it smiled back at him. It had been forever since he had been behind the wheel. Slowly walking out into the garage, Jason hesitated just a bit, but soon continued on to his car. He opened the door to the car and immediately sat down in the driver seat. It smelled the same.   He closed his eyes and slowly inhaled the smell. He smelled his wife's perfume. He smelled his son's snacks they would always bring into the car. Reaching into his jacket pockets he slowly retrieved three different pictures, one picture of each one of them. He gingerly and carefully placed the pictures in their respective locations, where they would usually sit when they traveled; Tracy, in the front passenger seat, and the pictures of the two boys in the back seats.

"You guys ready to go yet?" he asked.

"Jackson please don't hit your brother." Jason quickly, yet calmly stated while gazing at Jackson's pic through the rear-view mirror. Checking his mirrors thoroughly to make sure they were positioned in their right places, Jason started the car and immediately powered on the radio. He retrieved a CD from the visor and placed it in the CD player; Israel Kamakawiwo'ole's "Over the Rainbow," his family's favorite song. The song began to

play, and as the song played, he found himself becoming more relaxed as he closed his eyes and began singing along. He began reflecting back to all of those times he would sing this song to the boys, when their mother wasn't around to sing it to them.

Jason was a horrible singer, but even he sounded wonderful when he sang the song for his boys. They thought it was the best thing they'd ever heard. The song played in the background as Jason kept his eyes closed and sang along to it, not missing a beat or a word. The minutes quickly yet gradually crept by as the carbon monoxide from the exhaust pipe slowly made its way through the car and entered Jason's lungs as sleep slowly began to overwhelm him. ** It was becoming increasingly difficult to keep his eyes open at this point, as the carbon monoxide was quickly doing what he wanted.

This was the journey he was prepared to take, the journey in which he believed God forced him to take. This was the journey Jason felt as though the universe wanted him to embark upon, so that he could be with his family again.

He would no longer fight it. He no longer wanted to fight it.......

"Jesus, don't do this to yourself man." I whispered to myself while shaking my head. I was in utter disbelief at what I was reading.

"I'm sorry what'd you say?" Bradley asked while quickly looking up from his laptop. I shook my head and pointed down at the Nook.

"Nothing really.....It's just the guy in this story, well it's kind of hard to explain, but you know the character Jason we were discussing earlier, right?"

"Yeah." said Bradley while nodding.

"Well, it's kind of funny how earlier we were talking about him most likely wanting to commit suicide, well, he's essentially giving up, and is basically doing it."

"Well, you said it didn't you?" Bradley replied. "You said you see him doing that, yet you seemed surprised. Why?"

"I'm not really surprised, well a little I guess, but It's, well, shocking and of course I saw it as feasible, but as I stated when I said it, I don't agree with it."

"Well of course you don't agree with it," said Bradley "But can I ask you something personal?"

"Sure."

"Even though you don't agree with it, do you understand and even empathize a bit with him on his decision to go through with it considering, well...."

"I do," I quickly replied.

I knew where he was going with this.

"I understand," I continued. "but not really sure I truly empathized with him. As much pain as I'm dealing with right now, I just don't believe taking your own life is the answer to anything difficult we may encounter in this life, I just don't. I think ......"

I closed my eyes as the emotions begin to slightly overwhelm me.

"It's ok," said Bradley, "we don't have to talk about this if you don't want to."

"No, its fine. This is healthy for me, trust me. I just think, in order to start the healing process, you have to grieve adequately and appropriately when suffering a tragic loss. It's easier said than done of course, and honestly I don't think I've done it myself yet, and I know that time will come when I get back to my family, as we'll probably grieve together."

"Well, is the guy in your story, Jason—has he had time to grieve, or does he simply want to give up?" Bradley asked.

"I believe he wants to give up." I replied. "The pain is just too unbearable right now. I don't think he even wants to grieve at this point. That's a part of the healing process, and I don't think he's interested in going through any process right now that involves healing."

Sitting up in his seat, Bradley nodded as he leaned closer and began to whisper.

"When a man does not grieve properly, he barely even exists. This seems to be what's happening to Jason." I nodded my head as what Bradley was saying, as it being to register within.

"Look," said Bradley, "I just don't believe God created us just so we can end our lives whenever we aren't happy with what's going on around us, no matter how egregious the situation. Giving up isn't what we were placed in this vast universe to do, is it?"

"God? "I said as I shook my head through a smile. "God and I just..... As I told you before, I don't think we are on the same page about life or anything at the moment. Frankly, I don't think God and I have ever been on the same page. My daughter's death defeated me. I took a moment to pause. To truly gather myself.

"It's defeating me. It's a sharp feeling of defeat that I don't think I'll ever get over. It has taken a piece of my soul that will never return."

I stopped, took a moment to collect myself as my emotions began to get the better of me. I turned and glanced out of the window at the dark orange evening sky. It was clear, gazing out of this window during this flight would be a place I can turn to, literally, in order to escape, like the stars did for Jason.

"We can stop if it's too much." whispered Bradley as he leaned over close to me. I immediately shook my head.

"No, I'm fine. You must understand that I have to face this. The more I face this in the many aspects, from the many different views and concepts that I need to before doing so with my family, that can only help me to be as strong and as poised for them as I need to be."
Bradley immediately nodded his head.

"I understand."

"Look," I replied, "being defeated or feeling defeated is a temporary feeling no matter what you're going through. But, when you decide to simply give up, that's what makes it permanent in your world, that's what essentially gives your temporary circumstance, your brief trial that you're experiencing, life. I'm in the mind that no matter what you are going through or experiencing in life, it will be temporary if you want it to be temporary. This is something......."

I was exhausted but I continued to push through my emotions in order to complete my sentiment.

"This is something that applies to me as well. Though I don't think I can ever get over what I'm dealing with, the pain that I'm fighting through right now, the pain my family is fights through right now, I do know that the hurt and pain will only stay if we allow it. It will only be permanent in my life if I allow it and as hard as it is, I won't allow it. I believe Jason is doing essentially that. He's making his situation in his universe, in his world, permanent and I can't agree with it. This isn't the same for everyone. Sometimes it's all just too much and we give up. We're human. Everyone isn't built to withstand everything the same as everyone else. Me understanding that sentiment isn't the same as me agreeing with how one fights it, I suppose."

Bradley looked at me and began nodding his head as if he was in agreement with everything I was saying.

"Well feeling defeated isn't always temporary." he replied calmly. "Sometimes, it lasts forever but I get what you are saying. From your perspective, you believe this guy Jason has folded and allowed the universe to defeat him? You believe that no matter how egregious or difficult his situation now seems, the temporary nature of it is irrelevant now considering he's making it permanent with his sudden decision to just, give up?"

"Well, yeah," I replied as I nodded my head. "Pretty much. I believe this character Jason is no different than any of us. He's stronger than what he appears to be. I know he is. In this same story, he saved that DEA Agent's family in chapter one. He took on the entire group, all odds stacked against him, he did this to save the lives of people he never met. He's strong. Mentally, physically and emotionally he's strong. I just don't think he realizes just how strong he really is. I believe we are all stronger than what we appear to be during perilous times, it's just much harder to continue fighting when it's so much easier to simply quit. Jason is quitting. No one can truly understand with what he's going through, not even me, but I know that I do love living. Life can be hard, but what is the alternative? Killing himself isn't the answer for Jason in this story no more than it is for you or I for our life's struggles. I don't think he should kill himself."

Bradley slowly nodded his head while I was talking. I knew he agreed with me, somewhat.

"We all face different journeys, but I agree for the most part, my friend. So how does he kill himself?" Bradley asked with a curious look on his face. "And what's next in this story if the main character kills himself? Is there a secondary character?"

"Well, he isn't dead as of yet," I replied. "But he's in the process of taking his own life. He's in his car right now, inside his garage with the motor running. Don't really see a main secondary character just yet, but you bring up an interesting point."

"What's the name of that book again?" Bradley asked with a curious look on his face.

"I don't actually know. It was a gift from a friend, but they seemed to have put this book on this device without a title. I think the device is broken, to be honest with you, considering all the issues I've been having with it. I've given it my own title— *"Jason's Story."*
Bradley flashed a curious look and chuckled as he placed his glasses back on his face.

"Well, let me know how it turns out. I have to finish some more work here. I'll be in and out of focus on this over here, and sleep for the remainder of the flight. But I'm here if you have any questions or want to talk.

With that, Bradley smiled and focused his attention back onto his work. I quickly focused me attention back to the Jason's Story.

Jason's Story – Chapter Three—Continued

Sitting in his car, Jason stared at himself in the rear-view mirror for a few seconds as his eyes continued to get extremely heavy. He used what little energy he had to turn the car off and quickly exited the car. He immediately fell to the garage floor and began to slowly drag himself over to the garage door which was closed. He glanced up and noticed the button to open the garage door was about six feet from the ground.

Jason realized that he needed to get to that button in order to open the door as the effects of the carbon monoxide began to gradually overwhelm him. Lying on his back, Jason gazed up at the ceiling unsure of what to do next as the suddenly morbid situation he found himself in was impossible to escape. He no longer wanted to do this to himself. He didn't understand why this was the case. He seemingly had no way out of the garage as he laid flat on his back staring up at the ceiling as his eyes became increasingly heavier by the passing seconds. He saw no way out, maybe it was easier to just give up and allow it all to take him....

I had a hard time understanding this guy. That feeling was the only consistent sentiment I had within this story thus far. First, he wants to truly kill himself. He's committed and dedicated with going through with it, then suddenly, out of the blue, he doesn't. And now that he doesn't want to kill himself, it appeared as if he's going to accidentally kill himself. It was all too weird and too hard to take in at this point.

'If it was me,' I thought to myself, *'I would be looking for any and everything around me to grab in order to hit that button to open the garage.'*

"I'm sure you can find something in that garage to hit that button with man!!" I whispered to myself as I shook my head in disbelief. It shouldn't be too hard as I figured there had to be some sort of broom, rake or something in there that could aid him. I held my hand to my chest as I felt my heart racing rapidly.

This story had me completely engaged, and I was all in. I took a couple of deep breaths to calm my heart rate and fell back into the story......

Jason's Story- Chapter Three - Continued

Jason slowly glanced over onto the garage wall and immediately spotted a shovel leaning against the wall next to the door. He slowly began to pull himself over to the shovel to retrieve it. Finally reaching it, he gripped the bottom of the shovel with one hand, Jason swung the shovel towards the button but missed. He focused harder on the button as he started to become increasingly drowsy with each passing second. Time was precious but he took a moment to concentrate. He could feel the ability to control his limbs slowly slipping away. With all the remaining strength he had, Jason swung the shovel towards the button once more, this time, able to make contact. The garage door slowly opened, and when it was fully opened, Jason slowly dragged himself out into the driveway—eyes still heavy and unable to keep them open at this point. Jason made it to the edge of his driveway before completely passing out.

He struggled to open his eyes, but he could hear the sounds around him, clearly. As his eyes finally opened, the first thing he noticed was the ceiling. He slowly began looking around and struggled to understand what was happening or where he was. As he continued to gaze around, he began to slowly realize that he was in the hospital— it was all too familiar. The smell of the hospital reminded him of everything he wanted to forget. There were voices over by the room door. As he turned toward the voices, he suddenly realized how dizzy he was, and immediately laid his head back down on the pillow.

"He's waking up." Jason heard a voice say as he heard footsteps walking into the room towards him. Glancing up, he noticed what appeared to be a doctor along with Dave, and the bureau's psychiatrist—Dr. Sharon Reed.

"Jason, how we feeling?" the Doctor asked as he walked over to him and began checking the info on the machine.

"I feel very dizzy. Very groggy."

"That's normal." The Doctor replied. "You'll feel that way for a few hours, but it should subside within twenty-four hours. You were lucky to begin breathing fresh oxygen when you did. You were close to the point of no return."

"Jason, what happened?" Dave asked as he positioned himself in a chair next to Jason's bed. "Did you try to kill yourself, Jason?"
Jason looked away from Dave and gazed out towards the window. He took a deep breath and felt himself becoming emotional as tears begin falling from his eyes.

"Yeah Dave. I guess I did." Jason whispered dismissively.

"What happened, Jason?" Dr. Reed asked. "Did you simply change your mind?"
Jason turned back around to face everyone as his eyes widened.

"I don't know what I did." said Jason as he shook his head. "I don't know what happened. One minute I wanted out of here—I wanted to kill myself. Nothing was going to stop me from doing it, nothing, but the next minute, I was getting out of the car, and now I'm here. So, I don't know, you tell me. You guys are the Doctors."
Dave and Dr. Reed looked at one another in confusion.

"Jason, you need help." Dave calmly uttered. "Allow us to provide you with the help that you need." said

Dave.

"I don't need help, Dave." Jason took a moment to pause as he peered out of the window. "My family needed your help when I was unable to be there for them. I don't want your help, nor do I need it!" Shaking his head in disbelief, Dave glanced up at the Doctors.

"You guys want to give us a minute?"

"No!" said Jason. "No! You guys don't have to go anywhere, I don't want to talk to you, Dave. I have nothing to say to you, unless you're telling me why my family wasn't better protected. I don't want to hear anything from you."

"Jason, I'm sorry," Dave quickly replied. "I truly am. We failed you. I failed you. I failed your family, and I have to live with that failure every day for the rest of my life. I deal with those demons every day, but now I'm trying to help you, Jason."

Jason turned his head towards the window again and gazed out of it. Every word Dave was saying, he knew Dave truly meant it, and knew that he would eventually have to forgive him and deal with any personal demons he had to deal with in regard to forgiveness. He just couldn't do it at this time. He didn't have the strength or will to do it.

"I don't need your help, Dave. What do you guys want me to say? I don't want to kill myself. Not anymore. I thought I did, and I tried, I tried really hard to do so. I have no earthly idea why I didn't go through with it, I truly don't, but that's irrelevant now, considering I no longer wish to kill myself. I truly can't explain it. Stop asking me."

Dr. Reed hesitantly nodded her head as she inched her way closer toward Jason and maintained eye contact.

"Jason, there had to be a reason you changed your mind, what was the reason? What happen? What was going through your mind? I ask simply because, it was determined that based on the evidence, it appeared as if you thoughtfully and strategically planned this out, didn't you? You were found dressed in a suit. There were pictures of your family discovered in the car with seat belts strapped around them. That indicates planning, strategic planning. No one here is judging you, Jason. Though we don't know what you are feeling, agent Barrington, we do understand that it's difficult for you right now. We are here to help. We just need to understand what it is you want us to help you with."

"Just stop...." Jason whispered. "Just stop talking right now, please."

Jason slowly sat up in his bed as he looked deeply into Dr. Reed's eyes.

"Again—I don't know what it is you're looking for me to say. I don't know Doc. I can't tell you what it was. I can't tell you why or how. I just know that suddenly, I had this feeling inside me, a feeling around me that suddenly overwhelmed me and essentially yanked me out of that car. Yes, I physically got of the car on my own, but I just can't explain it. I truly do not know. It was like I was watching myself do this to myself, and I became sick and disgusted at how I was simply giving up on myself. It was like I suddenly felt as though I was much stronger than what I thought I was. It was as if there was something telling me that I could make it. Something telling me that killing myself wasn't an option. I felt like—there was more, and I was cutting my journey short."

Jason closed his eyes and slowly shook his head while the tears slowly fell.

"I just feel so defeated right now Doc," Jason sobbed. "But suddenly I want to fight. I don't know why or how, I just do. It hurts. The pain is still there, and it hurts, but this is me refusing to let it defeat me because I simply don't want it to. I just don't know what to do. There has to be more, so I don't know what you can help me with. I don't even know what I need help with. I just know my

mind is as opened as it's ever been, and I'm conflicted within myself as to what that that really means and yet the pain—it still lingers."

Dave and Dr. Reed glanced at one another with blank emotionally filled gazes. They knew they had a fight on their hands in order to get agent Barrington back healthy again in every way, but they had no idea what to do with what he'd just shared with them. None. They were glad he decided not to go through with taking his own life but was now concerned that he was gradually losing his grip on reality.

Jason's Story – Chapter Three - The End

I was happy Jason decided not to kill himself. I was also immensely intrigued with everything Jason said in that hospital bed. It was eerily and unmistakably similar to everything Bradley and I was discussing in regard to Jason's decision to kill himself. The more I thought about it, the more I smiled. I quickly found myself going back over Jason's words in the last part of that chapter just to be certain. And no matter how I read the words. No matter how much I read them out loud to myself, no matter how hard I tried to decipher them, I found myself back at the same place in thinking that it was a little bit too similar to what Bradley and I were discussing. I smiled, but not because it was funny, but because like Jason, I felt as if sometimes this grief buried within me had me slowly losing my grip on reality. My awareness was elevated slightly. This story had indeed grabbed me—I was all in.

Now, it was sending my already increasingly opening mind on a trip within itself, stopping only to question, second guess, or figure out any and everything that appeared to stand out or disrupt the normal order of everything around me, even in the smallest way—including within this story.

Those words, Jason's words, they stood out to me for good reason. I held on to the probable likelihood that I was dealing with a sharp case of coincidence here, but my mind, though suffering from grief, mental exhaustion, and fatigue at this point, had found something that stood out and wouldn't allow me to let it go for a reason that I wasn't cognizant of. Whatever it was, I couldn't let it go and knew I would be neck deep within it before it was all over. I proceeded with caution to begin chapter four of *Jason's Story*. A subtle smile instantly flashed over my face as I swiped to the next screen. Like before, no new chapter, no words, nothing. I gripped the Nook as tight as possible in frustration as I tilted my head back and took several deep breaths. I wanted to break the device in half at this point.

<u>Chapter Six</u>

A Toast Was in Order

I sat back in my seat, closed my eyes, and chuckled slightly. I didn't find this lingering "issue" with this device amusing in any way—quite the contrary. I found it to be extremely frustrating and annoying, to the point that all I could do was laugh to prevent from throwing it against the airplane walls. I glanced over to see if Bradley was noticing me having a mini meltdown, but he had already apparently dozed off for his first nap of the flight. The headphones, over his ears with the music playing, prevented outsides noise from interrupting his sleep. I began to look around to see if I saw anyone that would be able to help me. I wasn't able to see much sitting down. I sat back against my seat and took a deep breath.

"Someone should know how to work this god forsaken device." I whispered frustratingly to myself. I was about at my wits end with this device, but the story I was reading,

"Jason's story," was really intriguing and compelling. If anything, it was at least helping me escape from everything I needed to escape from right now—if only for the moment.

I slowly stood up with the device in hand, and slowly walked towards the back of the plane as if I was headed to the rest room. I was hoping to luck up and find someone, anyone, using the same device. I carefully surveyed the rows as I walked past, smiling at passengers, as I inconspicuously invaded their personal spaces with my wandering eye. I suppose I was looking for anyone that seemed technically savvy, a teenager perhaps. I slowly made my way upon two middle aged women, about five rows behind me, appearing to be enjoying what looked to be the same device. I wasn't sure if it was or not.

"Excuses me ladies," I whispered, bending down next to their seats.

"Yes?" the woman closest to the aisle replied.

"Is that a Nook you have there?" I asked behind a smile.

"Well no, it's a tablet, but not a Nook." she stated as she held up her device.

"Shit!!" I whispered, shaking my head dejectedly.

"Why do you ask?" the second lady asked in a soft

tone.

"Well, I'm having some issues with a Nook that I received as a gift. I just needed some help on how to use it. I'm not really familiar with it at all."

"I actually have one." the second woman replied.

"Wow, do you?!"

"Well yes," she exclaimed. "I'm sorry, but I didn't bring it with me, but I should still be able to help you with your issue, or I'll try my best."

"I would greatly appreciate that." I said as I placed my hand on my heart to express my gracious sentiments. I gingerly placed the Nook into the woman's outstretched hands.

"What's wrong with it?" she asked genuinely, powering it on as she spoke.

"Well, I've been having issues navigating to new chapters when I finish previous chapters. It's the weirdest thing. I've finished three chapters of the story that I'm reading so far, but like the previous two chapters, I'm consistently having fits trying to locate the next chapters. They seem to pop up whenever they want."

The woman looked over the device carefully and thoroughly with a curious look on her face.

"What's the title of the story?"

"Well—um, it doesn't actually have one. I'm not all that

sure why, but I didn't put the story on the device myself. It was a gift to me. The story was there already when I received it, but it's the story with a blank icon and no title."

"Ah, I see it. Yeah, that's weird." she said as she continued to examine the Nook. "Well," said the woman as she began shaking her head. "I've used these things for about two years now as I do tons of reading on them. My friend, I can assure you that this story that you're reading, it only has three chapters, no more."

"You sure?" I asked behind an immensely confused tone.

The woman didn't respond right away as she continued to maneuver through the device, swiped left, swiped right, and up and down. The curious look on the woman's face seemed to transform into a "frustrated" look as she took a deep breath. "Yeah, I'm sure." she said as she shook her head. "This story only has three chapters. Whoever loaded this book on here for you probably didn't do it right or loaded a corrupt copy of the book. There's nowhere for these chapters to be hidden. No reason for them not to be where they should be. No reason other than the device or the story file itself being corrupted. That's my only explanation, I'm so sorry."

She handed the Nook back to me and shook her head in confusion.

"I'm sorry I was unable to help you." She calmly uttered behind a warm smile.

"Oh, it's quite alright." I replied.

I stood up, thanked the two women again, then slowly made my way back to my seat. As I finally positioned myself back in my seat, I gazed down at the device, not really sure what to make of it, the story and everything else at this particular moment. I leaned my head back and I closed my eyes. I hadn't realized just how tired I was until my eyes were shut and I immediately began to feel the subtle burning sensation in my eyes somewhat subside as I left them closed for about a minute. I wanted to leave them closed forever as the exhaustion from the past forty-eight hours began to slowly overwhelm me. It was about three hours into the flight with just under twelve hours remaining. If I didn't have anything to read, focus or concentrate on to bide the time, then it would make for a long and uncomfortable flight. I wasn't in a mood for any of the movie options being presented. I really didn't want go to sleep, as I feared Natalie's face haunting me as soon as I closed my eyes.

I'm sure Father Miyake meant well with this gesture, but I knew this story would have no choice but to wait until I landed. It was indeed a highly intriguing story. I would certainly look to find it at a bookstore as soon as I touched down, as my interests had truly been peaked at this point. It was difficult to shake away all that I felt I had in common with the character Jason—the pain, the emotion, the struggle for potential healing. I understood when going through difficult times, especially when there isn't a precedent, you'd like some sort of "guide" to help make it through, and in a sense, I felt as though this story was that "guide" for me.

I had never experienced pain or trauma like this before, nor was I familiar with anyone who had. There was no one for me to call for advice as to how to get through this.

There was no one I could call to tell me how as a father and as a husband, what was needed to usher my family through this ordeal safely to the other side. I had no idea what I should do next or how I would get myself in a position mentally to be able to adequately deal with the emotions.

As I sat with my eyes closed, I began to focus heavily on my breathing. I began utilizing the breathing techniques the Doctor in Japan taught me in order to help relax, control my heart rate, and calm down in stressful times. The deeper the breaths I took, the more relaxed I started to feel. I was so relaxed that I didn't even feel the slight turbulence anymore as I was as comfortable as I'd been since stepping on this flight nearly three hours ago. The distant and faint sound of the plane lightly echoed through my mind as the cabin was extremely quiet. Too quiet. I needed something to occupy my mind as the quiet atmosphere was no good for me. Every time I closed my eyes, I not only saw Natalie's face, but the weeping faces of my wife and my other daughters. I slowly opened my eyes and glanced down at the Nook with a blank, emotionless gaze. I powered the device back on and slowly began gradually re-reading the first three chapters of the story.

I figured re-reading it would allow me to fill the void in my mind that was being ambushed by the silence.

I began reading the story from the beginning as if it was my first time reading it. It initially started as something I decided to do just to keep my mind occupied, something to combat the deafening silence, but it slowly began transitioned into something subconsciously pulling back into the initial chapters for other reasons. Reasons I was unable to understand or explain. There was something that I needed to grasp or understand, but that I was missing.

"What am I missing?" I softly whispered to myself as I shook my head—slightly confused.

My mind seemed as if it was, in a way, opening itself up more—consistently expanding, so to speak. I slowly began to clearly visualize the words from *"Jason's Story,"* in a way I hadn't done while reading it the first time. While re-reading, I continued with the helpful breathing exercises; inhaled deeply and exhaled deeply. The more I did it, the more relaxed I became, and the more the story itself began to open itself up to me in ways that was truly difficult to describe. The words began to take on a whole new meaning. The emotion from the story began to illuminate off the page this time. The words, this time around, uprooted a place in my soul and planted itself deep within me. I wasn't sure what was happening, but I liked the way I was suddenly starting to feel. I could feel a smile unconsciously stretching across my face. No, I didn't know how to explain it, but I was certain whatever it was, didn't really have an explanation, or needed to be explain. I was re-reading the story with a clear and sharp understanding of what I was reading, but for some unconsciously induced reason, it was now with an apparent different perspective and purpose.

The words were simply having a more profound effect on me this time around but why?

I noticed almost instantly during re-reading of the story that the beginning of chapters two and three stood out to me more than anything, as certain words, sentences, and verbiage seem to jump off the page at me. I couldn't exactly put a finger on any of it, but whatever it was, I couldn't seem to let it go. Certain words began to not only jump out at me, but for some reason they began to force me to immediately reflect on those conversations I had with Bradley while dealing with the issues with the Nook. The conversation I had with Bradley regarding Jason, and the sentiment that suggested that he should be upset with the bureau for not better protecting his family—it was the one that jumped out at me initially as I reflected on the discussion when he and I went back and forth on the topic.

I immediately closed my eyes and concentrated, as what I said to Bradley, and his response to what I said, immediately began to play back pretty vividly within my mind.

Bradley:

"......I always wondered about that. Like when someone who works undercover work for the Government go deep undercover like that, wouldn't their family be subject to bureau protection? Wouldn't it be risky to leave them out

in the open without protection considering how easy it is for one to have his cover compromised?"

Me:

"......Yeah I was thinking that myself when reading this story. I was thinking how the character, Jason, should be highly livid with his agency for not protecting his family, and he should demand answers. It's what I would do anyway......."

His words and my response took on a different meaning and feel after re-reading chapter two.

As I continued to read through the chapter again, I wasn't really certain how to piece together what I was reading as the words and the sentences bounced around my mind and ultimately landed in my subconscious with a thud. It was all so eerily familiar, and as I re-read the words it was hard to dismiss the feeling I was having. I briefly hesitated as I was slightly cautious of what I might discover next, but I slowly navigated to the beginning of chapter three to continue re-reading.

Jason's words immediately jumped off of the page at me:

".....You promised to protect them Dave!.......You promised you'd protect my family! That was YOU DAVE! You said that!......"

"...........WHY Dave? WHY DIDNT YOU PROTECT MY

FAMILY?!! ....Answer me, Dave!"

I slowly and instinctively nodded my head as I re-read Jason's response in chapter three.

"Interesting." I whispered to myself behind a smile as I began nodding my head.

I didn't know for certain what it was that I found "interesting." I also had no idea why I was being unconsciously pulled back into re-reading the first three chapters. I needed to make sure I wasn't thinking too much into all of it. It all seemed like a coincidence.

Simple logical flow of an intriguing story being laid out before me like any other normal story—nothing else. There *was* a pattern, a slight connection that I believed I was starting to put together. I also knew that it was very likely that this, whatever this was, it could be my mind desperately looking for something to occupy my time and break the counterproductive silence within my mind. I hesitated, but eventually forced myself back into the beginning of chapter three, as my brief conversation with Bradley about *"Jason's story"* continuously and vividly played back in my mind, while I continued to re-read the chapter.

It was as if the words this time around, defined themselves in such a way that made it easier and much clearer to understand.

I closed my eyes and began shaking my head, a bit perplexed. I had a very difficult time still shaking lose this feeling that had come over me. The deeper breaths I took, the more this unbelievable, unexplainable, surreal, lightheaded feeling seem to gradually embrace me. The feeling was as if I was dreaming, but wide awake inside the dream, in a way that was indescribable, and immensely surreal. The "feeling," was real, very real. But it didn't have the same "feel" as an emotion. It felt more like the feeling one would likely experience while standing on top of the highest idyllic mountain they could find on a mild spring night, starring out over the world, as the wind whipped gracefully across their face, as the feeling of weightlessness slowly overwhelmed them, causing them to rise higher and higher toward the star filled sky. All this while the unimaginable and untouched beauty and immensely surrealistic feel of cosmic inferiority, gradually wrapped itself around them as they made their way closer to the front door of the universe. It was difficult to explain and describe and I was happy I didn't have to describe it to anyone. But it was real.

I continued to re-read chapter three, and as I neared the part in which Jason was attempting to commit suicide, my conversation with Bradley once again began echoing in the back of my mind, one part in particular...

"......Honestly you probably couldn't blame the guy if he wanted to give up, or if he was possibly thinking suicide at this point. I can't see anybody going through something so difficult and not at least consider suicide, as morbid a thought as that was, in a situation such as this it was reality. Not saying it's what I would do, but I can see this guy Jason wanting to do something like that because of the unbearable pain he's dealing with........"

My words played back uninterruptedly in my mind as I scrolled back through the pages within the Nook. I slowly shook my head in disbelief. I was slightly astonished at what I was reading in correlation to what I had discussed with Bradley just moments before first reading the chapter. I knew what I was thinking. I knew what I was thinking was impossible, and I knew thinking it meant I was possibly dealing with my grief, emotions, and stress in a way that I didn't want to accept at this time. Maybe this "feeling" was the initial stage of a breakdown. I wasn't sure. I wasn't sure about a lot right now.

I wasn't sure about the odds of me suggesting suicide as being a legitimate option for Jason, and he actually attempting to pull it off. That was too close for me right now in my fragile mental state. It was all starting to creep past the "coincidence" stage for me which gave me more reason to believe that I was really starting to lose it.

Certainly—it's not hard to understand how a deeply emotional man would consider suicide after dealing with the type of pain Jason was struggling with. It is a story and stories have logic to them more times than not or they'll in some ways, lose the reader. So, I knew that it was extremely logical to assume that a man experiencing that type and amount of soul snatching pain would at least consider suicide. Not really going out on a limb to suggest such a thing. It was nothing more than logic.

This was easier to accept. But of course, there was something else about Jason trying to commit suicide that stood out to me. I just didn't know what it was yet. Sitting, gazing out of the window, I began to deeply ponder on what it was that my mind was trying so eagerly to put together within the cluttered rooms of my subconscious. If what I was thinking had any merit or validity to it whatsoever, then why didn't he go through with it?

Why didn't he kill himself? That certainly should've put an end to my "theory." A "theory" that I hadn't even officially admitted to having just yet. What made him stop? That truly was the question that needed answer.

It was a question that would answer more than just *that* question, which is why I slowly realized that there wasn't an answer to that question. I was exhausted. I was already beginning to subconsciously reflect on things I said to Bradley while discussing Jason's decision to commit suicide; something that actually not only didn't answer the question per se, but in fact, brought about more questions. *Me:*

"........Jesus man, don't do this............I believe this character is no different than any of us. He's stronger than what he appears to be. I believe we are all stronger than what we appear to be during perilous times. It's just much harder to continue fighting when it's so much easier to simply quit, and Jason is taking the easy way out. Killing himself isn't the answer for Jason in this story no more than it is for you or I........"

I closed my eyes, took a deep breath, and exhaled. I opened them while turning back towards the window and began staring out into the surreal setting sun that gracefully and majestically embraced the top of the ocean as the plane silently soared over the clouds.

Why *did* Jason all of a sudden change his mind? While reading the story, it didn't give a reason while he was trying to escape from the garage. The story didn't have any dialog into his thinking at that time. It was just a sudden and unexplainable change within his mind. Naturally, it's logical to believe that a man would, could, and should ultimately change his mind when on the verge of suicide. We're instinctive creatures—unconsciously wired to survive, but this felt different. Jason wanted to die and suddenly he didn't.

Was that me? Did I stop this man from killing himself after, based on what I'm starting to believe, being the reason, he tried to do it in the first place? What was I thinking in thinking this? This couldn't be true. The more I thought about it, the more I felt myself slipping away from reality and losing myself. How far off was my thinking on this?

"Wake up Steve, you're losing it." I whispered to myself.

The more I thought about "*Jason's story*", the more it forced me to think about it in a way that made it impossible to let it go, no matter how hard I tried.

As I stared out of the window, my counsel with Father Miyake slowly began making its way back into my subconscious. One part in particular began standing out to me as I thought heavily on it.

"*...The last thing you should feel is powerless. Half of the time we're so caught up in our day to day lives that we* *don't even realize the life, the power we have within ourselves, with our tongues and with our thoughts. But sometimes it takes us stepping out on faith in order to realize the power and ability we have. We won't know unless we open ourselves up and began speaking life into the universe to affect the things around us that appear to be incapable of being moved or changed. There are times as human beings, when we are opened to receive any and everything the universe has for us. Usually, these times are when our minds are completely opened for whatever reasons albeit good or difficult; open, nonetheless. It is then, that we have the ability to change everything, anything, but it requires stepping out of the norm and into faith."*

I slowly gazed down at the Nook sitting in my lap and stared at it like I was looking at it for the first time. It essentially felt that way. As I looked down at the device, Father Miyake's words hit me hard as I repeated them under my breath:

"There are no mistakes in this life. I truly believe it all happens for a reason, everything. You just have to be able to understand what that reason is and determine how that reason affects you going forward."

I peeked over at Bradley who was still asleep. I thought about waking him up and sharing the madness racing around it my mind, but I knew as a doctor, he would likely think that I was going crazy or had already gone crazy, or mad with grief.

And frankly, I wouldn't blame him. It honestly felt like the only logical explanation as to what was going on with me right now. I smiled as I thought about what I would say to him if I woke him up.

"Hey Bradley, I'm starting to believe that my thoughts and suggestions are influencing the story here, what do I do?"

There was no way I could share that with him. This was one of those things that you didn't tell anyone no matter how much you believed. I honestly didn't really know how much I believe it, another reason why telling him or anyone else was stupid. For all I know, he would take that info and think I was too unstable and essentially a risk up here on the plane to everyone aboard and have the air marshal strap me to a seat for the remainder of the flight. It's probably what I would've done.

"No thank you." I whispered to myself as I shook my head.

Peering out of the window again, it was essentially my place to not only escape right now, but the only way I could reset my mind in any way and get somewhat of a clear outlook on everything I was dealing with right now.

I began to wonder as to why exactly Father Miyake gave me this "story." What was it that he wanted me to get from this story? The more I thought about Father Miyake's potential reasoning for giving me this device with this story on it, the more his words of counsel bounced around my mind. I buried my head in my hands as I began to rub my eyes.

"What am I doing?!! What is wrong with me?!" I thought to myself.

I continued my gaze out of the window, lost in the clouds. The clouds were so vivid and full of life, shape, and substance as we flew over them. A sudden rush of energy moves through my body so fast it caused me to get chills. My right leg began to nervously shake as I quickly focused on my breathing while I closed my eyes.

"Step out on faith, huh?" I whispered.

"Okay." I murmured as I nodded my head.

I knew what I believed I needed to do. Somehow, I needed to put this insane theory of mine to the "test." I just didn't know how to exactly go about doing it; how to truly initiate it. I felt kind of like just even testing this "theory," I was somehow, in some way, admitting I was likely losing it. Even though I was alone, in a sense, with me and my thoughts, and no one would ever know what it was that I was insinuating within myself—it still carried an internal sense of admission that something was possibly wrong with me. I was reaching a point in which it didn't matter anymore as I now needed to know one way or the other.

I stared down at the Nook and focused on it without saying a word. It was as if I was slightly afraid of it, afraid to speak to it. It was as if my wife was the Nook and I needed to tell her that I threw the receipt away for the bag of products she wanted to return. In all actuality, I was more afraid of myself and losing myself than I was anything else at this point.

I closed my eyes and simply begin to speak. The first thing that came to mind about Jason and this next chapter, I said it;

"Jason's sister should come to live with him, to help him get back on his feet."

I whispered the words in a way that was almost secretive as if I was trying to somehow hide what I was attempting to do from myself. It was slightly comical and somewhat troubling. I woke the Nook out of its hibernation and swiped to proceed to the next chapter. Except there was no chapter magically appearing, no symbol for *"Next Chapter,"* there was nothing but the same—the end of chapter three. Not sure what I was expecting to happen after uttering those words, but I felt quite stupid for sitting, staring, and actually waiting for some kind of miraculous event to transpire within the story. I shook my head and smiled as I knew at this point, there was a good chance I had actually officially crossed over from grief to possible unstableness. It was beginning to become harder and harder to tell the difference between the two at this point, a real fine line.

"What am I doing?" I chuckled as I placed the Nook back down on top of the carry-on. I was trying not to laugh at myself, but it was very difficult not to as I began thinking about how silly I was acting. *'I desperately need a drink,'* I thought to myself as I sat back in my seat and exhaled. A sense of relief and calmness quickly fell over me. I didn't want to be crazy. Who does? I didn't want to feel like I was losing it. Me confirming that it was all coincidence and not some magical, weird, once in a million-occurrence happening, eased my mind and my spirit. Business flights served alcoholic drinks, and I figured now was as good a time as any to partake. I needed to relax and knew the drink would certainly help. I alerted the flight attendant. It didn't take her long to make her way over towards my row.

"Yes sir?"

"Mam would it be possible to get a drink? An alcoholic beverage to help me relax?"

"Of course," she replied cheerfully, as she handed me a small menu. "What would you prefer? We offer all types as you can see on the menu there."

"The Bourbon will be just fine." I said as she nodded in acknowledgement, retrieved the menu, and made her way back toward the flight attendant station. Didn't take her too long as she quickly returned with the drink.

"Thanks," I replied, "By the way, do you have something for me to read? A book perhaps?" She smiled and began shaking her head.

"I'm sorry sir, I don't. There's a selection of films available for you to watch."

"No thanks!" I replied as she quickly nodded and slowly walked away.

A toast was in order, I figured. I slightly and gingerly raised my glass towards the window.

"Here's a toast to my sanity, to you baby girl, wherever you are, just know that Daddy will always love you and will see you soon." I closed my eyes as the tears begun to fall just slightly.

"And to you Jason, who should be drinking to help mask that pain—Cheers."

The bourbon was smooth, but it had been a while since I last had alcohol, so it burned just a bit as it went down. Reaching for the seat tray in front of me I immediately noticed the Nook on top of my carry-on. I wouldn't have noticed it if it wasn't for the fact that the device had suddenly began to illuminate.

I slowly reached for the device and placed it on my lap. The screen saver was on, but the device was still illuminated. I curiously stared at the Nook until I felt my hand unconsciously moving toward the screen. I hesitantly placed my hand on top of the screen and swiped to the right. My heart skipped several beats as the first thing I noticed was the words; *"Chapter Four."*

<u>Chapter Seven</u>

A Reason to Live

* Hour Six *

It took me about two whole minutes to realize that I had fallen into a daydream. My eyes were essentially burning a hole through the Nook as I gazed right through the words *"Chapter Four"* at the top of the page. To say I was confused wasn't entirely accurate. It was now at the point where I was more annoyed than upset. The fact that I was sitting on this plane letting this device get the best of me, mentally, was slightly infuriating.

"Where the hell did you come from?" I whispered angrily to myself as I slowly shook my head.

The bewilderment and confusion behind this, frustrated me. I quickly and eagerly flipped back to chapter three and back again to chapter four to make sure I wasn't going completely crazy or mistaken. Yet sure enough, there it was—chapter four. I had no explanation for it. I slowly began to realize that the device was indeed truly defective. There was not much else I could do except chuckle at myself as I quickly dove into chapter four.

Jason's Story – Chapter Four

The stars seemed closer from atop of the roof, but he had always felt a closeness to the stars for as long as he could remember. He first became infatuated with them in his pre-teens. His love and curiosity for them forever stuck with him. He'd look to them in order to escape whenever he needed to get away. Maybe it was the thought of everything bigger than him - the thought that he'd never get to truly understand them in this lifetime. Or maybe, it was the fact that some were planets, some not, and trying to figure out which ones were which is was what intrigued him the most. He wasn't sure why he was infatuated with them.

They not only helped him escape from the world, but when he gazed upon them, it would clear his mind and help him think peacefully and more effectively. Right now, they took on a whole new purpose and meaning for him. Jason poured himself another glass of Vodka. As he stared up at the sky, he began to smile, almost facetiously as he raised his glass towards the stars.

*"Toast to you," he snickered. "You guys are up there or
....somewhere, looking at me and laughing at how pathetic
I've become since you left. I'm embracing it."
He was currently on his fourth glass, the alcohol currently
had him gripped by a rigid numbness but was honestly
starting to lose count as he knew it was needed to numb
the pain....*

I was speechless and I knew why. I just didn't know
how to put the actual reason into words or thoughts,
adequately. Placing my hand on my chest, I felt my heart
beating rather rapidly as I closed my eyes and begin to
utilize my newly discovered breathing exercises.

"Calm down, its ok Steve," I whispered to myself. "It's
ok."

I had no idea if it was going to be ok or not. I had no
idea what I thought was actually happening, and I didn't
know where to even start. Slowly, I got up from my seat,
made my way down the aisle toward the rest room. I felt
myself slowly starting to gradually lose it as I began feeling
slightly dizzy. I needed to make sure I didn't look like
how I was beginning to feel. I knocked on the door—no

one was inside. I immediately made my way inside, closed and locked the door behind me.

"It's going to be ok." I whispered as stared at myself in the mirror.

Everything was slowing starting to slip far away from *ok*. It didn't feel *ok*. Nothing about what I thought I was experiencing was ok. I made my way over to the toilet and sat down. I closed my eyes, lowered my head, and took a deep breath as I continued trying to calm my suddenly rapid heart rate. I knew why my heart was beating furiously, but I didn't know if accepting that reason would mean me accepting the fact that there was something wrong with me. Denial or blissful ignorance, neither one was working for me at this point. Something had to give. I would either need to accept what I believed was happening to me or accept the fact that I was gradually losing it. What was happening? Just what in the hell was I really experiencing? I sat on the toilet as my knee nervously shook uncontrollably at this point. I stood up to glance at myself in the mirror again.

"Ok Steve," I whispered, "Ok."

I nodded my head as if I was answering a question, but in reality, I was subconsciously accepting the fact that there was only one way to understand what I believed to be happening, and that would be to give up this seemingly self-destructing fight I was having within myself. I was in strong denial about what I believed to be happening. I naturally second guessed and doubted everything until I couldn't anymore, and this would be no different.

There was a legitimate thought in the back of my mind that suggested that all of this was in fact in my head, but what was wrong with wanting, needing to know for sure? It was all just too coincidental at this point.
The sudden knock on the door startled me slightly.

"Out in a second!"
Unlocking the door, I slowly made my way back down the aisle towards my seat. I had been in the bathroom longer than I'd realized, as I noticed the light outside of the plane had darkened since entering the bathroom.

The sky was clear, but the clouds were turning a dark color grey below us as if we were flying over bad weather. The sun was setting as evening gradually approached. We were headed east as the sun was setting in the west. We would get a good amount of darkness before running into the same sunset in the states. It was always the same whenever I flew to this part of Asia, the flying away and towards the sun, it played with your mind a bit, but it was something I quickly adapted to.

As I made my way closer to my row, I noticed that Bradley had finally awaken from his nap, typing vigorously on his laptop. He smiled as I carefully maneuvered my way past him and back into my seat. I was expecting him to say something, but he continued on with his work. I glanced down at the Nook and sighed. I remember mentioning something about him drinking, only to then discover him drinking to start chapter four. Coincidence? There was no way this was happening. I tested this crazy theory in trying to get Jason's sister to come live with him in the previous chapter, and that yielded no results. Why would anything else I tried be any different? Somehow, expecting some sort of logic to be wrapped around this ridiculous theory and concept that I called myself suddenly trying to accept, was probably crazier than the actual thought itself. I smiled the more I thought about it.

"Don't do this to yourself Steve."

I whispered the words to myself as if he was sitting right next to me. I sat back and tried putting it together in a way that was simple for me. What exactly did I think was happening?

Whatever this was, it seemed to be picking and choosing to apply my sentiments about Jason and the story. I didn't understand why or how, in fact I didn't understand any of it. This made it all more confusing. The story didn't respond when I requested that his sister come live with him, but it did when I suggested Jason needed to "*drink to numb his pain.*"

Looking up I smiled as I begin to ponder further on the thought I just had.

"Maybe it's the character? Maybe it's Jason?" I said to myself, somewhat excitedly.
I needed to test it but didn't know how. I grabbed the Nook and glared at the blank black screen. I didn't even think as much as the words simply forced their way out of my mouth.
"*Jason howls at the moon, jumps off the roof, and begins running down the street to let out his anger.*"

I uttered the words with a smirk on my face. I realized that it was slightly silly, juvenile, and potentially dangerous for Jason, if what I was thinking to be true was actually true. It could possibly cause him to injure himself, or worse, but I needed to see just how far my "influence" went, if I had any at all. What kind or type of influence and control did I have, if any? It was all too coincidental, and my mind was no longer allowing me to simply dismiss it all as a coincidence. I needed to know, if only to simply ease my mind. I cautiously powered the device back on and continued reading the fourth chapter.

Jason's Story – Chapter Four – Continued.

The Bureau instructed him to take as much time as possible. They told him that he could return whenever he was cleared by the Doctors and the Section Chief. Three months had passed since the suicide attempt, and not much had changed emotionally, besides the fact that he no longer desired to kill himself. He realized that killing himself wasn't the answer. He no longer possessed the drive, the will, to do much of anything at this point.

Sleeping was difficult—even with the medicine prescribed to him by the Doctors but waking up and getting out of bed every day was still much tougher. Dave took more of a committed and engaged role in seeing that Jason was making progress, no matter how tough the task and how grueling the challenge. Dave would make it his personal responsibility in picking Jason up and see to it that he made it to his therapy sessions with the psychiatrist. Dave would even stay for the entire session and attempt to discuss it with him afterwards, but it was to no avail. Jason knew Dave, for the most part, was doing it out of guilt. He also realized Dave legitimately cared about him and wanted to see him get back to who he was. Sometimes, he felt as though Dave was a bit overbearing in trying to push the healing process. Not only did he not feel as though he was healing properly, but he also wasn't exactly sure if he even wanted to heal. He still didn't answer the calls, the door, or his text messages. Sometimes, he stayed in the house and slept all day, waking up only to consume alcohol.

While around Dave, he knew Dave could smell the alcohol on him, but Dave never said anything about it.

He ate as little as possible. His appetite had vanished, and his weight was following right behind it. Nothing seemed to be getting easier and in fact, it all seemed to be getting harder. Harder to cope, harder to believe in anything, harder to see past his current circumstance. He hated the fact that he had given up on life but felt as though life had given up on him. He knew it probably didn't matter at this point, nothing mattered. He figured that wasting away sounded like the best option for him. He no longer wanted to kill himself, but he understood that not wanting to live was just as bad if not worse than actually killing yourself, but he didn't care. No matter how hard it was to fathom, he couldn't run from the fact that he believed he had nothing to live for.

This particular morning, the black drapes shielded the morning light from cutting through his room. He couldn't stand it anymore—the light. The sudden ringing from the cell phone annoyed him more than usual this morning. As usual, he allowed it to go to voicemail. Gazing over at the number, he noticed that it was the same number that had been calling for the past two days now. An out of state number, possibly Illinois. Reaching for the phone, Jason dialed his voicemail as he was now curious who was calling and why.

The voice didn't sound familiar at all:

"Hello Mrs. Barrington, this is the city of Chicago Child Services Department. We have been trying to contact you in regard to your daughter, Tara Brunswick, age thirteen. It's very important that you contact us immediately as this involves Tara's well-being. We cannot locate Tara's father, Mr. Jake Brunswick, and need to contact you immediately. My name is Mrs. Henderson with the Chicago Child Services Department, and my number is 708-444-4455. You can reach me here any time before 5PM CST. If I don't answer PLEASE leave me a message, and I certainly can call you back about this most pressing issue. Thanks."

Jason slowly ended the call, lost in his thought. Tara was Tracy's daughter, his stepdaughter. So, at this point, he was confused and conflicted. Tara had stayed with them every summer up until three summers ago when Tracy and Tara's father had a falling out. He accepted Tara as his own, loved her the same as his boys, and she returned the love. After ending the call, Jason stared at the phone, and began to quickly fall deeper into his thoughts. He figured the best thing would be to ignore the call—ignore it, and it would essentially go away. That's exactly what he was prepared to do. He carefully laid back on the bed focusing heavily on the ceiling, unable to shake free from what he just heard. He truly wanted to pick up the phone and call her back but didn't want to take that chance. Taking that chance with his life was one thing but letting someone else back into his life when he couldn't protect them or love them the way they would need, he just wasn't going to do it. He knew staying out of this would be the best thing for both he and for Tara. There weren't any doubts about that.

There was no howling. No jumping off the roof.

I wasn't sure what to think, but it was fairly obvious that my "sentiments" didn't have any impact on this story. It was a relief and sort of gratifying. I felt better about my chances of not being bat shit crazy. It was an insane thought in the first place, and I chuckled at the thought of me even considering it. It was a story, and I was simply the reader, nothing else. It was however, an intriguing and emotional story, so it was no wonder I found myself emotionally and mentally engaged with it. It was no different than any other story I had read in my life. No matter the book, I would always visualize the story and set the scenes in my mind, places that were the closest to me, primarily from my childhood.

While reading and visualizing the chapters, I would try my best to figure out how what was going to happen in the next chapter before getting there. It was something that I've always done. So, there was an explanation wrapped conveniently around the concept of coincidence that really wasn't hard to fathom.

I understood Jason's reservations for not wanting to take on the responsibility of his stepdaughter, Tara but as someone on the outside looking in, I knew that potentially adding this element to his life, it could possibly give him a reason to live again. He sure as hell didn't have one right now. So, my mind began to race. It began to piece together a puzzle that Jason was now actively running away from. Unconsciously, the thoughts lingered freely as the story and all that I'd read was right there on the forefront of my mind.

"He should pick up the phone and call Mrs. Henderson. Tara really needs him as much as he needs her." I thought to myself.

I truly wanted this man, this character, to get some sort of true healing. The more I read this story, the more I began feeling sorry for him, empathized with him. I found myself wishing I could instantly change things for the better for him, for this character. I wasn't sure about a lot of things, but I was certain that this girl, Tara, being back in Jason's life could only help him more than hinder him. I wasn't certain, but I knew the love I felt, the love I received from my daughters, was undoubtedly something that would help him become more of who he was before all of this, possibly even more.

I wasn't positive, but I knew deep down, it was the kind of love he desperately needed to experience. I opened my eyes and immediately returned to the story.

Jason's Story – Chapter Four – Continued

Jason suddenly found himself staring at the phone on the dresser for at least five minutes straight before finally getting up and pacing back and forth in front of the dresser where the phone was located. He unconsciously reached for the phone several times before pulling his hand back. He had no earthly idea what he was doing. He suddenly realized that he needed to call her back but didn't understand why this feeling had suddenly come over him. He didn't want this, but deep inside, he couldn't shake this strange and unexplainable feeling that he somehow not only truly wanted this but needed it. No matter how hard he wanted to resist, Jason found himself inching closer to the phone, until his hand was on top of the phone itself.

Tara needed help, not to mention, she was his daughter. Deep down he knew he would be doing the right thing, even though he didn't really want to. Realizing he was unable to fight anymore, he picked up the phone and dialed Mrs. Henderson's number. The line rang only once.

"This is Mrs. Henderson,"

"Hello Mrs. Henderson, this is...."

Jason paused and took a deep breath and pulled the phone away from his mouth as he exhaled. He couldn't understand what he was doing or why. He looked at the phone as if it was alive and he needed to prevent it from eating his face. Jason struggled to put the phone back to his ear as if his face and the phone were opposing magnets.

"Oh God what is this?!!" he whispered, confused. He gazed at himself in the mirror, instantly recognizing the perplexed look on his face.

"Hello?" Mrs. Henderson declared on the other end. He slowly and hesitantly brought the phone back towards his face.

"Mrs. Henderson, this is Jason, Jason Barrington. You don't know me, but I believe you may know my wife.....knew my wife; Tracy Barrington? I received a call from you regarding my late wife's daughter, Tara...."

I closed my eyes as I felt my heart beginning to race again. I tried my best to immediately start the exercises to control my breathing and heart rate, but this was gradually starting to overwhelm me, emotionally. I hadn't said anything this time, but I was acutely aware of the fact that I had thought it. A huge smile came across my face, but I wasn't sure if it was from excitement or shock. I knew this was happening—something was happening. I closed my eyes, sat back in my seat, and continued to focus on controlling my heart rate and breathing. The last thing I needed was another attack.

Whatever this was, I wasn't sure why it was happening to me. As I pondered on that, it was hard to get away from the inescapable possibility that this was all in my head. So many questions and I had answers for none of them. I pinched myself, hard, to make sure I wasn't dreaming. I never believed I was, but at this point, I was never more awake at any point in my life as I was at this very moment.

At the moment in my life, in which I should feel the saddest I'd ever felt, I had never felt more alive, and my blood has never pumped through my veins this clearly.

I wanted to tell someone, anyone, about what I believed I was experiencing right now, but there was no one to tell. I still didn't believe that this was happening. And I knew that this could still very well be just one weird, freaky, once in a lifetime, impossible coincidence, or at least that's what I was secretly and desperately trying to convince myself of.

Nevertheless, it was still one hell of a coincidence. It was difficult in trying to contain every emotion that I was dealing with right now. I slowly rested my head against the pillow on the window and returned to the story....

Jason's Story – Chapter Four - Continue

"Yes Mr. Barrington, and I'm sorry, but did you say that Tracy has passed away?"

The subtle yet genuine shock.in her tone was obvious. Jason took a deep breath and exhaled as he nodded his head.

"Yes mam I did. I've been dealing with a lot since her passing, and Tara and her father didn't really

communicate with us recently, even before my wife passed. It's no surprise that this info isn't known yet."

Jason listened as Mrs. Henderson spoke on the other end of the phone, but he really wasn't hearing her. He found himself in deep thought, attempting to piece together this mental puzzle he had suddenly found himself standing over. Just why in the hell did he decide to pick up the phone and call her after he truly and one hundred percent made his mind up that he wasn't going to do it? Where was this coming from? What made him do this? As he listened to what Mrs. Henderson was saying on the other end, he could only shake his head in disbelief and frustration as he knew something was wrong with him.

This, whatever this was, he was certain they had medication for it. And whatever it was, he needed to be on it as soon as possible. He had been feeling like this for quite some time, and a visit to the Doctor was long overdue at this point.

"What the hell is wrong with me?" Jason angrily whispered to himself.

"I'm sorry, what'd you say?" Mrs. Henderson asked. "Nothing," Jason quickly responded," What were you saying?"

He truly hadn't heard anything Mrs. Henderson was saying as he was so focused on his own inner thoughts.

"I was saying that legally, as the widower of Tara's mother, and since her father has disappeared, you are technically the legal guardian of Tara, if you so choose to be."

"Disappeared?" Jason asked.

"Yes, investigators are saying that over the past six months or so, he's been dealing with depression. We don't know where he is, but in the meantime, we have this girl who needs immediate care, or we'll have to place her in the system.'

There was a brief pause. A moment granted by her that felt like a chance for him to react. A reaction never came. She continued.

"Mr. Barrington, I understand you may be going through a lot right now considering your loss, so it's understandable if you don't think you are emotionally ready for this responsibility right now."

Jason remained quiet as Mrs. Henderson spoke, what she was saying was exactly how he felt, he truly didn't want this responsibility.

"Well, I'm certainly glad you understand that." Jason replied, relieved as she had essentially given him a guilt-free way "out."

"But I will say," Mrs. Henderson continued, "You are the only family she has right now, and she will find out about her mother's death eventually. I believe it would be healthier for her to hear it from you, and to grieve with the only family she has right now."

Jason sighed and closed his eyes. He knew what Mrs. Henderson was saying made sense, he just didn't want it to, as he continued to fight within himself on what he was feeling.

"Look Mrs. Henderson, I understand your point, and my heart truly goes out to Tara, it does, but I'm in no position to care for her right now. I'm sorry but I just can't."

"Trust me, I understand Mr. Barrington," she replied. "And I won't press the matter with you anymore. But, if you do change your mind, you know how to contact me. Once again, my condolences."

"Thanks." said Jason as he quickly hung up the phone.

It took practically all of his strength to get off that call, but it was the right thing, or least he believed it was. The battle within his mind was a furious one. On one side—something was telling him that he needed to do it. It was essentially the same side that subconsciously forced him to dial the number in the first place. On the other side—he wanted no part of this. He knew he wouldn't be able to care for Tara right now and believed that he would only add to her anguish and pain if he did.

Sitting on the edge of the bed, Jason had a difficult time trying to figure out just what was within him that compelled him to pick up that phone and make the call to Mrs. Henderson in the first place. He knew he didn't want to call her, but it was as if he couldn't stop himself from doing so.

It wasn't as if something was forcing him physically; it was as if a good portion of his mind was telling him what to do and his body was listening. It was more mental than anything. Staring at the phone as if he expected it to pop up and perform The Charleston. Jason returned to his workout. Deep down, he felt disgusted about not being able to care for Tara. He knew she would take her mother's death rather hard and wished he could be there for her the way she needed him to be. But he knew he was in no position to be there, as mentally, he was dealing with his own struggles. He realized that he was in no position to care for a child right now, not even close.

The battle he was now waging within his mind was the fiercest he'd ever experience in all his years. His mind was completely opened and clear as it's ever been at any point in his life, which in turn, made his pain, sorrow, and thoughts on his family much clearer, sharper and vivid.

Peering up from the story, I began biting my bottom lip as my nerves began to overwhelm me. I wasn't sure what to do next. Maybe, so just maybe, I really was going crazy. I mean for a minute there, it seemed as if this insane theory had legs, but then just when I start to even begin to believe, the rug was snatched right up from under me again. I seriously had no idea what to think at this point, but I was still certain that *something* was happening. If this had been any other time, place, or moment in my life, I might have not allowed this to affect me the way it was, but right now, at this moment, my mind was working on a different level, and for some reason, it wouldn't allow me to get off of this. It wouldn't allow me to simply dismiss this feeling I had about everything I was reading, no matter how unusual, impossible, and crazy it sounded or appeared to be.

I gazed outside of my window for a moment—I needed answers. How far was I willing to go to prove this theory to be real or to prove that I wasn't in fact going crazy? I didn't know, but something inside me was pushing me, and fighting it, only adding to the stress I was otherwise dealing with in my personal life.

As I peered out of the window, the light from the setting sun beamed gracefully through the airplane window onto my face.

As we slowly made our way through the sky, it felt as if we were at a stand-still. There weren't many clouds around, so it was hard to really gauge the movement from the plane with nothing to measure against. The sky continued to darken. I closed my eyes and for a moment; it felt as if I was back home, in my office. The ride was that smooth, quiet and relaxing.

I gradually began to wonder if it was something that I was doing or not doing that was causing the "inconsistent results" in the story and my insane theory that I was still holding onto. Maybe, I needed to do something else, something different? Maybe, it was the inconsistent way I delivered my words. I quickly flipped back through the story and began to look back on all the occurrences in which I believed the theory had shown its face.

The one thing that I began to quickly notice, as I found myself looking back through all the eerie incidents in the previous chapters, was that I was quickly yet unconsciously noticing that these occurrences seemed to arise after I shared well thought out and logical thoughts or instructions. Thoughts or instructions that centered on what Jason was currently going through or dealing with. Even the drinking on the roof, which at the time, made sense and was completely logical, as simple as it may had been. I would try again, it couldn't hurt. If only for potential peace of mind and some sort of closure on it all, I would try again. I had to.

I knew that Tara was probably the best chance Jason would have at somehow learning to live again. There were no guarantees, but I was fairly certain, and that certainty was based on what I've learned in being a father over these years. It would give him something to live for again—a reason to get out of bed in the morning and a reason to smile again no matter how rough it seemed. He desperately needed that right now. I wasn't sure how it would turn out, but I knew Jason needed something in his life to help him gain a sense of normalcy again, and Tara was that "something." He was fighting it and though I understood why, I couldn't accept that for him right now. I looked down at the Nook and closed my eyes. I noticed that it helped me to concentrate and focus better. I figured it was best if I spoke the words in lieu of thinking them.

My thoughts were so sporadic, random, unstable, and unpredictable—I didn't want to take that chance. I knew I needed to get a better handle on my thoughts. I didn't need spontaneous and sudden counter-productive or even dangerous thoughts deriving from my subconscious and entering into Jason's life. That would likely require more focused concentration and relaxing my mind.

"Jason calls Mrs. Henderson back and accepts Tara into his life as he understands that void in his world right now can only be filled if he stops running away from the things that can fill that void."

I whispered the words in a way that was clear and concise. The words came together perfectly, as they exited from my subconscious and mouth, and gradually entered the universe and atmosphere. I opened my eyes and immediately returned to the story.

Jason's Story – Chapter Four – Continue

Jason stopped in mid-pushup and simply stared at the wall in front of him.

"What?" said Jason as he starred at the phone.
He gradually stood to his feet, walked over to the phone, and stared at the phone as if it had just called his name. He began once again pacing back and forth in front of the dresser in which the phone was stationed. There was a lot he was dealing with, none more than the depression he was fighting through every day at this point.

"What are you doing?" Jason whispered to himself as he shook his head. "You can't be this stupid, can you?"

He knew that not only did this girl need him, but he needed her as well, probably more than she needed him— they needed each other. He wasn't living, not anymore. He was simply not dead yet, but he knew what he was doing now, he couldn't call it "living." He didn't have a family and now, neither did Tara. Both needed a reason to live, and she would be his. Jason stopped pacing and immediately stared down at the phone. He thought of

Tara as she received the news of her mother's death, and realized Mrs. Henderson was right, Tara needed to hear it from him. They needed each other. Jason picked up the phone and dialed Mrs. Henderson's number.

"Hello Mrs. Henderson, Jason Barrington here......"

Jason's Story: Chapter Four – The End

<u>Chapter Eight</u>

Tara Barrington

I had been smiling unconsciously for quite some time now. My face had begun to throb.

Wasn't certain what I was smiling at exactly, but I knew I had a reason to smile after finishing that chapter. Closing my eyes, I sat back and deeply exhaled. I opened my eyes and glared out of the window. The sun was slowly setting, and for a moment, we were stuck in time—everything was at a standstill.

The only thing moving was my thoughts. I wasn't certain what the universe was doing with me right now, but whatever it was, it would be something that would probably change my life forever.

Staring at the phone attached to the back of the seat in front of me, I immediately reached for it. I had no idea just how hard the family was dealing with Natalie's death. I hadn't spoken with them since *the* phone call, and the last communication I had with anyone, was with my mother-in-law, prior to boarding the plane, letting her know I would be home in fifteen hours.

My mother-in-law knew about the attack and the accident that left me hospitalized for two days. She promised me that she wouldn't tell Sabrina or the kids. I figured it was best not to throw anything else on them while I was apart from them. It was very difficult to not constantly think about Natalie.

The times I spent with her, the times she smiled at me, her face, and her voice. It was becoming increasingly difficult to get those images and memories out of my head, and I didn't know how long I would be able to keep myself together with those thoughts constantly lingering around my grieving mind.

Looking down at the Nook, I re-read the end of chapter seven. I had no idea where to go from this point. I wasn't sure what I needed to do. I assumed by the ending of the last chapter; Jason had decided to allow Tara into his life. I figure the best place to start next in a story that was obviously far from finished, considering Father Miyake stated that it had thirteen chapters, was the relationship between Jason and Tara. They both were suffering—emotionally. They both needed someone or something to help distract from the pain in their lives. There was a legitimate need for unconditional love, guidance, and emotional support. And that was just with Jason. Tara needed that all of that plus a lot more. Jason not only needed to be the father she needed and currently lacked, but he needed to allow her to be the daughter he so desperately needed at this point. It was something that would essentially write itself and only needed minimal "initiation" at best. I at least hoped so. I looked down at the Nook and slowly closed my eyes and took a deep breath and uttered the following words:

"Jason opens himself up even more, becomes the father Tara needs, and allows her to become the daughter he needs."

I spoke the words before slowly opening my eyes. Just like that, right before my eyes, the tab for *"Next Chapter"* suddenly appeared at the bottom of the screen.

The feeling when I saw that, was like someone had washed me from the inside out with a pressure washer. Knots formed in my stomach. Words couldn't describe the utter disbelief and shock, but I physically expressed these feelings by unconsciously smiling. As I smiled, I shook my head. In no way was I comfortable with what I was dealing with. It still had a shockingly surreal feeling attached to it that would stay with me for as long as I lived, but the substance of the story truly grabbed me, pulled me in and trumped the feeling of disbelief and shock. I wasted no time touching the screen to instantly reveal chapter five of *Jason's Story*.

Jason's Story- Chapter Five

*The smell of bacon woke Jason out of his sleep this
particular morning and caused him to quickly leap from
his bed, and sprint towards the kitchen full speed down
the steps—smashing his toe into the wall along the way.*

*"SHIT!!!" he yelled out as he quickly grabbed his left
foot and began hopping on the other.*

*He honestly didn't remember leaving the stove on
but, there had been times over the past year that his anti-
depressant medicine had caused him to sleepwalk at times.
There had been a time in which he left pots on the stove
before falling asleep, only to be awaken by the smoke
alarm. Jason made it to the kitchen, holding his toe in
both hands, as he grimaced in pain.*

*"I heard you hit something on your way down here, are
you ok?" Tara asked with a smile on her face.*

It took Jason a minute to gather himself.

"Yeah, I'm fine."

*He was visibly upset with himself for wrecking his foot.
Tara sense that Jason was upset, pulled back a little. Jason*

noticed it right away.

"I didn't mean to snap at you, but my foot hurts like hell right now, and it's....It's not your fault, its mine. I'm sorry."

"It's ok," she replied, "It sounded like it hurt. There was a slight pause as Jason settled himself.

"So, there's some bacon and eggs, you want some?" she asked while turning the bacon.

Jason was starving and felt like this was a great opportunity for them to talk. The adoption paperwork had gone through weeks ago, but they really hadn't had a chance to really talk like they needed to. Jason was still buried in his shell, and Tara was too afraid to crack it. Tara used to come around a lot when she was smaller. She and her father lived only forty-five minutes away, but that was about seven years ago when she was seven. She was familiar with Jason and loved him like a father, but after she moved to Chicago, distance and time drove them apart.

"Yeah I can use some breakfast," Jason huffed, while still rubbing his toe. "You have to excuse me as I'm still getting used to you being here. Although I'm getting better, it's quite possible that I forgot you were even here this morning, which is why I flew down here like that. Wasn't sure if I had left something on the stove or not." Tara nodded hesitantly.

Jason wasn't so sure if she even understood what he was trying to say so he immediately changed the subject. He calmly peered over into the pan that held the bacon.

"Do you even know how to cook?"

"My dad taught me how to cook." She replied behind a smile.

Jason noticed her demeanor changed when she spoke of her dad, so he quickly changed the subject, again.

"Your mother was a wonderful cook. She taught me." Jason uttered proudly.

Tara turned and smiled at him. Jason realized from his small discussions with Tara over the past two months, that she was not only wise but an incredibly fast learner. This morning, they shared a breakfast. It was a silent breakfast, for the most part. It's how their breakfasts usually went, whenever Jason found enough strength to even join her for breakfast on the weekends—which wasn't often. This Saturday was one of those rare days, and he figured since he was already down in the kitchen, he might as well join her.

"How's school?" he asked, attempting to break the ice.

His tone was warm, genuine and engaging.

Tara shrugged. "Its tenth grade, I've watched episodes of Jeopardy that are more challenging."

Jason gazed at Tara out of the corner of his eye. Not the response that he was expecting, but not really surprising.

"My mother—did you love her?" Tara asked while gazing down distractedly at her plate.
Jason slowly glanced up at Tara and smiled. He hesitated a bit as he found himself carefully searching for the correct words.

"I did. Very much so. She and the boys were my reason for....everything. They were the reason I strived so hard to be the best at everything. I didn't just love your mother Tara; I was in love with her. I was in love with everything about her. I loved the way she walked, the way she spoke, the way she got mad at me, and the way she loved me."
Jason found himself suddenly becoming emotional.

"What do you remember about your mother?" he asked her behind a forced smile.

"Everything," Tara replied without hesitation. "Everything. My mother and my father separated when I was four, and I remember everything about her from the time I was born until the day she and my father split."

"From the time you were born?" Jason asked perplexedly.
Tara didn't glance up from her plate.

"Yes. I remember when she would sing to me. She would always sing "Over the Rainbow" to me. I remember when she would change my diapers, and I even remember when she would kiss me endlessly after she would bathe me. Vanilla and peaches, that's what I remember her smelling like—always. I would go to sleep with my face buried in her neck, and her scent would put me to sleep."

Jason folded his arms, sat back in his chair, and nodded at every word Tara shared. He visualized every vivid word she uttered. It was all so familiar.

"She didn't just sing to me, but she would also read to me." Tara continued. "Whenever I asked her to, she would read to me. When I was four, I remember no matter what book I would bring her she would read it to me. The sound of her voice would make me feel, I don't know—feel better about everything."

Jason suddenly realized that Tara was becoming emotional and was beginning to cry. He truly didn't know what to do and began to feel somewhat uncomfortable. He forced something, anything out of his mouth to help break the uncomfortable and awkward feeling he was experiencing.

"Your mother was very beautiful and made everything in our lives better than it all probably deserved to be."

Jason stared at Tara, looking for any reaction from her.

"She brought me out of bad shell I was in, and I wanted to give her more."

"How did they die?" Tara asked while finally looking up from her plate. "What happened?"

There wasn't a single part of Jason that knew how to answer that question without fighting back tears. He certainly didn't want the vision of Tara's mother and stepbrothers dying in the explosion, bouncing around her head.

"You don't have to tell me, and I honestly don't think I even really want to know." Tara continued, while grabbing Jason's hand. "I just miss them."

"I know you do," he replied somberly. "I miss them too."

Jason could see the emotion starting to overwhelm Tara. He immediately rummaged through his brain to find something, anything to comfort her with. He was bad with this stuff, but as of late, his mind was working on its own.

"Tara, I need you to understand that you're my daughter. As unorthodox or unusual as all of this may seem to you and me, you are my daughter, and I'm your father and I'm happy about that. I need to know if you want me as your father, and if you are as happy to be my daughter as I am to be your father?"

Tara slowly looked up from her plate. Jason noticed a tear slowly falling down her right eye as Tara began nodding her head.

"Yes." Tara replied gingerly, "You've always been my dad and I've never forgotten you. Yes, I'm happy you're my dad but, I'm sad because I miss mommy. I miss her so much. My dad and my mom are gone, and I just feel so alone."

Tara began to weep quietly as Jason stood up to embrace his daughter, her sobs became louder, sharper.

"You're not alone Tara, I'm not going anywhere, this I promise. I love you and I will always be here for you. You understand that?"

Tara slowly nodded her head as she embraced her father. The minutes at that breakfast table for Jason and Tara turned into hours as night ultimately caught up to them. Tara made her way to bed as Jason spent hours cleaning the hours before making his way onto the roof. As always, a bottle of Vodka and a blanket accompanied him. Jason gazed directly up at the same cluster of stars he always found when he frequented the roof. He would lie on his back, gaze up, escape, and allow his mind to open up to all his eyes could see. It was hard not to ponder on many things, but more so, his family. How much he missed them. Were they watching him? Where were they? As much as he tried not to contemplate deeply on these things, as much as he tried to prevent the painful thoughts and memories from settling into his subconscious, it was very difficult to tame the thoughts, and fighting them off was as difficult a challenge as anything he faced right now. A lot of it had to do with the way his mind had been working as of late. A feeling of surreal openness on levels of indescribability, that rival nothing he'd ever experienced before.

"It's cold out here."

Tara's sudden voice gave Jason a quick scare. Tara startling Jason was instantly hilarious to her. She began giggling as her head was halfway out of the window. Jason held his hand to his heart in dramatic fashion.

"I thought you were sleep. And don't laugh, you want your father to have a heart attack?"

"I don't." Tara giggled softly. She began making her way through the window and onto the roof, smiling at her dad in the process. "My heart isn't as strong as yours," Jason said, as he guided Tara through the window—onto the roof.

"Eh, I was just resting." she responded behind a genuine smile.

Tara looked up towards the sky and began nodding her head.

"I see why you come out here at night. The sky is clear, and you get a great view of the stars out here. This is pretty awesome."

Jason got quiet as he nodded. He was thinking—searching for words.

"It is surreal. It helps me relax and concentrate on.........everything. It forces me to think about things, certain things I wouldn't normally think about as my mind look for ways to put everything together—things I would normally miss when I'm not up here."

Tara glanced over at Jason, slightly confused.

"What do you mean?"

Jason chuckled slightly.

He had a feeling his verbiage would spark a serious interest from within Tara, who he understood to be extremely curious.

"Well," Jason uttered as he held his skyward gaze, "since losing your mother and your brothers, the only thing I can think about is death, what happens to us when we die, or where we go when we die. I believe the answers lies somewhere up there within the stars. After it all happened, I found myself longing to be with them— wherever they are."

Pausing, he glanced over at Tara then back up towards the sky. He noticed the look on her face—she was concerned.

"I'm better now," he quickly continued. "Much better. Though I don't necessarily long to be with them, I still have questions that linger. The answers are definitely up there. I don't know why or how I believe it; I just believe it. I don't have a real reason as to why I believe this or feel this way, but it's something I've focused on and been infatuated with all my life. When I lost them, it magnified my intensity, my passion. Nothing looks the same to me anymore—especially out here."

Tara continued gazing up toward the sky as she nodded her head, acknowledging what Jason was saying.

"What makes you believe that the answers are up there?" she asked while motioning upwards with her head. Jason shrugged.

"Like I said, I don't know. You'll probably need to live a lot longer to understand why I feel the way I feel, and you may live the rest of your life and never understand why I feel this way. There are things about this world, Tara that you will have to learn as you continue to live, and there are things about this world that you will never learn or understand. They won't teach you this in school, but the universe is so vast and huge that I believe when we die, we begin a whole new journey.

That journey takes us on a ride through the endless parts of the universe that we can only dream of traveling to while we're alive."

Tara grinned as she thought heavily on what her father was sharing with her.

"Well, I know I have a lot more learning and living to do," she replied. "And yes, there are things that I don't understand that I want to understand. I do get what you are saying. I'm not saying that what you are saying isn't right, but I believe in God. My Grandmother taught me about God. I believe that if what you say is true, then God is in the background, or at the control of that journey you say we take after we leave here."

She focused her attention back up at the star filled sky. Jason took a deep breath and smiled.

"Me and God, if he or she even exists, aren't on the same page right now, Tara."

Tara glanced down at her father with a look of slight bewilderment.

"You blame God for what happen to my mom and the boys?"

"Oh no," Jason replied while keeping his eyes focused on the sky. "I don't blame an "all powerful" omnipotent

being for not being able to protect my family from being
slaughtered. Surely, it's asking too much for them to be
able to control the weather and protect my family at the
same time, right? Of course, I don't blame them, why
should I blame them? It's not like they have the power to
prevent these things, right?"

Jason knew it was a good possibility that Tara probably
wouldn't pick up on his facetious tone, but he threw it out
anyway.

"I get it. I do." Tara replied genuinely, "My science
teacher back in Chicago used to tell me that the Universe
is much bigger than you and me—bigger than all of us.
We lost a classmate two years ago. My teacher said to us
that; "The universe gives and takes as it pleases, and God
has given the universe the authority to do this......"

Slowly, I peered up from the nook and closed my eyes.
Their words seemed so familiar, but why? I've seen them
or heard them somewhere before. I was trying to figure
out how and why those words were hitting so close to me.
It only took a matter of minutes of reflection before
eventually realizing that the words I was reading, were
eerily similar to what Father Miyake shared with me in our

counsel back in Japan. The words weren't just similar, but the more I pondered on it, the more I realized that there didn't seem to be many differences in what she was saying and Father Miyake's words - it was almost essentially verbatim.

The thought of it being a coincidence certainly positioned itself at the forefront of my mind, but the thought of my own naivety positioned itself there as well. At what point would I start realizing that these "coincidences" were happening far too frequently in rather short periods of time? When was I willing to understand that at some point, these coincidences I'd been experiencing the past few hours weren't just "coincidences"? I felt as if I was beginning to tow that fine line between insanity and denial in a way that I was yet to completely understand.

I continued the story.

Jason's Story – Chapter Five – Continued...

"*You believe God didn't do much to protect our family, but I don't think I agree with that,*" *said Tara as she gazed into Jason's eyes. "I don't know, but I guess I believe in something greater, something better when we die. I don't know how to explain it, and maybe one day I will, but I just believe that my mother and my brothers were needed in another part of God's huge universe. Just because I believe in God, doesn't mean I don't believe in what you are saying. I just believe that everything, no matter how good or bad, happens because the universe makes it happen, and there's limited things we can do to alter or change this no matter how hard we try. Maybe, just maybe, we're not to understand any of this until we begin that next journey?*"*

The look on Tara's face was one of passion as she spoke. Jason recognized it. Tara's mother used to have the same expression on her face when speaking passionately about something. Jason didn't know if Tara was dialed in to what they were discussing because of her passion, or if he had been oblivious to the fact that this is who she was all the time.

What she said not only made sense, to an extent, but it was well thought out. It was still surprising to hear this come from her, someone as young as her. That's when Jason realized that he didn't know Tara as much as he knew he should at this point, and they probably had more in common than either of them realized. Hearing her talk with the logic and substance behind her words only reaffirmed that sentiment.

"Well, I thought I had an open mind," Jason stated behind a grin. "Where did you get that from? The way you speak— that point of view?"

Tara glanced away from the stars for a moment and looked back into Jason's eyes.

"I'm not sure," she said. "But I do a lot of reading, always have. Mom used to read to me when I was younger. I remember you used to read to me as well."

"Yeah," Jason replied, "You loved anything I read to you, no matter what it was. It was cute. You used to run into the room with the TIME magazine screaming; "Read me a story!"

Tara chuckled, "I think I remember that, and ever since then, I just loved to read. My Grandfather had this encyclopedia collection that was really good. His library consisted of all types of books, and I didn't do anything but read those encyclopedias whenever I had a chance and that was all the time. I really didn't do much else. I didn't have many friends."

Jason could see the passion in her eyes, and realized now, more than ever, she was not only very intelligent, but she seemed to be dealing with a lot of pain inside, like him. For the first time since Tara came into his life, he saw someone that needed to be healed as much as him.

The reasons were different of course, but he understood that pain is pain.

"Well," said Jason, "what you say makes a lot of sense, but right now, it's really tough for me to believe in that. God has really done a number on me. It's just really tough to believe that right now."

Jason closed his eyes and raised his head to the sky as he began to feel himself becoming more emotional.

"Belief in something bigger than you," replied Tara. "Takes more than just some sense of open-mindedness or courageousness. It takes you willing to accept one of two possibilities—that either the universe is entirely too big for you to matter that much, and one minute you're here and the next you're gone, having not affected or influenced a single person on this planet, or, you simply believe that the universe in fact recognizes every single person, and we all *play a part. A part in not just our lives and our loved one's lives, but the lives of others, even those you have never met, and those you will never meet."*

Nodding his head slowly, Jason looked deeply into Tara's eyes and knew she meant every word she was saying, passionate about every syllable. He smiled as he stared into his daughter's eyes. He thought about how proud Tracy would be to have a daughter not only this intelligent, but this full of creativity and life. The wall Jason had up was starting to come down brick by brick as he realized that he was in this for the long haul with Tara.

She needed him as much as he needed her. The sooner he accepted his responsibilities, the better father he could be to her, and the more accepting of her as his daughter he would become. It wasn't easy, it was a slightly weird and uncomfortable situation, but he knew it was what he wanted—it was important. There was a reason he picked up the phone and brought this girl into his life. Despite not truly understanding exactly why he did it so abruptly and almost unconsciously instinctive, he was happy he did it and wouldn't change anything about that decision.

That night, the two of them spent the rest of night on the roof gazing at the stars and discussing everything from life to their favorite TV shows and movies. It was something that was well overdue between the two, but it was also something that was needed, to help heal; to help understand that both of them had someone that they could not only depend on, but to love again as well.

Chapter Nine

Agent Jessica Phillips

* Hour Eight *

<u>Jason's Story – Chapter Five - Continued</u>

*W*aking up in cold sweats was something that happened regularly since losing his family. The nightmares weren't as bad as they used to be, but they still happened rather frequently.

"Dad, I made you coffee. I'm headed out!"

Jason heard the front door slam shut.

Peering out of the window, he saw her running towards her bus stop—greeted by a few friends. It had been about sixteen months since Tara had come to live with him and just like he knew it would, her presence forced him to change who he had become after the tragedy, in so many ways. She was very engaging, and people seemed drawn to her; an extremely likable person, much like her mother. It was headed towards the end of the winter months as the frigid air and snow still lingered.

"Attention passengers, we're heading into some inclement weather, and the turbulence will probably get rough. We will try to make it as smooth as possible as we make our way well above the storm. Thanks."

Looking up from the Nook, peering out of the window, I noticed that the clouds had become much thicker and darker.

"Hey, how's it going?" Bradley asked.

"Weather turbulence." I replied, "But they're flying above it, I believe. I imagine it'll be over soon."

"About nine more hours to go it seems." Bradley uttered through a yawn.

Bradley placed the headphones back over his ear and went back to typing. Time was no longer an important factor with me at this point. What I was currently experiencing had practically caused time to completely stand still for me. I was so completely caught up in this story, that nearly everything outside of it seemed so distant. I carefully rested my head against the pillow on the window, propped the Nook up on the tray on the seat in front of me, and returned to the story.

Jason's Story – Chapter Five – Continued

Jason glanced over toward the dresser and noticed his cell phone going off. He knew this time of day, it wasn't anyone but Dave calling to come pick him up for one of his bureau mandated therapy sessions.

The sessions had been going much better as of late, but he still hated going to them. It provided him with someone to talk to, but at times, he felt like the Doctor had done all that could be done with him. It had been sixteen months since he first began the sessions. Seventeen months had gone by since he lost his family. It honestly felt like yesterday.

Time hadn't really moved all that much for him. He still desperately longed for his family and missed them terribly. Time really wasn't doing much to heal the wounds on that end. He wasn't as bad off as he was sixteen months ago and in fact, he was doing a lot better, but that was primarily due to Tara being around more than anything else.

She required that someone care for her and be there for her during what she was going through and dealing with, so Jason had no choice but to become what she needed.

Dave was on the other end of the phone but on this day, he wasn't calling about therapy. It was the call Jason had been waiting on for at least half a year now.

"Jason, Chief needs you down here for a briefing and final evaluation. You need this. I need you to be ready for this, you copy?"

"Yeah, I copy."

Call ended as Jason sighed. This was the call he had been waiting on for quite some time, and here it was. He honestly didn't know if he was as ready as he'd hope he'd be upon getting the call. He of course wanted to get back to work, but now that the time had presented itself, he wasn't sure. He figured at this point; it could only help with the healing process.

To get back to doing what he was good at, but truth was, he wasn't as confident in himself as he was before it all happened. The ugly thought that crept in the back of his mind was; if he couldn't even protect his own family, how would he protect anyone else?

How could he do his job effectively? Self-doubt and low self-esteem were his biggest enemies at this point. It would actually be the first time he had seen or step foot inside the Federal building in nearly two years.

For the past year and a half, he only went to his therapy visits and back home. The past sixteen months he'd refused to go anywhere near the building. Staying away was a part of the healing process.

The seven months prior to that, he was deep undercover with Malvieo's crew. It had been quite some time since he'd actually laid eyes on the building. As he stood outside of the building, he stared at it like it was the first building he'd ever laid eyes on. He still hadn't let go of the disdain and ill feelings towards the bureau for what happened to his family, but he certainly had gotten much better at pretending he had.

He had forgiven Dave, quicker than he'd forgiven himself, actually.

"Jason?" the voice calmly called out to him from behind.

Quickly turning around, Jason immediately noticed a woman walking towards him. As she got closer, her face started to become clearer and more familiar. He stared at the woman as she approached him with a soft smile.

Brown hair, confident, about five feet five inches tall, pretty face and baby smooth skin —a sight for sore eyes. The closer she came, the more familiar she seemed. "Jason? How are you?" She asked in a genuinely concerned tone.

"I'm.....uh...I'm pretty good?"
Jason's response actually sounded more like a question than a statement, making it relatively obvious that he had no idea who she was.

"You don't remember me do you?" she chuckled. She could tell by his demeanor that he hadn't the slightest idea as to who she was. She was beautiful. Her smile was radiant. He'd seen the smile before—he was sure of it.

"Of course, I remember, um, nothing about you." Jason replied while chuckling. "I apologize, but my memory isn't that good nowadays."

"It's ok," she said, "I'll give your dumb ass a hint...."

"Wait, Jessica?!!" Jason quickly exclaimed. Her hint was perfect.

"Ha, yes," Jessica stated behind a huge smile. "I knew the "dumb-ass" would help you remember."

"Oh wow, of course I remember. How are you?"

"Well, I'm good." Jessica replied, "I can't really complain, and you'd probably start to walk away if I did. I'm ok though."

The more she talked, the more the memories started to return.

Agent Jessica Phillips. It had been years since he had seen her. They both entered the FBI Academy in 1991.

*They had essentially fallen for one another just one week
into the Academy. They were immediately impressed
with one another. She was originally from Norfolk,
Virginia, but later moved to Michigan. Tough, smart,
beautiful, and charming, were some of her best attributes,
but her dominance in the water and marksman exercises
was what really caught his eye at the Academy. It was the
reason he never truly forgot about her.*

*The guys were falling all over her from the very first
day. After smashing the Academy's underwater test, one
in which she managed to hold her breath for nearly five
minutes, she got the attention of the Director himself.
Jason was completely oblivious to the fact that she already
had her eye on him, yet somehow, the attraction was
instantly mutual and genuine, but never really blossomed
into anything serious. Before it had a chance to grow, they
were assigned to field offices in opposite ends of the
country—he in LA, while she was assigned to the Atlanta
field office.*

*"I heard what happened to you," Jessica calmly
uttered in a soft tone.*

"I just want ..."

*Jessica paused and didn't bother hiding her emotions as
she put her hand up to her mouth while suddenly fighting
back tears.*

"I just can't. I can't imagine the pain. You have my deepest sympathies and condolences."

It was tough for Jason to watch Jessica almost break down like that without it affecting him emotionally. He himself began to fight back his emotions. All he could essentially do was nod his head in acknowledgement of her heart felt sentiments.

"Thanks. I appreciate that, and I'm getting through it. It's going on two years now, and I'm finally learning how to begin to deal with the pain. At least I think I am." Jessica smiled as she listened to him. This was the first time Jason had really talked to anyone or said anything like that out loud. He hadn't been around many people over the past seventeen months, so she was really the first person outside of Dave and the Doctors to show real genuine emotion for what happened for him.

"What are you doing here? Jason asked, "I thought you were down in Atlanta?"

"Well, I was. I did four years down there and requested to be reassigned here to be with my mother after my father passed two years ago."

"I'm so sorry for your loss." Jason quickly replied. It was a surreal moment for Jason; having to turn right around and offer his condolences to her. Having to put his pain and hurt aside for a moment, just to return the *emotion she'd just provided him. Jessica's father meant everything to her—it was all starting to come back to him, the more he reflected on it.*

Jason had the pleasure of meeting her father a few times during the Academy. Graduation was when he actually discovered that her father was a police captain for the city of Lansing, Michigan.

It was the proudest day of the old man's life, witnessing his daughter graduate from the academy at the top of her class. He was the reason she was such a wonderful marksman. He'd taught her how to shoot since she was ten years of age and she was so good, so dialed in when it came to shooting. She could shave the back hair off a fly with a bullet, twenty feet away.

"Thanks." said Jessica through a smile, "I've handled it better than I thought I would, but my mother, that's another story altogether.

Jessica carried a smile so big; Jason instantly fell in love with it. He realized that if he were to cover his ears, he'd have no idea she was talking about the death of her father. That's who she was, always smiling though her words—always. Jason remembered that she always carried this engaging personality and had this positive glow around her no matter what was happening with her or around her.

"So yeah, I'm here," she continued. "On the seventh floor, Counter Terrorism Unit. What about you?"

Jason shrugged his shoulders as he shook his head.

"Not sure. I guess I'll know after today. Since everything happened, I've been on leave. I didn't really want to come back, but they gave me the opportunity to come back whenever I was ready. I think they are trying to determine today if I'm ready or not."

"Well, are you.......ready?"

Jessica's sharply inquisitive tone was a bit of an eye opener. It was at this moment he realized what he was about to jump back into.

Jason hesitantly shook his head as he closed his eyes. "I don't know, Jessica. I truly don't."

"I understand completely." Jessica nodded.

Jason knew just by looking at her, she understood exactly what he meant. She was cognizant of the procedure, the evaluations, and the briefs an agent needed to go through before returning to duty after going through something so traumatic.

Jessica suddenly glanced down at her wrist as a bracelet she was wearing began beeping loudly.

"Fancy watch." Jason uttered jokingly.

Jessica chuckled as she shook her head.

"Yes!! It's my special wonder woman bracelet." she

chuckled. "No. It's actually a GPS locator bracelet. It's for my mother. I got her one so I can keep tabs on her. She was not happy about wearing it because it's not "fashionable," so to show solidarity and support, I ordered one so she would feel better, and it worked, she just loves wearing it now because I make it look so cool."

"You really do." said Jason jokingly.

"Yeah, there was an incident two years ago in which she walked out of her house and was found wandering almost a mile down the road. It was then discovered that she was in the early stages of Alzheimer's."

"Oh, I'm so sorry to hear that, Jessica."

Jessica shrugged gently, but clearly fought to hide her emotions.

"Like you said, I'm dealing with it. Life—we have no choice, right?"

"Right." Jason whispered while nodding.

"Well, I'm headed up, you want to go up with me?" she asked.

Jason took a deep breath and exhaled as he shook his head.

"No, I'm going to wait out here for a little bit. I have to meet up with Dave and I want to catch more of this sun before I go into the "dungeon" for my visit with the Chief.

Jessica nodded but Jason had a feeling that she wanted him to say "yes."

The instant and mutual attraction was fairly obvious, but it was clear that she was dealing with her own pain at the moment.

Jessica smiled as she slowly turned and walked off. She turned back, waved at him, and begin heading toward the front of the building. Jason couldn't be certain, but he could tell by the way Jessica was looking at him while he was talking, she was reminiscing on the academy days when they were together. He wasn't sure if the look she was giving him now was one of sympathy or attraction. At this point, he understood it probably didn't matter. He was entirely too fragile to handle anything close to a relationship at this point. He didn't want to be hurt again. He didn't want to love and lose—not again. The best way to ensure that he wouldn't, would be to keep his personal relationships to a minimum, and that's what he was planning to do. Jason glanced up at Jessica and saw that she had turned around to look at him again. When she saw him look up, she smiled and turned back around heading towards the door again.....

I immediately peeled my eyes from the story, smiling. I found myself once again questioning Jason's personal judgment and decision making while simultaneously understanding that it was indeed a very delicate situation. There were too many variables to consider, and no easy answers or ways to "fix" this character's broken life right now. I knew Jason was at the point where positive and meaningful relationships were certainly vital in helping him with the healing process, a process that he was clearly struggling with.

To help him heal the way he needed to be healed, completely, it would take more than just wishing and wanting it all to somehow get better, it would take actions. I found myself a bit surprised at how dismissive Jason was to these potential meaningful relationships that were staring him in his face. I was curious as to how and why he didn't see how beneficial they would be for him. Of course, I understood that sometimes, we're oblivious to seemingly obvious and potential moves that stand to positively benefit our lives.

But I also realized that my unimaginable position, where I currently found myself juxtaposed Jason's, was perfectly and cosmically placed. Indeed, this position, from the outside perspective, afforded me the inconceivable ability to help Jason recognize all that he's unable to see from his own perspective. In this particular case, I was literally on the outside looking in, as I was reading and experiencing this man's life with the unexplainable and improbable ability to actually do something about it. I smiled.

I couldn't believe how my mind was currently operating. It was as if it was effortlessly grasping concepts, ideas and logic, in ways that I could never possibly fathom. Which wasn't saying much considering in all of my adult life, I didn't give much thought to anything outside of my job or my family.

Wasn't exactly hard for my mind to become more open than it's ever been, considering I was a tragically closed-minded man for the most part. I sat back in my seat, closed my eyes, and began thinking about Jason's situation as objectively and logically as I could.

I wanted to try to see it completely from Jason's point of view as best I could and try to at least understand what he was thinking. I began to breathe and relax myself and my mind as much as I could.

Ever since the start of this unbelievable experience, I haven't felt the same in any way shape or form. My mind seemed to continue to push the limits and openness of my subconscious, and it was as if I had no way to stop it from doing so or no way to control it. I now understood that the decisions I was making were directly impacting this character's "life," within this story, but what good is it to have this ability and not utilize it the way I wanted to, or the way I thought was best for the character? The story was still a story. It was still filling itself out despite what I added in Jason's life, which made it all the more confusing. The story appeared to be laying out the history between Jason and Jessica rather perfectly for me, and it was as if I completely understood their relationship just by the little details I read. I was well aware of the fact that Jason was reluctant to take on any more meaningful relationships because he was afraid of getting hurt. I wasn't sure what the "appropriate" time was to begin a relationship after losing a spouse. I didn't know if it mattered or not considering Jason needed something more to live for, a lot more.

He needed to know what it felt like to be happy again, what it feels like to know that the world hadn't completely forgotten about him. He needed to know what a family was again. The only way for him to know was to start completely living again, and Jessica, along with Tara, was essentially another really good and seemingly logical step in that direction. If I had anything to do with it, I would see to it that Jason made it back to who he was before— before I began the story.

I took a deep breath as my eyes remained closed. I wanted to make sure that the words that I uttered into the atmosphere were the words that would truly help this man, this character, and not harm him or derail his healing process in any way.

This story, this experience, was beginning to become heavier by the chapter. The responsibility seem to be growing with each turn of the page, and the risks seem to be getting greater as more and more people started to become a part of Jason's life. I knew this was a direct result of decisions being "made" by me, because of words being spoken by me, and that feeling was beginning to weigh heavier on me.

At this point, I had no idea if I had already gotten over the "shock" at what was apparently happening to me, or if my mind was so cosmically elevated at this point, that the sheer thought of all of this being impossible was something that my mind wouldn't allow me to even consider.

My thoughts were working on such a level of high unconscionable state of awareness that whenever I begin to think about the possibility of this not being real, or that it was all in my mind, or that it was all coincidences—my mind would seemingly start fighting within itself. I presumed it was an attempt to reject what it saw as illogical denial on my part.

At this point, my mind seemed to be unconsciously and effortlessly operating under the logic that any and everything was possible.

Up until this point, I'd never thought this way at any point in my life, nor had my mind ever pushed such logic into the forefront of my subconscious.

The possibility of me currently dreaming, still lingered in the back of my mind, but I had never experienced a dream as vivid, as clear, as colorful and emotional as this in all my years on this earth. I did know that if I was in fact dreaming, it would be ok for me to awake from this nightmare at any moment. It would be ok to wake up to know that my daughter was still alive.

There was nothing I wanted more right now than to know that all of this was nothing but a nightmare, but the longer I sat and felt the vibration from the plane, inhaled the oxygen from inside the plane, the more I fought to keep my personal pain buried deep within me, the more I realized just how real the pain of Natalie's death really was. This was no dream; this was only a nightmare in the metaphorical sense.

I glanced down at the Nook. I suddenly found myself inconveniently at a loss of words. I honestly didn't want to read any further until I knew exactly what I needed to say in order to get Jason to do what I believe he should be doing–allowing Jessica into his life. Chapter five appeared to be a long chapter, the longest of all the chapters thus far. Was it a reason for that?

Was there something of great importance Jason needed to do this chapter?

I sat pondering on just how I needed to word it to make certain that it was said correctly and logically. I smiled at the thought of how difficult it had become to simply say words, words that should otherwise be so simple or easy to utter. As humans, we relish the thought of having this type of "power" over someone else, and here I was, with the "ability" to essentially do whatever I wanted for this character, and I didn't know what to say or how to say it. I slowly closed my eyes again, began to concentrate, and began to dig deep within my subconscious.

After much digging, I finally opened my mouth and spoke the words:

"Jason can't ignore or fight the feelings he has towards Jessica. He goes after her and pulls her into his world."

Simple words, simple thought, simple logic. After uttering the words, I opened my eyes, glanced down at the Nook and continued reading.......

Jason's Story – Chapter Five – Continued

He watched her until she disappeared through the building doors. He continued to stare at the doors she had walked through, stuck in a daydream, thinking about what could've been if he wasn't so strangely apprehensive. He found it extremely difficult to simply ignore or dismiss the feelings he suddenly felt upon seeing her again. He shook his head as he battled within himself on what it was that he believed he wanted to do, but he knew deep down inside, there wasn't much he had emotionally, to offer right now.

That was something that he didn't want to really accept, but deep down he knew accepting it was probably the best thing. It was the right thing.
Jason gradually made his way into the building and up to the seventeenth floor.

"Jason, you sure you're ok?" Dave asked gingerly. They were the only two in the elevator headed up to Section Chief's Keegan's office on the seventeenth floor. Jason stared at the top of the elevator ceiling, it was a mirror, and Jason couldn't take his eyes off of it. He wasn't' interested in his reflection, it was more the current

weird and unmistakably surreal feeling he couldn't explain that had come over him.

"The hell is wrong with me?" Jason angrily whispered to himself as he shook his head.

"What's that?" Dave asked.

They were passing the sixth floor. Jason abruptly scurried toward the elevator buttons on the wall and immediately pressed the button for the seventh floor.

"Jason, what the hell are you doing?!!" Dave snickered.

"I honestly have no idea." Jason shouted out distractedly, as he quickly sprinted through the opening elevator doors.

An unquestionably confused Dave immediately sprinted closely behind Jason.

"Jason!!" Dave whispered as loudly as he could as he followed closely behind, "Jason, stop God dammit! The hell are you doing?"

Jason wasn't hearing Dave as he found himself walking rapidly and slightly franticly, popping his head through office door after another, looking for the Counter Terrorism Division. He walked inside of the fourth office. The office wasn't crowded at all, but there were more than a few people inside, enough for Dave to worry about Jason doing something erratic or even dangerous.

"Agent Barrington STOP!" Dave barked while grabbing his arm tight.

"Just what in the hell are you doing, son? I'm trying to get you back on the team, get you back reinstated and you're already going section eight on me?"

"Dave, its ok," Jason chuckled, "Just trust me, please?" Dave looked into Jason's eyes and saw something. He didn't know what it was, but as he focused in on the eyes, he didn't see a man that was unstable or who was losing it. He saw something else, something he couldn't explain— something that most likely didn't need an explanation.

He slowly and cautiously released the grip on Jason's arm as Jason calmly continued his search through the office. Jason gazed around the entire office until he arrived at the desk of one Agent Jessica Phillips. She was busy doing work, so she hadn't really notice him standing next to her desk.

"Jessica?" he whispered.
Jessica immediately glanced up from her computer and noticed Jason, a smile immediately flashed across her face.

"Jason? What are you doing here?" she asked behind a slightly confused expression, as she quickly glanced around the office. Jason didn't know what to say or how to say it.

His initial thinking was that he truly had no idea why he was suddenly standing in this woman's face or why he was even in her office. He was speechless and didn't know why. As he began to search the halls of his subconscious, he realized that though he didn't know why he was suddenly in her presence, the only thing he did know was that he needed her but didn't want to look the fool in telling her that. He closed his eyes and slowly began shaking his head as he had a very hard time understanding what was happening.

"You..... um, when you were outside, I um ..."
He struggled to get the words out.
Jason smiled a nervous smile and continued to shake his head as he couldn't believe how quickly he was making a fool of himself.

"When you were downstairs and I was downstairs too, you know—when we were outside? We were outside together, remember?"

Jessica could only smile as she listened to Jason babble. Jason noticed her smile and instantly knew she could have stopped him, but realized she was probably enjoying it way too much.

"You asked me, you said; "Do you want to come up with me?" and yeah..... I said "no" but I did, I did wanted it—I mean...... I want to come up with you."

Jason nervously took a deep breath and exhaled.

"Jason," Jessica interrupted Jason as she was now clearly struggling to prevent from laughing out loud at his performance. "Jason, can you hear me?"

"Yes." said Jason as he took another deep breath and slowly exhaled. Jessica smiled as she quickly began writing on a sticky note, and immediately handed it to Jason.

"Just call me, Jason, please?"
Jason stared at the note and didn't move. The moment was immensely surreal and also slightly confusing. It felt so right, but he couldn't exactly explain why or how.

"I will," said Jason as he slowly backed out of the office with his eyes locked on Jessica. "I'll call you."

I slowly glanced up from the story, and honestly couldn't do anything but smile.

I didn't know what to say, but I wanted to say something, anything to someone. It was an immensely euphoric and exciting feeling, and holding it in was becoming difficult, but as much as I wanted to share what I was experiencing with someone, I knew I couldn't.

"Ok." I whispered softly behind a smile.

I was smiling for a variety of reasons; I just didn't know which one I wanted to actually admit to. I truly didn't know how to describe what I was feeling. I assumed it was similar to winning some sort of competition, but much more gratifying and surreal, and on another level. It was hard to not only put it into words, but it was hard to even put it into rational thought.

I didn't know what or how to think about what I believed I'd discovered and was currently experiencing through this "story."

As I pondered on it a bit more, I realized that it all started to make sense and somewhat slightly come together for me.

Slowly, I was starting to realize that I had assumed that the story, that "*Jason's Story*," was subject to be influence essentially by any and everything I said to him no matter how I said it, or how I delivered and phrased it.

But it seemed as if that wasn't the case. It was gradually starting to seem like not only could I not influence anything or anyone in this story outside of Jason, but it was becoming apparent that the deeper I went into this story, the more elaborate and logical my thinking and verbal "instructions" would need to be in regard to any "influence" or "control" I had over Jason. I wasn't sure of a lot right now, but there were some things that were becoming clearer for me with every chapter of this story I read.

I wasn't certain, and needed a bit more confirmation, but my mind seems to suddenly allow me to notice that apparently, when the chapters ended, the next chapters didn't seem to appear until I spoke or even thought something meaningful and logical into the story—into Jason's life. This is what seem to ultimately initiate the next chapters.

As I reflected back to the beginning of the story and my reading of the first few chapters, it was as clear as day. The thought of me missing something so apparent, so obvious, made me smile as I shook my head. I couldn't believe it.

"How did I miss it?" I chuckled to myself. Glancing over at Bradley, I noticed he was still asleep. I wanted desperately to tell someone, anyone, about what I was experiencing, about what I was reading, about Jason, but I knew nothing good could possibly come of that. It was beginning to feel almost like a puzzle, and I questioned whether or not I honestly had the mental, physical, and emotional energy to keep it up as I felt myself becoming more drained.

My eyes burned from a combination of lack of sleep and the constant staring at the screen over the past few hours.

I really hadn't gotten much rest before boarding, because of the nearly two-day counsel "session" I had with Father Miyake back in the hospital. I rubbed my eyes in an attempt to rub the burning sensation out of them—to no avail of course.

The story was doing more at this point than just taking my mind off the personal pain I was currently dealing with; it was also distracting me from my apparent fatigue. For now, I figured it would be all I needed to help make it through the flight, sanity intact.

I picked up the Nook and immediately jumped back into the story.

Jason's Story – Chapter Five – Continued...

"The hell was that?" Dave asked, the confusion sharply smeared across his face.

The two men headed towards the elevators.

"You really did all that for that?" Jason slowly began to shake his head. "Dave, if I knew I would tell you, but I don't know. "There's something going on with me."

Dave nodded his head in agreement.

"I know there is, and we'll continue to get you the help you need.... "

"No!" Jason chuckled as he interrupted Dave. "I'm not.....I'm not talking about that. It's like ever since I lost my...."

Jason quickly began to gather himself as he began to get emotional. He tilted his head back, closed his eyes, and took a deep breath. What he was attempting to say not only wasn't coming out easy, but he knew Dave wouldn't understand. But there was a need on his part, to at least attempt to explain it to Dave at this point.

"Ever since it all fell apart for me," Jason continued. "I

don't see things the way I used to see them prior, and for the life of me, I can't' understand why."

Dave focused deeply into Jason's eyes as tears began to slowly fall down Jason's face. Dave knew when Jason was being sincere. He taught Jason, schooled him, and worked with him long enough to know when he was being genuine.

As he looked into Jason's eyes, he knew that he was being real, and that Jason would need him now more than ever, but it was difficult accepting what Jason was saying as it was all so confusing and hard to understand. As he stared into his eyes, he saw the same thing now as he saw moments prior while in Jessica's office—sincerity and genuine belief in what he was saying and doing.

"Jason, what do you want me to say? Dave replied confusingly, as he placed his hand on Jason shoulder. I'm not sure what to say to that, I'm just not. I only want you to get back to where you were. I want you to get healthy."

Shaking his head, Jason closed his eyes. He knew it would be difficult in trying to get Dave to understand how he was feeling. Dave's responses and reaction didn't surprise Jason at all.

"Dave look, I know you don't understand what I'm trying to say...."

"Of course I don't understand what you're trying to say Jason because..... look, I believe you, I do. You haven't felt the same since the incident, I get that, but damn son, you experienced an immensely traumatic event and now you starting to come out on top of it. Don't look back now, just—don't go back there. I didn't say anything when you adopted Tara. I didn't say anything because I thought and still do believe she will help you get back to where you need to be and you can be the parent, the father she needs in her life. But even that was a rash and unexplainable decision. A decision that needed more input than just your own, because of everything that has happened to you emotionally. You don't agree with that?"

"I do agree Dave," Jason replied as he shrugged his shoulders, "You're right about that. I had no intentions of doing it, if that makes any sense? But it was something that I found myself unconsciously doing. I can't explain it. I'm happy she's here though. That's all that matters now."

"As am I. I'm glad she is adding some light to the darkness that has surrounded you," Dave quickly replied, "but the point still stands son."

No matter how much he tried to explain to Dave how he had been feeling as of late, no matter how hard he tried to put it into words, he knew Dave wouldn't understand, *no one would probably understand.*

Section Chief Stanley Keegan, Dave's boss, only by definition. Dave really didn't answer to Keegan as much as he answered to the Director himself. Keegan "allowed" Dave and his team the leeway to do what they needed to do as long as they brought in the results, which they did. Keegan simply stayed out of Dave's way as it was well known that Dave and his team went over Keegan's head and answered primarily to the Director.

Though this wasn't anything "official," it was clear, and Dave and Chief Keegan bumped heads quite a bit over it.

The meeting with Chief Keegan lasted for about an hour, and Jason walked out of Keegan's office with a certain sense of confidence, but also with a certain degree of doubt weighing down on him. Keegan's decision – reinstatement. Three months of desk duty back under Dave's supervision.

Field agent analyst support duty to help get his mind back into the swing of things, get up to speed on what

Dave and the team were doing, and to simply ease him back into the starting lineup.

Jason welcomed the move for more than one reason, but the most important reason, was that he didn't really trust himself to be as effective as he needed to be out in the field. He was glad to be back with the team but couldn't understand or explain why he was doing some of the stuff he had done recently and that concerned him.

He didn't know why he was making sudden, unexplainable, and rash decisions about important things in his life. It was difficult to understand just why this was happening, which was one of the reasons he knew he really couldn't trust himself out in the field at this time. Not until he figured out what was really going on with him. Nevertheless, going back to work was something he dreaded for the past year or so, but as of late, he found himself missing what he used to do, missing his team, and simply tired of being stuck in the house all day, every day. Keegan told him that Dave would ultimately decide when to put him back in the field, but Jason had a hard time envisioning a scenario in which he would be ready anytime soon. No matter how much he wanted to be.

A week had gone by since bumping into Jessica, and Jason had gone out of his way to not call her—to practically avoid her. She wasn't aware that he had been reinstated to work and that was the way he wanted it. He was glad to see her but didn't know what to say to her or how to say it and he was afraid of failure.

The confidence he had before, was no more. No matter how much he tried to force it back within himself, it just wasn't there anymore.

Jason sat up on the edge of his bed as he held Jessica's number in his hand. He caught himself staring at it, trying to figure out what to do with it. He pondered on if it was too early to try to jump back into something meaningful as doubt found itself creeping back into his mind.

It was going on two years since losing his family, but it honestly felt like everything happened just yesterday. Everything was unfortunately still fresh in his mind and his world, no matter how much time had passed.

He found himself staring right through the slip with Jessica's number on it. He found himself in a daze thinking about what he could possibly say to her if he were to call her. It had been a while since he had courted a woman and talked with one over the phone, and at this point, he felt he had nothing truly positive to talk with her about.

"What are you looking at?" Tara asked suddenly.

Her voice startled Jason as he quickly turned around to discover that she had quietly entered the room and was in position to see that he was holding and staring at

Jessica's number. He didn't know if he should answer Tara but didn't want to lie to her.

"Um.... It's..... I'm not sure what this is" said Jason as he lazily shook his head and shrugged his shoulders. Tara walked over to Jason, sat down beside him, and slowly retrieved the slip from his hand. He wanted to pull it back and pretend like it was nothing, but it was too late.

Tara was too smart for that and doing so would only peak her inquisitive nature even more. Tara had been with him almost two years now, and they had undoubtedly grown closer during that time. Jason had also gotten much better at reading Tara and understanding how she thought, but he had no idea how she would react to discovering this.

"Jessica," Tara stated as she quietly read the slip of paper, "Who is Jessica?"

Jason glanced up at Tara and didn't say anything. He closed his eyes and began shaking his head.

"Dad, why are you sitting here staring at this number? Do you want to call her? Who is she?"

Jason shook his head as he closed his eyes and tilted his head up towards the ceiling.

"She's an old friend. An old colleague, Tara, and quite honestly, I don't know if I want to call her or not. I'm afraid to call her, for more than one reason.

Tara had one eyebrow raised in curiosity as she wasn't quite sure what Jason meant but nodded her head any way as if she did.

"Dad," she chuckled, "you're sitting here on the edge of the bed, staring at this paper with this number on it. I don't get it."

Jason sighed and continued to shake his head as his forced smile gradually disappeared. Looking Tara in her eyes, he didn't know how she would react if he told her who Jessica was and his "true" intentions, but he had in fact grown to trust Tara and she wasn't afraid to get her opinion.

"She's an old friend, an old colleague of mine that I bumped into a week ago, and I have yet to call her. I didn't know if I should call her or what I would say if I did call her. I was trying to be sensitive to your feelings as well. I just wasn't sure how you would feel about me........"

"Being with someone other than my mother?" Jessica's asked inquisitively.

"Well, yeah," Jason replied as he nodded his head. "I wasn't just afraid of how you would feel about that, but I'm afraid of how I would feel about that. I'm not sure how long I suppose to be grieving for your mother and how long I should allow it to govern my life. One year? Two years? Forever?"

Tara could see the discontent in his face, but it wasn't just a look of discontent, Jason seemed lost and had no idea where to go and what to do with this.

"Mom isn't here anymore. But you and I, we're still here. What else is there to discuss? We have been sad for them for quite some time now, but we have to live our own lives. Moving on doesn't mean forgetting about them, does it?"

Tara looked her father in his eyes before handing Jessica's number back to him and slowly making her way back towards the door as she turned around and paused.
"It doesn't matter what anyone says about your life Dad, not even me. It's your life and no one can live it for you. I want to see you happy; I want to see you smile. That's what will make me happy."

With that, Tara quickly made her way back over to him, planted a small kiss on his cheek, smiled, and exited the room just as quietly and quickly as she entered it. Jason glanced back down at Jessica's card as Tara's words echoed throughout his head. He slowly picked up the phone and began to dial Jessica's number. By the third ring, he was ready to hang up the phone, but Jessica's voice caught him by surprise.

"Hello?"

"Um, Jessica?"

"Yes?"

Jason sat breathing as he didn't know what to say to her. It was an awkward silence and he hated it. He quickly looked around the room in a slight panic for any type of inspiration to help him say something, anything meaningful to her.

"Jason?" Jessica whispered quietly into the phone ending the awkward silence.

"Yes?" he quickly responded.

"Can I tell you a story?"

Jason was so taken aback at her sudden, odd request that it took him a minute to register just what she had asked him.

"Um, sure." Jason finally responded.

"My father was a practical man," Jessica began. "A simple man who didn't give much thought to things outside of us, outside of his family. If he couldn't see it, touch it, smell it, or taste it, it had no place in his world, except at the end of his life—the very end to be exact. One day, while I sat next to him at home as he lay dying, he woke up out of his sleep for fifteen seconds right before he died, fifteen seconds he spent with me before he left us. He saw my face; he was calm as he smiled at me and said, 'Hey,' she whispered, "I remembered smiling at him and responding; 'Hey?'

"He looked me in my eyes and said; "she begins again with his end...."

"I looked him in his eyes—bewildered and confused. 'Dad, what are you saying?' I asked him.
He hesitated and smile at me then said: 'It's more amazing than I thought.' And after those words, that was it—my father was no more."

"Do you have any idea what he meant by that?" Jason asked curiously.

"Not exactly," said Jessica. "But my family have debated this for some time now, and my mother believes that he was saying that with his passing she will be able to begin again—to live again. Her life will not only not end with his passing, but it will begin again, but honestly, we'll never know. It's one of the mysteries of the universe that he took with him."

"Jessica I'm sorry. I know how close you were to...."

"It's fine," Jessica quickly replied. "I'm at peace with it Jason. I tell you this story because I want you to know that life never makes anything easy for you, sometimes it makes things very difficult. The trick is that you have to find important life lessons from within each difficult situation or it'll drive you crazy. My father; the man that didn't believe in anything outside of what he could see, but to see his face and hear him saying what he said that day in the hospital bed, showed me that through pain and difficulties, life will always give you a chance to discover something meaningful from within those circumstances, something fruitful, and full of substance. Though what my father said didn't make any sense to me at that moment, I know what he said was very meaningful and one day it would make sense."

Jason could hear her voice crack as she spoke on her father. He could hear the passion, the emotion. He laid back on the bed and closed his eyes thinking about what Jessica just shared with him.

He honestly understood what she was getting at but didn't know what he was supposed to take away from what happened to his family. He decided that whatever it was, he would spend the rest of his life searching for it and do whatever it took to find it if it was out there to be found.

"Jessica, I appreciate that," said Jason. "You don't know how much I needed to hear that."

"Trust me," Jessica replied. "I do. Now that we've gotten that out of the way—Hi."

"Hi," Jason responded as he gingerly laid back on the bed, glancing up at the ceiling while smiling. "How was your day?"

Jason's Story – Chapter Five—The End

<u>Chapter Ten</u>

The Crossroads
* Hour Nine *

I t was a truly satisfying feeling.

A relatively proud feeling. The gratifying feeling in which you know you're potentially responsible for something as great, meaningfully, and positively substantive as the journey Jason and Jessica were about to embark upon.

I swiped the screen of the Nook over like before and of course—no chapter. New chapters not being there after I finished previous chapters, the concept didn't get any easier to understand or accept as the story went along. It was just gradually becoming less shocking. I quickly found myself in a precarious position. No matter how opened my mind had become as of late

I was worried about my ability to remain a consistently creative asset to this story. The more I read, the more it was fairly obvious that my creativity was desperately needed as much as any part of my mind at this point. Initiating chapters undoubtedly required a certain amount of creativity wrapped delicately around logic, and that's what made it all so difficult. I for one, wasn't good at this sort of thing, which is why I was never great at writing.

Any school projects my daughters had, requiring a certain amount of creativity, I delegated it to their mother, always.

This was slightly different. This was more than just simply creating the next chapter in some assignment to be turned in for a grade, this was.....well, I had no idea what it was when I sat back and really thought about it.

The more I actually thought about it, the more I realized I hadn't really actually thought about it.

I slowly gazed around the plane. The more I thought about what was happening, the more I found myself somewhat afraid of what it all could potentially mean. I once again found myself back at the possibility that I was either going crazy or everything I was experiencing, was actually really happening. If that was the case, it meant that something bigger was happening here, which in itself, was just as scary a thought. Either way, here it was, right here in front of me, and for some reason, I felt compelled to do something about it. I was happy that Jason had now found the courage to call Jessica, and they seem to hit it off pretty good, initially. I only figured that the most logical move from this point would be to further expand on their relationship. I wasn't sure if that was the ultimate purpose of the story.

There had to be some purpose to all of this, I'm sure of it, but right now I didn't see it. It raised within me, a philosophical question of sort.

When "reading" or experiencing someone's "story," at what point can you stop reading? Is there a point in their life in which something happens that brings about the "end" of your position as the reader?

Father Miyake's note stated that there were thirteen chapters, but was I obligated to see them through?

I slowly turned and gazed out of the window as I found myself thinking heavily on all the possibilities.

The more I thought about the way Jason described how he was feeling, how his mind seemed to be elevating, and shifting on another level, the more I believed I understood exactly how he was feeling. It could actually quite accurately define the way I was currently feeling, and had been, ever since leaving the hospital. It truly was a feeling that I'd never felt before—that made it difficult to describe, even to myself.

Quite honestly, it didn't have any sort of "feel" to it. It was more like a different state of being or existence, but within the mind. I was beginning to feel as though my mind was expanding, big enough to hold everything. Not only expanding but adapting to every critical challenge around me currently. In this case, that challenge happened to be this story I was reading. It was impossible to describe to myself, so I was pretty happy that I didn't have to explain or describe it to anyone else.

Considering what I now knew, I figured the best course of action, would be to do my best to "initiate" and get through all thirteen of the chapters, no matter what it took.

As I continued gazing out of the window, I began contemplating on the most important question at the given moment; "*what was next for Jason?*" I wasn't entirely sure, but I figured since I was the one charged with painting this initial picture or scene, and with making adequate changes in this character's life, I might as well try to paint carefully and responsibly. In my mind, the only place to logically go, from this point, was appropriately placing Jason and Jessica in the best possible position for them to have a chance at a successful relationship.

Both Jason and Jessica needed to open themselves up in order to receive the love and affection from the other, but I was aware of the notion that I could only "influence"

Jason and that's essentially what I would do. I would try to make it easy for Jessica to love Jason.

I closed my eyes. I found it easier to concentrate and focus when closing them before speaking the words out into the universe that seem to so inexplicably affect this character's life.

I took a deep breath with my eyes still closed and spoke:

"Jason opens himself up and becomes more accepting of Jessica's love and affection as he in turns gives her every bit of himself."

I slowly opened my eyes and glanced down at the device. It was surreal, as the notification for the next chapter immediately faded into place at the bottom of the page. I pressed the icon to begin the next chapter. I wasted no time jumping back into the story.

Jason's Story—Chapter Six

"So, what are you going to do?" Agent Brask asked behind a sincerely concerned tone.

"Nothing." Jason replied, shrugging as he gazed aimlessly down at his desk. "Boss said I'm still on desk duty so, nothing."

He found himself thoroughly annoyed at the fact that he wasn't cleared for field duty as of yet, but it some weird way, he was ok with it. He still wasn't sure if he could trust himself in the field at this point.

"Hey, hold your head," Brask replied as he extended his hand towards Jason.

"You'll be fine."

"Thanks man." Jason whispered as he extended his hand towards Brask's and completed the fist bump. "Now get outta here and watch your ass out there."

Brask was the more experienced agent out of the group. Having served under Dave the longest, Brask was only a few years older than Jason. He took the team lead now that Jason was sidelined.

Brask quickly made his way out of the building towards ground level as the team waited to pull out. Jason was allowed to brief with the team, but that was as far as he was allowed to go.

This night, Dave and the team headed out to make an arrest and finally close on the case agent Willingham had been undercover on for the past six and a half months. From thirteen floors above, Jason gaze down at the federal vehicles that quickly carried his team away. There was an overwhelming sense of failure falling over him as he watched his team pull away.

It was now going on nineteen months total and Section Chief Keegan still didn't feel as though Jason was ready for field duty.

Nineteen months—not typical time frame as far as standard medical leave, but there was nothing "typical" or "standard" about his case and Jason accepted that.

His visits with the therapists weren't doing much for him. He felt as though he'd already done much of the healing on his own, along with the help of whatever hidden strength he suddenly and recently found buried deep within.

Watching his team pull away, Jason peered out over the view of the city as nightfall had completely covered the town. He found himself becoming lost within the city lights as he began to reflect on the past seven months and how much his life had changed, primarily for the better, over that time period.

Jessica and Tara had grown immensely close over the previous three months. Jason would at times take a step back and admire just how much they quickly seemed to begin to care unconditionally for one another.

He began to reflect on the turning point in he and Jessica's relationship. A conversation that opened his eyes and essentially changed their relationship. He remembered that night that took place a few months ago.

The conversation was so vivid, as if it was happening at this very moment. He remembered the look Jessica had in her eyes, the tears that slowly fell down her face, and the horrible feeling he had inside as he watched her open herself up to him in a way that no woman had ever done for him, this soon.

What is this?" he remembered her asking him. " Is this real, Jason? What are you so afraid of?" she said, shaking her head as she gazed deeply into Jason's eyes.

Jason remembered not being exactly sure how to answer her question. At the time, he honestly didn't know just what he was afraid of. He realized that at this point, he was afraid of everything—afraid of life. He remembered *realizing that he was essentially in the way of his own happiness.*

"At this point, I don't know. I don't know what I'm afraid of Jessica. Life? Love? I really can't say anymore, and I don't know why I don't know. I'm simply not the same person I was before my life changed."

She guided his face back so that she could see his eyes, as she nodded her head.

"I know Jason, I know. You don't think I'm afraid as well? I am afraid, but that doesn't mean I allow it to stop me from living or allow this fear to control me or my happiness. It's been a half a year since this started and I honestly feel more distant from you now than I did when I first saw you again, outside the federal building."

Jason distinctly remembered gently guiding her face towards his, grabbing her hand and placing her hand over his heart.

"This......is real," he whispered emphatically. "The only thing I know right now is that I'm alive, you're alive and we're both here right now—at this moment. I'm afraid of losing you. I'm afraid of losing Tara. I'm afraid that I can't protect you guys the way I need to because I barely believe in myself anymore. That's what I'm afraid of, Jessica. Not love."

"You don't need to protect us, Jason." Jessica quickly

replied while shaking her head. "Protect us from what? Tara needs a father more than she needs a bodyguard. I need you to love me more than I need you to feel obligated to protect me, Jason. Just tell me something real."

Jessica stared deep into his eyes as she spoke.

"Over the past half year, we've fallen hard for one another and I'm thankful for every moment of it. These past several months feels much longer than that. This is real to me, Jason. Everything I see within you and around you, around us, is real to me. Is it real to you?"

Jason remembered struggling to get a word out as he tried finding the right words. He didn't know what to say or how to say it.

"Listen to me," Jessica whispered sternly, "I want to protect you as much as you want to protect us, probably more, but I can't do that, that's not my job. The only thing I can do is love you, Jason, but I can't do that if you don't let me, or if you don't believe in me, believe in us. I'm not here to replace anyone, I can't do that. I can only be who I am for you, and if that's not enough, then I have to respect that, but I have to respect if from a place that isn't next to you."

He remembered gazing deep into her eyes as she spoke.

There was something in her eyes that night that comforted him in a way he hadn't been comforted in a long time. He saw passion, honesty and love, and it was as real as if he could reach out and touch it. He gently placed his hand on Jessica's face and gingerly rubbed her cheek with his thumb. Her face felt moist from the tears as he grabbed the other side of her face with his other hands and continued to peer deep in her eyes.

"It's real." Jason finally replied. "And I know it's been difficult to understand, but I can't pretend as if I'm not afraid of loving you and possibly losing you. I hate being afraid and I hate the hold that this fear has on me. I fear because I love you and I don't want to lose you."

"You're not going to lose me, Jason." she whispered as she gently placed her hand on his heart. "I'm not going anywhere, but I need you, I need what's in here,"

That was the day, he and Jessica met at a crossroads and left together in one direction. It was after that night that Jason knew he had to stop dwelling on the ghosts of his pasts, literally and figuratively. This feeling that had recently came over him had not gone away, and he was still yet unable to explain it. But whatever it was, it made him feel as if he wasn't himself, made him see things, life, and the world, from a different perspective.

He wanted desperately to tell Jessica how he was feeling, but like Dave, he realized he truly didn't know how to adequately describe the feeling. The more he thought on it, the more he realized that he actually remembered feeling this way as far back as the night he was undercover in the van over two years ago, the night in which his entire life changed.

This was something he was dealing with for the past two years, and he still yet had difficulties trying to explain why, even to himself.

No one understood how he was feeling, and he knew there was a good chance that no one ever would. It was that night, a few months ago, that he decided to stop feeling guilty about wanting to love again. It was that night, a few months ago, in which Jason the victim, no longer had any place in his life It was that night, a few months ago, Jason realized that the universe not only took what it wanted, when it wanted, but it also gave when it wanted, planted the seeds of life in our worlds whenever it wanted, and he could do nothing but accept it.

"Ladies and gentlemen, this is your Captain speaking. The crew will be coming around in about twenty minutes time *to offer you a light snack and beverage. The second inflight movie will begin shortly after that. I'll talk to you again before we reach our destination. Until then, sit back, relax and enjoy the rest of the flight."*

Unconsciously, I was rubbing my tired eyes as the captain's voice unnervingly shook me out of my intense focus on the story. I glanced over at Bradley who was still yet sound asleep. I took another sip of my drink as I surrendered a sincere yawn into the airplane's atmosphere. Resting my head against the pillow propped against the window, I returned to the story.

Over the past half year, he witnessed Tara and Jessica's relationship grow into something special and that meant more to him than anything. He knew they loved him, but he wanted Tara to have someone other than him to rely on, confide in, and to listen to. Jessica was that person, or at least he believed she was.

"I got some good news to share with you..."

The text from Jessica read earlier that day. He had no idea what it could be and didn't want to speculate. He wanted to find out sooner rather than later as he slowly drive home, by way of the scenic route. It was hard not to reflect on the past half year and not be extremely thankful for what he now had, considering all that he'd lost. He reached his neighborhood as he slowly pushed down the street, his house suddenly coming into view. He saw Jessica sitting on the porch next to a few boxes; her stuff.

She was officially moving in and was still in the moving process. She smiled once she saw him.

"You finally made it home I see." she said behind a soft grin on her face. "I saw you driving slow as soon as you hit the corner. Why?"

Her tone was in jest, but Jason had no idea he was driving as slow as he was. He was so lost in thought, he hadn't even notice. "Yes mam I did," Jason replied. "I had a lot on my mind—a lot to think about."

"Oh yeah?" replied Jessica, "Like what?"

"I don't know, but I'm working through it." Jason quickly replied. "You have a lot of stuff!" Jason said behind a smile as he glanced around at the many boxes Jessica had sprawled over the porch.

"Not too late to change your mind." Jessica uttered behind a slight chuckle. Jason gently grabbed Jessica's hand as he began to gently usher Jessica into the house.

"Not happening." he replied. Here, let's go inside for a moment."

They made their way into the house. A house that was slowly becoming a home. Jessica had been hesitant to move in over the past few months, but Jason was persistent, and so was Tara, who had taken a serious liking to Jessica, as quickly as Jason had. Jessica had been on a few assignments with her division that caused her to have to leave he and Tara for days at a time. Jason found himself desperately missing her whenever she did.

"I love how you and Tara have been getting along." said Jason.

Jessica smiled as she began unpacking one of her boxes.

"She's a wonderful kid." she chuckled. "Smart, and believe it or not, gives me better advice than any of my friends ever had."

"You know," said Jason. "I wasn't going to call you that time you gave me your number—you remember that?"

"Yes, of course I do."

Jason took a moment to pause as he reflected on that moment.

"I came home, sitting in my room, and I was staring at your number, practically staring through it. Tara walked into my room and saw me holding and staring at your number. She basically told me that I needed to begin living again. She basically told me to start acting like I'm alive. She told me, that as much as she loves and misses her mother, that her mother is no longer here, but I still am, and that I should, well.......call you. Without her saying that to me, I don't think I would've ever called you."

Jessica found it hard not to smile as she thought about what Jason was sharing with her.

"Well, I'm glad she did that," Jessica replied, "and that's something I can share with her sibling in nine months, when they get here. What do you want me to do with my books here?" Jessica quickly asked as she held up a few books.

Jason chuckled as he shook his head.

"No mam. I might be slow, and you might be faster than me in some things, but I'm not **that** slow, and you aren't **that** fast. Screw the books. Rewind the tape. Play the previous track. Run it completely back and cease all operations..."

"What? What I say?!!" she asked with a bewildered look on her face as she grinned.

"You know what you just said, mam. Repeat that for me please." Jason replied behind a nervous smile.

"I said, I will share with Tara's siblings, the fact that

their older sibling was responsible for you calling me, and how wonderful a sister she is. Chances are, they will probably find out before I need to tell them though."

"Wait, what do you....What are you trying to.....How serious are you?" Jason asked while trying to contain his excitement.

"Yes Jason," Jessica whispered. "we're having a baby. This baby is a beginning for us. That's what I want, but I need to know if this is what you want."
Jessica's illuminating smile was radiating off the walls as she spoke. Jason fed off her excitement.

"You sure this is what you want?" he asked, gazing deeply into her eyes, " I mean, you have a lot going on at the agency, this pregnancy will take you out of the field, and I know how much field work means to you over in CTU."

"I'm sure." Jessica snickered. "We women have been balancing these things forever. We're having a baby; I'm not losing a limb. My career will be there if I want it to be."

Jason chuckled as he slowly glanced over at a box over parked in one of the corners. It was one of his old boxes from the old house that he never unpacked. It held the pictures of Tracy and the boys.

He slowly retrieved one of the photos and stared down at it as he could feel Jessica's eyes fixated on him.

"I'm sorry," Jessica whispered while looking Jason in his eyes. "If I could bring them back right now for you to heal that pain that's inside of you, I would. You know that, right?"

Jason nodded his head as he focused in on Jessica's eyes.

"I miss them. I do. I can't lie," Jason said. "but you're here.....you're here right now, and you and I have something real and new and it's ours, and I know in order for us to have any meaningful or productive life and relationship I will have to allow you all the way in. That doesn't mean I don't miss them. That doesn't mean I won't always love them....."

Jason paused as Jessica could sense the emotion starting to overwhelm him. She began gingerly rubbing his face. "It's ok. I know you do, and I need you to understand that I'm not here, in your life to replace them or their memories. That's not what I want to do and that's not what I'm here to do."

"I know," Jason quickly replied, "And you being in my life has saved me in more ways than one. I only hope me being in yours will be just as moving and important."

Jason held onto Jessica as if a storm was coming and he didn't want her to blow away. In a sense, a storm was *approaching and Jason was supremely oblivious. Usually being more cognizant of his surroundings, Jason was blissfully unaware of the armed assassin, gingerly and quietly making his way through the back door into the kitchen.*

Jason and Jessica shared a passionate embrace, their minds were on one another and nothing else at this point as the gunman, with his silencer equipped, semi-automatic weapon raised, aimed and ready to shoot, quietly made his way through the kitchen. He made certain not to make a sound as he wanted to catch his targets off guard.

Jason and Jessica were just two rooms away in the living room, but seemingly had no idea that their lives were currently in extreme and immediate danger......

"Wait, what?" I whispered, as I quickly glanced up from the Nook. I wasn't sure what to say or do.

The sudden pressure to do something, anything, to help Jason and Jessica, caused my heart rate to rapidly increase. I was generally good under pressure for the most part, especially on the job, but to say this was different, would be an understatement. Jason and Jessica, their lives were clearly currently in danger, but I didn't know what to say or how to say it, in order to sufficiently address the threat.

What could I possibly say? What should I do? I found myself panicking as quietly as I could, as I nervously peeked over my shoulders to make sure no one was witnessing my subtle panic session. Neither Jason nor Jessica had a clue they were in immediate danger, but I knew, and didn't have the slightest idea as to what to say to help them.

This was certainly beginning to become a bit overwhelming and somewhat stressful. I nervously shoved my nails in my teeth and began biting down on them.

Not a single logical thought was coming across my panicked mind at the moment, so I began to dig deep within my mind to try to dig up something, anything, to speak into this story to help this unsuspecting couple. *"Uh...... Um..... "*

I stammered as the words were there, but I found myself panicking and they just wouldn't come out. I closed my eyes and took a deep breath.

"A tree smashes through the house and ......um....falls on top of the gunman?"

I whispered to myself in a soft yet panicked tone.

Deep down, it honestly felt more like a question because of the extreme uncertainty that it was wrapped around.

I was beginning to feel rushed and as if I was losing control, but I had to remind myself that I hadn't any real control of any of this thus far. I immediately returned my focus back to the story......

Jason's Story – Chapter Six - Continued

They were of course oblivious to the danger just a few feet away from them. With each step the intruder took, he was a step closer to his targets, who were now just a few steps away in the next room.

The intruder held the silencer equipped nine-millimeter up and steady as he slowly made his way through the kitchen and closer towards the adjacent room Jessica and Jason were in. He was a professional. Jessica guided Jason's face closer to hers with her hand.

"I'm not here to make you forget about anything or anyone. I'm here to start a new chapter with you, new memories. I'm not trying to finish a previous chapter because I can't do that, that's not why God allowed us to find each other again."

Jason looked deep into her eyes and saw the sincerity that he needed to see. He didn't question her love for him, he questioned his love for himself, and that was what prevented him from opening up to her completely, but not anymore. The more he looked into her eyes, the more he smiled as he thought about how happy he was about her carrying his child.

"What are you smiling at?" she asked behind a grin,

"Have you been listening to me?" Nodding his head, Jason placed his hand on her stomach. "This, this is what I'm smiling at. I realize that you aren't here to replace anyone....."

I closed my eyes and shook my head as if I was shaking off a headache. The words I'd spoken weren't having any effect on the story. I instantly found myself once again, questioning everything. I knew what I believed to be happening, was in fact happening, but the words coming out of my mouth didn't seem to have any effects on the story, the seed of doubt began to gradually swell within the halls of my mind. I had a feeling that the story would force me to "witness" these people, these characters whom I have grown close with while experiencing this story, possibly being killed.

I wasn't interested in reading or witnessing that.

What do I say? My heart started to race, I continued to panic as I smacked my forehead hard over and over to try to push it out of me. I closed my eyes and took a deep breath and whispered to myself:

"The gunman trips over a chair he doesn't see in the kitchen, alerting Jason and Jessica to his presence."
I opened my eyes and focused in on the story once more.

Jason's Story – Chapter Six – Continued

"I know you can't, and I don't want you to," Jason continued, *"And if I did anything to insinuate that in any way, I apologize. I miss them, without a doubt, and will always keep a place in my heart for them. It takes a lot to start a new chapter after going through something so difficult, but it makes it worth it when you're starting that chapter with someone that's worth starting it with."*

At this point, the intruder was close enough to hear Jason and Jessica's words, essentially waiting for the perfect time to strike. He wanted to make sure he had both of them in his line of sight to eliminate any possibility of one of them making some sort of escape. He listened carefully to their conversation, as Jason and Jessica begin walking back around to the other end of the dining room, away from his location, which was perfect, as he had the element of surprise, if he flanked back around to meet them and get the drop on them.

The gunman gradually made his way back through the kitchen as he planned to greet the unsuspecting couple on the other side. The intruder listened carefully and quietly as he stood patiently in the kitchen. He heard the unsuspecting couple conversing and laughing in the living room, discussing something that he couldn't quite make out as they weren't speaking that loudly. He waited for the perfect opportunity to strike, hoping to catch them in an extremely vulnerable position.

"...I do remember that." Jason chuckled, "But you were the one in the academy that failed the marksman competition. You remember that?"

"Ha! Nope." Jessica chirped. "I was tops in everything, and I can still hold my breath longer than you."

They began carefully going through some of Jason's old things from the bureau that had been packed and sent home after everything happened. It was the first time he had taken time out to unpack it all.

"They boxed it all up." Jason uttered distractedly, as he peered down into one of his boxes. "Dave boxed them up and they didn't think I'd come back. I mean who really comes back after something like this?" he whispered *while looking through the box.*

Jessica nodded.

"You do. You....... did." she said as she gently caressed his hands.

"Hmmm, what's this?" she asked as she quickly retrieved a Kevlar vest from one of the boxes.

"Ah ha. That my friend, is my good buddy "Winston" Jason whispered inconspicuously while grinning and nodding proudly.

"See this?" he asked as he pointed at a dent in the front of the vest. "That is from a 357 Magnum blast from about thirty feet away during my first assignment in Los Angeles shortly after graduation."

The intruder was a professional. He really didn't need to peek around the corner to know how close or far away the couple was, sound was all he needed, and they provided plenty of it. They gave him more than he needed. Their voices gave him everything he needed as he settled in prime position to strike.....

I quickly glanced up from the story. What the hell was I doing? I closed my eyes and sighed and turned towards the window.

"*Come on Steve,*" I whispered to myself. "*They need you. What the hell are you doing? Help them!*" I couldn't "*control*" the story, this I had already established, but Jason, he was the one that I seem to be able to "control." So essentially, it was up to me and ultimately my mind, in how logic would play into this. That thought alone, would determine just how effective I would be in saving their lives. I had pretty much established that if it wasn't logical to his current situation or position within the story and essentially within his life, Jason's subconscious wouldn't accept it. That at least appeared to be the case.

I tilted my head back and stared at the ceiling, closed my eyes, and began to take deep breaths as I concentrated—hard.

I hadn't contemplated long when it suddenly hit me. I believed I knew what I needed to say and how I needed to say it, and if this didn't work, I knew that I was probably either losing my influence on this character or worse—I never had this "influence," and I am truly crazier than I initially thought. If I couldn't influence the intruder, I could at least try tipping the scale in Jason's direction a bit. I glanced over at Bradley who was focused intensely on his computer. I figured now was as good a time as any to ask him a hypothetical question wrapped loosely around this seemingly impossible experience, I now found myself a part of.

"Can I ask you a question?" I asked Bradley. Bradley immediately and curiously leaned over closer towards me and smiled. "Sure, go ahead."

"Well," I replied, attempting to remain as calm as possible. "Say that, and just work with me here and open your mind a bit, but say one day out of the blue, you're reading a story, a real story about a man with real world problems and while reading this story....."

I paused as my heart raced. I was nervous. I felt like I was wasting the same exact time that Jason and Jessica were now running out of. I didn't want to seem panicked as I spoke to Bradley. I chuckled at the thought of me actually asking him what I was about to ask him.

"This may sound crazy," I said as a grin immediately flashed across Bradley's face.

"Trust me," he replied. "In my existence, I've heard it and probably seen it all. Trust me its fine, go ahead."

I chuckled, as I understood completely that there was no turning back now. I had clearly piqued his interest.

"Well, say while reading the story you discover that for some strange unexplainable and cosmic reason, you suddenly have the uncanny ability to control the main character."

Bradley smiled but gazed at me with a slight look of bewilderment. He appeared to turn his head on a slight angle, like a confused puppy searching for the source of a sudden noise.

"What exactly do you mean by "control"?

"Well, exactly that." I replied. "Essentially controlling the main character's thoughts and actions, to the point in which it starts to affect the entire story."
Bradley nodded his head consistently as I spoke.

"Ah I see," said Bradley as he focused in on every word I uttered. "Well, I would first determine what kind of problems he or she are facing or what particular direction the story is headed. Then I'd guide the story or try to guide the story in a direction that seemingly fixes these "problems" you say they're dealing with."

I smiled. What Bradley was saying was logical, considering I believed that I was already doing exactly that. It was just a bit surreal in hearing him essentially co-sign what I'd already decided to do.

"Well," I replied, "You see, here's the catch. You can't control the story. You can't control other characters, the environment, or anything around the character at all, just the character himself. Nothing else."
Bradley smirked.

I could tell by his expressions and mannerisms that he was highly intrigued in the questions I was asking him.

He was intensely focusing in on every word I uttered.

"Well see," he chuckled, as he wagged his index finger at me like a scolding parent. "Now it starts to get really interesting. If you couldn't control anything around the character, and can only control the character himself, then it would probably drastically reduce the impact you can have on his life, or in this hypothetical case—his story."

"Why do you say that?" I asked curiously.

Bradley continued.

"I for one believe that people's lives are heavily impacted and influenced by their surroundings, environment and those around them. That's why God is believed to be in control of all of it, everything. I don't believe it's feasible or even logical that God only controls us and not the environment and surroundings, or that he only controls the environment and surrounding and not us. If this is the case, I believe it drastically reduces the impact God has on our lives, and I honestly don't believe God has those limitations, but we do. Put it this way; if you suddenly discovered that someone was controlling or influencing you in some sort of story, would you approve of the job they have done thus far into your life?"

The question was unexpected indeed but made me think more than I wanted to.

"I truly don't know." I stammered.

"Have you ever heard of the saying; *"Everyone has a story"*? Bradley asked.

"Yes I have."

"Well," Bradley continued, "I don't think we put too much thought into that saying, but it's true. Everyone born of this universe—everyone. You, me, we all have a story, the only question is, who's reading? And more importantly, who wrote it?"
Bradley's words were more than just food for thought for me. With the unusual way my mind's been currently working, his words only pushed open the doors of my mind, that much wider.

It was very easy for me to get lost in the thoughts that he was sharing with me. I unconsciously stared deeply at the Nook, while Bradley's words echoed through my mind. I still didn't know what this was and stopped trying to make any sense of it. It was becoming much easier to dismiss logic and simply accept it, but what exactly was I accepting? Nothing was any clearer now than when I read the first words of the story. I wasn't certain if I'd done what Bradley suggested. I truly wasn't sure if I'd been "fixing" Jason's story or life, or essentially making it worse.

I was becoming more and more comfortable talking with Bradley as the plane ride went on.

He had a nurturing soul, wrapped tightly in a warm comforting shell of wisdom. I knew I couldn't quite share with Bradley what was really happening with me and this story, but I would try to continue garnering as much wisdom from him as possible. I didn't want to share it for more than a few reasons, but I realized that Bradley had extensive wisdom that was proving to be valuable. Knowledge that I could potentially utilize accordingly, to help guide Jason through what he was dealing with. Was it just a coincidence that I found myself sitting next to a man that was so knowledgeable and seemingly so understanding?

At this point, I was beginning to realize that coincidences were merely cosmically and universally planned moments in time and space that arrive at unplanned times and immediately interjected themselves in our world. Either way, here he was. Why wouldn't I allow his wisdom to help guide me through what I was dealing with? I was doing this alone for the most part, and because of my emotionally fragile state, I didn't fully trust myself to be able to completely and objectively do what's best for Jason without consistently incorporating my own life and emotions into this story and allowing that to guide the way I influenced Jason's decision making.

Bradley was still staring at me, waiting on a response to what he'd just shared with me.

"Do you mind if I asked you another question?" I whispered softly. I didn't want to feel like I was bothering him, even though he wasn't giving off that vibe, yet. Bradley smiled.

"We have seven more hours on this flight my man, trust me, your questions are preventing me from going crazy on here." he whispered behind a soft chuckle.

"Ok, say, though you can control and influence the character in the story, just how effective can your "influence" be if you are unable to get the character to do what you want him to do whenever you wanted them to?"

I wasn't exactly sure if I had worded the question adequately for Bradley as he had a confused look on his face, but he nodded.

"Hmm, what do you mean? Elaborate a bit for me."

I slowly leaned closer to Bradley to get more comfortable, and to hopefully relay my question more clearly.

"Stay with me," I said behind a soft chuckle, "I probably won't make this as clear as I need to. Say for instance, in this story, you're reading how the character is about to be attacked as someone is trying to kill him. This person that is trying to kill him has, unbeknownst to the main character, broken into his house. You're reading this and know that the attacker is close to harming the main character, but you are also aware that the character is oblivious to this. You are unable to make him aware of the attacker's presence."

"Wait," Bradley quickly replied with a look of confusion on his face.

"Why aren't you able to make him aware of the character's presence?
I shook my head and sighed.

"Primarily because something is preventing the reader from placing sporadic, illogical and spontaneous thoughts in the character's mind without there being some kind of logical explanation, connection or reasoning for him to accept these thoughts. Am I making any sense at all here?"

I chuckled as I asked him this. I knew I had to have sounded just a tad bit crazy. I wondered if it sounded as crazy to him as it felt to me.

"Yes, yes you are. I actually see what you're saying." Bradley said. "So, let me see if I understand this so I can answer adequately. It sounds like you're saying that; said person or reader that's "*controlling*" the character, wouldn't be unable to fully control the character or make them do whatever they want, if what they are trying to get them to do doesn't essentially incorporate any sense of logic, meaning, importance, or relevance into their current situation and or circumstances?"

"Yes!!" I exclaimed, "Say this is the case, how can you get the character to do what you want, go where you need him to go, even say the things you need him to say?" Bradley seemed to concentrate heavily for a minute and seemed to focus deeply on every word coming out of my mouth as he was pretty much all in at this point.

"Well," Bradley finally replied, "Technically speaking, you would only need to get them to think logically about their situation or life and if.....If they're smart and are cognizant of their surroundings and place in life, in any way, conventional wisdom suggests that they will do the rest. It requires a bit of trust. Trust that all you need to do is to place them in the most logical situation to succeed. It's almost the same concept or strategy parents utilize when they send their offspring off into the world, after providing them with the necessary information and tutelage over the years to be a successful, productive adult. It's not exactly the same, but in your hypothetical situation, it's probably as close as you are going to get."

I nodded as Bradley spoke. The nodding was part reflexes, and the other part was me wholeheartedly agreeing with Bradley. It made perfect sense, almost too much sense. Reading the last few chapters of *Jason's Story*, I realized that I had to be elaborate with Jason, as he wasn't responding to simple, elementary thoughts or suggestions.

I knew he required more detail, but what Bradley suggested actually made more sense and explained why Jason at times, didn't respond to certain things I'd previously suggested, and why I was now having a hard time getting Jason to respond to anything I was now speaking into his current dire situation.

I knew a lot of it had to do with the fact that reading this part of the story and realizing that Jason's and Jessica's life is in danger, I simply found myself panicked and saying the first things that came to mind in order to help his dire situation.

That wasn't getting it done for Jason. I needed to be more logical, as it was clear Jason wasn't allowing just anything to be spoken into his life, and I guess I understood that.

"Wow," I said slowly nodded my head. "I guess I never looked at it that way. Thanks."

"No problem." Bradley said as he gingerly placed his glasses back on his face, "Excuse me, as I have to go to the private men's room." I smiled at Bradley's odd word usage, it reminded me of my grandfather. My Grandfather would speak as if he just stepped out of an Earnest Hemingway novel.

I didn't even want to look down at the Nook at this point, not without thinking about what I needed to say to immediately alter Jason's and Jessica's current life-threatening situation. I instead found myself gazing out of the window as the late-night Pacific Ocean skies were as surreal as I'd ever seen them. I'd taken this trip at least twice a year for the past few years and this was the most serene, the most euphorically beautiful I'd ever seen the skies and the clouds.

I quickly focused my attention back on Jason and his current situation. I began contemplating heavily on what it was I needed to say. I closed my eyes and began thinking as it gradually began to come to me piece by piece and thought by thought.

The thought was simple yet logical and it was perfect or at least I thought it was. I thought about Bradley's words while I thought about what needed to be said. I contemplated on all variables involved, while keeping it logical but limitless. I glanced out of the window and again and spoke;

"Jason hasn't been in the field in a while, so he puts the Kevlar Vest on to show Jessica how good he looks in it."

I smiled as I spoke the words.

I thought it was genius, and if this didn't work, I would be dumfounded. I knew for that most part that Jason was a good, moral, and loving man, but he was still a man.

If I know one thing about men, it was that we're never too old to show off for women, never. I still found myself flexing every now and then for Sabrina, probably more than I should.

With Jason not being in the field for such a long time, this was the perfect opportunity for him to scratch that itch that I knew still lingered. A chance for him to show off what he deemed to be his favorite vest to this woman he cared deeply about. It of course was about ego and pride, both of which, no matter what a man has been through in life, would find a way to incorporate it within his everyday life, even if on the smallest of scales.

On the surface, it seemed elementary, but it was seed that I planted that needed to grow into something that would hopefully save their lives. I knew of no other way to make Jason aware of the armed intruder currently in his house, so I'd try to do the second-best thing, which was try to at least to somehow to slightly even the odds if there was ever a way to do so.

It made sense to me, but I hope it worked as I didn't know what else to say or how else to say it. I accepted the possibility that it would eventually come to a point in the story in which I wouldn't be able to save every one of these characters, but at this point, and with this current situation, my options seemed to be limited.

I didn't know what I was trying to accomplish by getting Jason to put on his Kevlar, but in my mind, it was the only potential way of logically and inadvertently protecting himself right now from a potential bullet with his name on it, hiding somewhere within the next few words or so I was about to read. It would hopefully give him a chance to use his instincts.

I took a deep breath, opened my eyes and returned to the story.

Jason's Story – Chapter Six - Continued

"How's it look?" Jason asked while carefully sliding the vest on. "It's been a while since I've put one of these on." Jason figured Jessica was yet to see him in his Kevlar since they met again, and he always loved the way the Kevlar fit him, and he figured she would as well.

The vest had a snug feel to it and Jason glanced in Jessica's eyes and realized she couldn't take her eyes off of him. Jessica smiled as she rubbed her fingers over the vest. She gently rubbed her hands over Jason's chest area immediately causing him to blush.

"It fits you perfectly," she whispered behind a flirty tone. Jessica quickly paused as her smile quickly vanished. She looked past Jason and took a deep breath..... "Jason!!!" she yelled.

Jason immediately turned and instantly noticed the gunman standing in the door of the living room, gun in hand, aimed at he and Jessica.

Before the gunman could squeeze, Jason shoved Jessica out of the way, hard. Jason's push had such force on it, that it lifted Jessica off her feet and sent her a few feet into the other part of the living room, away from the gunman. At that same time, the gunman, who had Jason's chest in his aim, opened fire. Jason took a shot to his chest. It instantly lifted Jason off his feet and onto his back against the wall into the front of the living room. The pain was intense.

Jason immediately grabbed his chest as he struggled to breathe. With essentially no time to react, he saw the gunman running toward him to get another shot off. The gunman quickly entered the living room and aimed his silencer equipped semi-automatic weapon in Jessica's direction. He immediately discovered that Jessica wasn't there. Jason struggled, but gradually made it to his feet. The pain made it difficult to breathe as he gripped his chest. He was hurting but needed to eliminate the threat in order to save both his and Jessica's lives. The gunman, quickly noticed Jason making the move to his feet, rapidly turned his gun back on Jason, and fired multiple times.

The shots hit Jason in the chest again launching him back into the wall and dropping him on his back once again. Jason fell backwards, yelling in pain, grabbing his chest, it all was happening too fast, really fast. The wind seemed to be knocked out of him as he struggled for air. He quickly opened his eyes as saw the gunman walking toward him with the gun aimed high, this time at his head, as the gunman realized that Jason was wearing a Kevlar. The gunman got the shot off, but the bullet hit the ceiling as Jessica had flanked around the side of the gunman, and kicked the intruder's hand, forcing the arm and the impending shot upwards.

As the gun flew out of his hand, he quickly retrieved a large knife from his back from under his jacket, and immediately lunged for Jessica. She was too fast for him. She quickly stunned him with a tightly clinched fist *to the throat that stopped him in his tracks. He grabbed his throat as he began to choke, struggling to breathe.*

Jessica immediately followed the chop with a vicious drop kick to the face that sent the gunman airborne and caused him to fall back on top of Jason who still clutched his chest in pain. Jason, not wasting any time; immediately placed a vicious choke hold on the assailant and began squeezing tighter and tighter. The gunman struggled mightily, but the hold was too much for him as he dropped the knife to free his hands. He aggressively attempted to free himself from the chokehold, but the more the intruder struggled and fought, the tighter Jason squeezed. Jason squeezed tighter and tighter until he felt the life of the gunman slipping further away from his body.

Jason's Story- Chapter Six – The End.

I was literally hanging off the edge of my seat when I looked up from the Nook, shocked from what I just read. That was the end of chapter six.

I couldn't believe the way it had ended, but if there was any reason to no longer doubt the power and ability I had to alter or change this story, the way the last chapter ended was that reason.

"Wow, that good huh?" said Bradley. I quickly sat back in the seat and tried to somewhat compose myself. I glanced over at Bradley and hadn't realized that he was staring at me.

"Why do say that?" I asked as if I didn't already know.

"Well you were hanging off the edge of your seat with your mouth open while you were reading," Bradley said while smiling. "Hey, it's quite alright. I've read a story or two like that in my lifetime."

I smiled, looked at Bradley and began shaking my head.

"No. Not like this one, you haven't."

<u>Chapter Eleven</u>

The Strange Man

I had a difficult time trying to figure out just where I was, mentally, at the moment. Physically, I was flying high above the Pacific Ocean, headed to my home in Florida but, mentally and emotionally, I had no idea where I was, and I wasn't even sure how to begin to figure it out. Exhausted. I closed my eyes and rested my forehead in the palm of my hands.

I couldn't determine if I was mentally or physically tired, or if I was dealing with a combination of both.

I knew part of my emotions lie firmly planted in the middle of someone else's story, in the middle of Jason's world, in the middle of his life. As much as I tried to no longer be a part of it, I found myself crawling deeper into it. I gripped the Nook as I gazed at the blank black screen with my reflection staring back at me. I had no idea who I was looking at.

This feeling, I couldn't understand it, and I wasn't sure if I even wanted to. The emotion and the vivid imagery of *Jason's Story* had overwhelmed me.

The sheer focus of this story on love and family, wrapped itself around me like a warm blanket and kept me warm during a time in which I was dealing with the universe's cold bitter ways. I had a place in my soul that wanted to have the type of family restoration Jason was experiencing right now, even though he suffered a lot, more than anyone could even dare to imagine.

I peered aimlessly out of the window, and though I was thousands of feet in the air over the Pacific Ocean, I felt lost, but it was gradually starting to feel like I was exactly where I needed to be.

Looking down at the Nook, I realized that based on how the last chapter ended, I had no idea how to begin the next chapter, chapter seven. What was I to say? I smiled as I thought about how this wasn't getting any easier, the further into the story it went.

Just when I thought the last "trial" involving Jason and his "story" was the hardest thing I had ever focused on in my forty plus years of life, I run into something else seemingly much more complex and difficult.
I couldn't begin to even fathom how Jason and Jessica's life was going to change after how the last chapter ended.

I knew deep down inside that I did the best I could to save them, or to prevent harm from coming to them, or their family. But the more I read this story, the more the story pulled me into its world.

The more I experienced this story, the more I felt as though I was consistently stepping over the line of no return. It felt as if I had fallen so deep into the story, I wouldn't be able to find my way back at this point even if I stopped and never read another word. I stared at the Nook, contemplating.

What was next for Jason and Jessica? I knew there wasn't a chapter seven waiting. Chapter seven was in my head, in my subconscious—I just had to dig it out.

"You're going to burn a hole right through that thing," said Bradley as I immediately turned towards him. He was staring at me with a smile, his glasses in his hand. "You alright?" he asked behind a concernedly fixated gaze.

"Yeah, I'm fine." I smirked.

I can only imagine how weird I must've appeared, simply staring into the blank screen.

Bradley probably already knew I was bothered by everything I was dealing with personally, so he probably didn't put too much into anything I believed to be "weird" or "abnormal." I knew he knew something wasn't right, but I appreciated him talking to me anyway. Hell, he could've asked to be re-seated, but he didn't. He's here, still talking with me, and I appreciated that. I needed that more than I realized at this point.

"Man, I'm just so caught up in this book," I said as I nodded hesitantly towards the Nook.
"I see."

Bradley replied behind a chuckle. I slowly glanced over at Bradley and realized for the first time, he didn't really look much like a Doctor, retired or not. I found myself suddenly intrigued by him. I hadn't realized it until just now. The way he spoke, the way he acted, even with how wise he appeared to be, it all suddenly intrigued me. "Bradley, why did you stop practicing medicine?" I asked curiously. "Were you bored or was it just that time? Time for a change?"

Bradley quickly froze. He looked at me liked I just asked him a million-dollar question on a game show. He abruptly closed his laptop, placed his glasses on top of the laptop, and turned towards me.

"You mean why am I'm no longer a doctor?"

"Yes." I quickly chuckled as I nodded.
His question and verbiage was quite confusing, but not surprising, considering Bradley seemed a bit obsessive

compulsive and extraordinarily detailed when it came to certain things.

"Well, none of those, really," he replied as he looked me in my eye. "My profession as a doctor, ultimately met its end, because of unfortunate circumstances and situations I no longer had the ability or strength to fight. It's truly a young person's profession, to be honest."

The words he spoke surprised me. I was relatively certain that I had a confused or bewildered look on my face at this point as he began to chuckle at my reaction. I guess I wasn't expecting him to answer that question in the slightly confusing manner in which he did.

"You seemed surprised." he responded. "To be honest, it was all a bit surprising to say the least. Those around me were surprised because of how suddenly it all happened. It was a situation in which I felt as though I no longer had a choice. It was something that I'd gone through and came out on the wrong end of. I truly believe the universe simply had different plans for me. Hard to accept life's struggles at times. We go through them, accept them, and deal with them. That's what I did."

I was confused. For a moment, I had to remember just what it was that I asked him. His answer didn't really line up what I was expecting but knew there was more, and I was simply missing it.

"What do you mean?" I replied confusedly, "What happened? If you don't mind me asking?"

Bradley stared past me in a deep, emotionless gaze. He was daydreaming and appeared to be immediately reflecting back on everything we were now discussing.

"Oh of course I don't mind." he finally replied after a seemingly lengthy pause. "I misdiagnosed a patient of mine."

Bradley gazed past me out of the window. He appeared to be lost in deep reflection. He lowered his head as he continued.

"The patient, a father, husband, and friend of mine, fell dangerously ill."

"So, he was your friend?" I asked.

"Yes. Companion, friend, colleague. Not only was he my friend," Bradley softly uttered as he peered intensely into my eyes. "But he was like those that are closest to you—he was my family, as you would say. I lost my family, so his family took me in like their own for that last year of my studies. He and I became brothers."

Wasn't that difficult to see that this was something that still haunted him. It was as if the warm person I'd grown to "know" over the past few hours or so, had turned into a shell of himself. It wasn't that hard to see the emotion as he spoke about it.

"We got older," Bradley continued. "And eventually went our separate ways in life, seeking out our own path, but we kept in touch. His family always considered me one of their own. With he and his family, is where I spent the most of my time."

Bradley kept his eyes closed as he spoke. It seemed as though the jubilation that I believed I saw when I first asked him this question was in fact real, but not for the reason I thought. He was happy to talk about it, but not because it was something that brought him joy or something that he loved to discuss, but because he seem to need to talk about it. It was obvious that it was healing him in a way that I couldn't understand.

"About ten years ago," Bradley continued. "He came to me not feeling well and I examined him. My advisors all agreed with my diagnosis. We immediately started him on treatment, but it wasn't working. The treatments had no effect on his illness whatsoever, so we started him on a higher volume of the treatment.

"What was wrong with him?" I immediately asked.

"I have no idea," Bradley replied. "To this very day, I have no idea what was wrong with him, but I believe it was a form of what you call "*Cancer*."

Bradley paused once more, taking a moment to gaze out of the window before continuing.

"After a few weeks, his health rapidly deteriorated. Those that were closest to him......"

"His family?" I asked, inquisitively.

Bradley nodded, hesitantly.

"Yes, his family." Bradley replied, slightly uncertain. "At that point, they thought it necessary to get a second opinion, at which time it was discovered that my friend.... "

He paused as he continued to gaze past me with a blank gaze into the cloud filled night sky, as if I wasn't even there. More importantly, he seemed to be taking time to gather himself as he clearly fought through his tattered emotions at this point. The emotions seem to gradually overwhelm him, but I didn't know if I admired him or pitied him for being as strong as he was and not succumbing to his emotions, considering how tragic and unfortunate the story appeared to be so far.

"It was discovered that my friend had some sort of rare, very rare infection, as you would call it. I didn't catch it in time. The treatment I provided for him had an adverse effect on him and his condition and it was too much to overcome in such a short period."

I had a hard time reading Bradley's face right now, and I didn't know which one of us I should feel sorry for the most; me for having lost my baby girl, or Bradley for having believed that he "killed" his good friend, his brother?

I actually found it somewhat difficult to contain my emotions while listening to him. It was very difficult to swallow. He stopped talking, but his head continued to slowly shake yet, he didn't utter a word—he just gazed right past me and barely blinked.

"The pain I felt," he continued, "After I essentially took the life of my closest friend, was something the strongest numbing agents couldn't numb. I was in a really bad place. His loved ones threatened to take everything from me but gave me the option to simply retire and never practice my craft again and leave with my "good name" intact. They promised if I retired, they wouldn't come after me. So, I did the only thing to do. I did what I had to in order to protect me, those closest to me, my name, but more importantly, those that I cared for. I had to protect them. So, I retired from the practice that I loved. The profession that I loved so dearly; I gave it up. I didn't have a choice. Before I allowed the unfortunate circumstances to continue to bury me, I knew I had to do something. My profession, my way of life, everything I built, was attacked, but not by those closest to my friend, but by circumstance, and I needed to not only attack it back, but I needed to get out in front of it before it destroyed me and everything I loved. It had attacked me and those that I loved, so I needed to find a way to counter it, to get out in front of it and that's essentially what I did."

The look on Bradley's face was an empty, cold expression that held no emotion.

"Man, I'm sorry that happened to you, I truly am." I whispered softly, as Bradley nodded his head. I knew he appreciated my sympathies especially considering what I was going through. I could tell it was still hurting him though. I could tell that it was something that he tried to bury, to no avail. The raw and real emotion that I saw on this face, magnified the story and his feelings ten times over. It showed me that everyone has a story, and you really don't know someone's story until you *know* someone's story.

Something Bradley said while sharing his story with me stuck with me in a way that wouldn't allow it to leave my subconscious.

I glanced down at the Nook as Bradley's words replayed over and over in my mind; "*My profession, my way of life, everything I built was attacked, but not by his family but by life, and I needed to not only attack it back, but I needed to get in front of it before it destroyed me and everything I loved...*"

It grabbed me and held on to me as I fought within myself, within my mind, to understand just why his words stayed with me.

I glanced back at Bradley who had laid his head back on the seat and was reflecting as he stared at the airplane ceiling. I knew he was deep in thought regarding what he just shared with me as was I, but for different reasons.

I now knew why his words were so important to me and I couldn't let them go. I was now correlating everything I was dealing with in my life to Jason and what he was going through. I didn't know if that was a good or bad thing at this point.

I found myself so intensely dialed into *Jason's Story,* no matter how much I tried to convince myself that I didn't want or need to be. I knew deep down, I not only wanted to, but I knew not finishing what I started regarding this story, just wasn't an option for me.

"Hey, are *you* alright?" Bradley asked.

I quickly glanced over towards him and caught him staring at me with a concerned expression on his face.

"Yeah man, I'm ok." I replied, as I tried to relax my tense posture.

Bradley had this caring, nurturing spirit about him, it wasn't that difficult to notice. It reminded me of my father-in-law and how he was with my girls. Everyone always wanted to be around him because he made you feel like he cared no matter what he was dealing with personally. No matter how hard life had hit him, he'd come around and made you feel like your issues were not only more important, but made you feel as though everything was going to be alright.

That's the vibe I got from Bradley.

"You still reading that story?" Bradley asked with a semi-perplexed look on his face.

"I am," I chuckled, "It's getting better and better as I go. I feel like I was supposed to read this story."

Bradley had a weird way in which he spoke. It was all so strange. It was something that I noticed but hadn't really paid that much attention to. But it was becoming more noticeable at this point. It was almost as if he'd just recently learned the English language within the past few years or so, but I didn't notice an accent. I wanted to ask him about it but didn't want to offend him.

Bradley suddenly chuckled and shook his head as he placed his earphones back on his ear.

"I'm due for another nap," he said smiling through a yawn, "wake me up if anything happens, or if you want to talk, or when it's time to eat."

I snickered and nodded my head in acknowledgement as Bradley turned his music on, closed his eyes, and leaned his head back on his seat and began resting.

I hesitantly gazed down at the Nook. I couldn't and didn't take my eyes off of it.

I was contemplating on what I needed to speak in order to get chapter seven to appear, but of course, I had no idea. I had no idea what move to make or card to play at this point on Jason's behalf, but what I thought I didn't know, I realized that I probably *did* know as Bradley's words started to echo in my mind once more.

I suddenly began to understand that Jason, his family, his way of life, and everything close to him was just attacked. And like Bradley did with his situation, Jason needed to get in "front" of it before it destroyed him and everything he loved.

"That's it!" I whispered to myself with slight excitement, "Jason needs to get ahead of this—whatever *this* was."

If he didn't, I could see this quickly getting away from him, and with eight chapters remaining, anything could happen rather quickly. I glanced out of the window, took a deep breath and closed my eyes;

"Angry and confused as to why he and Jessica were attacked, Jason goes on the offensive in trying to figure out why he was attacked in order to truly protect his family."

I whispered the words as I continued to gaze out of the window. I closed my eyes and took another deep breath and slowly exhaled as if I was sending the words, my thoughts, into the atmosphere accompanied by my weary air from my lungs. I slowly powered on the Nook and turned to the last page of chapter six. And just like that, the icon to get to chapter seven suddenly appeared. I smiled as I nodded my head in acknowledgement and immediately began reading chapter seven.

Jason's Story – Chapter Seven

"Dad!" Jason could hear Tara's frantic voice from outside. "Dad!? Jessica?!!"

Police and federal vehicles outlined the front of the house as on looking neighbors stared curiously at the scene.

"They're inside, they're safe." the officer replied, as he ushered Tara into the house and into the living room where Jessica, Jason, and Dave were all huddled.

"Dad?!"

Jason saw Tara and immediately embraced her. He pulled back and noticed the distraught look on her face. He realized that she was probably confused and scared at the entire chaotic and confusing scene.

"What happened?!!" asked Tara in a frantic tone as she surveyed the scene inside the house. Jessica gently grabbed Tara's hand and began rubbing her hair.

"It's ok Tara, everything will be ok." Jessica whispered softly.

"What happened, Jessica?" Tara asked as she gazed up into Jessica's eyes. Jessica gazed right back into Tara's eyes. She knew she couldn't lie to her.

"Your father and I were attacked by someone who broke into the house—we don't know who or why."

Tara's breathing increased as she listened to Jessica's words. Jessica noticed tears starting to swell in Tara's eyes.

"Come here," said Jason, as he gently pulled Tara towards him and embraced her once more.

"Listen to me," Jason said. "We're fine. I won't allow anything to happen to you two. You are the only family I have, and I won't allow it this time." Jason began fighting back tears as he spoke. He glanced over at Dave who was examining the weapon used by the gunman.

"What are we doing?" Jason asked Dave as he held on to Tara, "What is the next move here?"

"Well first," Dave exhaled. "We need find out who this guy is. Prints are being processed now. We also have to get you and your family to safety. The bureau will handle that, we'll keep it in-house. This place is off the books, so I have no idea how they found it, but we're going to move you and your family."

Jason shook his head slowly as he took in Dave's words.

"Dave, I'm not hiding anywhere, not anymore. I need to get out on top of this. I need to get ahead of this before there are any more threats to me or my family."

Dave immediately nodded his head.

"I copy, and I'm with you on getting out ahead of this, but let's at least get Jessica and Tara in protection, please." Dave pleaded.

"Wait, what? No "Jessica relied sharply, "I'm not leaving you. I'm not hiding."

Dave immediately looked at Jason, as Jason immediately respected and understood the logic behind Dave's suggestion.

"I'll be outside," Dave uttered, as he quickly made his way out of the house. Jason knew Dave was making his exit to give him the privacy needed to speak to Jessica.

Taking a deep breath, Jason gazed over towards his family—the two most important people in his life right now. The only two people that he loved unconditionally and who he would do anything to protect. He could see the detailed concern on Jessica's face as she gazed into his eyes, patiently waiting for a response. He knew she was also looking for some sort of comfort, some sort of reassurance that everything would be ok. Considering the news she just shared with him about being pregnant, she had every right to be concerned—everything was different.

"Baby," Jason uttered softly as he softy gripped Jessica's hands, "you two are the most important people in my life, and I need to know that you guys are safe right now. At least until I can get ahead of this and find out what's going on."

Jason gently caressed Jessica's face. He knew she would resist and fight him on this, he just couldn't take that chance. He couldn't take chances with the life she now carried inside her. He would stand firm on this, and she saw that in his eyes. Jessica finally nodded, to acknowledge Jason's sentiments. It wasn't hard to get Jessica to understand that this was the best for them right now considering she was familiar with the agency and knew the procedures. She knew they would be safe with the agency's protection. She of course found herself more concerned with Jason's well-being.

"Just like you don't want to lose us Jason, we don't want to lose you," she calmly replied. "But I can't sit down and hide, you know I can't do that. I have a job to do."

Jason smiled and adored the passion he saw in her eyes. He loved her for it, but he couldn't take that chance. Not this time.

"I know baby, trust me I do." said Jason. "I love your passion and I understand what you're saying, but I need you to be safe and I won't take chances with your life, or the kids. Please, just let me find out what's going on. I need you to look after Tara while I try to figure this out. I need to know that she is safe, and I will only feel comfortable if she is with you. Can you do that for me?"

Jessica closed her eyes and sighed. She wanted to object to what Jason was suggesting, but her overall sense of logic, her sense of reasoning, wouldn't allow her. She slowly began to nod her head as she gradually opened her eyes.

"Yes," she replied hesitantly, "I can do that."

Section Chief Stanley Keegan rubbed his eyes as he began to shake his head in a slight state of confusion.

"What is this? What did I miss, Dave?"

Chief stared at Dave with a thoroughly confused look on his face. Keegan was one that didn't miss much, and when he asked a question, it was usually rhetorical. Most of the time, he already knew the answers to the questions he asked. This time however, he appeared legitimately confused. Dave stood over by the window and continued to gaze distractedly out of it, an intentionally dismissive gesture on his part. He'd heard what the Sect Chief asked him but didn't feel the need to respond.

Dave and the Sect Chief didn't have the best working relationship, or any relationship for that matter.

It had become increasingly clear over the past couple of years that Keegan wasn't too fond of the respect that Dave garnered from the higher ups within the bureau.

Keegan, was at times, kept out of loops on most of Dave's cases, sometimes important loops. At times, due to the high value targets and high-profile suspects Dave and his team went after, and to prevent leaks from jeopardizing the cases, Dave reported directly to the Director himself.

Keegan burned internally about that. It was well known within upper circles within the bureau, that the only reason Keegan got the position as Section Chief was because Dave turned down the promotion, twice, before it was eventually offered to Keegan.

This was something that Keegan was never able to shake.

"What do you mean?" Dave asked in a subtle and nonchalant tone.

Keegan gradually made his way over toward Dave who was still positioned by the window and continued to gaze out of it.

"Dave, look at me," Keegan uttered sternly, as he started to shake his head. "Your best agent was almost assassinated, and I want to know if you have the balls to look me in my face and pretend you don't know what's going on."

Dave slowly turned from facing the window to face Chief Keegan who was visibly yet subtly fuming at this point. Dave glanced over across the room at Jason who was still perplexed at the tension between the two.

"We don't know." Dave replied, as he maintained sharp eye contact with the Chief. The two men were about two feet apart as they sharply gazed into each other's eyes—neither one flinching.

"What the hell is this?" Jason quickly barked. "Someone just tried to kill me, inside our home. The hell are we doing this pissing contest right now for? What the hell am I missing here? I need for someone to tell me why in the hell my family was just targeted. If you can't find out why, or if you two want to stand here and juggle each other's balls, then I will walk and figure this out on my own. That I promise you. Both of you know me well enough to know how serious you should take my promise."

An annoyed Jason immediately headed for the door to exit Keegan's office.

"Agent Barrington wait," Chief Keegan yelled, "Look, just sit." he said, motioning towards the seat.
Jason paused as he glared at Keegan.

"Please, Agent Barrington." Keegan pleaded.
Jason gradually made his way back from the door as he looked at Dave who had a blank, emotionless stare locked in on Jason. He was very good at knowing what Dave was thinking for the most part, and he knew Dave hated to deal with Keegan. He knew Dave probably preferred to take care of this within the team, but he also knew that Dave respected order and chain of command, for the most part.

"I'm sorry this happened," Keegan said as he shook his head. "And if it seems I'm being insensitive to what has happened, please believe it's not intentional, and I apologize."

Keegan made his way back behind his desk, sat down in his chair and sighed. "But there is protocol and procedure that we have to follow. I have order to maintain and that's what I'll do."

"I understand," Jason whispered frustratingly, as he began nodding his head, "but I need to get in front of this to make sure my family stays safe. I need to find out who that was and why I was attacked. I can't risk the lives of my family again—I won't do it this time."

Chief Keegan was ready to respond to Jason, not before being interrupted by his phone ringing.

"Excuse me," Keegan whispered while reaching for his phone.

Dave glanced over at Jason and began slowly shaking his head. Jason nodded his head to acknowledge Dave's subtle gesture. Chief Keegan hung the phone after what appeared to be a brief conversation with the caller and began typing in his computer.

"That was ASAC Robertson over at the DEA. Apparently, they've apprehended a cartel member who conveniently showed up on their front porch, and he won't speak to anyone. No one but you, Agent Barrington."

The Chief glared at Jason while nodding his head and slowly glanced over at Dave.

"Dave," Chief uttered behind a facetious smile, "if there's something going on here that you're not telling me, I don't give a shit how many friends you have, I'll make sure your retirement comes a lot sooner than you'll like, you got that?"

Dave's expression didn't change as he stared at Keegan with an empty, emotionless gaze.

"What is the move here, Keegan?" he asked, completely ignoring Keegan's previous statement. "The hell am I supposed to tell my agent to do?"

"Agent Barrington," Keegan replied, "You will be escorted over to the DEA to speak with whoever this guy is and get as much info as you can from them. This can probably be what you need to in order to get in front of this like you want to. I'm immediately placing you back in the field. I want you to have all resources at your disposal to handle this. I hope you're ready. I just ask you to use sound judgment and keep me in the loop on everything." Keegan walked out from behind his desk to approach Jason.

"Rules and protocol, agent Barrington. We have them for a reason."

Jason slowly nodded his head and glanced over at Dave. He noticed Dave was once again staring out of the window, clearly bothered by something, if not everything right now.

"I'll have an agent escort you," said the Chief as he placed one hand on Jason's shoulder.

"No, I'll take him." Dave replied, who had now turned to face Chief Keegan and Jason.

"Negative." Keegan quickly responded. "I need you on a Jet to Chicago, immediately, to head up an operation linked to the Juarez-Ortega Cartel. There's a good chance the recent activity is related to what is happening here, and I need you heading up a task force. Details will be waiting for you on the Jet as always. You can take your entire team with you outside of agent Barrington here. Agent Barrington will have all the support he needs here."

"Bullshit," barked Dave, "Agent Barrington is a part of my team, my best agent and my responsibility. I'm not leaving him after he was just attacked, are you crazy?"

"You'll do exactly what you are ordered to, Special Agent in Charge Watson." Keegan quickly replied. "And just so we're clear here, I don't answer to you, you answer to me. You turned down this position. I didn't, so I tell

*you what to do, and I don't care who you're friends with."
Dave smiled facetiously as he nodded his head.*

*"You don't actually believe that do you? That I take
orders from you?" Dave snickered. "I allow you to say
words to me. If I decide it's in the best interest of me and
my team, I'll follow them. I don't answer to you and
there's nothing you can do about that. You're
incompetent, you're clueless and you have no idea what
you're doing, and what you're ordering here, isn't in the
best interest of Agent Barrington or my team, so I will
have to respectfully decline your...."*

*"Dave," Jason shouted, "for Christ sakes..... Please.
Let me do this. Just ......go. I'll take care of this. Please?"
Dave slowly smiled and carefully turned his back on Jason
and Chief Keegan and began gazing out of the window
once more as he let out a long sigh.*

*"Who is with Agent Barrington's finance; agent
Phillips and his daughter?" Dave asked sternly.*

*"They are under the bureau's protection," Keegan
replied. "In a secure location until we can figure out their
next move." Keegan glanced up from his computer and
immediately looked at Jason with a serious gaze.*

*"Agent Barrington, you sure you're up for this?"
Keegan inquired. "There's nothing wrong with sitting*

down for a while and being with your family. I know how difficult it was almost two years ago when....."

"I appreciate that sir," Jason replied—quickly interrupting Agent Keegan. "But we both know that running and hiding with my family probably won't be the best thing for me or them, if there's a legitimate threat out there. I'll go find out who this guy is, what this guy wants and how he's connected to what happened today."

Chief Keegan nodded in agreement as he returned his focus back to his computer. Dave and Jason quickly exited Keegan's office and began gradually making their way down to the truck. Jason didn't say anything to Dave just yet, but he could tell by the look on his face that Dave was bothered.

"Want to tell me what the hell that was back there?" Jason demanded as they boarded the elevator.

"Keegan has had it out for me for a while because I don't answer to him, and that chaps his ass." Dave huffed hesitantly.

"You and I both know, the more agents in on this, the worse this gets for us. We need to handle this. I don't really trust anyone else; I never have."

Jason knew how anal Dave was about not trusting agents outside of the team, so he understood why Dave was a bit annoyed and slightly paranoid with it all.

"Something just doesn't feel right about any of It." said Dave as he shook his head, unable to shake the sharp feeling of confusion that blanketed him. "It all feels different in a way. It just feels so sudden. Hard to trust anything at the moment."

Jason stared at his boss, his mentor of ten years and although he wasn't feeling what Dave was feeling, he knew Dave had a real bad habit of being right about these things. Jason agreed that whatever this was, it didn't feel similar to anything they'd been used to over the years. It was so abrupt, so sudden and out of nowhere, almost hard to believe. The two men made their way towards the parking deck to head into opposite directions as Dave grabbed Jason's arm.

"Look son," Dave whispered. "Don't trust anyone, and if it doesn't smell right....."

"Then it's probably not fresh." Jason quickly replied.

This was something Dave had said to the team countless times over the years. It was ingrained within him at this point. Hell, he even found himself saying it more than Dave. Dave took a small step back and smiled at his agent.

"So, you do listen, huh?"

"Probably more than I should sometimes." Jason chucked.

Jason saw the sincere concern on Dave's face, something he wasn't used to seeing from his mentor.

"Listen," said Jason, "You're worrying and I'm not sure why. I'm well trained. What's the point of training us the way you do, if you're going to worry when it's time for us to handle things on our own?

Dave quickly nodded his head in agreement.

"I don't know," said Dave, as he glanced up towards the sky. "Like I said, something just doesn't feel right about any of this and it's like everything is happening entirely too fast. So, I understand you feel as though I have prepared you for this. But there are things that I haven't prepared you for. Things that we are never prepared for."

"Like what?"

"Like," Dave calmly replied. "Despite everything you've been through, despite all the pain, what if the universe is once again calling on you to pay? When I lost my mother years ago, I thought it was the end, but almost two years later, I lost Ann. Losing my mother and my wife so close together like that made me realize how big of a price I paid and for what?"

"Let's just stop there." Jason sternly replied. "Fuck the universe. I've paid enough. I've sacrificed so much. I refuse to sacrifice anymore. I'm done. I don't' want to pay anymore, Dave. What more else do I have to give?'"

The emotion radiating off Jason's face was incredibly sharp. Dave was unable to escape it. Shaking his head, Dave smiled.

"Jason, there's a lot you've yet to learn in how everything around us works. There's a price to pay. Everything comes with a price, but we as inhabitants of the universe are usually afraid to pay. But being afraid to pay this price, won't stop the universe from charging us and collecting. It's not about you Jason. It's not. True salvation, salvation that causes positions to shift, change or transform within the universe, comes at a steep price. But, when you pay that price for others, it's the most rewarding, fulfilling and cosmically gratifying feeling your soul was ever initially created to experience."

Dave nodded as he put his bureau issued flight jacket on as Jason continued to stare off, thinking about everything his mentor just shared with him.

"Watch your back," Dave continued. "Keep your eyes open. None of this feels right." Dave glanced up at the sky, took a deep breath and closed his eyes. "I've seen it all, been through it all, and this is the first time in about thirty years in which everything has felt wrong. Hard to explain, so I won't."

Jason extended his hand towards Dave.

"I'll keep you updated on things here." said Jason. "When you touch down in Chicago, call me. I should have an update for you."

Dave extended his hand towards Jason and completed the handshake. Jason watched as Dave hopped into his truck, sped off, and headed out of the parking garage, until he disappeared out of sight. Jason sighed while grimacing in pain as the gunshots to his Kevlar in the middle of his chest still throbbed. For a brief moment, he'd forgotten about the throbbing pain. He opened the trunk of the SUV, retrieving a semi-automatic 9-millimeter and an extra clip. He holstered the weapon, closed his eyes, and calmly took in the moment. It had been a while since he had actually holstered his gun. He missed the feeling of having his gun on his side in its holster, and he didn't realize how much he missed it until holstering it. He opened his eyes and gazed up towards the sky. The sky was as gray and gloomy as he had seen it in a long time, as if a storm was approaching. The air was crisp and mild, but the wind blew just enough for him to notice the trees and branches swaying back and forth. He took in the moment and allowed the wind to gently smack across his face, making sure to inhale the fresh air with each passing crisp gust of wind. Jason couldn't get Dave's *words out of his mind, as he peered out towards the gray, surreal sky, Jessica and Tara's faces instantly popped into his mind as the emotions quickly began to consume him. He retrieved his cell phone from his hip and immediately dialed Jessica's number. It rang once.*

"Hello?" Jessica answered.

"Sweetie?" Jason replied.

"Jason, what's going on? Where are you?"

He could feel the genuine concern in her voice. It was so rich and full of sincere emotion that radiated through the phone and touched him. It was as if she was standing right in front of him. Jason knew that Jessica was calm and cool. No stranger to field duty over the years, she was relatively composed and relaxed, for the most part. It was pretty difficult to shake her up, but he realized how this situation differed from any other she had experienced. He understood the many variables in play here, and all that was at stake now. He heard in Jessica's voice, something he had never heard from her—fear. Her voice was low, yet the nervousness in her voice was sharp and very obvious. She wasn't trying to hide it.

"I'm up here at the office. I just met with Keegan and Dave."

"Ok, what's going on?" she replied anxiously.

"Baby, I know you're worried." Jason calmly replied. "I don't know what's happening, but I'll find out. I'm headed over to the DEA to meet with them, then I'll meet up with you guys. "

"Baby, please tell me what's going on," she replied behind a slightly frantic tone. "That doesn't sound like standard protocol."

"Jessica, sweetie, I don't know what's going on, but when I do, I will tell you—you know I will. But in the meantime, I need you to keep calm for Tara and for the baby. If she sees you panicking, she will start panicking as well. It's going to be alright. I'm not going to let anything happen to you, Tara, or the baby. None of this sounds like protocol sweetie because there is no protocol for this in Keegan's eyes. We have to figure out the threat and eliminate it, you know that."

"Well, let me help you." she pleaded, "I can help you more, being out there with you and you know it."

"I can't." Jason quickly replied, "Keegan has already shut you down until we figure out what's happening. Plus, I need you out there looking after Tara. Not to mention, after what happened two years ago......."

"Stop. Don't say it," Jessica replied somberly. "I understand. Just.... get here as soon as you can. They're taking us somewhere outside of town, but I'm not sure where, yet."

"I'll get there as soon as I can," said Jason. "I promise. I love you."

Jason ended the call and gradually rubbed his hand over the front of his vest again, grimacing in pain. The vest was still intact, but he wasn't surprised, this vest had saved his life before, a few years ago. It was tough and apparently lucky. He began to take it off, but after a second thought, he left it on. It had not only saved his life today, but possibly Jessica's and the baby's as well. No harm in keeping it on until he left the meeting with the DEA.

Jason hopped into the SUV and began making his way downtown towards the DEA building.

It usually took about twenty minutes to drive from the federal building to the DEA building downtown, but that was with traffic, but today there was no traffic, and the streets were clear. As he pulled up to the front of the building, he was instantly greeted out front by two DEA agents.

One of the agents approached the vehicle as Jason exited it.

"Agent Barrington?"

Jason quickly nodded his head in response to the agent's inquiry.

"Follow us, please."

Jason immediately followed behind the DEA agents. They hopped on the elevator, and gradually made their way up to the tenth floor.

"This way." said the second agent as he motioned towards what looked to be an interrogation room.

They slowly ushered Jason into the room that looked in on the interrogation room by way of a two-way mirror, as he was greeted by other agents. Jason looked through the tinted glass inside the room and saw a man, in handcuffs sitting at a table. He didn't recognize him at all. There were no distinguishing marks or tattoos, nothing.

"Has he said anything?" Jason asked.

"Nothing." replied one of the agents.

"What do you have on him?" Jason replied, as he peered through the window at the man hand cuffed to the table.

The agent shook his head before Jason could even finish asking the question.

"That's just it, there's nothing on him, literally. He doesn't even register with the census bureau. The IRS has nothing on him, he's never owned an address in this country, a bank account, no ID, nothing on file with the DMV."

"So who the hell is he?" Jason asked calmly.

The agent shook his head once more even before Jason could finish asking the question.

"He's not pulling up in any international database," the agent replied. "He looks to be American." Jason had already pegged the guy as an American. It was clear that he was an American, but something was a bit off with him.

Jason gazed straight into the man's eyes as he entered the room. They were empty, his face emotionless, as he stared directly ahead towards the mirror. No facial movements, no expressions—nothing. Jason gradually walked into the room, shutting the door behind him. There was another DEA officer standing on guard in the corner as Jason acknowledged him before sitting down across from the man.

"Hello sir—how can I help you?" Jason had his arms folded as he gingerly leaned against the wall.

The man finally snapped out of his blank stare and focused his attention and his sights directly on Jason and smiled. He was clean cut and shaven, about 6'2, maybe one hundred and eighty pounds. He appeared to be wearing only jeans and a shirt with the sleeves rolled up. Jason noticed his hands as they lay cuffed on top of the table. They appeared to be very clean, no wrinkles, almost as if they were baby hands.

"Agent Barrington," the man's voice was sharp and deep. He sounded like he could've been from the eastern part of the country. New York or New Jersey was a possibility.

"I was sent here to share something of critical importance with you. After I'm done sharing this information with you, you will release me."
Flashing a cynical smirk, Jason began facetiously nodding his head.

"Well, ok, we'll see about that, but first thing's first, why don't you start by telling me who sent you here to share this "information" with me."
The man's smile grew wider after hearing Jason's question, but he didn't answer as he simply peered deep into Jason's face.

"Who sent you?" Jason barked, this time sterner and clearer.

Slowly the man began shaking his head as if he was saying "no," but didn't utter a word. Frustrated that his time was probably being wasted, Jason figured he'd use a bit of reverse psychology on the man.

"Sir, I don't think I can help you." Jason uttered as he slowly stood up to make his way towards the door.

"Agent Barrington," the man finally responded. "The life we live is nothing but infinite time and space. As much as we try to understand it, our minds will never be able to fully grasp the limitless possibilities that exist out here in the universe or outside of the universe. Since your day of birth, you are fed and forced to accept a certain view of the world around you. Naturally and instinctively, we accept, receive, and become accustomed to it–never questioning it, never asking the logical, important and pertinent questions."

"Oh yeah?" replied Jason facetiously behind a smirk, "What questions might those be, sir?"

The man smiled at Jason and nodded his head but didn't seem interested in answering Jason's question as he simply continued talking.

"We are so bound by our daily, earthly lives, that we never take time to step back and try to truly take in the universe. The universe is a living organism, a living body, an endless, infinite body of immense possibilities created by God. God created it and designed it to communicate with us. This communication requires us as a race, as a species, to think outside of this earthly box we consistently find ourselves unconsciously and mentally anchored in."

The strange man took just a brief moment to smile as he appeared to be collecting his thoughts before finally *continuing.*

"Case in point agent Barrington; if I was to tell you that right now, at this very moment, there are two different people in two different parts of the multiverse, directly affecting you and your family's existence, and there's not much you can do about it, would you even stop to grasp the remote possibility of such a suggestion? Or would your mind simply dismiss it and not even spend one second on the thought, considering how "crazy" it sounds to your earthly mind?"

Jason immediately chuckled as he shook his head in disbelief. He had already made his way to the seat directly across from the man while he was busy talking, but that didn't make him feel any more comfortable. He had no idea what the man was talking about or if the question he ended with was in fact really a question or a rhetorical one.

"Umm," Jason murmured, behind a forced smile. "I'm really not actually sure what you want me to say here."

"You don't have to say or do anything other than answer the question that I asked, agent Barrington."

"I'm sorry, what was the question again?" Jason snickered.

He was already becoming restless and was quickly losing patience with the strange man. He wanted to know what this man knew about anything worth knowing about, especially about the intruder that attacked he and Jessica about an hour ago.

"My question was," the strange man continued. "If I was to tell you that right now at this very moment, there are two different people in two different points of the multiverse, directly affecting you and your family's existence, and there's not much you can do about it, would you even stop to grasp and consider the remote possibility of such a suggestion? Or would your mind dismiss it and not even spend one second on the thought considering how "crazy" it sounds to your earthly mind?"

"I don't know." Jason quickly responded. "I um, I guess I would have to wonder why you think I would simply accept something so insane from you, a stranger that I've never met?

The man smiled as he began nodding his head—his way of acknowledging Jason's words.

"Is this what you wanted to share with me?" Jason chuckled facetiously, slowly standing to his feet. "I mean, because if this is what you needed to share with me, I should probably not waste anymore of your or my time."

"Agent Barrington, I will only share this with you once." said the man as the smile quickly disappeared and a serious yet empty look appeared on his face.

"As you and I sit here, right here—right now, speaking with one another, there is an inhabitant of your multiverse, this inhabitant may or may not exist inside or outside of your own Universe; I'm not certain either way. This inhabitant or "author," is currently writing or has already written a story—a story full of characters and a real storyline. This "story" that this "author" is writing or has already written, Jason, it is your story. There is also another "inhabitant," that may exist inside or outside of your universe, and that is unbeknownst to this "writer," that is currently reading and altering this same story, your story, your life, as it's been written, in an attempt to counteract, if you will, the seemingly inevitable fate the "author" has written out for you."

Jason, trying his best not to erupt in laughter, stared at the stranger, curiously raising one eyebrow as the man continued to speak. He could tell the man was serious, but also realized the man was likely battling some sort of condition or disorder and would probably need some sort of medical or psychiatric attention.

"Trust me, I understand your skepticism here, agent Barrington. It is logical to question what you don't understand, and I don't blame you."

Jason glanced up at the guard in the room as he noticed the guard trying not to laugh as well.

"So, it's not just me?" Jason jokingly asked the guard who simply shook his head.

"My purpose, agent Barrington; isn't really to convince you that what I'm saying is true, as much as it is to simply share this information with you and allow you to do with it whatever you decide. The story, your story, will continue whether you believe what I'm saying or not. How long it continues, and what actually happens, will be totally up to you."

There was no response, as Jason simply stared at the man without so much as blinking his eye. He wasn't sure if he should get upset or simply see how far the man was willing to take this.

He knew the agents behind the glass were probably getting a kick out of this.

"Agent Barrington, the universe is such a magnificent and immense wonder on a grand scale of immense and infinite possibilities. The universe that we live in, is simply a tiny part of a multiverse, and we are all connected to one another in ways you can never imagine, believe, or

comprehend on any conceivable levels of your mind.
Some life out there in the multi universe, is writing or has
written your story, while there's another life in another part
of the multiverse, reading it as it's being written, but
seemingly wielding the ability to alter and change what's
being written. "This writer or author of your story, Jason,
has decided to kill you off in his story. It's nothing
personal, as you're simply a character in his story and for
some reason or another, killing you is an important part of
their story's completion. Your family, Jason, will be used
by this writer to accomplish this, if necessary. There is no
logic as to why this writer is trying to accomplish this in the
way that they have decided to do it, and frankly, it won't
or never will make any sense to your earthly mind."
Jason shook his head again in disbelief as he smiled at the
strange man. He didn't know how to even begin to want
to understand what the strange man was conveying to him.

"What do you know about what happened at my
house today?" Jason asked. "Can you answer that for me?"

"I don't know anything about that." The strange man
replied. "But whatever you see here, it's not really what it
seems. What looks to you like someone trying to harm
you and your family, is simply the story falling in line to
what its author has written. It only seems as if your
worldly dangers are trying to take you out of here agent

Barrington, but it's bigger than you and your family at this point."

"Ok," Jason quickly replied, as he slowly began to pace back and forth and continued to shake his head in disbelief.

"I'll play this game with you to help speed things up a bit here. Humor me for a moment. Let me ask you a question, If what you say is true—if what you say has any merit to it whatsoever, and I'm some "character" in someone's book, and this, "someone," this "author" is writing my story, my life, wouldn't that mean that the writer is not only writing what you and I are currently saying right now in this room? Wouldn't they now be aware of the fact that you've made me aware of all of this? Wouldn't that throw something into the mix of your whole 'cosmic, the universe is all, and all is the universe, we are all one with everything,' bull shit you're feeding me right now? I mean you can't seriously march in here on your loony tune stallion and sell me something like this without providing some real answers, or proof."

Nodding his head to acknowledge Jason's question, the strange man once again flashed a genuine smile.

"Well, now you're asking the appropriate questions, agent Barrington. Let's just say, the specifics of this particular conversation we are currently having is unintentionally unknown to the author of your "story" as they have simply written this part of your story, this part of your life in third person format, and has chosen to simply designate this particular part of the story, this conversation, as a simple general interrogation on your part."

"So, wait," Jason chuckled, "You're telling me that the author of this story, my story, has no idea what is being said right now between us?" Jason chuckled slightly as he let out a sigh. "Come on my friend, if I wasn't confused before, I'm sure as hell confused now."

"You're not confused, agent Barrington," the man replied. "You're simply refusing to accept what you already know to be true. I assure you, before this is over, before you fully realize the magnitude of what is actually happening here, in your life, you will open your mind the way the universe meant for us to do so when we were created."

"Oh? Will I?"

"Yes, you will. The author has chosen not to write any specifics regarding this conversation in lieu of writing it out as a simple general interrogation. This author, for their own reasons, decided to simply write that you entered this room with me, we spoke for a brief period, and that you'll leave the room with a bewildered look on your face, confused and shocked because of what apparently *happened during your interrogation while you were in here with me. The writer is simply deciding to leave it up to the imagination of the reader, but in this case, the one reader that's reading it, unbeknownst to the writer of course, is already aware of everything. Which is why as long as you are in this room, you and I can speak freely, and the "author" will not be aware of what is said. Whatever is said in this room, Jason, the writer is completely unaware because of how they have written this part but you, I, and the reader whoever they may be, are very much aware. The author, like they've always done throughout the universe's history, has inadvertently given the Universe this moment and time it needs to make the inhabitant whose story is being written, acutely aware of the fact that their life is in fact a story being written. This moment, in this room, Jason, is that time for you. It is that moment for you. So, here I am. So, Jason, now is the time to ask me any questions you may have. As soon as you step foot outside of this moment, outside of this room, I can no longer help you or answer any questions. No one can. The only person who can "help" you, is this reader, and that person, that inhabitant of your multi-verse that is reading and altering your life, your story, may or may not be up to the task to see this through to the end. As in some cases, they may not even be all that aware of their ability to help you. The reader won't be able to communicate with you at all. It has been known to be possible, but it requires both the reader and the "character's" minds to be on the same level subconsciously and cosmically—simultaneously. I can almost tell from our conversation thus far, that you are fighting against opening your mind, so communication with your reader will likely never happen."*

It was too much. Jason tried his best not to break out in gut wrenching laughter, but it was getting more difficult with every word the stranger shared. Jason couldn't help but to notice the serious look cemented on the man's face as he shared this information with him. It was what made it all much more comical than it probably was. Jason began pacing around the interrogation room hoping to make the guy nervous or even uncomfortable.

"So, let me get this straight sir," Jason finally replied.

"You say this writer is writing my story, writing my life, correct?"

"That is correct."

"So, tell me—what's to stop this "writer" from essentially going back, reading what's been written and what's been altered by this reader, who you claim is reading and altering the story? I mean, this reader is essentially reading and altering the story that the writer,

who you say is in another part of the universe or multiverse, is writing. This writer, what's preventing him from realizing that their story has been altered? You mean he won't notice what's happening to his story? I find that hard to believe."

The man began slowly and calmly shaking his head as he began to chuckle.

"Again, my friend," said the strange man. "You're looking at this without fully opening your mind, which is why you're standing here mocking every word I've shared with you since you've walked through those doors and that's ok. I'm not your friend or enemy, agent Barrington. I don't love, hate, like, or dislike you. I don't know you and don't care for you. I don't wish you well or harm. You are simply someone that needs the information that I have— information I'm not exactly sure how I came across. Let's already assume, agent Barrington, that in this writer's "world" or the part of the universe that they're in, their book, your story, your life, has already been written, it's finished—it's completed. This is not only very possible, but more times than not, very likely. Time, agent Barrington, doesn't work or operate on the same level of existence in every part of the multiverses. This story could very well have already been written and completed and the author isn't aware of the fact that it's being altered in

any way. Let's just also assume for one moment, that the person reading and altering your story, the person who we can both assume, is the one hopefully trying to save your life —this person who is reading or experiencing this story, your story, is either knowingly or most likely unknowingly, mentally in tune or "communicating" with the Universe thus, allowing him the "ability" to not only read this completed story, but alter it as well. It's the only way, in the history of the known universe, in which it has ever been possible for a reader to alter a story."

Jason stared at the strange man and shook his head. There was no part of him that believed this guy, but that didn't stop his mind from thinking logically and objectively around every word this guy was sharing. It was all coming at him entirely too fast. Jason occasionally glanced over at the mirror as he knew the other agents behind it were probably unwell with laughter. The strange man continued.

"Your life, agent Barrington, your story, there is a possibility that it is complete in some part of the multiverse. It is completed because the writer has finished it, but the universe is now trying to make you aware of it. The universe has its own reasons for doing this, reasons we'll never know in this lifetime. I don't know any specifics, I just know one way or another, you will die, and

your family will too, if the person reading and altering your story doesn't make the necessary alterations or changes needed to completely change the ending of your story. Open your mind, Jason. Your life and your family's lives will depend on you consistently doing so from this moment on, I assure you it will."

Jason truly had no idea how to respond to what the strange man just shared with him. He had no idea what to say or how to even say whatever it was that probably needed to be said at this point.

He was speechless. Not because he was in deep thought on what this stranger was sharing with him, as he found it increasingly difficult to believe anything the man was saying, but because he was cognizant of the fact that this stranger, whoever he was, had a certain genuine passion about which he spoke and seemed to honestly believe every word that he uttered.

"You'll have to forgive me," Jason finally replied. "If I can't take what you're saying at face value, my friend. My job is literally to question everything and believe nothing, except the facts."

"Of course," the strange man replied, as he smiled. "But your job also requires you to utilize instincts and gut feelings as well, does it not?"

"Who are you?" Jason asked, completely dismissing the

man's question, "You have no identification, no record, virtually no identity. So, who are you? What is your name?"

"You won't believe this," replied the man, "but I truly don't know. I have no idea who I am, what my name is, or how I got here, but clearly this moment with you is why I'm here. If I had to guess, I would say that the universe brought me here to share this information with you to maintain order and balance in the universe. Somebody, something, some force out there wanted you to have this information and I'm simply here to provide it. The first and only thing I truly remember is showing up at the front of the DEA building with this information on my mind, I can't seem to recall anything before then."

"Look at me," said Jason behind a stern tone. "Enough already. Why don't you tell me why you're really here? Who sent you? Someone real and not some imaginary "author" in the universe. Who sent you and why are you here? What the hell do you know about what happened at my house today?"

The strange man nodded his head as Jason spoke as if he was answering a question.

"It's ok Jason, if you have your doubts and are skeptical. Looking at it objectively and logically, I can't say that I wouldn't have the same doubts and skepticism.

Your mind is open agent Barrington but, whatever you experienced today, it has caused you to partially close a door within your mind. A door that has been open for nearly two years. You asked me a few minutes ago; 'why should you simply just accept something like this from me, a stranger that you've just met?' Well, it's essentially like school. When first attending, you're meeting your teachers or professors for the first time, but they educate you anyway and you accept it. You allow them to teach you and provide you with information that you need, earthly rules actually mandate this as the best way to educate you. There's nothing wrong with that, just like there's nothing wrong with your accepting what is being presented to you here at this moment from someone you don't know."

Under normal circumstances, Jason would've been patient. He had interrogated dozens of suspects over the years, but this, he felt as though he had no time for.

"I just want you to know that normally, under different circumstances, I wouldn't mind being in here with you," said Jason, "but it just so happens that today isn't a good day, and I haven't any more time to waste here. So how about this—let's say I believe you," Jason smiled. "And for the record, I don't, but let's say that I do. Why? What is the overall purpose of all of this? Am I supposed to simply lie down and die? Am I supposed to

allow this "author" to simply kill me and my family off?
Tell me, what's to stop me from taking this gun, killing
myself, and completely ending..... "
Jason's voice faded off as he began thinking heavily,
slipping into a mini daydream as he began to quickly
reflect on the not-too-distant past. The stranger
immediately recognized the look on Jason's face and
began smiling.

"Let me guess;" the stranger replied softly, "you've
already tried to kill yourself, huh? Let me take another
guess—you suddenly and abruptly found yourself unable to
go through with it and unable to explain why, right?"

The man smiled as Jason's expression became more
distant. Jason sat staring off into the near distance as he
was slightly stuck in his mini reflection, thinking about the
day he tried to commit suicide in the garage, but suddenly
and abruptly decided against it—a sudden and
unexplainable change of mind. He didn't want to admit to
the stranger that he was possibly correct in any way, but
he still to this day couldn't actually confirm what
happened that day he tried to kill himself.

He couldn't, with any certainty, say something or
someone prevented him from sitting in that car and killing
himself that day, but something happened. He hadn't
really thought much about it as he figured it was best to

leave it in the past, but the stranger mentioning it, forced him to at least think about it for the first time since it happened.

Gazing at the stranger, he noticed the serious yet subtle look on his face as he awaited a response from Jason, but Jason knew better than to engage this guy or to give him what he wanted. He still didn't know who he was and whoever this guy was, he wasn't going to allow him to completely mind screw him.

"That incident happened nearly two years ago, my friend," Jason said as he shook his head "If what you say is true, shouldn't this "author" have tried to take me out of here a lot sooner than today?"

The man began shaking his head before Jason could even finish speaking.

"Your story," the strange man replied. "Has likely been completed my friend. I truly believe that is the case here and there is no time frame on any of this. None of this works by your earthly definition of time. All of this is non-linear. What was almost two years ago for you, can easily be two hours ago for some other inhabitant across your multiverse. What was almost two years ago for you, could easily be two chapters ago for the author."

Jason sat back in his seat as he began to contemplate somewhat deeply on the words this man was sharing with *him. Jason glanced up at the security guard and noticed that even his expression on his face had changed as he too was probably seeing the logic within the man's words.*

"Why are you here?" asked Jason. "What country are you from? Tell me why there isn't a file on you in any database out there? Whenever I come across someone such as yourself that appears to be hiding or running, I must ask the question; why are you trying to hide and what are you running from?"

"As I told you before," the strange man uttered confidently. "I can't answer those questions with sincere certainty, but I believe my purpose for being here is clear and simple, and I've shared that with you. It's up to you do what you will with the info that I provided."

Jason snickered at how calm and somewhat confident this stranger appeared to be. He had seen it a thousand times with countless suspects. They confidently spew off ridiculous nonsense with their poker faces, only to be eventually escorted off to jail kicking and screaming. This guy would be no different, but Jason knew there was a solid chance he would probably be escorted off to a hospital.

"Tell me something," said Jason as he smiled back at the stranger. "If what you're saying has merit, and you want me to believe you, answer me this—how is this

possible? How is any of this possible? Why is any of this happening? What is the purpose? Just tell me why, because it's not making any sense, you're not making any sense, and I truly want to understand you and why you're really here."

Shaking his head, the stranger continued to smile as he slowly began to stand up, prompting the agent on guard to instinctively reach for his weapon and Jason to reach for his.

"It's ok," Jason quickly said to the guard as he motioned towards him to relax. The guard gradually removed his hand from his weapon and nodded his head to acknowledge Jason's "instructions".

"It's ok. Isn't it my friend?" Jason utterly nervously to the strange man.

The strange man nodded his head as he turned and smiled at the agent then back at Jason. Jason however, kept his hand on his semi-automatic weapon.

The strange man wasn't making any threatening moves or gestures, he simply gradually and calmly stood to his feet and closed his eyes while taking a deep breath.

"You want to know how any of this is possible?" he asked with his eyes still closed. "How is any and everything your mind can imagine not possible, Jason? I

can't tell you why or how all of this is possible because I don't know why and unfortunately that's most likely a question we'll never get answered in our lifetime. But I believe because of the infinite and unknown possibilities that exist out in the immense universe, that anything that we can think of is not only possible but is probably already happening in some part of our multiverse. That's how immense it is.

"As I told you before, agent Barrington, though I'm able to share quite a bit of information with you, I'm unaware as to where this information derived from. The information that I am providing you is coming from somewhere. I cannot with all honesty tell you from where because I do not know. Everything that is happening here is by cosmic design, nothing now or has it ever been what it seems. The only thing I do know is that whoever or whatever I am or came from, I know that this isn't my first time here doing whatever it is I'm here to do."

"What the hell does that even mean?" Jason barked as he shook his head—confused. He gazed at the strange man as a sense of intrigue and doubt waged a fierce battle within his mind.

"Agent Barrington," the strange man continued. "I've already insisted that you open your mind, I suggest you get on that rather quickly. You're asking the wrong

questions. I won't be around to answer them when you start asking the right ones, the important ones. You, agent Barrington, essentially have two inhabitants in the multiverse fighting over the lives of you and your family. Only one of them "knows", albeit not much, as I'm certain they are probably more confused than you are at this point. Nevertheless, this inhabitant knows about it now and that person is the one that is currently reading it and trying to keep you and your family alive. It's up to you to convince this person that he or she is fighting for a good reason and not in vain."

"Why are you calling them "inhabitants"?" Jason asked curiously, "What in any kind of hell do you mean by that?"

"Every inhabitant of the multiverse, agent Barrington, aren't exactly human." The strange man chucked. "There is a story that your "author" has written, a story they created and since you don't know how that story was written, you are going to have to simply live your life and go about things like you normally would until this story is complete. Unfortunately for you and your family, it appears that the writer's version of a completed story, doesn't have you alive in it."

Jason stared deeply into the strange man's eyes—he saw nothing but sincerity as the strange man continued speaking.

"Agent Barrington before I go, I should make you aware that there's a ninety percent probability that whoever has written your story, has already killed you. In the cosmic sense of the meaning and literal sense, wrapped loosely around the elements of time—you're already dead. It just hasn't caught up to the universe's official orders set for you as of yet. And that is most likely due to the fact that whoever is out there reading and altering your life, altering your story, has done an adequate job of countering the writer's finished and completed storyline. "The reader of your story is likely the reason you and your family are currently alive, but I assure you, conventional wisdom and the laws of the universe says this reader won't be able to continue to do so for much longer. You have been able to escape death thus far, agent Barrington, but your path is set and clear as it ends in death, but not your family's, they are still in danger of succumbing from the turbulence of your already written destiny."

"Wait," Jason replied, "My family, what the hell do they have to do with any of this?"

The man nodded his head to acknowledge Jason's question.

"There is still hope for them, agent Barrington. There is a way to see that they stay alive to live their own lives. There is a way to see that their fate is altered in a way that takes them out of the cross hairs of your story and onto their own paths, their own stories, written by someone whose plans may be much different than what the writer of your story had for you."

Jason gazed into the man's eyes for what felt like an eternity. He knew the man believed he was telling the truth. That caused a bit of pause within Jason as he began to slowly take it all in. He didn't know if what this man was talking about had anything to do with what happened at his house, maybe it didn't or didn't, but he wouldn't be doing his job as a father, as Jessica's fiancé, if he didn't at least see if there was any correlation at all.

"Say I want to believe you?" said Jason. "Because I honestly do. How exactly would I "save" my family? Whatever you claim this is, it's putting my family at risk, yet I'm the only one whose destiny has been determined, right?"

"This is correct," the strange man stated, slowly nodding his head.

"So, hypothetically speaking of course, how can I get them on their own "path" and off mine? On their own destiny?"

The strange man smiled as he closed his eyes and took a deep breath.

"Now my friend, you're asking the only question that matters. It's a really complex moral dilemma. As complex as you'll ever experience in this lifetime my friend. Simply put, Agent Barrington, one of three inhabitants of this multiverse will have to die in order to save your family."

"What?" Jason exclaimed behind a perplexed expression, "What does that mean?"

"In order to save your family, agent Barrington, someone will have to die, and it will have to be at least one of three inhabitants. The first way—is if the author of your "story" dies, no matter if the story is already completed or not. If the writer dies, it will universally and automatically shift the story into the universe's hands, and you'll be able to immediately change your destiny. If the story is already written, that doesn't mean the writer is already dead, it just simply means your story is already written. The second way—you have to personally take someone's life, but not just anyone's, agent Barrington. You have to personally take the life of someone that has taken something precious, meaningful or substantive away from you. That "something" can be anything of value, it can be anything or anyone. The third and final way agent Barrington—you have to sacrifice yourself for someone and not just anyone. You have to sacrifice yourself for someone that you've never met and will never physically meet. And by "sacrifice," I'm indeed referring to the ultimate sacrifice, agent Barrington, by giving your life for them."

Jason stared at the man for a moment to get an honest read out on his emotions and they never changed. His expression stayed that same as he peered back into Jason's eyes as the small smirk on his face was just enough to give Jason slight chills.

"You do realize how insane this all sounds, right?" asked Jason as he chuckled nervously. " Why would all that be necessary? Who the hell makes these rules? I have to kill someone that has taken "something precious" away from me? Like what? A toy? A car? The repo man? You do see how nonsensical all this sounds, right?"
The man smiled as he closed his eyes and began nodding his head as Jason inched closer to the strange man in an attempt to rattle him.

"So, what if I pull my gun out right now and really kill myself?" Jason asked. "Huh? What if I kill myself in order to keep my family safe and get them off of my "story"? How about that?"

The man began shaking his head before Jason could even finish.

"That won't work, agent Barrington. For starters; the inhabitant that is reading your story won't allow it and second, the universe will only honor that act if you are doing it to save the life of someone else you will never meet – a sacrifice. Your death by any means other than what the author of your story has already written out for you or the universal sanctioned self-sacrifice I mentioned to you, won't alter the destiny of your loved ones or take them out of harm's way."

Slowly backing away from the man, Jason began shaking his head. He thought carefully on what the man just said. The more he thought about it, the more it was clear that this man was struggling with reality.

"Who the hell makes these rules?" Jason laughed as he was unable to hold it any longer. "Who the hell comes up with this stuff?"

"That, I do not know." The strange man uttered through a smile. "The only thing I do know, agent Barrington, is that you now have the information that you need, the information that I needed to convey to you, so now" said the stranger, "I must be going."

"I can assure you my friend," said Jason. "The only place you'll be going when you leave here is either to the hospital or inside of a jail cell—nowhere else. Just until we figure out who you really are and where you come from?"

The stranger continued to smile as he sat back in his seat.

"It's truly been a pleasure speaking with you today, Jason. I hope you remember what I've shared with you, it's very vital that you do. I truly wish you the best, hope your choices from this point are logical, and hope that whoever is currently guiding or altering your steps, can guide you and your family to a place of peace and happiness. Goodbye agent Barrington."

And with that, the strange man whose cuffed hands were in front of him, snapped out of the handcuffs, immediately leaped out of his seat and quickly darted over towards the guard. Before the guard could react, the stranger head butted the guard in his face instantly knocking him to the ground as the guard held his face and yelled in agony. He grabbed the guard's gun and let off two shots into the guard's chest, killing him instantly. The stranger wasted no time whipping the gun around to aim at Jason, but by that time it was already too late as Jason had already gotten the drop on him.

Jason had the man in his aim through his 9-millimeter and let off two shots from his weapon, one to the head and one to the neck, instantly ending the stranger's life. Jason held a sharp aim on the stranger without flinching.

The interrogation door swung open as armed DEA agents began storming in with their weapons aimed.

Frozen in confusion, Jason still had his aim on the stranger who was already dead. Slowly lowering his weapon, Jason gradually holstered the semi-automatic weapon and slowly began walking out of the interrogation room, unsure of what just actually happened.

Jason's Story- Chapter Seven—The End

Chapter Twelve

Hypothetical Understanding

I must've subconsciously powered down the Nook as I truly didn't remember powering it off. As I snapped out of my mini daydream, I immediately noticed the nook sitting on top of my carry-on with no recollection of even placing it there. I assumed I subconsciously placed it there after zoning out due to the weighted concept that was introduced to me during that last chapter. There was a part of me that couldn't bear to even glance at the device, not even for a second—after all I'd read in that last chapter.

It was entirely too much going on in my mind right now, and I desperately needed something, anything else to focus my attention on. I had no idea what it was that I just finished reading, but whatever it was, I had trouble truly wrapping my brain around every word of it. I didn't even know how to begin to do so. The more I began to think about it, the more it was all gradually coming together in the once place that it needed to—my mind. I had both hands placed firmly and nervously on top of my knees at this point as my nerves had me squeezing both of them. I caught myself rocking back and forth in my seat.

Did the strange man in the room with Jason actually acknowledge my presence? He alluded to a *"reader"* that was reading and altering the story. Was I even the least bit naïve to think that he wasn't referring to me? Who or what else could that strange man been referring to? Maybe I was still thinking all of this was simply one big coincidence? I slowly and somewhat inconspicuously gazed around the plane as I felt everyone's eyes on me. I couldn't help but feeling like they all knew what was happening. Everyone. They knew what I was experiencing, what I'd just read, but in all reality, they knew nothing.

Everyone on the plane was nearly asleep aside from the few passengers still up reading and working under their own personal lights. I glanced over at Bradley who was asleep, with music blaring in his ears. His left leg seem to move to the music which indicated he probably wasn't too far deep in his sleep to not be disturbed. I desperately needed to talk with someone, anyone, and Bradley was the only person that essentially knew, somewhat, what I was experiencing. I took several deep breaths as I gazed out of my window, contemplating heavily on what I needed to say to Bradley to even begin to help me with what I was now faced with. While doing so, I slowly began to realize that I hadn't even accepted the impossible words and the seemingly impossible logic of what I just read with Jason in the interrogation room. I hadn't even thought enough on it to even have an sufficient and logical discussion about it with Bradley. At this point, and after what I just read, I no longer wanted any more parts of this story in any way. I was tempted to let Jason and his family meet whatever fate they were destined to meet. Why did I need to do this? Why me? Who was I that had the Universe's authority to alter someone else's life—someone else's story? Who gave me that right? I didn't want it. What about my story? Who was responsible for tearing my world apart from the foundation right now?

There was a lot going on in my mind, and I didn't know where or how to start deciphering it all. This last chapter had done something to me, and I wasn't even certain what that "something" was. I just knew I was beginning to question everything I've believed in and more, and that scared me. I was becoming more emotional as the hours went on with this flight and this story. Jason's story was doing this to me, and I hadn't the faintest idea as to what my next move should be.

Jason didn't appear to believe what the strange man shared with him, but it was something about the man's words, the way he spoke, what he said, the confidence attached to it, in which I knew there was enough logic attached to it, to make me think. **My leg shook nervously. I put my hand up to my head and gently massaged my frontal lobe. There was a headache, I could feel gradually coming on. I inconspicuously peeked through my opened fingers and glanced down at the Nook sitting on top of my bag. I figured in a way, I was attempting to fool myself. I believe deep down, I was trying to pretend the device was no longer there. I didn't want to look at the device, so I did the next "best" thing. I looked everywhere around the device, occasionally landing my eyes on the actual device itself. I was going out of my way in attempting to ignore it, but it wasn't working. I wasn't fooling myself.

My mind was working on a whole different level, so of course I knew better, I was thinking as clear as ever. I'd never had this much clarity when it came to grasping and thinking about anything and now, my mind wasn't just racing at one hundred miles per hour, it was as if life, my circumstances, this story, Jason's life, was under a microscope. I didn't just see it clearly, but I was seeing it fly past in a way that no one could possibly understand. That was another reason I felt so alone right now, and why I knew I desperately needed to speak with someone about this. I glanced over at Bradley who was still resting comfortably. I slowly leaned over towards him and gently tapped him on his shoulder. Bradley slowly began to sit up yawning, as he removed the earphones from his ear, looking at me, he began to grin.

"Hey, Steve?" he mumbled as he began looking around the plane.

I immediately forced a grin on my face as I didn't want to seem too distraught as Bradley, in just my short time knowing him, has proven that he was very good at reading people.

"I apologize for waking you." I whispered.

"Oh man no," Bradley replied. "I told you, long flight and all. I would rather talk than to be sitting here slumped over, bored out of my mind, drifting in and out of sleep."

I casually glanced over to his laptop and nodded my head.

"How's the writing coming along?" Bradley chuckled slightly as he began shaking his head. "It's ok, everything will probably work itself out. How's that book coming?"

I hesitated, probably longer than I should have. It was unintentional, but noticeable nonetheless, as Bradley clearly recognized the hesitation. He raised his right eyebrow as he let out a slight snicker.

"Does that mean it's really interesting or something else?"

I smiled, but really, I was at a loss of words and didn't know how to answer his question without displaying the emotion that had been building within me as I read the past hour or so. I calmly shook my head as Bradley waited patiently for an answer.

"I'm not sure how I feel about this book my friend, because my mind is everywhere else right now."

"Of course." said Bradley as he quickly nodded his head in agreement.

"It's not just in what I'm dealing with in losing my baby girl, it's everything right now, and I don't know if I'm doing a great job at keeping it together."

Bradley's grin gradually disappeared and a look of extreme yet genuine concern immediately blanketed his face. The doctor in him seemed to instantly make its way to the forefront.

"Steve, I need you to let me know how I can help you. I need you to be honest and tell me what it is I can do to help you through this?"

I closed my eyes and slowly shook my head. I didn't have an answer to that question. I knew Bradley was being genuine, but I didn't know how to respond to his words.

"I appreciate that," I finally said. "I do, but right now, I don't know if what I'm dealing with in my daughter's death has caused some sort of unconscious nervous breakdown, and I just don't know it, or I'm just flat-out losing it?"

"Why do you say that?" asked Bradley.

I hesitated as I calmly turned and peered out of the window, gathering my thoughts. I slowly turned back towards Bradley as he remained focused on me, undoubtedly waiting for a response to his question. I could tell by his expression, whatever it was that I was trying to tell him, he was very interested and concerned. I was struggling to get it out, for more than one reason. The battle I was waging within my inner consciousness, in hopes of adequately piecing together an appropriate response, was playing itself out on my face, and Bradley was witnessing it. I couldn't hide it and frankly, I didn't want to anymore. I was tired, extremely tired, and holding all of this in hadn't worked so far for the past six hours or so.

"Do you believe the universe simply just gets to a point where it interferes and interacts with our lives?" I asked him.

I couldn't quite understand why I asked him what I asked him, but I knew at this point, my mind was working methodically. If the question derived from my subconscious, it was likely a question that I needed an answer to.

"How do you mean?" Bradley replied, confused. I paused for a moment as I tried to put together the right words to answer his question. "Quite honestly I don't know what I mean exactly, just thought you might have had thoughts on something like that."

"Well," Bradley stated as he rubbed his beard gingerly, as he gathered his own thoughts. "I think you're asking if the universe has more of an impact on our lives than we actually are aware of?"

"Yeah. I guess."
He peered at me with a confused look on his face, as if he was trying to figure out what I was getting at, trying to read more into me as the question had caught him a bit off guard.

"I don't know." he replied. "I think it's logical to assume when it comes to the universe, anything is possible." Bradley chuckled slightly as he raised his eyebrow while gazing at me.

"Pretty strange question, Steve. Why'd you ask that?" I took a deep breath and dove right into what I felt like I needed to say to get it over with.

"Bradley, I'm......uh, going to ask you more questions," I stammered as I shook my head. I couldn't believe what I was prepared to say. "These questions I ask you, please, I need you to understand that I need you to not judge me or be concerned about me in any way. I am fine. I need you to open your mind and answer the questions, logically, honestly, and from your heart. This is what you can do to help me my friend. Your wisdom in regard to my questions, is the only thing I need right now, nothing more. Can you promise you'll do this for me?"

Bradley looked at me with a look of slight confusion at first, but after he noticed the sincere and honest look on my face, I think he realized how serious I was. He gently nodded his head as a small smirk flashed across his face. He hung his head for a moment as I heard him take a deep breath. He slowly glanced back up at me as his smile got much wider and seemed more genuine.

"Yes Steve, I can do that, I promise."
I still had a battle going on inside of me. I fought diligently and silently in trying to figure out just what it was I was

going to say to or ask Bradley. I still feared the inescapable possibility that I might have lost it, but Bradley seemed as opened minded as any person I had ever met, and I knew if I was going to take a chance on someone believing me on what I was currently experiencing, it would be someone like him. Someone that not only has an opened mind, but that has gone through some surreal, difficult trials in life. Bradley had most certainly experienced all of these and that much was clear, just in the six hours or so I had come to know him.

He gazed over at me, waiting for me to begin asking the questions. I didn't know where to start, but I figure since we were already discussing the universe, we might as well stay there.

"Do you believe the universe is alive?" I asked. "Alive" as in conscious and aware of what is going on in every part and corner of it? "Alive" as in cognizant of every human's or non-human's state of existence? "Alive" as in actively controlling all of our lives in a way that may be difficult to understand or grasp on a normal, conscious level of thinking?"

I gazed into Bradley's face, into his eyes, and he simply smiled as he gently nodded his head.

"What are you asking, Steve? Are you asking if I believe if the universe has more control over us than we know or even care to know? Are you asking me if I believe if the universe has a proactive role in the lives of every living organism inside the known universe? Are you asking me if I believe that our fate is not controlled entirely by us, if at all, but instead controlled by the universe, the subconscious and unknowing forces the universe have charged with doing just that?"

I smiled as I listened to Bradley. He asked what I presumed to be semi-rhetorical questions as he looked deep into my eyes, he appeared to be waiting for a response from me from his question.

"Yes," I replied, "That's essentially what I'm asking you—I think."

"The answer is yes Steve, I do."

"Why?" I quickly replied, "Why do believe that? What reason do you have, or what have you experienced in your life causes you to believe the way you do?"

"Well," he quickly responded behind a smile. "If you're looking for some surreal, euphoric, and epic tale of me experiencing one of the universe's many marvels and possibilities, and how it left me in awe, and a believer in the many possibilities that exist out in the vastness and immenseness of the universe, then sorry to disappoint you, I don't have one. I honestly don't need one. No one should need one of those stories or experiences to make them see what they are currently walking under and walking in everyday that they are alive on this planet. If it just so happens to take one of these experiences to ultimately open their eyes then fine, but I truly believe the world, the universe provides you with more than enough evidence that the universe is alive. It's just a matter of opening your mind and yourself up to receive it."

It was very clear Bradley understood what I asked him, which was yet another reason I knew discussing this with him was probably in my best interest, considering how wise and open minded he appeared to be. He uttered the words that I needed to hear, and somewhat confirmed my leap of faith I was taking by confiding in him at a moment when I wasn't sure what was real and what wasn't. I was still yet debating whether or not I would tell him everything, but I knew I would at least tell him enough.

Slowly, I nodded my head, acknowledging Bradley's words as he spoke with such clarity and confidence. His sentiments provided me with the strength I needed to continue. I gazed past him while I carefully constructed my own thoughts, mentally putting together what I would say to him next. I could see him staring at me as he eagerly awaited my response. I had drawn him in, and he was here to stay until I provided him with more information—information that would seemingly make sense of the way I was acting. I gazed around the plane, and I felt somewhat comforted by the fact that most if not everyone that I could see was either sleep or deeply engaged in their own work. Even the passengers directly behind and in front of me were fast asleep. I guess it was a sense of security in that if I wanted to completely confide in Bradley, I could without fear of someone hearing and judging in more ways than one. I smiled as I looked Bradley in his eye as he took a sip of his tea. I continued with my questions.

"Say for instance," I continued. "I tell you that, utilizing the "concept;" "*anything is possible,*" a concept that you mentioned and seem to understand perfectly and believe in, hypothetically of course, I have this story that I'm reading, and while reading this story, I get further and deeper into this story when I discover that.... "

I paused as the words weren't easy to let go of. It was almost as if speaking them out loud for the first time – which I was. It was at this moment, I started to understand just how crazy, how impossible, how unbelievable it all sounded. I closed my eyes and smiled as I continued.

"You discover that this story is more than just a "story." You discover that this story is actually someone's life, and that you, that I, the person that is reading this story, actually has the ability to alter said story by "controlling" if you will, the main character and nothing else?"

Bradley let out a slight chuckle. "This 'hypothetical' story," he replied. "Is this the same story we were discussing earlier? You know, the one about the suicidal federal agent that lost his family? The one that led to our mini philosophical discussion about suicide, life, and faith?"

I smiled, but I knew there was no way I would be able to convince him otherwise, he was reading right through me. I gently nodded my head as I was certain he was asking a question he already knew the answer to.

"Yes, this is the same story."
As he shook his head, Bradley closed his eyes and sighed.

"Well, I guess after getting over the initial shock, which is easier said than done when experiencing something so surreal as this, I'm guessing I would be in denial for a while. I would certainly have to make sure that I wasn't dreaming or experiencing some sort of mental break down that was affecting my state of mind."

I could tell by the way Bradley was looking at me; he was examining me from afar. I assumed he was doing so and didn't want to officially do so as to not offend me. But after the way I've acted since reading this story, and after how he has witnessed it all, I didn't blame him for his concern. I appreciated his demeanor, respect, and understanding of what I was dealing with, even though he didn't officially "know" I was dealing with it. I knew he realized there was something going on with me, but I didn't know to what extent he knew, as he was a very calm and collected man. Considering everything I was sharing with him and asking him, which was all too surreal and sublime, I was pretty content with the way he was interacting and responding to what I was presenting to him. I didn't know what I expected from him, but I guess it was probably what he was currently giving me.

"I would also," Bradley noted, "try my best to understand why this was happening to me since I for one believe the universe most likely works in a very specific way that is precisely detailed and methodical. I believe it utilizes a direct "order" that is created for each and every one of us. I would believe that there would have to be an end reasoning, result, or specific designed purpose as to why I was suddenly granted this cosmic and highly inconceivable "ability," and my overall goal would be to discover what that is, and I would do so by any means."

"But why would you believe the universe works this way?" I asked, as I began looking around. "How do we know that none of this isn't all in our minds?"

"What do you mean?" Bradley replied.

"Well, you seem so confident that the universe just works by these "rules" and "laws," but why are you so confident it works this way?"

"Well, I don't know," Bradley stated. "I believe confidence is the cousin of faith. Just because I'm confident in something, doesn't automatically make it right, but I'm confident for a reason. I like to use logic when thinking about things that are bigger than me, and let's understand something here my friend—the universe is something that is far greater than any of us, so we really don't have to be sure anything "works" in any way when discussing the universe. I've haven't always thought this way, but as you grow, live, and mature, you learn, but everyone learns differently, in different ways."

I felt my smile growing wider as he spoke. Wasn't exactly certain why I was smiling, but a lot of it had to do with the fact that I wasn't just understanding everything he was saying, it was as if I was seeing it as he spoke it. It was a level of comfort falling over me as I listened to him speak, I wasn't exactly certain why.

"Travel with me for a moment," he whispered, as he raised his arms towards the sky, attempting to paint a picture for me. "We're on Earth, a planet inside our solar system, a solar system that still possesses unknown and undiscovered parts that we aren't close to understanding. Our Solar System is inside a Galaxy.... "

"The Milky Way Galaxy," I uttered calmly.

"That's correct." Bradley confirmed. "The Milky Way Galaxy. Outside of our Galaxy and right next to us is another Galaxy, Andromeda. That galaxy almost certainly holds its own Solar Systems. Our galaxies are two of probably hundreds of thousands that exist inside a super cluster. We're essentially talking about one hundred billion galaxies in our Cosmos, my friend. That's more possibilities out there than your mind will ever imagine in all the years you have been alive plus the years until you die. You will never imagine all the possibilities that exist out here in the Cosmos, but that shouldn't stop you from at least accepting the notion of infinite possibilities. That's what I do. That's what I know. That's where my confidence comes from, and nothing shakes the confidence I have in that concept."

Bradley took a sip of water and nodded his head as if he was, in a sense, agreeing with himself. I rubbed my eyes as they were not only tired, but they still burned. They had been burning for the past three hours or so. I just didn't take time out to even notice but having this moment to stop and reflect on what I was actually experiencing allowed me to realize just how tired I really was. What Bradley was saying not only made sense, but I firmly believed it was what I needed to hear.

I found it eerily strange, how similar he sounded to the strange man Jason was speaking with in the interrogation room in that last chapter, but unlike Jason and the strange man, I was more inclined to, and had every reason to buy into if not fully believe what Bradley was sharing with me because of how astute, confident, wise and logical he was, and because of the confidence I had in him, just in the small time I had come to "know" him.

Bradley gazed at me with a calm, patient yet inquisitive look as if he was calmly saying; "next question?"

I smiled because I knew I was hesitating, maybe even stalling, but I needed to make sure I gathered my words and thoughts appropriately before asking him or sharing them with him. I wanted to be very careful not to make him think I was crazy, but part of me felt like we were already past that point. What he said seemed feasible even though it was hard to make earthly sense of it or anything I was dealing with right now. I seemed to be grasping everything at this point, quicker than I ever had at any point in my life. That strange feeling, I had been experiencing the past five hours or so, seemed to have opened up my understanding to a level that I was afraid to even admit I was on.

"So, hypothetically speaking," I said. "Say if I was given this "cosmic" ability, as you put it, right now, during everything I'm dealing with emotionally. I was charged by the universe, as you suggest, with reading and "finishing" this story, but not just "finishing" it in the direct sense of the word, but "finishing" it by adequately and responsibly completing this story. Completing a story that is essentially someone else's life. Doing so, while dealing with the personal emotional overload I currently find myself dealing with at this very moment and while reading, experiencing, and responsibly altering the story to see that the main character sees what I believe to be a happy ending. But, while doing so, the story starts to get immensely deep, and too emotionally overwhelming for me in a way that I believe now not only forces me to question everything, but causes me to emotionally drown, even more than I already was prior to reading said story. What if I told you that I didn't want to have any part of this story anymore because of the emotional weight that I felt pressing down on me? What if I told you, that the responsibility and confidence and certain level of creativity needed to continue to adequately guide this main character's story and life was something I no longer felt I had within myself? Considering I felt this way because of my emotional state, and that I could no longer make sound, logical, decisions for this character and his family. What would you say to me?"

The way Bradley peered right through me, I knew he realized it was more to these hypothetical questions than I was letting on, but he wouldn't break and wouldn't sway from what he promised me—no matter how much I knew he wanted to. He gazed at me as he raised one eyebrow and smiled. I knew he realized that there was more to all of this than I was sharing with him. He shook his head and took another deep breath as he smirked, slightly.

"Steve........"

Bradley paused. He appeared to be at a loss of words as he shook his head and peered past me through the window as if he was lost in thought. I had no idea what he was thinking, but he was too wise and inquisitive to not want to simply do away with the hypotheticals and ask me what was "really" going on. In a sense, he was probably regretting what he had promised me.

"Steve, there isn't an easy answer to your question. But I would first tell you that ultimately, no one can tell you what or what not to do when it comes to something so emotionally engaging. No one can and should judge you, no matter what personal decision you decide to make, considering how emotionally fragile your personal ordeal has made you and you honestly shouldn't care if they do. I ...... "

Bradley paused suddenly as he shook his head. It was clear that he was struggling to find the right words to express to me. I realized I had hit him with a highly complex and difficult conundrum, and when looking at it from a completely objective and realistic point of view, shouldn't really have an easy answer, if any earthly answer at all. I knew his responses and answers weren't going to be as quick as they were with the previous conversations we had in the past few hours or so, but I knew I had no one else that could help me shift through what I was currently experiencing, not to mention he seemed to quickly understand and grasp the relatively complex things I shared with him.

"I would also tell you," Bradley continued. "That you have every right to feel that way. I would applaud your initial altruistic and subservient outlook and state of mind towards this newfound ability and surreal yet invaluable responsibility that you had been "given." I would also have to look at it from a perspective that is beyond what you and I can physically and mentally begin to comprehend right now or even want to, and that's where I'm afraid I might lose you."

I immediately broke out in a quiet chuckle. I shook my head as I laughed in a slightly and soft hysterical tone, almost forgetting where I was and that everyone around me was resting. Bradley seemed a bit surprised by my reaction to his statement as he immediately motioned for me to quiet down.

"Shhh," he instructed, quickly placing his finger to his lip. "What's so funny?" he inquired through a smile. I laughed, but it wasn't funny, and it certainly wasn't as funny as Bradley probably believed I thought it was considering how hard I was laughing, apparently. I wasn't laughing because what he said was funny, I broke out in laughter because of the sheer irony of Bradley suggesting that he might "lose me." I laughed because I was the one afraid of "losing" him with what I knew, with what I was experiencing, with what my mind was dealing with at this point. It was funny, but not nearly as funny as I wanted it to be.

"Trust me," I said. "It's not me that is in danger of being "lost" here, but to be honest, you don't really sound like someone that gets lost that much when it comes to things other people would usually get lost in, but I digress, why don't you try me. You won't lose me, trust me."
"If you had this unbelievable "ability," hypothetically speaking of course," Bradley whispered, "And you had

been exercising this ability after discovering it, proactively altering and guiding this character's steps, life and story up until a point where it's actually gotten you emotionally compromised and weak, then I believe it's your moral responsibility to see this, cosmically appointed assignment, if you will, through to the furthest point of your understanding and abilities. I think if you started it, knowingly or unknowingly, you are morally bound by the "rules" of the universe and morally obligated to see it through until you can't anymore or until the end. That would be the way I see it, hypothetically speaking of course."

I nodded my head. Not necessarily in agreement, but more so "understanding" than anything else. I understood what he was trying to convey to me, I just didn't *want* to understand it. I took a deep breath as I closed my eyes, I could feel Bradley staring at me, waiting for my response. It was obvious by his tone and verbiage that he knew more. Honestly, I wouldn't be surprised if he knew exactly what was happening to me just from the emotional context clues, I'd been inadvertently sending out since first discussing this story with him.

"I can't." I whispered dejectedly as I rubbed my eyes.

"I'm sorry, what'd you say?" Bradley quickly replied. I stopped rubbing my eyes and stared at him. He had one eyebrow raised again while he leaned in slightly to get a better angle on my response as he appeared to not hear me, but I knew he did, he simply wanted me to repeat myself. So, I did, this time, I didn't whisper.

"I can't! I can't do it." I repeated as I shook my head. He nodded his head, quickly—as if he was expecting the response that I'd given him. He nodded in a way that suggested that he understood what I was saying, but it came across as slightly facetious. I expected nothing less from him at this point, considering it appeared as if there was no way I was going to convince him to believe anything contrary to what he believed. Most importantly, with me saying to him that, "*I can't,*" I all but officially made it clear that we weren't discussing hypotheticals anymore.

I didn't realize that right away, but after we sat in silence for a few seconds staring at one another, it began to slowly hit me—what I'd said. I looked for any type of response, expression, or movement on his face that would provide me with a hint of what he was thinking after hearing me utter the words *"I can't,"* but I got nothing. He nodded his head as he gazed at me and smiled, but it was as if he was looking deep within me and not at me. I closed my eyes and took a deep breath.

"This isn't hypothetical my friend." I murmured, as my eyes remained closed. "I need you to understand clearly what I mean when I say that. I need you to realize that the person you're sitting next to and having a conversation with is either crazy as all hell, or he is experiencing one of those infinite cosmic "possibilities" that could happen to anyone or any being, in any part of the immense and vast universe."

My eyes remained closed as I spoke in a whisper to him. What I was saying, I certainly was trying my best to keep anyone else from hearing it, so the more I said, the lower my tone got, but Bradley understood it all. I slowly opened my eyes as Bradley was staring at me with a relaxed grin on his face. He began slowly nodding his head again but was yet to say a word. I knew I had put some heavy stuff on him the past hour or so we'd been talking, and I had no idea what to expect from him.

There isn't etiquette for something like this. There wasn't a rule book out there on how to act or respond when someone hits you with something like this, so I couldn't really blame him for being speechless, or if he simply requested to have his seat changed because he feared for his safety, hell, it's what I would consider doing after hearing me talk for the past fifty minutes or so.

"Why can't you?" Bradley finally asked.

Slowly I shook my head as I didn't have an immediate answer. Even if I was expecting the question, I still wouldn't have an immediate answer to it because it was all too emotionally overwhelming.

"Because," I replied hesitantly. "The impossible fact that I have this character's, this man's life, the lives of his family in my hands—literally, is more than I can carry and handle right now, emotionally and mentally.... "

I stammered on my words a bit as I paused and struggled to find the right ones as Bradley gazed deep into my eyes as I spoke, patiently waiting for my next words. I continued.

"Because of what I'm dealing with personally. Along with the sheer weight of the fact that I'm still in shock and disbelief that it's all actually happening to me. I don't want to be responsible for this man losing his family again. It seems as though I've tried to guide this man, this character, responsibly and accordingly, but I don't have him in a place that I can confidently say, he's better off because I was somehow cosmically interjected into his life. I can't say without a doubt that right now, whoever this character or man is, that I've added any substantive or positive value to his life. I just can't, and I feel as though I should stop it now before I make it worse."

The pause that followed my words unfurled a weighted ton of silence down on the both of us. Bradley looked as if he genuinely accepted all I was saying to him and yet part of him needed me to understand more.

"Have you ever started a project at work," Bradley asked, "and simply gave up or stopped in the middle of it because it got too challenging?"

"This is not the same and you know it" I declared.

"Why isn't it?" he asked, "You don't know this character, this man, no more than you know random floor plans that fall into your lap on one of your projects. This character may only be real within the space of your universe and nowhere else. If you're a finisher, be a finisher, but if you going to start something so incredible, so surreal, and life altering, then you must do what it takes to finish it. What if someone did the same to you and your life? What if the universe felt as though your life was too emotional and stressful for it to be bothered with it anymore, and it simply decided not to pick up your story and continue it anymore? What do you think would happen?"

"Well, I already feel as though it has done this," I whispered calmly as I could feel the tears slowly starting to flood my eyes. "I believe the universe, God, everything, has given up on me and losing my baby girl was proof of that."

Bradley took a deep breath and flashed a subtle smirk as he nodded his head. It was one of those respectful "*ok, I don't think you're getting it, but I'll try something else*" kind of smirks.

"So, your daughter's untimely demise is "proof" that someone or something out there has given up on you, is this what you're trying to tell me?"

"Yes," I quietly snapped at him "This is what I'm trying to tell you."

"If this is the case," said Bradley, "When that man, that character whose life you have been guiding and altering, felt as though the world turned against him after he lost his family, why didn't you give up on him, like you say life has to you?"

"Because I didn't know what I was doing or saying, initially." I replied through a nervous stutter. "I was doing it unconsciously. I had no idea what was going on."

"But, when you did discover what you can do, you didn't stop. Why not?" Bradley asked

"Because I saw something better for him. I wanted better for him, and I believed deep down he wanted it too."

"So, you saw something unfinished and incomplete, correct?" said Bradley.

"Yes."

"So, tell me again why your daughter's death completes your story, but his family's death didn't complete his? Tell me why the universe can't see something unfinished and incomplete within your story?"

I was at a loss. I had no answer to what he was asking. I was hurt, and the pain of Natalie's death burned inside me once more, just like it did when I first awoke up in the hospital in Japan. In a way, I felt as though I didn't ask for this ability, this responsibility, so I shouldn't be obligated to do anything more from this point. However, I realized that Bradley had a point. I hadn't given up on Jason and in fact, I wouldn't even allow him to give up on himself, and now all of a sudden, I was giving up on the both of us.

"I'll just say this," Bradley whispered, as he inched closer toward me and focused in on my teary eyes. "If we as occupants of the known universe are in the position and possess the skills, abilities, and resources to help those that are in need, and we choose not to for whatever reason, why are we here? There is nothing more universally surreal, euphorically beautiful, important, and meaningful, than when those who have the ability to make the lives of those around them who are in need, better and actually do it. I've never witnessed, in all my journeys, and with any and every teacher, patient, acquaintances, or friend that I've had the privilege to meet in all the years I have been alive, the unnatural and shear unmatched, flawless state of existence, at that exact moment in time and space in which someone realizes that they don't just have the ability and resources to make someone's life better, but they actually have the "power" to make someone's story better. It's a priceless moment to be able to witness something like that, and we should all be so lucky. So, I thank you Steve, for giving me that opportunity to do just that. I thank you for the opportunity to allow me to witness that today."

Bradley smiled as he finished his thought. He placed his glasses back on his nose as he gazed at his computer screen. He gently placed his ear buds back into his ears and refocused his attention back to his laptop as if I wasn't even there—as if I hadn't uttered a single world. Bradley's last few words were the ones that left the deep sting in my spirit, the copper-like taste of defeatist failure in my mouth. I wanted to hide somewhere considering how ashamed I was starting to feel about it all. I knew there was a bit of a reverse psychology within his words, but for the most part, he wasn't wrong.

I wanted Bradley to be wrong in everything he said, but he just wasn't. I gazed at him for what felt like an eternity. His focus was now off me and back onto his laptop, he returned to typing while his music blared in his ear. It was as if he was purposely tuning me out, as if I didn't even exist. I knew what he was doing, and I understood. There really wasn't anything else to be said on his part. I slowly nodded my head as I turned towards the Nook that lay sprawled out on top of my carry on. I glanced back at Bradley who was still focused on his PC. I looked back towards the Nook and started shaking my head, disgusted with myself.

Disgusted with how easily I was prepared to give up on something so extraordinary and so unimaginably impossible. I used to read stories to Natalie all the time. She was always engaged in the stories, and if I were to read her this story, she would undoubtedly want me to finish it to help Jason and his family live happily ever after. Tears began to fall down my face as I hesitantly reached for the Nook sitting on top of my bag. I didn't know if I was prepared for this or not, but that didn't matter anymore. I was going to do my best to finish this. I was going to see Jason's story to whatever end awaited him, no matter how long it took.

I placed the Nook in my lap and glanced back over to Bradley who was still focused on his PC, but this time there was a smile flashed across his face. I didn't assume right away that he was inconspicuously smiling at me, I just assumed he was smiling at whatever it was that he was working on. I glanced out of the window as the late-night sky appeared brighter than usual. We had been flying for almost seven hours or so. The moon was now lightning up the sky gracefully. I glared up at the moon through the window. It honestly felt as if it was following us. I nodded my head at the moon, in a way to acknowledge its unearthly presence. I focused my attention down on the Nook which sat gingerly on my lap. I powered it on and turned to the end of chapter seven.

As I expected, there was no chapter eight. Jason needed to get to his family, and I would do my best to see to it that this was his initial focus of this next chapter. I closed my eyes and spoke.

"*Unable to shake off the unusual information shared by the strange man, Jason understands that he needs to immediately secure his family, ASAP and attempt to make sense of all that is happening around him.*"

I opened my eyes, and before my eyes could even touch the screen of the Nook, the icon for chapter eight was staring me directly in my face. I took a deep breath and rejoined Jason's story.

Chapter Thirteen

The Conundrum of Agent Terrell

Jason's Story—Chapter Eight

Still stuck in a state of surreal disbelief and slight shock, Jason gazed down the brightly lit hall as DEA agents continued to pour into the interrogation room to render aid to the strange man that he just shot and killed, along with the other agent on guard in the room. He had no idea what his next move should be as he tried grasping the reality of what just actually happened. DEA ASAC, Henry Robertson was on his way to access the scene. Jason knew he would need to speak with him to provide an official statement as to what actually happened. It was hard for Jason to shake it off, but he knew he needed to remain focused. The more he pondered on the man's weird and eerie words, the more he realized he probably needed to be with his family, to make sure they were safe. It all started to feel as though everything was happening entirely too fast. It felt almost designed.

He reached for his phone to call Dave, but paused, as he couldn't understand what was more confusing—what the strange man had been babbling about for the past thirty minutes or so or, the fact that this strange man just pulled a "suicide by cop"? There wasn't a doubt in Jason's mind that the man's plan in the end was to get him to kill him. It took a minute or so for Jason to gather himself as he stood standing staring off down the hall as agents continued to access and control the scene.

Jason already found himself thinking back on the stranger's chilling words— "I'll share this with you, and then you will release me."

Jason shook his head in confusion as he thought heavily on what the strange man shared with him. He was unable to completely shake it out of his subconscious. Jason grabbed one of the agents that was behind the two-way mirror from the interrogation room.

"You guys didn't think what he was saying was weird?" Jason asked, curiously. The agent immediately shook his head and shrugged his shoulders. "Yeah right." the agent said with a bewildered look on his face,

"I'm serious," Jason snapped behind a stern tone. "You didn't find that shit weird?!!"

"What are you asking?" the agent replied sharply, as he looked Jason in his eye.

"That babble he was speaking in there," Jason replied.

"You guys didn't think that was weird and confusing?" The agent stared at Jason with a perplexing gaze. "Not sure what you're getting at here agent Barrington, but it's cool— your actions were completely justified in there. There's no need for....whatever it is you're doing right now."

Jason was somewhat confused and slightly bewildered by the agent's response. He slowly peered back into the room, the agents and medics were still tending to the stranger and the other wounded agent inside the room. He immediately began reflecting back on what the strange man shared with him while inside the room. As the DEA agent began to walk away Jason immediately grabbed his arm.

"Hey, what did you see while I was in there?" The agent glanced at Jason curiously and began shaking his head in apparent disbelief.

"After you," he said as he motioned for Jason to enter the viewing room behind the two-way mirror adjacent to the interrogation room. The agent immediately walked over to the video recording station, and immediately began to rewind the recording as Jason curiously looked on. The agent stepped back as the recording began to play. Jason gazed onto the screen in shock and disbelief as the recording eerily appeared to show Jason walking into the room to speak with the stranger and not even five seconds later, it showed the strange man standing up, attacking the other agent on guard in the room, and Jason being forced to kill him just like he had in the room, minus the entire conversation he and the strange man had while in the room.

"What the hell is this?" Jason barked as he gazed sharply at the DEA agent. " What is this? Why isn't our full conversation on this video?"

"What conversation?!" the agent quickly snapped. "There was no conversation, agent Barrington. Stop this— stop talking this way. Don't do this or you'll force my hand. I'll have to report how strange you're acting here. You walked into the room to talk with the gentlemen, and he obviously and clearly went crazy not even five seconds after you walked in and you couldn't even say one word to him. There was no conversation with him. The question

that I should be asking you, agent Barrington, is why?
Why would he request your presence only to force you to
kill him merely seconds after meeting him?"

Shaking his head, Jason suddenly found himself
slipping into a subtle euphoric state of disbelief and denial.
He completely understood the current confusion and
skepticism on part of the DEA agent, as the agent was
right, it didn't make any sense, it didn't add up. He knew
for an undeniable fact, that he most definitely had a nearly
forty-five-minute conversation with the strange man, so
watching that five second video forced his mind into
overload in an attempt to figure out what was happening,
and to try to make sense of it all.

The more he tried to make sense of everything, the
more it made no sense at all. Every word the strange man
said to him, quickly began to play back in his mind as he
gradually began to make his way out of the building. He
didn't necessarily believe the man's words, but that didn't
stop the man's words from sticking with him and echoing
repeatedly throughout his head. It was beginning to feel
like one of those surreal moments in which you were
dreaming, you knew you were dreaming— except in this
case, you weren't dreaming, because you knew it was real.
Whether it was real or not, was something Jason was yet to
fully determine as he found it easier to begin questioning

things he wouldn't have questioned, prior to him stepping into that interrogation room.

"Agent Barrington!"

The voice was deep and crystal clear, forcing Jason to immediately turn towards the direction in which it derived from. He was immediately greeted by DEA Assistant Special Agent in Charge Henry Robertson.

"ASAC Robertson." he said as he extended his hand towards Jason.

"I know who you are sir." Jason replied as he extended his hand in return and firmly shook the ASAC's hand.

"Agent Barrington, you mind telling me what in the hell happened here?"

"I can't say sir," Jason sighed, as he shook his head.

"Have you had a chance to review the recording?"

"I have and that's why I'm asking." said Robertson,

"Did you know this man? Why would he try to kill you onsite?"

Shrugging his shoulders, Jason was immediately perplexed as he struggled to dig up an adequate response to the ASAC's question. He truly didn't have one, but it was certainly a fair question that deserved a legitimate answer.

"I can't say sir. I had never met the man in my life. I don't know what happened in there, but when I find out, I will let you know." Jason turned to walk away, but before he could, ASAC Robertson yelled out to him.

"Hey," cried ASAC Robertson, as he gazed directly into Jason's eyes. Robertson had a serious demeanor about himself. He was easily over 220 pounds and stood about 6'2 or so. He didn't appear to be that much older than Jason if at all. Clean cut, with a bit of gray in his hair and facial hair, but it wasn't that easy to tell his age.

"I'll need an official statement from you, just type it up and send it over as soon as you can."

Jason nodded as began to walk away but noticed a deep and concerning look on Robertson's face as he seem to be struggling with thoughts that needed to be released. Robertson wanted to say something but didn't seem to know how.

"I never got to thank you personally for what you did that night," ASAC Robertson finally uttered. "Almost two years ago, in saving agent Merriweather's family. Thank you. If there's anything you ever need, just let me know. This entire agency owes you a debt."

Jason nodded. There wasn't much to say. That day was almost two years ago, but it was as if it just happened last night, and seeing the genuine gratitude on Robertson's face, began to instantly bring out a bit of buried emotion from that night that he didn't have the energy to deal with, at least not at the moment.

Jason turned and began casually sprinting towards his truck parked in front of the building. The only thing on his mind— getting to his family. It was the only thing that was pushing him at the moment. He needed to get to them, to make sure they were safe, to keep them safe. After the discussion with the strange man, he now needed to pull back and figure what was happening. Pulling off into the middle of the suddenly busy downtown intersection, Jason immediately came upon what appeared to be congested traffic caused by construction that forced the traffic to an immediate stand still.

Jason hesitantly retrieved his phone from his hip and dialed Keegan's number. The phone rang once but went immediately to Keegan's voicemail. Jason hung up and began to dial Jessica's number, but before he could dial the final number, the sound of a loud blaring car horn was heard to his immediate right as an approaching vehicle slammed on brakes to prevent from slamming into Jason's car. Startled, Jason immediately dropped the phone as the car stopped about two feet away from his door. He closed his eyes as his heart raced rapidly. He attempted to control his heart rate by calming himself down with steady, controlled breathing. With his eyes closed, Jason was now more in tuned to the sounds around him as he worked to steadily calm himself.

He began looking around for any noticeable detours, but there were none in sight. Sitting back in his seat, Jason began to think about the strange man's words. Putting together what actually happened in that room, was something he found himself struggling mightily with at the moment. As the traffic jam had him at a standstill, Jason took that time to slowly exit his vehicle and stood directly in front of his truck as he slowly peered up towards the sky. The sky's dark overcast had grown darker. It was about 2 PM, but the dark clouds made it appear as if it was much later in the evening. The wind was blowing hard enough to confirm that a storm was indeed on its way. Looking up towards the sky, the strange man's words began to vividly play back in his mind.

"What if it's all true?" he whispered to himself as he gazed at the surreal and euphoric overcast above him.

Jason lowered his head and began gradually looking around at the other cars that were stuck in the jam as well. The faces of all the drivers, the passengers, everyone that he could spot as far as his eye could see, just didn't seem the same to him at this point. How far fetch was the concept that someone was writing his story, his life, while someone else was reading and altering it? It didn't make sense, but neither did what just happened back there in the DEA building. Jason snapped out of his surreal daydream, made his way back into the truck, retrieved his cell phone and tried Dave's number again. It rang twice.

"Jason, talk to me," said Dave.

"I don't know what just happened over here, Dave, and I will have to talk to you about that later, but right now, I need you to secure my family."

"Keegan is handling that." Dave replied. "I'm on my way to Chicago. Keegan has agent Terrell and Willingham on the protection detail. I trust them, so should you."

"Dave, just listen." Jason quickly responded, "You were right. None of this feels right. You always said when something doesn't feel right, you go with what you know and feel. Well, this doesn't smell fresh. I know something's wrong, and I feel really bad about it. I'm currently stuck in traffic, and I can't get to my family at the moment—I need you to make sure they're safe. I need you to do it or I fear the worst, Dave. I need you to personally do this for me, Dave. I already feel like it's too late."

Jason could hear Dave letting out deep winded sigh on the other end of the phone.

"What the hell happened over there, Jason? What's going on?"

Jason immediately shook his head as he couldn't even begin to find the right words to describe what he just experienced. There was a struggle within that currently prevented him from dismissing everything that was now slowly consuming him. The feeling suddenly surrounded him all at once and yet, he had no idea how to describe what it was that was happening. He knew something was wrong. He knew none of all that he was currently standing in, felt right. As soon as he exited that room, everything changed, and it was changing more and more with each passing minute he stood outside of the DEA building. It was confusion and enlightenment all in one. Nothing was disorganized and yet, it was all cloudy. He took a minute and let out a few sighs and gathered himself. The air around him felt different. He didn't know what to say or how to say it, he just knew it was all wrong.

"I don't know, Dave." Jason replied hesitantly. "But whatever it was, it's stuck on me. I can't shake it. When I find the words to explain it to you, I'll do so but right now...... my family."

"Where are you right now?" Dave asked.

"I'm about a block away from the DEA building," Jason replied. "But there's no getting to me right now, just get to them. Just get to my family."

"Circle back to the city." Jason heard Dave instruct someone on the other end. "Jason, sit tight, I'll rendezvous with Terrell and Willingham and retrieve your packages. Sit tight and keep your line open. I'll be in touch."

"Listen to me," Jason quickly responded, "I need you to promise me, promise me that no matter what happens to me you will protect them, you will protect my family."

There was silence on the other end of the line, and Jason knew Dave wanted to ask why he was saying what he was saying, but he never asked. Instead of inquiring as to why Jason was speaking so somberly, Dave simply uttered two words.

"I promise."

And with a promise made, Dave ended the call.

Agent Terrell answered the phone and received the instructions given to her from the other end. She nodded as she acknowledged her orders given to her by her boss.

"Yes sir, I understand." she replied nervously as she hung up the phone.

His orders were precise and detailed as to what he wanted her to do with Jessica and Tara. She would follow them to the letter. She glanced over at agent Willingham who was acutely unaware of the orders she'd just received, and she knew it best she kept it that way. On the other end of the phone wasn't her boss—Special Agent in Charge David Watson, but instead—Joseph Serrano, the head of the Serrano Cartel and one of the most notorious Cartel bosses in Mexico.

"We're about fifteen minutes out." Willingham barked into his com.

Agent Terrell didn't know if she was truly prepared to do what she had been ordered to do, but at this point, she had no choice as the Serrano cartel had a chip that she couldn't bargain against; her three-year-old daughter, Chasity, who was taken four days ago from her home. Terrell's first instinct was to get her boss, Dave and her team involved, but was of course threatened not to do so if she wanted to keep Chasity alive. She was all too familiar with this cartel and their barbaric tactics. She was all too familiar with the fact that their victims, sometimes included children. She knew better than to risk it as her daughter's life was already in extreme danger and she wanted to do nothing to further the risk. She simply followed instructions under the promise that her daughter would be returned to her unarmed if she did. Serrano's instructions echoed in her ear; "Take care of your partner and escort them to the drop point."

She had no idea what they would do to them, but right now she didn't care all that much as her judgment had become extremely cloudy. Fact was, she truly did care.

Agent Jason Barrington was more than just a teammate or a co-worker to her, he was essentially family. That's what burned. That's what was emotionally tearing her apart right now, and it was hard to contain her emotions right now in front of her partner.

"Do you know where we're taking them?" she asked Willingham. Agent Willingham immediately simply shook his head. "Nope. Boss said we'd get that info once we have the packages in tow."

Agent Willingham was generally laid back for the most part, but very efficient at his job. He was very tactful and detailed—Dave trained him very well. He was also her friend, but she knew the harsh reality was that in order to get this done, she would have to take him out, and she didn't know how she would live with herself after doing such a thing to someone whom she loved and respected.

She began to feel sick to her stomach. Everything played out a lot smoother in her head the past few days or so, but now that everything was starting to happen, and with her every thought being on her kidnapped daughter, Chasity, and the videos they sent of Chasity on the other end of their guns, it was starting to be too much.

Agent Willingham grabbed his radio COM on his collar. "Five minutes out from retrieving the packages sir."

"Copy." Dave responded.

It was all happening entirely too fast and agent Terrell knew she essentially had no choice if she ever wanted to see her daughter again. As she closed her eyes, she saw her daughter's face, her smile, she could even smell her hair. It was starting to emotionally overwhelm her even more and she knew she couldn't allow her emotions to do that at this point. The packages were tucked away at a downtown hotel as the two agents gradually pulled up to the front of the hotel. "You go secure the packages, I got to hit the men's room." said agent Willingham as he quickly exited the truck. Agent Terrell knew this was a prime opportunity for her to execute her plan and immediately jumped on the opportunity to do so.

"Sure, I'll let you know when I'm headed back down with them" she replied.

Agent Willingham quickly exited the vehicle and
disappeared into the hotel lobby, heading towards the
lobby restroom. Agent Terrell waited until she couldn't
see him anymore as he disappeared around the lobby
corner before she carefully followed behind him, making
sure to keep her distance. She inconspicuously observed
agent Willingham entering the restroom, and immediately
and gingerly made her way up to the door of the restroom
and peeked in. There didn't seem to be anyone else inside
as she slowly and quietly entered the restroom, turning
and locking the door behind her. She carefully peeked
around the corner and saw that agent Willingham
occupied one of the stalls. She quickly made her way
towards the last stall, the stall that was positioned directly
next to the stall that agent Willingham occupied. She
made her way into the stall as quietly as possible and
proceeded to squat down, making sure she not only had a
view of agent Willingham's leg which she did, she
confirmed that his leg was indeed in arm's reach. Once on
the floor, agent Terrell retrieved the Taser from her
holster. She immediately shoved it firmly into the upper
calf of agent Willingham, causing him to immediately drop
to the floor ceasing from the Taser shock. Agent Terrell
held on and didn't let up until agent Willingham was out
cold on the floor. Agent Terrell laid motionless on the

floor as she was in shock and utter disbelief as to what she had just done. It was all too surreal. She had to take a few seconds to calm her breathing and her nerves. She laid there trying to catch her breath, but quickly realized she needed to move fast before agent Willingham came to. She quickly exited the stall and looked around slight franticly. She noticed that there wasn't a closet or anything to drag Willingham into, so she needed to be more creative. She carefully dragged Willingham's body into the middle stall. He was much heavier than he appeared, and it was essentially a struggle to get him into the stall. Utilizing all her strength and leverage to properly lift the seemingly dead weight, she stood behind him and was able to prop him up. She struggled mightily, placing him on top of the toilet seat, positioning him in a way that it appeared he was using the toilet. She locked the stall from the inside and made her way from the stall by crawling out underneath. She wanted it to appear as if he was just another patron occupying a stall and for the most part, it's exactly how it appeared as she glanced back, one last time, as she gradually made her way out of the restroom.

Quickly exiting the rest room, agent Terrell headed for the fifth floor to retrieve the "packages" Jessica and Tara.

"So, where's dad?" Tara asked with a confused look on her face.

"Not sure," said Jessica "He called on his way downtown to the DEA and said someone was on their way to pick us up and take us to him. That's the last I heard from him over an hour ago. He just called a few minutes ago, but the phone rang once and hung up. I tried to call back, but it's going straight to voicemail."

Tara sat quietly on the bed while shaking her head. So much was going through her mind at this point, so much that she couldn't seem to quite understand. She needed her father, she needed him there to comfort her, to talk to her. It was something they both had gotten better at doing with one another over the past year. She didn't understand what was happening—she wasn't sure why they were in the hotel right now. She knew Jessica wasn't being completely honest with her, but she did realize that she was probably doing so in order to protect her, but it didn't make things better, at all.

"What aren't you telling me?" Tara asked. Jessica slowly shook her head but didn't say anything.

"Why don't you think you can tell me what's really going on? You don't think I can handle it?"

"That's not it, sweetie. I just don't, want...... I don't know. I don't want you worrying. I don't want you to be afraid." Tara walked over to Jessica, grabbed her hand, and began to gently rub it.

"The only thing I'm afraid of," said Tara, "is being without my family. I've lost both my mother and father. I'm afraid of that happening again. I love you and dad, and I don't want to be without you guys, but not knowing what's going on, frightens me and I'm not sure how to handle it. I'm missing school, so I know whatever's happening, it's serious enough for me to be missing school. Plus, you're carrying my little sister or brother, and I don't want anything to happen to you."

Jessica noticed Tara becoming emotional as tears begin to fill her eyes. Nodding her head, she wanted to do nothing but comfort her. Jessica nodded her head and figured now was as good a time as any to at least tell her why they were there.

"Tara, we're here because......"

** KNOCK KNOCK **

The loud knock on the hotel door startled both of them.

"Who is it?" Jessica cried out while quickly retrieving her 9-millimeter and immediately began checking her magazine.

"Agent Zoe Terrell. Jessica, I work with Jason and Dave. I'm here to escort you and Tara to a safe location."

Jessica remembered agent Terrell, distinctly. It was a few months ago when she visited Jason at his office and the whole team was there. Looking over at Tara, Jessica could see the fear on her face. She knew Tara had an idea that they were in some sort of danger. She knew there wasn't much she would be able to consistently keep from her at this point, but her first instincts and her first responsibility was to keep her safe.

Jessica gave Tara the "what do you think?" look. Tara hesitantly returned the gesture with a shrug. "Where's Jason and Dave?" barked Jessica. She'd crept closer to the door, her weapon pointed to the ground, ready to take an offensive position.

"They're both waiting on you at the rendezvous point. They won't let me know where that is until I have you guys secured." Terrell bellowed from the other side of the door. Jessica nervously glanced at Tara who nodded her head as she began grabbing their bags and reaching for the Kevlar vest. Jessica made sure her 9mm was secured in her holster on her hip. She opened the door with the 9mm in her hand, finger on the trigger. "You have to forgive us," said Jessica, "At this point we have every reason to be paranoid and don't know who to trust."

"I understand," agent Terrell said, as she carefully surveyed her surroundings while ushering the two women out of the room and into the hallway. She tried to remain as calm as possible, but felt her stomach turn every second she thought about what she was being forced to do. She led the two of them out of the hotel, and inside the truck where she once again assured them of how safe they were. Jessica was extremely nervous and kept her hand gripped on her 9mm. She didn't want to appear too nervous in front of Tara, but she knew Tara was already cognizant of the tension within the situation.

"I just got the rendezvous directions from Dave," Terrell stated as she pulled away from the hotel. "We'll be there in about thirty minutes. Your cell phones, I need you to remove the sim cards and destroy them, immediately. Jason believes the GPS signals may have been compromised."

Tara glanced at Jessica who nodded her head in agreement with agent Terrell as Jessica understood that this was anti-tracking protocol. Both Jessica and Tara

quickly complied with agent Terrell's orders. Terrell put
the truck in gear and headed down the highway with the
packages in tow and their fates seemingly sealed.

The turbulence was just a bit uneasy. I glanced out of
the window and noticed we were flying through a bit of
thick clouds, as the plane gradually began making its way
above them. It was this area over the Pacific in which the
clouds were higher than usual. I noticed it every time I
made this trip. As I gazed out over the clouds, I found
myself thinking about where I was in *Jason's Story*. It was
starting to become clear to me as to why the recording
showed only the last minute or so of Jason's meeting with
the strange man in the interrogation room. I believe that
the information that he shared with Jason was truly only
meant for Jason and myself. It was all becoming so clear
with every turn of the page. Whoever or whatever sent
that stranger to share that information with Jason, did so
fully knowing that I would read everything that was being
said and would provide me with a perspective that would

either break me or fuel this "guidance" or influence I had over Jason, but the question remained as to "why?"

As I stared out of the airplane window, I wasn't exactly certain how I was truly feeling at this point as I was simply taking everything as it came. I felt as though Jason, even without my guidance or influence, was beginning to question and accept some things he normally wouldn't. There were some things that stood out to me right away within the chapter I was currently reading. Jason entered the DEA building and mentioned how the streets were clear, no traffic. Now, he walks out of the building and suddenly there's bumper to bumper traffic due to some construction. I didn't trust this "traffic jam" and it felt strange and eerily intentional, as if it was purposely placed there to prevent Jason from moving forward to do anything, like get to his family. I was afraid of what would happen next, what I would read next if Jason sat there simply waiting on it to clear up, even though I knew it was likely that it wouldn't clear it. If Jason and his family were meant to meet their demise in this story, it sure as hell wouldn't be while I was stuck with this ability to do what it was that I was doing.

This theory that whoever created, wrote or was writing *Jason's Story*, wanted Jason and his family dead, was just that—a theory. But I figured it was now time to test that theory. Part of me didn't understand why, if the writer or creator of this story wanted certain characters dead, wouldn't they simply do something that would instantly kill them? Why not simply just write in a hurricane or a tornado and take out whomever they wanted to? Why the show and dance? Why string it along? It was all so confusing but challenging at the same time. I felt as though I was up for the challenge. I was no longer afraid, even though I believed, because of everything surrounding this immensely incredible experience, I had every reason to be afraid, but I wasn't.

Jason's family was in danger, and he had no true idea as to how close to home the danger to his family now lie. I needed to get Jason to his family, in order for them to have a chance. I had to get Jason to understand the severity of the danger his family was now in. I also reflected back to earlier points in the story, in which I discovered that Jason only accepted logical guidance from me and simply trying to somehow make him somehow "know" what was going on with his family, wasn't an option as that method had yet to work thus far. I needed to logically guide Jason into thinking what I needed him to think in order to save his family. **This had become more difficult than I ever thought it would. The initial feeling of "amazement" and shock from what I was experiencing with this device and this story, had now been replaced by stress and doubt. I knew if I were to put this story down, this device down, Jason and his family were dead. I knew that Jason told himself that he didn't believe what the man in the interrogation room told him, but I also knew that Jason shared with Dave earlier that he felt 'different.' The way he described his feelings.

The euphoric, surreal, mind-opening feelings he was experiencing, were eerily similar to how I was currently feeling. That was enough for me to believe that Jason should have no problems understanding and utilizing the small logical steps I would provide for him. It at least gave me a bit of hope. This traffic jam Jason was sitting in didn't sit well with me at all. I distinctly remembered Jason stating how clear the traffic was on his way to the DEA building. Now all of a sudden, the traffic jam? It certainly didn't feel right, and it shouldn't sit and feel right with Jason either. The last thing I wanted was to continue to read and death suddenly sneaks up on Jason knowing fully well I could've prevented it by simply opening my mouth or my thoughts to help guide him adequately. Was this the reason I was reading this story? To help this man, this character, navigate through his own story that was apparently already written?

I knew Jason was thinking hard on what the strange man shared with him. I knew he had to feel what I felt about this sudden "traffic jam." I glanced down at the Nook and closed my eyes.

"Jason, begins to open his mind like the strange man insisted and he realizes that this traffic jam isn't what it seems and begins to question its legitimacy."

I slowly opened my eyes, took a deep breath like I was getting ready to do something that required a decent amount or energy or adrenaline, and I immediately jumped back into the story.

Jason's Story—Chapter Eight – Continue

"Open your mind agent Barrington."

The strange man's words lingered around in the halls of his mind. How does one open their minds? Jason thought to himself. It sounded like something easier said than done. Jason closed his eyes, sighed and imagined his mind literally opening up. The result was instant and surreal. Quickly opening his eyes, Jason understood that opening one's mind was as simple as literally doing the exact action, subconsciously, with no thought behind it.

The feeling he'd been experiencing for quite some time now seemed to have been magnified now with him opening his mind further. Looking around; it was starting to get increasingly difficult to shake this feeling that this sudden "traffic jam" didn't hold any true logic with it. Clearly it was more than what it appeared to be. Prior to going into the building, Jason didn't remember seeing any construction that had such a tight jam, but now all of a sudden, here it was. Jason nervously smiled as the feeling of light paranoia suddenly draped over him, but it was now coming to that point in which he was now fighting against his own instincts and his training. Dave taught him to accept and trust his instincts. He taught him to give everything and everyone the benefit of the doubt until they leave you no other choice. Jason was beginning to feel as if maybe, he was trying too hard to dismiss what the strange man shared with him—dismiss his instincts. The more he thought about what the man said, the more logic started to creep into the picture, into his mind. Ever since he woke up in that hospital bed and was given that news that his family was dead, his mind had a feeling of elevation, as if it was on a different level of thinking, and he had no way to explain it or no one to share it with that would possibly understand.

This feeling to Jason, was like a mixture of being medicated, and the surreal moment he witnessed as a kid, waking up to snow on Christmas morning. It was a weird sense of elevated euphoria wrapped tightly around an unforgettable daydream that he was seemingly unable to shake loose from. But this feeling hasn't gone away, and ever since it fell over him, it's as if he grasp and understood everything clearer, faster and better than at any point in his life. Which made the continued dismissal of the strange man's words, slightly illogical and difficult to understand. He realized that he was using more energy in trying to dismiss or refute the strange man's words and not taking time to logically put it together from every angle and aspect. It was as if he was having a hard time trying to come up with a logical reason as to why this man was lying or why none of it made any sense. The moment he stopped, thought for a brief second on why what this man shared with him the information he did, his mind didn't waste any time putting it all together in a way that made it easy to accept.

He closed his eyes to slow his thoughts down, right now, one thing didn't seem plausible at all, and that was this "traffic jam" due to "construction." Jason looked at his cell phone and dialed ASAC Robertson's number. It rang three times.

"ASAC Robertson here."

"Robertson, this is Agent Barrington here..."

"Agent Barrington, you got that statement ready to send over yet?"

"No sir, not yet." Jason replied, "Sir, I don't know if you heard what happened at my house this morning, but I was attacked, along with my fiancée. Something is happening and I need to make sure my family is safe."

"No, agent Barrington," Robertson responded, "I hadn't heard what happened. All we heard that there was an incident involving an FBI agent this morning, I assume your department wanted to keep specifics under wraps for

good reason. What is it that I can do for you, agent Barrington?"

"Well, there is a traffic jam due to some construction right around from your building sir..."

"Construction?" Robertson quickly uttered behind a confused tone. "When there's construction this close to us, we are made aware beforehand, as it affects a lot of how we handle things from a security standpoint. This is news to me. I haven't heard anything. Where are you?"

Jason nodded his head at what the ASAC was sharing with him now. It somewhat confirmed his suspicions. This wasn't a traffic jam—there was something more happening here.

"What the hell is going on?" Jason softly whispered to himself as he gradually yet nervously gazed around at all the cars that surrounded him as if they held some sort of answer.

"What was that, Agent Barrington?"

"Nothing. Sir, I need your help to get to my family as soon as possible and if I don't, I fear the worst."

"You fear the worst? Why? Where is your family, Agent Barrington? What's going on with them?"

Jason took a deep breath, as he wasn't sure how to answer Robertson's questions. He wasn't quite sure where they were, considering he hadn't received that information *from Keegan yet, which was standard protocol even for family members. They were likely still in transit to their secure location and protocol stipulated in situations like this, locations used for protection, weren't disclosed until the packages were actually secured in the locations. But this was different. He needed to secure them now, before they got to their location. He no longer trusted anything at this point and outside of Dave, he didn't trust anyone – not anymore.*

"That's just it sir, I don't know where they are, but I know they're being taken to a secure location, and I fear soon it may be too late. I don't know what's going on, but this morning I was attacked at my house, and now I fear for my family's safety."

Robertson took a deep breath.

"This is highly irregular, agent Barrington. But, if you're asking for my help, if you're telling me that your family needs your help, I won't say no. I trust agent Watson, so I trust you. Look around and tell me if you see the Thomas Raine Memorial Park?"

Jason glanced to his left and noticed the park on the other side of the street.

"I do." Jason replied.

"Get to that park. A helo will pick you up from the north field and take you where you need to go. I'll have one of my agents' get your vehicle back where it belongs."

Robertson took a moment to pause and took a deep breath before finally exhaling.

"Agent Barrington—what you did for agent Merriweather that night, this doesn't even come close to repaying that debt. His daughter, the one you saved that night? She's my Goddaughter. She is going into her second year at Stanford right now because of you. I owe you agent Barrington, and one helicopter ride to help you secure your family doesn't make us even. I don't think there's anything that I can do to truly repay you, agent Barrington."

The emotion in ASAC Robertson's words was sharp and precise.

"Thank you, sir." Jason quietly and emotionally whispered into the phone before ending the call. Jason caught himself becoming slightly emotional and tearing up as he listened to Robertson.

He quickly gathered himself as he made his way to the back of the truck to retrieve the G-36 assault rifle from the trunk storage compartment, secured it on himself as he put on his FBI field jacket to conceal the weapon. As Jason gradually sprinted over towards the park, he found *himself starting to panic just a bit. He took a deep breath to help calm himself. Standing in the middle of the field, as he waited for the chopper, Jason noticed the clouds becoming thicker and the sky becoming darker. He glanced down at his cellphone and tried calling both Jessica and Tara's phones, repeatedly—both lines repeatedly went straight to voice mail. That didn't help settle his restless and troubled spirit. He tightened his Kevlar vest and checked his ammo. The sounds of the helicopter could now be heard in the distance. Wasn't too long before he was able to spot the DEA's helicopter headed directly towards him coming in directly from the south.*

Agent Terrell raced down the busy late evening highway, acutely cognizant of the fact that she was thirty minutes past the rendezvous time Serrano had given her. The time she was given to make contact with Serrano's men in order for them to receive the "packages."

Terrell gazed up towards the sky and noticed the dark storm clouds increasingly making its way over the area.

Serrano's top guy had already been trying to reach her for the past twenty minutes. Calling her back-to-back as she was supposed to have handed the packages off to them at the rendezvous point by now. She didn't answer their calls and she knew they would soon start to question her commitment to the agreement. She was fairly certain that they not only knew of her whereabouts, but they were probably trailing her right now. She gazed through her rear view, she didn't see anyone following her, but didn't notice the SUV in front of her gradually slowing down, causing her to quickly slam on her brakes. The truck maneuvered around the side of agent Terrell's SUV, abruptly slowing to get even beside her. The driver inside signaled for her to pull over, but Terrell pretended not to see him and continued driving. Terrell sped up in an attempt to get ahead of them and somehow lose them, but they managed to keep pace with her. Pulling up right beside her, they rolled the windows down. She thought about calling backup, but she'd put herself in such a precarious situation with no out, that it was impossible for her to envision a scenario in which she got out of this without getting arrested or killed. She accepted her fate either way.

"Agent Terrell, pull over now!!" the passenger barked out towards her as they raced side by side down the

highway. Glancing over at them, Agent Terrell gave no response or indication that she'd heard them. She continued to race down the highway, pulling ahead of them once more. She peered through her rearview and saw them pulling back. They trailed her for about five minutes before returning to her left side, as she glanced over, she immediately noticed the passenger hanging out of the window with what appeared to be some sort of automatic weapon. Terrell didn't have time to react as the gunman immediately let off shots into her tires, causing Terrell to instantly lose control, forcing the truck to flip uncontrollably off the side of the highway. Agent Terrell felt herself going airborne, upside down—it was all happening so fast.

The crash was instant and rough as the SUV ended upside down after tumbling over several times. Though in pain, agent Terrell was conscious and somewhat cognizant of her surroundings as she was still strapped to her seat by way of her seat belt. She immediately heard cars honking as they sped by, but even though she was upside down, she immediately noticed the two men from the truck rapidly approached the vehicle, carrying automatic rifles aimed directly at the vehicle.

Agent Terrell began to reach for her semi-automatic weapon, but the pain in her shooting arm was intense and caused her to scream out in pain as soon as she tried making a move for it. The two gunmen paused for a moment upon hearing her scream. The first gunman hopped down into the ditch and proceeded to open the door to remove the "packages" from the back seat. He struggled to get the door opened as it had jammed after being upended but, he eventually managed to jar it open. Aiming his assault rifle inside, he immediately realized that there was no one in the back of the truck. The gunmen immediately gazed up at his partner, bewilderedly. Enraged, the first gunman immediately opened Agent Terrell's door, reached in and begin dragging her out into the ditch. The pain was intense as agent Terrell let out screams of pain while being dragged onto the side of the vehicle. She had suffered a broken arm and collarbone and multiple lacerations over her face. The pain was multiplied after being dragged onto a clearing off the side of the road.

"Where are they?!" The first gunman barked. Agent Terrell didn't respond. The pain made it somewhat difficult to respond and focus as she simply stared at the two men and shook her head.

"Agent Terrell, where are they?"

"Go to hell!" she huffed hesitantly through bated breaths. The first gunman began shaking his head as he kneeled down next to her.

"So unwise, agent Terrell," he calmly whispered. "Your daughter will die. Don't be stupid, one call from me and..." he paused, giving agent Terrell time to truly understand what was happening.

"Where are they?"
Emotion and dread overwhelmed her at this point. Between the physical pain, the thought of her daughter being killed, and what she was being forced to do, her emotions had reached a boiling point. The first cartel gunmen stood up shaking his head as he smiled.

"You're a fool, agent Terrell. We're going to cut your daughter up, and send you the video, this is your last chance, where are they?!!" Shaking her head, Agent Terrell closed her eyes and begin to weep.

"You go to hell!" she repeated, as tears made their way through her tightly closed eyes.

The second gunman slowly stood up, retrieved his phone from his jacket pocket, begin dialing a number, and gradually placed the phone to his ear.

"This is on you." he said while smiling.
With the phone to his ear, he started to speak the words that would end the life of Agent Terrell's daughter. Agent

Terrell cried out and shook her head as the vision of her daughter's lifeless body bounced around in her head. She shook her head repeatedly as she was in a state of extreme denial at all of this at this point.

"No!! No!" she yelled while slowly shaking her head. Fighting every urge and emotion within herself, she couldn't bring herself to beg them to stop. She refused to open her mouth. She'd had enough at this point, she was exhausted. She couldn't beg them to not make the call, but she knew deep down, what she was now doing, it was the right thing. She closed her eyes and began to talk. She said a prayer for her little girl, for Chasity. God was the only one listening at this point. She had already decided that she wasn't going to hand them over before getting the call from Serrano.

She had spent the entire night prior praying and asking God to receive her daughter into his arms. She spent the entire night prior; crying, praying and accepting her circumstances—this was her fate. She remembered the pain Jason had suffered through after losing his family and there was no way she would do that to him again. She would rather die willingly than to have Jason suffer that pain again much less be personally responsible for it. She was much more hesitant in regard to Chasity's life, but her options were limited, and Jason and his family didn't *deserve this, no one did. She had accepted a lot about death during the ordeal she experienced with her first daughter, Miracle, a few years back. She was afraid but committed to her decision.*

"The girl," the gunman began.

"No!!" cried Agent Terrell instinctively.

"Then give me what I want!" he calmly ordered.

She shook her head and closed her eyes.

"No. I won't"

The gunman placed the phone back towards his mouth.

"The girl. I need you......."

Agent Terrell wept as she waited for him to speak the rest of the words, but he never did. He was unable to finish his words as he was instantly interrupted by the bullet that ripped through his chest and the second one that entered the back of his head and exited the front. The phone fell from his hand, and he immediately dropped to the ground. The second gunman attempted to quickly hide behind the overturn truck but didn't make it far as the next bullet quickly tore through his thigh. He immediately dropped to his knee, screaming in pain and begin to wildly return fire from his automatic rifle in the direction from which the shots were coming from as he continued screaming, hitting a few passing vehicles in the process. Two more bullets entered the scene as they found their target. Entering the gunman's chest, the force from the bullets leveled the gunman off his fee. He was dead before he hit the ground. The pain was extreme for agent Terrell, but she was fully aware of what was happening. The crash caused some head trauma as blood dripped over her eyes blinding her view a bit, but she managed to lift her head up, as painful as it was. She managed to lift her head just enough to get a good look across the busy intersection. She spotted someone standing on top of a vehicle, aiming what looked to be an automatic weapon in her direction.

As she focused her eyes and her sight became clearer, she realized instantly that it was Dave, her boss. He stood firm across the four-lane highway as cars sped by while others begin stopping to render aid. Gripping his automatic rifle and holding his focus, he continued to aim the weapon without blinking or budging; waiting to see if the threat had been eliminated.

The samaritan's voice got closer and closer.

"Mam, are you ok? Mam?"

The voices from those approaching to render aid, along with the approaching sounds of sirens, was the last bit of sounds agent Terrell heard before passing out.

Jason's thoughts suddenly raced down a deserted highway within his subconscious at a thousand miles per hour. A highway blanketed by an immense shade of darkness. A metaphoric yet vivid night sky filled with endless stars, planets, and galaxies. He gazed up at the night sky within his subconscious looking for answers that clearly couldn't be found out in the real world, outside of his mind at this point. Something was happening and the more he stood still and began to reflect, the more that fact became increasingly evident.

Though his mind was racing, it somehow found a way to gradually slow down just enough to comfortably sow everything that happened in the past few hours, deep within the fertile soil of his subconscious, instantly reaping "answers" that seemingly had no place in earthly time or space. So lost within himself, the sound of the approaching helicopter didn't seem to be enough to pull Jason out of his deep thought and extreme focus. Standing in the middle of the park, his physical eye locked in on the city's evening skyline. While he subconsciously focused his mind on the night sky above the highway, his mind found itself slowing down. He found himself quickly reflecting on everything that had transpired over the past few hours or so, in an attempt to piece together logical and solid answers that would help alleviate the confusion he was suffering from.

The unlikely experience of getting attacked twice in one day, having to kill twice in one day, along with being told that his life essentially wasn't real, and everything he's ever known was, is practically a lie, kept his mind temporarily cemented in a place that he now found extremely difficult to pull back from. The sound of the helicopter got increasingly closer and louder as it made its way closer to its target. The pilot had no trouble spotting the lone FBI agent wearing an agency issued jacket in the middle of a seemingly empty evening park field. It was Jason who was the one that wasn't as cognizant of his current surroundings as he usually was, as cognizant as Dave trained him to be. The approaching helicopter wasn't enough to break Jason out of his deep and surreal concentration, but the phone vibrating on his hip was. He instantly glanced down as he retrieved his cell phone. It was Dave.

"Dave? Talk to me."

"I need you at St Luke's Hospital immediately." Dave stated firmly. "The team is on their way to get you."

"What do you mean? Why?"

"There was an incident, Jason. You aren't safe out there right now. It seems Joseph Serrano is out for you and your family. "

"Joseph Serrano?" Jason barked under a confused tone. "What? Dave, where's Jessica and Tara?!"

"I don't know," said Dave. "Agent Terrell and Willingham were escorting them to the safe house when they were attacked. Jason listen to me; Agent Terrell was compromised."

"What do you mean "compromised"? What's going on? Where is my family, Dave?"

"Agent Barrington, listen to me. Agent Brask and Willingham are currently en route to get you. Do not move. They are headed towards the direction of the GPS signal on your SUV."

"That's not necessary, ASAC Robertson has already sent a helicopter to come get me and take me to find my family."

"Agent Barrington listen to me; the DEA and the FBI have been compromised. I'm not saying Robertson has been, I'm just saying, now isn't the time drop your guard.

Do not get on that helicopter, do you copy? Do not get on that chopper!"

Upon hearing those words from Dave, it seemed as if the sound of the helicopter instantly got louder. Part of it felt as if it was primarily in his head, but he wasn't certain anymore. Jason immediately turned and spotted the helicopter getting in position to land.

The story was hard to turn away from at this point. I found myself understanding what Jason was feeling and going through, to a certain extent. The feeling of not only uncertainty, but also confusion, can weigh heavy on one's mind especially when you begin to question everything. It seemed as if, in the process of attempting to take it all in and make sense of everything, he was unintentionally letting his guard down and putting himself at more risk than he needed to. The story itself was already trying to kill him, he was essentially making it easier for it to do so. I shook my head as I realized this wasn't going to be difficult, it was going to be virtually impossible. Trying to keep this man and his story, alive, I was up against it all, and I was struggling in trying to determine what obstacle I needed to focus on and knock down first. Jason was dealing with unknown variables and factors, and if there was a time, he needed to keep his guard up, it was now. I closed my eyes and began to contemplate on what I needed Jason to do before reading another word.

I needed him to stay alive and the best way to get him to do so, was to make sure that he remained aware of his surroundings. I understood the need for him to simply stop and think in order to attempt to figure out what was happening, but it seemed he was doing it at the wrong times considering the risk he was dealing with. I figure I try to get him to raise his awareness at least for the moment. I spoke the words as if I were a filmmaker directing a scene.

"*After hearing Dave's words and warning, Jason immediately becomes more cognizant of his surroundings. He keeps his guard up. He remembers his training. He remembers who he is.*"

I finished whispering the words as I slowly opened my eyes and returned to the story.

Jason's Story - Chapter Eight – Continue

The sound of Dave's voice was rapidly getting drowned out by the sound of the approaching helicopter. Jason slowly pulled the phone away from his ear and immediately begin to become instantly cognizant of his surroundings, something he realized he should've done as soon as he entered the park. He was in no position to drop his guard at this point. Dave's words weren't expected, but he had received them loud and clear.

The agencies were compromised, his family was unaccounted for, and his team's loyalty was now an immediate concern—possibly even Dave's at this point. It was all becoming so clear, the louder the helicopter got—it was about seven feet off the ground at this point. It was as if the propellers from the helicopter were somehow blowing away the clouds and dust that covered the unguarded spaces in Jason's mind and begin to rapidly and somewhat thoroughly clear a path for his mind to receive whatever the universe was sending. The words of the strange man from earlier began to play back in his mind. They had attached themselves to the insides of his mind and he was picking them apart word by word, line by line;

"Open your mind Jason, your life and your family's life will depend on you consistently doing so from this moment on, I assure you it will."

The words were so vivid, it was as if he was hearing them in real time. That feeling; that weird, euphoric, unexplainable feeling of mind opening surrealistic subconscious weightlessness he'd been experiencing, but ignoring for quite some time now, was not only deep and enriching, but it had a very good piece of his thoughts, of his mind right now and it wasn't letting go.

The park was wide open. Too wide. Not only was it wide open, but it was currently, conveniently empty. Not a soul in sight, and prior to the helicopter arriving, he didn't pay attention to how eerily quiet it was. Probably didn't mean much but could very well mean a lot. Jason gripped the G-36 automatic weapon from his waist and instantly placed his finger on the trigger as the helicopter landed on the ground about twenty feet to the left of him. Under normal circumstances, he would block the wind from the propeller from hitting his face, but now it was as if he didn't feel a thing. He was so dialed in and focused on his surroundings; it didn't matter.

Everything moved in slow motion. He wasn't missing anything as he was seeing everything. He'd already dropped his guard and walked right into the middle of something he should've picked up minutes ago. He immediately began to formulate options to now rectify his mistake.

Immediately, his peripherals picked up movement from the bushes about fifty feet in front of the helicopter, to his far right. Peering to his right, in the direction of the movement, Jason had trouble making out who it was exactly, but it was clear their movement was hostile. It was more than one, aggressively heading in the direction of the chopper and Jason. Jason immediately signaled for the pilot to take off. Oblivious to what Jason was instructing him to do, the pilot continued to wave Jason onto the chopper. Jason immediately sprinted towards the chopper, made it to the door, and quickly swung it open

"Get the hell out of here! Go, NOW!" he yelled as slammed the door shut.

The pilot didn't ask any questions, he saw the panic on Jason's face and immediately took off. As the chopper gradually lifted off the ground, it slowly revealed the other side of the park, and it also instantly revealed four armed men who immediately raised their weapons, aimed, and began firing in Jason's direction. No time to return fire with the G-36, Jason immediately dipped to his right towards the heavy bushes and dove over them as he took cover from heavy fire.

The park was surrounded by office buildings on all sides with a busy intersection wrapped loosely around it – in the middle of downtown. Jason quickly surveyed his area as he used the thick bushes and tall cement flower beds to hide and began to access his surroundings. There was no way to run toward any of the buildings, or even the intersection without running in an open field without cover. It was practically dark out at this point so nighttime was a small ally, but if he was a betting man, and this were Serrano's guys, they were most likely equipped with night vision equipment. The gunfire continued, but the muffled sounds indicated that there were silencers attached to the weapons. It was a sound that Dave taught them how to recognize, Jason was fairly good at it. There was the park bathroom about thirty to forty feet in front of him. It was made of brick. If there was any viable place to make a stand, it would be there. No time to waste, Jason immediately hopped up and sprinted towards the bathroom as the gunfire returned in his direction.

He dropped, rolled, and zig-zagged to keep from giving them something easy to hit. Hitting the corner of the park bathroom, Jason immediately took cover as the gunfire once again ceased. There would be nowhere left to run except out of the park from this point. Ahead of the bathroom, it was about one football field length of nothing but open green that led out of the park to the main street. Jason knew if he made a run for it, the odds of him getting hit were high. Odds were, even by accident, with as much time they would have, he would get hit. Carefully, he peeked around the corner as the gunfire began again, hitting both sides of the park bathroom. There was no legitimate way to get out of this, at least none that he could see. Going inside of the bathroom wasn't an option as it would essentially trap him like a mouse. Running full speed toward the other end of the opened field was suicide. That option was out. He would have to go out fighting. Jason checked the ammo in his G-36, full clip—one to spare in his jacket pocket, plus a standard issue semi on his hip with two clips on his person and full clip in the mag.

Jason closed his eyes and immediately saw the faces of Jessica and Tara. The faces of Tracy and the boys were right behind them as he held his eyes closed. The sound of footsteps approaching, as the crunching of the park leaves grew louder and closer. His phone suddenly vibrated—it had enough force to garner his attention as he quickly reached for it. It was agent Brask.

"Man, where the hell are you?!" Jason whispered loudly into the phone.

"Twelve-o-clock." Brask quickly replied,

"What?!" Jason barked.

"Dude, look to your twelve—genius."

It was dark, but bright enough for Jason to immediately see agent Brask standing at the edge of the park next to a black suburban. Someone was on top of the suburban, Jason couldn't exactly make out who it was.

"Barrington, you have rapidly approaching heat on your six. I don't have a clear shot. You got to step out. Give them something to hit."

"Yeah, no shit!!" Jason shouted nervously.

"I need you on your feet and to run this way now," ordered Brask. "I need you to flank toward your left when you hit the green, and stay hitting that direction, almost like running a post pattern in football, do you copy?

"Copy!"

Jason didn't question or second guess. He had nothing else to lose at this point. He understood he would be dead if he continued to sit there. Jason understood that the post route agent Brask wanted him to run was a tactic the team learned in training with Special Ops. Brask needed a clear line of sight to chop down the threat that surrounded Jason and running the post would help clear up the sight and keep Jason out of harm's way. He immediately got up, ran, and hit the post, full speed. The gunfire from behind Jason began briefly, but the group on his rear immediately caught the heat from the rapid fire from the direction of agent Brask and the suburban. Jason stopped and turned around as all four gunmen were on the ground. He sprinted towards agent Brask as he immediately spotted agent Willingham jumping down from a top of the suburban with his fingers still gripped on the SR-25 Sniper Assault Rifle. Jason didn't say anything as he was out of breath and his heart still racing. The only thing he could do was wrap his arms around both of his teammates and hugged them.

"Nice shooting." Jason said to agent Willingham. "It's what I do." Willingham responded behind a confident smile.

"Come on," said Brask. "We got to get you to St Luke's."

<u>Chapter Fourteen</u>

I Forgive You

<u>Jason's Story - Chapter Eight – Continued....</u>

*T*he smell of the hospital room was all too familiar to agent Terrell. It was practically her second home nearly five years ago while her daughter, Miracle, was housed on the Oncology ward for close to four months. She got used to the smell during her daily visits, until she couldn't smell it anymore. That smell was the primary reason she hated and avoided hospitals now, and it would always be synonymous with Miracle's trial she went through during those four months before her passing. That same smell was what seemingly woke her from her deep sleep. She didn't feel any pain but felt the drowsy effects of apparent pain killers. Opening her eyes, she immediately noticed Dave standing over her.*

"How you feeling?" Dave asked. Agent Terrell didn't answer, but simply nodded her head as she began to tear up. "You should've let them kill me. I fucked up."

He had seen a lot in his tenure as Special Agent in Charge, and even more as the leader of this particular unit. Even in his years as a special agent, he had seen and been through some things that some agents would probably never be able to wrap their minds around. A young special agent coming into the bureau during the Cold War, there wasn't much that he hadn't seen or much that he didn't know how to handle, this however, was something different.

He had always had a sharp handle and tight grip on his team. It was the reason he had garnered so much respect from them and from the higher ups in the bureau, but when he peered into agent Terrell's teary eyes, he knew he had missed something. That was difficult for him to admit. He knew what he was getting from agent Terrell right now, indicated that there was something deeper in play here, something she wasn't telling him.

"Talk to me Terrell, what am I missing here?" She began to weep as Dave gingerly held her hand. She calmed herself a bit and began slowly shaking her head. "You remember when I lost Miracle four years ago?" she asked softly.

"I do," replied Dave. "I remember you showing all of us what strength really was. I remember that very well."

"When Miracle passed, it turned me inside out, but I knew I needed to keep my head above water and not drown because I wanted to live and not die. When Chasity was born, it gave me something other than my career, to live for. Everyone knew what Miracle's death did to me, and everyone knew just why that made Chasity immensely vital to my wellbeing. Which is why I know that Chasity being kidnapped five days ago wasn't a coincidence. They knew how important she was to.... "

Terrell paused, and begin to breakdown, finding it difficult to even continue.

"Whoever did this, they knew I would do anything to get her back, even if it meant betraying you and this team, betraying even my own family, which is essentially what I did."

Dave closed his eyes and shook his head. He knew it was something bad, but not this bad. This was "worst case scenario" bad and here it was, staring him right in the face. He realized that what she was saying was painfully accurate. If someone had taken her daughter, it was only because they knew she would crawl through hell to get her back because of what she'd experienced in losing Miracle a few years back. Dave knew it also meant that someone on the inside had provided the kidnappers with that information.

"How bad is it?" Dave replied. "What are we dealing with?"

"They took my baby," she cried. "They took her and threatened to kill her if I didn't give them Jason's family. I couldn't tell anyone, I couldn't say anything, or they would kill her. I can't lose her. I couldn't handle that sir."

Terrell wept as she covered her face with her hand. Dave closed his eyes and lowered his head. He realized Serrano's reach was long but didn't think his team was capable of getting touched. He had a hard time dealing with the clear possibility that his naivety and misjudgment, not the Serrano Cartel, may have been the biggest threat to everything he stood and worked so hard for. He continued to peer into Terrell's eyes and wondered if he himself wouldn't have done the same if he were in Terrell's position.

"What do they know?" he asked.
Terrell slowly shook her head.

"I don't know, but I gave them Jason's address. I don't know what we're going to do. I didn't know anything about what happened at Jason's house today. I was supposed to take Jessica and Tara to a drop off location to hand them over to Serrano's men, but that's when you *found me on the side of the highway. I just couldn't do it. I knew what I was doing would destroy Jason. He too had suffered unimaginable loss, and it wasn't fair for me to be the reason he did so again. I suddenly was willing to let my daughter go in order to make things right, and right now I don't know what's going to happen to her. When he was making that phone call to kill my baby, just before you shot him, I saw my life and her life flashed before my eyes."*

Terrell continued to weep as Dave grabbed her and hugged her. He hadn't really hugged anyone like this in years, since hugging his daughter Maggie after his wife passed a decade ago. Dave felt himself becoming overwhelmed with emotion. Overwhelmed partly because of how much it hurt to see Terrell, an agent he became extremely closed to during the ordeal with her cancer-stricken daughter, cry out like this. He also understood that if she was taken across the border, then it would be very difficult to get her back.

This was an extremely fine line that could potentially affect diplomatic relations between two countries if it got out. Dave realized that this would be something the government wouldn't entertain as far as negotiations go, despite the fact that agent Terrell was one of their own; it wouldn't matter. Before Dave could say anything to her, she gingerly laid back on her bed and closed her eyes, weeping, as Dave held onto her hand.

Agent Terrell woke as she felt someone holding her hand, quickly looking over, she expected to see Dave still standing there, but instead saw Jason.

"How you feeling?" Jason whispered.
Staring at Jason's honest face, agent Terrell instantly become consumed with guilt and emotions. She closed her eyes and slowly shook her head. It was the only "response" she could muster up at the moment.

"Boss said the Doctor said you're going to be fine mam," he said with a grin on his face. "You're tougher than this and have been through much more than this. What actually happened out there?"

Jason had a look of deep curiosity on his face. Terrell knew she owed him all, including the truth. She shook her head while letting out a long emotional sigh, dreading what it was that she needed to say. She understood that she had to tell Jason everything, no matter how hard it was to admit her betrayal.

"You've been through a lot with losing Tracy and the boys, and what you went through afterwards—my heart. I wept for you every night after that. It hurt me because over the past eight years we've become close, like family and when you lost them, I felt as though I lost a piece of me as well."

"Zoe, I know this. I do. You're going to be alright. You're going to bounce back from this."
She gripped his hands tight as she began to stare deeply into Jason's eyes—unable to hold back her tears. She shook her head. Jason was a bit confused by her demeanor, but not too confused as he knew, and understood her being shaken up after what she had just been through. He also knew she had seen a lot of action in the field before. This was different, deeper, and infinitely more emotional.

"Zoe, what's wrong? What are you holding on to?" Jason asked, confusedly.

"What did Dave tell you?" she replied.

"He didn't tell me much. Just said you were going to be fine and that you needed to talk to me when you woke up. He's down the hall briefing the rest of the team. Should I go get him?"

"No." she quickly replied as she shook her head. "Don't"

She closed her eyes. What she needed to tell him wasn't coming so easy. It wasn't something that was easy to say. She lowered her head while slowly shaking it, but Jason didn't release the grip he had on her hand. He didn't know what this was and why agent Terrell was in the extreme emotional state she was, but he knew he wouldn't leave her until she told him. Holding on to her hand as she held her head down and quietly wept, Jason glanced out of the room window. He noticed that the city's night skyline was more illuminated than ever before. The day's events were still playing back in his mind, and he hadn't even taken a moment to breathe. As he gently rubbed agent Terrell's hand, Jason could feel the pain that weighed on her, but there was more. This wasn't as "simple" as it appeared to be, and his opened mind wouldn't allow that feeling to escape him. As he caressed her hand, he began to slowly put together pieces within his mind. Pieces that he probably normally wouldn't be able to put together. His mind, in its "new" state had no trouble gradually putting it together the more he thought as he stared out of the window. He turned back towards agent Terrell as she stared up into his eyes.

"Zoe, look at me." he gently grabbed her face and guided up so that her eyes locked on his. "Zoe, where is Chasity?" his eyes locked in on hers. "Where is she? Is she home?"

Shaking her head, the tears begin to flow harder and faster.

"I need to know if you forgive me?" she asked as her eyes remained tightly shut. Peering down at her, Jason nodded his head. He felt his eyes slowly closing as he began to try to understand the root of agent Terrell's question. It only took a brief moment of dedicated focus and concentration as it really wasn't hard for his mind to piece together what was actually happening. Didn't take much to put together why Dave wanted him to speak with her alone, why she was as torn up as she was considering any other time, she was as tough as anyone he'd ever met.

Jason was very skilled at utilizing the simplest context clues to adequately survey scenes or situations and utilize them to his advantage but, with the elevated levels his mind was apparently working on as of late, this one was fairly easy—yet, it was the hardest. He didn't find it necessary to make her repeat what he already knew.

"I need you to forgive me, Jason. I love you and would never do anything to hurt you, but I've done something unforgiveable, and I need you to forgive me for that."

Jason gazed at his emotional and tearful teammate, friend,

family of eight years, and simply nodded his head as the tears began to fall down his face as well.

"I forgive you Zoe.' he said behind a smile, "I do." They embraced for about two minutes as she wept on his shoulder, until she forced herself away from his embrace and looked him in his eye again.

"Just tell me," Jason asked. "Are they alive? Are they safe?"

"Your family is safe Jason," Terrell replied. "I made them dump their phones and sent them North. I gave Serrano their numbers, so they were tracking them up until I had them destroy their sim cards from the phones. I have no idea where they are. I told Jessica to get somewhere safe and contact you or Dave when they did. I instructed her to stay off cell lines and to only call your or Dave and not to trust anyone else."

Jason let out a sigh of relief. He knew Jessica would take care of them until he was able to get to them. It burned, realizing that once again he had placed his family in harm's way. He had a hard time shaking the guilt. With Jessica being pregnant and Tara probably being afraid, it was difficult for Jason to not to assume and fear the worst, but with all that on him, he was more concerned with agent Terrell's current situation.

*"I thank you for that, Zoe. I do. But Zoe, I need you to tell
me where your daughter is. I need you to do that for me.
Where's Chasity?"*

Terrell shook her head slowly as the tears fell freely.

*"I don't know. I don't know where she is. I know that
I have to accept the possibility that she's probably dead.
She paused, as the pain saturated her entire existence.
Everything that she was unable to hold onto in that
moment was eating her from the inside out.*

*"It burns just thinking about it, Jason." She whispered.
"I don't want to think about it anymore. I just don't want
to even think about anything anymore."*

*As he peered intensely into her eyes, the look of
genuine uncertainty and unfiltered dread washed over her
face. Her hurt and pain was achingly evident to Jason. She
was not only scared, but it was as if she was defeated. Her
soul was slowly leaving her body. She laid back down on
the hospital bed as the nurse came and in appeared to
inject something into Terrell's IV as she continued to
weep.*

*"She'll be asleep soon." the nurse whispered as she
nodded at Jason.*

*Staring down on her, Jason stood there next to her
bed, holding her hand as she gradually cried herself to
sleep. It was one of the toughest things he had to witness*

as of late, considering he was all too familiar with the immensely painful, emotional, and dark foundation in which her now burning soul had been structured on. Staring down at her as she slowly drifted off to sleep, Jason immediately noticed Dave standing outside of the room, motioning for Jason to join him outside.

Jason gently laid agent Terrell's hand down on the bed, leaned over and gingerly kissed her on her forehead. He quickly made his way out of her room as he could see the somber look on Dave's face.

"Talk to me Dave. What's going on?"

"I believe your family is safe. We were tracking the GPS on the truck. We lost the signal near exit 42 on highway seventy-five north. You have any idea where they might be headed?"

Jason immediately shook his head.

"I know Jessica's parents had an old house up for sale in the country, somewhere in the north near Gaylord, but we never made it out there together, so I don't know its location or anything. She only brought it up once or twice, it's off the grid—kind of. My guess is, that's where they'd be headed."

Dave instantly retrieved his cell phone and placed it to his ear.

"I need every address on file for agent Jessica Phillips and her parents for the past twenty years."
Dave ended the call as he looked curiously into Jason's eyes.

"What's the play here Barrington? Why do I have this feeling there's something you're holding back from me? What's going on?"

Jason closed his eyes and sighed. He didn't know exactly how to express to Dave how he was feeling. He'd tried before and Dave brushed it off and didn't understand. He knew Dave could see the concern on his face, there was no way to hide it.

"There is something I know I have to do," said Jason as he continued to gingerly shake his head with his eyes closed.

"But I don't know why I feel as though I have to do this." Placing his hand on Jason's shoulder, Dave struggled in attempting to figure out what was actually happening with Jason. Nothing felt normal to him, and Jason didn't appear to be the same agent he'd known for the past few years or so.

"Talk to me Jason," Dave whispered. "I can't know what this is if you don't talk to me."
Slowly opening his eyes, Jason could see the sincere sentiments that sharply outlined his boss's face.

"I don't have the energy to adequately express what's happening to me, Dave," Jason replied. "And I don't even know if I want to anymore. I just feel so different at this point. I've felt this way since after trying to kill myself. I don't know what this is or what's going on, I just know no one will understand and maybe no one is supposed to."
Dave suddenly retrieved his cell from his pocket and began reviewing the information that was just sent to him.

"We have three addresses on file for Jessica and her parents. There's an old house that's apparently on the market up in Gaylord. That's right off of highway seventy-five, in the country. That's our best play."

Dave had already turned down the hall to assemble the rest of the team: Agents Brask, Burba, and Willingham. They immediately made their way down back towards Jason as they were prepping to leave–preparing to find Jason's family. They headed for the exit, but before Dave could reach the exit door, he realized Jason wasn't behind him–he was still sitting in a chair outside of agent Terrell's room, staring aimlessly into the room.

"Agent Barrington," Dave sharply chirped. "We have a chopper en route, let's go."
Jason slowly peered up and began shaking his head at his boss.

"What about agent Terrell, sir?

Dave shook his head and took a deep breath as if he had been dreading having to discuss this.

"That's going to be left up to the Director and the Section Chief." Dave replied. "It's out of our hands. It has now become a diplomatic concern that is beyond our reach."

"Sir, I don't agree with that." said Jason through a sincerely agitated tone. "I think we need to do something."

"What will you have me do, agent Barrington? Huh? There's rules and protocol for this and this is the one time we must follow them, for the sake of her daughter. To at least give the girl a chance."

"No." replied Jason as he stubbornly shook his head, "if you do this Dave, the girl won't make it and you know it."

Dave paused and closed his eyes as he sighed frustratingly.

"She's as good as dead, Agent Barrington!" Dave whispered. "You and I both know when she made that deal with them, what the end game was. She should've come to me. I can't help her now. I can, however, help your family."

Jason nodded his head as Dave words bounced around his mind, but in no way was he in total agreement with his boss, his friend, his mentor. At this point, Jason found himself still trying to make some sense of the day he was having and tried desperately to mentally place it all in a box, to sort out but his mind was moving entirely too fast to do so. He knew he needed to get to his family as they certainly needed him, but it was no longer that simple.

"Dave, I can't think that way. I just can't. I need to ask you for the........"

Pausing, Jason shook his head as tears suddenly filled his eyes as what he was about to ask Dave was immensely difficult and seemingly impossible to put into words, but he knew what he wanted to do, was what he had to do.

"I need you Dave, to trust me more than you ever had at any point since I've been a part of this team. I need you to trust me more than you ever had at any point since you've known me. I need that from you Dave."

Dave stared at his agent of ten years with a blank empty gaze as he sighed. He squinted his eyes as if he was looking through Jason's soul, trying to get a better understanding of what was happening here. Slowly nodding his head, Dave closed his eyes.

"Ok Jason," Dave huffed, "I trust you. You know that."

"Sir, the Bird is here!" Agent Brask's voice echoed through the com.

"Copy." Dave quickly replied as he remained focused on Jason, waiting for a response.

"Talk to me Jason, what is this? You need to tell me what this is because right now, we need to be out there finding and securing your family. Why are you standing there hesitating, son? Whatever this is, you need to tell me, and make it make sense."

Jason shook his head unsure of what to say as he sighed and closed his eyes. The words were there. The thoughts were there. The logic was there but none of it made sense on the surface—only internally.

"I don't know....."

Jason paused. He struggled, in this moment, to piece together what was needed to convince David to support the unthinkable.

"Dave, I need you. I can't make this make sense because I'm still struggling to do so myself. My family needs you and I need you to promise me that you will protect them like your own. I need that promise from you."

Dave emotionless yet steady gaze was still fixated on Jason's face as his confusion was topped only by his intrigue. He didn't blink, or so much as breathe heavy, as he found himself focusing in on Jason's eyes. He didn't know what this was or what was happening, but whatever it was, he knew it was real, at least in Jason's world it was. Jason's eyes told Dave everything he needed to know.

"Ok Jason." Dave whispered through a confident nod. "I'll do that, now do something for me. Tell me just what the hell all of this is. Can you do that for me? Help me help you. Trust is one thing Agent Barrington, but I still need to understand. Will you ever be able to tell me what the hell is going on with you, son?"

The look on Dave's face as he spoke wasn't that hard for Jason to read or understand. It was one of clear genuine concern, love, and also confusion.

"Just give me something—anything," Dave continued. "To help me understand what you're going through, to help me understand what this is. I need to know if this is something real or something I should be worried about."

The look Dave was giving him gave Jason chills. He realized that Dave was thoroughly confused. Jason hated not being able to truly express what was going on with him to his closest confidant and mentor, but what was happening was too much, too heavy to put into words.

"All I know is, whatever this is Dave, it's bigger than you and I. Just the past few hours or so, I've come to the inescapable conclusion that there are things we'll never understand, and were never made to understand, but we don't have to understand those things to realize it's about everything that's greater than us."

Pausing, Jason pointed towards Agent Terrell's room and closed his eyes as his emotions began to gradually swallow him.

"That woman in there. My friend, my partner, my family—she has suffered enough. When she lost Miracle, you saw how far over the edge it pushed her. I can't stand here, selfishly and think about what I'm dealing with without constantly coming back to what she's currently consumed with. She needs us. She needs me and I need you."

Dave smiled and slowly nodded his head as he slowly digested Jason's words. He understood what Jason was trying to get through to him. He didn't' necessarily agree with it but he understood.

"I trust you, Jason." Dave finally replied. "I've seen a lot the past thirty years, and believe it or not, you're showing me something new. Congratulations, son, you're the first to do that in two decades. I understand. I get it. I trust you. Now tell me what it is you want to do."
Jason rubbed his chin, thinking heavily. He nodded his head as he peered deep into Dave's eyes.

"Chasity," Jason replied softly as he nodded his head. "I need to bring her home."

Jason's Story – Chapter Eight—The End

Chapter Fifteen

Ciudad Juarez

I had missed the Captain's announcement that we were headed for a rough patch due to inclement weather. The turbulence was consistent and slightly rough, seemingly deriving out of nowhere. We were a little past Hawaii at this point, essentially halfway through the flight. It was still pitch black outside the window, but the raindrops could be seen with clarity.

"Once again, we apologize for the bumpy ride. We're going to try to get above this to smooth it out for you. Thanks for your patience."

The captain's voice echoed clearly throughout the plane. Looking over at Bradley who appeared to be reading, he must've saw me gazing over at him as he slowly turned towards me and smiled.

"How's it coming along?" he asked behind a subtle grin.

I honestly didn't know what he believed he knew, but apparently, he knew quite a bit, and that was ok. It was ok because he seemed to not only understand everything I tossed at him, but in a way, it felt as if whatever I was currently experiencing, he was more in tuned with it than I was.

My erratic behavior, this impossible story, this unlikely ordeal, it all seemed to somehow tap into some immensely passionately curious side of him that had likely always been there. Though there was seemingly no doubt that there was a bit of skepticism, concern, and doubt within him in regard to it all, he was now aware of its reality in my world. Deep down, I knew *he* knew that whatever this was, it was real, it was bigger than us, and it was really happening. I finally shook my head in response to his question. That brought about a smile from him. The turbulence shifted my focus from the end of the last chapter, but only for a moment.

Jason and his story quickly returned to my mind again. If I admitted that I agreed with Jason's decision to go after agent Terrell's daughter instead of focusing solely on his own family right now, I wouldn't be telling the truth. On the other hand, if I tried telling myself that I didn't understand why he decided to do it, I would also be lying to myself. In the depths of my mind, my personal pain and personal loss, seemed to factor deeply into this "understanding" I had for Jason in deciding to do whatever he could in order to try to spare agent Terrell from what looked to be inevitable, unspeakable, unimaginable pain.

The fact that this woman had already suffered an unimaginable loss with the death of her first daughter, coupled with what I was dealing with personally, in the deep parts of my subconscious, I was actually satisfied, and in a way, relieved that Jason decided to do this. Admittedly, I didn't see this coming from Jason. Very surprising, but I understood.

"Thank you," I calmly replied, as I gazed over at Bradley while slowly nodding my head.

Bradley looked at me and didn't even pretend to not understand why I was thanking him. I figured we were way past that at this point. Pretending to not understand why I was really showing gratitude, would be insulting to both of us and slightly counterproductive to anything we had discussed at this point. He knew why. He was a very wise man, and I knew that he had no problems reading through that "*thank you,*" but his expression didn't change. If he was reading through it, he was doing a fine job at hiding it.

"Steve; you don't have to do that." he calmly whispered.

"Just know that whatever it is you're currently dealing with or experiencing, there's a reason for it. You will have to find out what that reason is, even if it takes you the rest of your life to do so."

I knew that as uncluttered as my mind had apparently found itself on this current "journey" I was experiencing, I would probably truly never understand what any of this was or its purpose—if there was even a purpose to any of it. Deep down, I knew that at some point, this would all come to an end, and all of this would simply just go away, and there would be no more to it. No purpose, no reason, no cosmic life lesson planted here by some unseen force, and ultimately, no point. I also knew however, that at this point, essentially anything and everything was possible, and my mind had waged such a battle within itself the past twenty-four hours, that I now felt it was prepared for any and everything.

"Thanks for.......I don't know, believing in me?" I replied. The emotion in my voice was evident as I spoke. I knew Bradley could feel it. I heard it. I felt it. A soft smile gently flashed across Bradley's face as he carefully removed his glasses.

"Steve, it'll probably make things easy for you and help you with whatever you're dealing with if you start to believe more in yourself and what you're capable of despite what you're personally going through. Easier said than done but, difficult times are universally designed to not only test us but help us evolve while bringing out the best in us in the process. At least that's what I've always believed."

The look he gave me confirmed my thoughts. I believed that though he lacked precise and exact details of what I was dealing with, he was probably more cognizant of my situation than he let on. His words however also indicated that in a way, he not only understood in his own way, what was happening to me, but none of what I was conveying to him didn't appear to come across as unusual or even strange to him. I wasn't sure what that meant, if anything at all.

"Steve, I'm not going to ask you about this story you're reading again, but if you have any questions, or if there's anything I can do to help, I'll be right here, next to you. At least for the next seven hours I will."

His smile was comforting as he placed his glasses back on his face, turned and focused his attention back on his work, and placed his headphones back into his ears. I stared at him for a few more seconds but found myself actually daydreaming, thinking about his words. I didn't know how well I was handling this. How does one actually handle something so unbelievable and practically impossible? I'd done a surprisingly solid job at not breaking down so far, but with the unpredictability of the entire story, I wasn't sure how long I could keep it all together.   There would be no "breaking" on my part—not from this. What awaited me at home—that was something different, something I wasn't looking forward to. Something I knew could potentially break me and quite honestly, something my mind had temporarily drifted away from, primarily due to this story. I noticed that the plane had apparently made its way above the turbulence as the calmness had returned to my surroundings. My mind began focusing on Jason and what he was planning to do. I was highly intrigued about his incredibly bold decision to help Agent Terrell. I knew it would probably be somewhat simple to logically influence him out of this decision as it wouldn't be too hard to get him to "understand" how important it was to make sure that his family was safe again, but I wasn't going to do that. I was going to allow this to play out the way Jason wanted it to. I would remain steadfast. I was torn in my decision to do so, but I wasn't going to waver.

As a father who had recently lost a child, I realized I not only understood what agent Terrell was going through, but as I read through the story, I passionately and emotionally empathized with her to the point that I could feel the burn from within her. The same burn I felt when my world came crashing down just two days ago. It still burned. It's likely a feeling that never goes away, and I didn't expect it to, anytime soon.

The fact that Agent Terrell had lost a daughter to cancer, really had a lot to do with my understanding of Jason's decision. The feeling of the unimaginable pain and unthinkable torture that had befallen agent Terrell, had tightly wrapped itself around my heart. It felt as if the heartbeats were magnified immensely. If she lost her daughter Chasity, a few years after losing her first daughter, Miracle to cancer, it would undoubtedly put her in a place that she would never be able to return from. If I even attempted to stop Jason from trying to prevent agent Terrell from experiencing that kind of immense pain and severe soul shattering despair, it would simply defeat the purpose of me holding this device in my hand and trying to adequately put this story together for this character, this man, for so many reasons, and I couldn't escape this feeling.

This—whatever this was, it was clearly about more than just Jason. That started to become clearer the more the story progressed. I sat back and closed my eyes. I found myself contemplating deeply on how this story, this man's life, a life that I was currently a part of, if given a choice, I probably wouldn't want anything to do with. This story impacted more than one character, more than one person. It impacted those on the pages of the story and those outside of it. If that wasn't clear to me before, it was unquestionably clear to me now. Opening my eyes, I woke the Nook up out of its sleep and just for standard practice, I attempted to navigate to the next chapter, chapter nine. Just like the six previous chapters before, it wasn't there. I carried my eyes up towards the ceiling of the plane, exhausted. I took a deep breath and exhaled as I closed my eyes, tight. I wanted Jason to at least really think about what he was wanting to do before actually going through with this. I would have him at least do that. I believe I owed him and his family that much. I owed all of them the courtesy of trying to see if making this move was what he really wanted to do. This decision he was making carried a lot of weight with it for various reasons and had the potential to invite more life-threatening dangers into his life. I owed it to him and to his family to see if this was something he truly wanted to do or if he was diving headfirst into this because of the way his mind was operating, and he was more emotional than he realized. I wanted him to understand and essentially think about the potential repercussions of his actions no matter which way he decided to act. What else did I need to say? I quickly spoke the words.

"Jason takes a moment, thinks logically about his decision to help agent Terrell, and how it will affect his family."

Opening my eyes, I immediately placed them on the Nook. The way the notification appeared reminded me of the old eight-ball I had in high school. I spoke and the notification appeared—no shaking required. It was surreal on every level, but the shock phase had passed. I relaxed myself in my seat and jumped back into the story...

Jason's Story—Chapter Nine

The meeting with Dave's colleague—Travis Miller, was to be held under the Yarborough Street Bridge. Jason stopped in agent Terrell's hospital room by her bed as he gently rubbed her face. The face even seemed to frown as she slept. God only knows the nightmares she was currently having right now. Nightmares no loving parent deserved to have. As he glanced down at her face, he began to think about what he was about to do. He wanted to think about it logically and make sure he was doing the right thing, but he knew there was no legitimate way to determine what was right or wrong at this point. It was all about what made sense and what didn't, and it didn't make sense to stand idly by while his friend lost another child, especially if he had a chance to do something about it.

"There is no logic to any of this anymore," he whispered as he continued gently rubbing her face. "I'll bring her back to you. I forgive you." Jason leaned over and gently kissed the forehead of agent Terrell, made his

way out of agent Terrell's room, ultimately out of the hospital, and immediately made his way to the meet with Dave's longtime colleague, Travis Miller.

Dave reached out to Miller, albeit apprehensively, after realizing just how serious Jason was about his decision and realizing that there would be no changing his mind. Dave had introduced the entire team to Miller about six years ago, but never really disclosed what it was that he did exactly. It was known that Miller was ex- Military Intelligence—twenty plus years on the job, and he and Dave served in Desert Storm together. Dave talked highly about Miller, talked quite a bit about him, and held him in high regard. Like Dave, he was "old school," but very wise, savvy, and knew a lot about a lot.

Dave never confirmed, but Jason always knew that Miller moonlighted as a "cleanup" guy. A silent mercenary for hire for high level, unknown US government officials that wanted "jobs" done off the record. He was really good at what he did. Miller owed Dave quite a bit as Dave provided Miller with valuable federal intel that helped with his assignments, yet Dave was never one to call in a favor unless he really needed to. This was the one favor he wouldn't hesitate to call on as he understood that Jason was his best and smartest agent. He wanted him to have the best possible chance at success.

Dave, agent Brask, agent Burba, and a few other agents were already on a chopper headed north to find Jessica and Tara. Jason made his way toward the Yarborough Street Bridge, under the cover of night. He couldn't help but to think about his family as he drove closer to the bridge. No man in their "right" mind would make this decision, but Jason knew he was no longer in his "right" mind. It was tough for Jason to deal, but he trusted Dave more than he trusted himself. Dave promised him that he would get them and protect them, and Jason knew he could hold Dave to that, despite what had happened in the past. That promise made his decision to help agent Terrell that much easier. Dave's words echoed through Jason's head as he made his way to meet Miller; "He has a team he works with—they don't play by the same rules we do."

He was on his way to meet Miller and Miller's trusted team. There was no doubt in Jason mind that the tactics Miller and his team utilized were frowned upon, unconventional if not, illegal. Jason never brought it up or talked about it with Dave because Dave never brought it up or talked about it and there was probably a good reason for that. Jason knew two things regarding Miller—he was good at what he did, and his services was apparently in high demand.

A matted black truck, presumably Miller's, pulled into the empty lot underneath the bridge about twenty feet away from Jason's vehicle. Jason pressed lightly on the gas and slowly made his way towards the vehicle as he pulled up to the driver side window.

"Get in." Miller instructed, as he continued staring straight ahead.

Jason didn't waste any time as he put his car in park, exited the vehicle and made his way to the passenger side of Miller's car. Miller immediately put the truck in drive and began to slowly drive away from the lot, away from the bridge. The silence was deafening. The faint sound of the engine was the only thing that could be heard as the two men made their way down the highway. Jason glanced over at Miller inconspicuously out of the corner of his eye. Miller stared straight ahead. No expression, no facial movement, nothing.

"Dave said you were instinctive," Miller finally uttered without taking his eyes off the road. "He also said you were sort of a maverick."

"Oh?" Jason replied while shaking his head, "Not sure how true that is. I believe in getting things done that need to get done, just like Dave. And from what I hear, just like you."

Miller glanced over at Jason and cracked a small grin. He was clean cut, older gentlemen. He appeared to be in solid shape. Jason wasn't certain, but he knew Miller was around the same age as Dave. There was a bit of gray that canvassed parts of Miller's hair and beard, but not much. Miller extended his hand towards Jason. Jason didn't waste any time returning the gesture as the two men shook hands.

"I never said being a Maverick was a bad thing." Miller uttered as he raised his eyebrow and returned his focus back on the road. "I need to introduce you to the team. That's where we're headed now."

The ride was short. It took about ten minutes to reach the meeting point. They pulled into the parking lot of what appeared to be an old drive-in movie theater. Jason immediately noticed a black SUV parked in the middle of the parking lot which appeared to have a few occupants inside.

"These guys are all pros." said Miller as he continued to look straight ahead towards the SUV. "Two of them are retired Navy Seals. One of them is retired Military Intelligence and served under me for about five years. The other is CIA—he specializes in Intel and other shit, and he's arguably the most important member of my team. Miller slowly turned and gazed at Jason.

"I don't really know you, but I trust and owe Dave. I owe him and then some, so when he called and asked me to take lead on this, I didn't hesitate. He assured me that you are more than capable of handling yourself. That's good, because a job like this requires us to get in and out while keeping our heads on a swivel. This is short notice, agent Barrington, but this is what we do, how about you? You really prepared for what has to be done here?"

Jason gazed out of the passenger window as he pondered on Miller's question. It was a valid question but deep down he knew that this was something that he had to do. He wasn't about to sit around and allow agent Terrell to have to pay for whatever was happening in his life or apparently his 'story.' There was no way he would sit by doing nothing and simply wait for this pain, this hurt, to find its way into agent Terrell's world. He wasn't sure why he was thinking the way he was thinking, but his mind wouldn't allow him to walk away from this right now, and it was difficult in trying to fully understand why. Jason turned slowly to face Miller as he began to nod his head.

"Yes, I am," Jason replied confidently. "Will you help me?"

Miller smiled. The smile was genuine. He slowly nodded his head as he reached above the visor, retrieved a manila folder, and handed it to Jason.

"*Cyprus, my intelligence community asset, has intel that suggests the girl is possibly being held in Ciudad Juárez, Mexico.*"

"*How did you come across this Intel this fast?*" Jason quickly replied. "*And what kind of intel?*"

"*Well, agent Barrington, we're very good at what we do,*" Miller replied. "*But this one we can thank Dave for. Apparently when he saved agent Terrell yesterday, one of her attackers placed a call out to someone that has the girl. Whoever that person was, they answered, and that's all we needed. The call was traced directly to a location in Ciudad, from that phone call.*"

Jason held the map up towards the car light, immediately noticing the red circle around a location inside the city of Ciudad Juárez.

Miller continued...

"*Satellite imagery suggests that there hasn't been any movement in or out of that property at all since the number was dialed. Which means, dead or alive, the girl is likely in there, and since they haven't heard from who they needed to hear from, my best guess is; they have her alive while awaiting instructions. It's only a matter of time before they realize those instructions aren't coming, and when they do, they will kill her.*"

Miller paused as he looked as if he wanted to continue speaking but paused to collect his thoughts.

"You are correct agent Barrington," Miller continued.

"We won't be waiting around to do this. We leave tonight."

Jason slowly looked over at Miller as Miller peered back at him. Jason knew Miller was most likely testing him. The test to see if he would flinch upon hearing they would leave right away, a tactic utilized by Jason when interrogating suspects for as long as he could remember. Introduce a potential stressful situation to a suspect to gauge their reaction. Jason didn't flinch, he didn't even blink.

"So, I guess I should meet everyone, yes?" Jason replied. Miller nodded his head as he immediately flashed his lights. The occupants of the SUV began slowly exiting the vehicle and collectively made their way in front of the truck. Miller introduced Jason to each of them. Jason surveyed the entire group as they were being introduced. They all looked the part, but for a job like this, nothing short of dedicated and slightly unstable pros would suffice. They all seemed focused and dialed in on Jason's stance, expression and demeanor—they were well trained. After about ten minutes into the meet, it was clear that they were pretty sincere and committed in getting the job done. On the surface, Jason wasn't sure, in such short notice, how Miller was able to get his group's commitment in doing a job like this for someone they didn't even know, but Jason found himself impressed. He knew it was very possible to step outside oneself for the dedication and commitment towards others, he made a career out of it.

The group: Case Bradford and Ty Ford were ex-Navy Seals, ex-Military intelligence officer Harry Raymond and a CIA contact that went by the name of Cyprus. They were all aware of the risks, aware of the fact that this was strictly off the books. They were aware that if they were caught, it could potentially damage the relationship between two allied countries. They were aware of the fact that not only their freedom and lively hood was at stake, but undoubtedly their lives. But Miller seemed to have already garnered the unwavering commitment from each one of them. Each one of them considered the risk to save the child, very much worth it. It was a group fitting to do some effective damage and frankly that's exactly what was needed to get this job done at this point. Jason recognized the serious, intensely focused looks on the faces of the team. It was the same look his team exhibited when preparing to do their jobs. Miller gradually walked back towards the driver side of his truck and opened the door.

"We leave in an hour." Miller said as he hopped into the vehicle.

The team quickly made their way back toward their truck as Jason made his way onto the passenger side of Miller's truck.

"We have a Jet ready at Grady Airfield," said Miller.

"You sure you want to go ahead with this? She could already be dead. You thought about that?"

Jason glanced out of the window as he contemplated heavily on Miller's question. He of course had already thought about this possibility and found himself struggling to dismiss it. But that thought, as morbidly depressing as it was, it wasn't enough to deter him from going through with it. Jason slowly turned towards Miller and nodded his head.

"Yes, I have." Jason calmly responded. "She needs to be back with her mother one way or another. We bring her back, no matter what. I can live with trying and failing."

Miller slowly and confidently nodded his head to acknowledge Jason's words.

The flight into El Paso, Texas was about three hours from Michigan, but it was enough time for Miller to go over the plan with Jason and the team.

"Listen up." Miller barked, as he stood in front of everyone. "Once in El Paso, we will rendezvous with an asset of mine who will get us about five clicks outside of Ciudad Juárez. We'll post up at a designated spot just outside the city and we'll set up there. This is a sensitive extraction. We protect the package at all costs. She won't be able to protect herself, so we have to be cognizant of that while extracting her. We shoot to kill, and we watch each other's back. Options gentlemen are always great, but not making it back home......."

"*AIN'T ONE OF EM!*" The group barked in unison. Jason was admittedly nervous considering he was getting closer to the only real action he'd been a part of in about two years, not counting the attack on him and Jessica, and of course getting shot at in the park. Jessica and Tara weighed heavily on his mind. He couldn't help consistently wondering if he was doing the right thing or not. Every time he closed his eyes, he saw their faces as if they were standing directly in front of him. He knew and trusted that Dave would do everything in his power to see that his family was safe. He had no doubts about that. Silence fell over the team as they all sat quietly loading and checking their weapons as the plane rapidly pushed its way to El Paso.

The late-night drive to the country was a calm and peaceful one for what was undoubtedly a long, stressful day for the two ladies. Jessica didn't ask any questions when agent Terrell told her what to do. For some reason, looking into agent Terrell's eyes, she knew at that moment, she had no choice but to trust her. She saw the sincerity when she looked into them, she saw the fright, and that was enough for her not to ask questions.

"I'm so sorry!!"

Agent Terrell's chilling last words to her and Tara, after instructing them to get into a truck and drive away. Those words haunted her as she gazed into the horizon that stretched across the highway as she and Tara headed north up the highway. She and Tara had been driving for about an hour, headed north towards her mother's old house just outside Gaylord, Michigan. It wasn't her mother's house anymore. She had moved her mother closer to her and was in the process of selling it.

"Where are we?" Tara whispered softly as she began awaking out of her sleep.

"This is my home," said Jessica behind a smile. "Where I grew up."

Tara surveyed the property as they slowly pulled onto it from off the highway. The scenery instantly reminded her of stories she'd read when she was younger, stories set in surreal country settings. It was night, but the house had adequate lighting that lit the property well. In the back—a lake with ducks walking freely about. A tire swing hanging from a tall oak tree on the other side of the pond. A deck that led out into the pond like she had seen in the movies where kids would get a running start and launch themselves into the water. Just looking at the property made her smile, made her feel good inside. It made her forget about the world, if only for a moment.

"What's so funny?" Jessica asked.

"Nothing." Tara snickered. "It's just, this place. Reminds me of a place where I always wanted to live. This is the place that was in my dreams, in the stories I read. I wish I grew up somewhere like this."

"Well, I was supposed to sell it," said Jessica. "I just hadn't gotten around to finding a buyer for it. Would you like it if I didn't sell it, and we made this place our home instead?"

Tara's smile widened but pulled back as if she was careful not to get too excited. This was something she now did unconsciously. Her way of proactively protecting herself, protecting her emotions.

"That would be awesome." Said Tara as she fought back a smile.

"Ok," said Jessica. "When this is all over, I'll discuss it with your dad and see what he says. But if that's something that you really want, then I think I can probably convince him."

Pulling around to the back of the property, Tara realized that the back yard was bigger than she initially thought.

"Wow! This back yard is huge!" Tara exclaimed.

"I know, right." Jessica replied. "When I was younger, my parents would have events and functions back here. I even remember them bringing a mini carnival back here to celebrate my middle school graduation. I invited all of my friends. It's something I'll never forget, and I want you to have memories that you'll never forget, good memories, lasting memories."

Tara smiled at Jessica as Jessica maneuvered the truck to a complete stop near the back door of the house.

"I'm so glad he found you," said Tara. "He truly has been a different person since you've been here. When I first came to live with him, he wasn't the same person you see now. He's happier. I can't wait until my little brother or sister gets here; I know that will make him even happier. I never knew my brothers all that well before they died, and my biological father didn't have any other kids."

Jessica could see the emotion on Tara's face and felt it in her words. She knew they both were under enough stress. She knew she needed to keep Tara encouraged and uplifted.

"I know you're going to be a great sister," Jessica quickly replied. "You're already a wonderful daughter, a wonderful person."

The quiet atmosphere was deafening to Tara as they exited the vehicle and made their way into the house. It was something she wasn't all that used to, being from the city. The air itself smelled differently. The sky even looked different. The way the wind brushed up against her skin wasn't the same. She gazed at Jessica walking in front of her and immediately noticed the Kevlar vest she was wearing and the 9-millimeter semi-automatic weapon in the holster on her hip.

"Do you do the same work as dad?"
Jessica chuckled.

"Not really. Not anymore, I used to. I used to be out in the field doing what your father does, but not anymore. I lost my father a few years ago and while he was sick, I asked to be taken out of the field, so I'd more time to *spend with my mother and ailing father. I didn't want that burden on my mother. So now I do a lot of work. I'm what you would call an "analyst." We basically have the important job of sitting around behind a desk being extra bored all day."*

They shared a laugh at Jessica's expense as they gradually made their way into the house. The beeping from the alarm commenced almost as soon as they stepped into the house, as Jessica immediately went over the wall near the kitchen and immediately turned off the alarm.

"Well, this is home." Jessica said, smiling.
Tara walked gingerly toward the living room and slowly sat down on the couch. The troubling look on her face was immediately noticed by Jessica as she made her way over to her.

"What's wrong?" she said as she sat down next to Tara.

"I'm scared," Tara whispered, "We haven't heard from dad in a few hours and that's not like him. That lady in the truck was acting so weird and so scared when she was telling us what to do and where to go. I don't know why, but I'm scared."

Moving closer to Tara, Jessica gingerly wrapped her arms around Tara and embraced her. "Want to know something? I'm scared too. It's perfectly normal to be scared in uncertain situations, but you know what? I'm not going to let anything happen to you, I promise you this."

Tara appeared to be somewhat comforted by Jessica's words as Jessica continued to embrace her. It had been a while since she had been embraced by someone that genuinely cared about her, but Tara quickly began to remember what it felt like as Jessica held onto her. She remembered this feeling from when her mother use to provide her with the same type of affection and comfort years ago. For quite some time, she feared and accepted the fact that she would never experience this type of feeling, this type of love and affection again, but here it was.

Here was the woman her father had fallen in love with, holding her, comforting her like she was her own daughter. It was hard for Tara to completely understand this, but the only thing she knew, and felt right now, was loved. That was the only thing that matter, that was the only thing that pushed away the fear.

"I stay here sometimes while we're out here doing repairs on the place," Jessica said as she peered around the room.

"And we usually keep some frozen food in the deep freezer. What say we raid the deep freezer to see what we can whip up for dinner?" Jessica asked as she still held on to Tara. Tara nodded her head.

"Sounds good to me."

The stars had blanketed Jessica's country home on this mild summer night. Inside the house, Jessica and Tara begin preparing themselves a meal after a long day. Outside—one of the six gunmen that were already on top of the property, quietly and gradually made his way to the front of the house to try to get a peek inside. The gunman and his four cohorts were carrying automatic weapons. Peeping inside of the house, he didn't see much movement in the front room, but he could hear the faint voices deriving from the kitchen. He signaled for three of his teammates to circle around to the back and side of the house and the fourth, he signaled for him to stay put. Their orders were clear; apprehend the two women alive. Jessica dropped a handful of fries in the deep fryer.

"I used to love making French fries with this old deep fryer," she chuckled. "The fries would come out perfect every time."

Digging her hand in the fresh batch that Jessica just dumped out, Tara couldn't wait as she grabbed a few hot ones and begin throwing them in her mouth fighting through the heat in order to enjoy them. Jessica giggled as she watched Tara attempt to maneuver the fries around in her mouth in an attempt to combat the heat.

"You should see how funny you look with those fries dancing around in your mouth like that." Jessica said while laughing. Placing the empty plate down next to the deep fryer, Jessica slowly walked over to Tara as she removed her Kevlar vest.

"Hey, I wanted to see how this vest fits on you." she said to Tara as she held the vest up in front of Tara. Tara didn't have much of a reaction to Jessica's unusual request. It wasn't as if she asked her to try on a necklace or a pair of pants. Tara felt as though it was truly an odd request.

"Oh, ok." Tara replied, as she lifted her hands so Jessica could get it on her. Carefully fastening the vest around Tara, Jessica secured it before stepping back and nodding her head in apparent approval.

"How does it feel?" Jessica asked.
Tara began rubbing her hands over the vest while looking down at it, admiring it like it was a dress.

"Feels fine. It's kind of tight and feels snug." she said while rubbing it.

"Can I take it off now?" she asked while smiling.

"NO!" Jessica barked in a sharp tone. Her sharp response startling Tara.
Tara's smile quickly faded. She glared at Jessica and started to ask why she couldn't remove the vest, but before

she could get the question out, Jessica grabbed her hand tight and immediately pulled her closer to her so that Jessica's face was merely inches away from hers.

"Listen to me," Jessica whispered. "I need you to go downstairs in the basement. My father's old office is down there, directly towards the back of the basement. I want you to go in there, lock the door, and don't come out until I come get you, only me, no one else you understand?"

"No, I don't. Who else would......."

"What did I say about trusting me, Tara? I need you to trust me, and no matter what sounds you hear you don't come out."

Jessica words were clear and stern. She saw the fright on Tara's face as she kissed her on her forehead.

"Go. Now." she said while motioning towards the basement.

Tara gradually moved towards the basement and turned and looked at Jessica. "Go!!" yelled Jessica. Quickly turning and opening the basement door, Tara turned back towards Jessica.

"I love....."

Tara started but was interrupted by Jessica's abrupt aggressive actions. Jessica swiftly unholstered her semi-automatic weapon from her holster, aimed it at Tara's head, closed one eye, and fired one shot after the other.

Tara instantly ducked as the sound of the gun shots startled her, forcing her to immediately dive and take cover under the nearby kitchen table. Looking over, she saw Jessica, who was still aiming and firing her weapon toward the opened basement door. She suddenly heard the sound of someone falling down the basement steps.

"Who was that?!! What was that?!!" Tara screamed as she looked towards the opened basement door.

"I don't know." Jessica replied as she raced over to shut the door and began barricading it. "Whoever it is, I'm sure there's more of them outside."

"What are we going to do?" asked Tara with a frightened look on her face. Jessica didn't answer immediately as she headed over to the back door to barricade it. "We're going upstairs." she finally responded, as she grabbed Tara's hand as they two sprinted towards the steps.

Jessica peeped through the front door to get a look outside on the way up the stairs. It was just dark enough out to not be able to see that far out into the front yard. As they walked past the front room windows, the sound of broken glass being stepped on could be heard coming from the kitchen. Jessica had Tara by her hand, pulled her up the stairs, and into one of the bedrooms at the end *of the hall quickly shutting and locking the door behind them.*

"What are we going to do?" Tara asked again this time with tears falling down her face.
Jessica grabbed Tara's face and wiped her tears.

"I need you to stay here. I promised you I won't let anything happen to you. But you're going to have to trust me and do as I say. Do you understand me?"

Tara quickly nodded her head. Jessica looked around the room franticly. It was hard for Tara to figure out what she was looking for exactly.

"What can I do? Let me help you." Tara uttered as she grabbed Jessica's hand.

"Think Jessica," Jessica whispered forcefully as she continued looking around the room. She finally planted her eyes on the closet door. She immediately made her way towards the closet and opened the door. Reaching into the closet she retrieved a pump action Remington 870 shotgun that belong to her father. She blew the dust off the weapon then immediately grabbed a box of shells from the top of the closet and stuffed two hand full of shells into her pockets. Placing the shotgun strap around her body she then checked her semi-automatic weapon. Jessica pointed towards the phone.

"Pick that phone up and dial 911."

Racing over to the phone Tara picked it up and begin dialing 911, she listened for a moment as her face begin to frown.

"I don't hear anything." Tara said.

"The lines....." Jessica replied, "Shit. Whatever you do, don't take that vest off." She instructed Tara as she made her way toward the door. Tara quickly sprinted over to Jessica and stopped her before she left the room.

"No," she said as she began taking off the vest. "You take this vest and wear it; you have to protect my brother or sister now."

"Tara, put the vest back on!"

"No! Tara cried, "Take it, PLEEEEEASE!! Take it! Do it for me. "

Jessica focused in on Tara's eyes and saw something that brought tears to her eyes. It touched her in a way that she knew she'd never be able to explain or understand. The honest sincerity she saw radiating off Tara's face was undeniable and unmistakable. It was something worth fighting for, something worth cherishing.

Nodding her head, Jessica grabbed Tara and hugged her.

"I love you." she whispered into Tara's ear.

Jessica took the vest out of Tara's hands and secured it on herself.

"I need you to stay here and don't come out until I come get you, do you understand?"

Tara quickly nodded her head. Jessica quickly exited the room.

Jessica, in a crouching position, pushed down the hallway, one foot in front of the other, shotgun up at eye aiming levels, finger on the trigger—ready to fire. She heard footsteps downstairs as she quietly and gingerly pressed her shoulder up against the wall, and slowly made her way towards the top of the stairs. She stopped to see if the footsteps could still be heard. Pressing her back up against the hallway wall, she remained as quiet as possible, listening for any continued movement downstairs. She steadied her breathing as she realized just how heavy her lungs were working. She heard what appeared to be whispering and footsteps but couldn't determine what direction they were coming from. The only way down was down the stairs.

To the left was the living room, to the right—a wall. Her options were limited. She knew if she went down, she would lose any tactical advantage and anyone in position below her would get the instant drop on her as she would be out of position to adequately defend herself, it was too risky. She knew in all likely hood that the intruders were *downstairs plotting and waiting. Waiting to see if she made a mistake.*

She understood they knew she had a weapon so they wouldn't take any risks. Looking down the hallway, Jessica noticed a chair covered in a sheet. She placed the shotgun around her upper body with the strap, tightened it, and retrieved her 9-millimeter. Sprinting towards the chair, Jessica snatched the chair, and quietly made her way to the top of the stairs and tossed the chair down the steps. The chair didn't quite reach the bottom of the steps before it was hit with gunfire from the left side of the steps. Jessica picked up the sound of two separated weapons firing—there were two gunmen.

With the gunfire directed toward the chair, Jessica lifted and aimed the 9-millimeter as she quickly and carefully made her way down the steps. She immediately noticed the two gunmen firing unmercifully in the chair's direction. She aimed her semi-automatic weapon in their direction. They immediately noticed her, but it was already too late as her distraction had worked. She now had the drop on them. She immediately began to let off shots from the 9-millimeter. Her bullets found their targets hitting the gunmen in the head and chest. The bullets caught them by surprised as their reflexes immediately caused them to fire their guns but ended up hitting one another in their immediate state of panic. Not wasting any time, Jessica entered the living room as she immediately holstered the 9-millimeter, raised the shotgun, with her finger on the trigger. Her father had taught her how to utilize the shotgun properly when she was twenty, prior to her attending the academy, so she would have a leg up, needless to say, it certainly helped as she ended up being the best marksman in her class. He taught her how to shoot with handguns since she was in high school, but only taught her how to shoot with the shot gun for the sake of her entering and graduating the academy.

She had no idea just how many gunmen there were, but footsteps still could be heard outside—she assumed the worst. She assumed that there was more than she could handle out there. She was afraid, but focused. She had seen plenty of field action before, but she had seen it with backup. She had no backup now, and she didn't want to die and leave Tara on her own. She promised Tara she would protect her, and that promise was truly pushing her at the moment, that and the fact that she was now with child.

Lights suddenly illuminated the front of the house. The lights sharply cut through the living room and lit the whole front area. Jessica had no doubts the lights were coming from some truck of some kind. The lights forced

Jessica to take cover beside one of her mother's tall china cabinets just so her shadow wouldn't be seen on the outside.

"*Agent Jessica Phillips!!!*"

The voice was loud and appeared to have a deep south American accent to it. With her back against the cabinet, her heart began to race. Whoever this was, knew her name and knew she was FBI, but who was it?

"Agent Jessica Phillips. No one here wants to hurt you. You've seemed to have taken out three of my men and I can't have any more of that. There doesn't have to be any more killing. I'm going to need you to put your guns down and come out here—both of you. We don't want to hurt you. Do not force our hand here, agent Phillips. You have five minutes to come out, or we're coming in."

*In Mexico, five miles outside of the city of Ciudad
Juárez, the team set up behind an abandoned warehouse,
sufficient enough cover to allow Cyprus to unleash a
miniature spy drone into the air. It took about six minutes
before the drone was relaying valuable intel from the area
back to the group.*

*"Ok, listen up," said Miller, "heat signature from the
drone confirmed that there are about five bodies in the
house. Obviously, no way to confirm the package is in
fact inside. The concrete wall around the property
appears to be about seven feet tall, but we'll get a
confirmation on that when we get closer."*

*"So, we're going hot with no confirmation of the
package?" asked Jason.*

Miller slowly nodded.

*"Like always, we'll tactfully utilize logic and our best
judgment. There's obviously something of importance in
that house, something worth protecting. There's not only a
consistent rotation of four armed guards, but there's two
SUVs that are patrolling the property as well. They've*

passed the house at least six times since we've had eyes up. Bradford, you're going to get close and ID the package, confirm the package, and pull back until it's clear to retrieve her. Once we've ID the package, Cyprus will take us dark. Drone has picked up what we believe to be a generator in the back that will almost certainly go live once we move." **Jason handed Miller a photo of Chasity as Miller immediately raised it high enough for the entire team to see.

"This is the package." Miller barked. "This is who we came to bring back home. Raymond, you and Ford will then move in, disable the generator, eliminate any threats and provide suppressive fire for the extraction team. Bradford and I will enter the premises and retrieve the package as Raymond and Ford will cover our six on our retreat. Agent Barrington, you and Cyprus will lay out suppressive fire from the front and cover the package extraction along with Raymond and Ford. We move fast and clean, and if it isn't the package or one of us, we eliminate it without hesitation."

Without delay, the group acknowledged Miller's plan. Miller inconspicuously gazed into Jason's eyes to gauge his reaction after hearing the plan. There was an ice cold look on Jason's face as he glared down at the Drone relay monitor. Miller knew Jason was not only as committed as his own team in getting this done, but he appeared to be intensely dialed in. He wasn't certain what was driving Jason to risk it all for a child not of his own, but after realizing the countless times over the decades in which he had done the same, he found himself understanding more than he needed to.

The five-mile ride into town was silent as everyone focused on what needed to be done, gathered their thoughts, and checked weapons and ammo. Riding in the back of the SUV immediately caused Jason to instantly reflect on that unfortunate night that changed his life nearly two years ago. It was a case of slight Deja vu for him as the quiet, somber ride took him back to that night.

The seven-minute ride was more than enough time for him to get lost in his own thoughts as the faces of Jessica and Tara flashed vividly throughout his mind. Every time he closed his eyes, he would see their smiles, hear their voices. He could even feel their embrace whenever he'd hugged them in the past. The more he thought about them, about what he was doing, about the past twenty-four hours, the more he began to feel as if everything seemed to be a huge cosmic puzzle that was slowly and gradually falling into place. Subconsciously, he was starting to put it together faster than it was actually being put together outside of his mind. The more he thought, the more the strange man's words weighed down on him.

The SUV pulled into the back of what looked to be a small convenient store. The property was further down the street, about two football fields' length away from their current location. Jason peered through the night vision binoculars as Bradford wasted no time covertly making his way towards the house. The rotation of patrol vehicles was very consistent, like clockwork, but Bradford was very good at his job. The cover of darkness aided him tremendously as he covertly made his way towards the property next door to the house. Bradford gazed through the scope of his silencer equipped MP5 with his thumb on the safety and his finger just below the trigger. He effortlessly made his way up on the top of the roof of the property next door to the property that held the package.

"In position now sir," Bradford whispered over the com,

"Getting eyes on now."

Jason gazed around the group and noticed that everyone seemed to be comfortable and relaxed, for the most part. He understood this is what they did and what they were used to, but he wasn't as calm and relaxed as they were. There was a lot going on within his mind and it was difficult in trying to keep it together while remaining focused on the important job right in front of him.

"I have confirmation of the package in the back bedroom sir." Bradford whispered over the com.

"Re-confirm package." Miller quickly replied.
There was a brief period of silence as Miller released his com, closed his eyes and sighed.

"The package is re-conformed sir. It's her."

"Copy!" Miller echoed into the com. "Bradford, wait for the signal from Cyprus then you and Ford move in and secure the package. Once you've secured the package, we'll hit them with a diversion, then lay out suppressive fire for you to retreat with the package."

"Copy." Bradford softly replied.
Jason gripped his MP5 tightly while waiting for Cyprus to dump the lights. He was seeing everything clearly. Chasity's life was on the line, so he would use that clarity to his advantage. Jason listened over the earpiece as Miller counted down from five to signal Cyprus.

"5................4...................3..................2....................1"

There was no hesitation on Cyprus's part as he immediately cut the lights. The team waited in position as the silence was deafening. The sounds of slight panic *could be heard from within the compound as there was probably a mad scramble to get the lights back on. Five minutes, which felt more like five hours to Jason, passed as there was still no communication from Bradford. Jason nervously gripped his weapon tightly as he kept his eyes closed. His mind reflected back to the property layout on the drone heat signature screen. It replayed the rotation of guards around the house, even the 15 seconds between the trucks that patrolled the house. His mind was putting it all together. As Jason began to fall deeper in thought, Bradford's voice could suddenly be heard over the radio com....*

"Package is secure, I repeat package is secure. Falling back to the rendezvous point."

Jason wasted no time as he dropped the night vision goggles over his eyes. He and Cyprus immediately crouched down, weapons aimed, one foot in front of the other and carefully push their way to the front of the property to lay down suppressive fire. The sound of the cartel gunmen in the dark, screaming orders to one another in a panic, kept Jason on his toes, head on a swivel as he peered around rapidly with his MP5 up at eye aiming level ready to eliminate any threats. Jason could hear the sound of silenced MP5 rifles, undoubtedly coming from the team, along with the return fire from the cartel, which wasn't muffled at all and made the party official.

Looking eastward, Jason spotted the two security trucks approaching the property at full speed. Not wasting anytime, Jason sprinted into the middle of the street as the trucks quickly headed towards him. Dropping to one knee, Jason aimed the MP5 and immediately opened fire on the front of the first truck. Multiple shots hit the windshield and the front grill of the truck, causing it to veer wildly off the road and headfirst into a tree. Jason dumped a few more shots into the truck just to be safe as the sound of another truck could be heard behind him.

The second truck made its way in his direction as Jason quickly stood up turned, focused his aim towards the truck and begin letting off more shots. The gunmen on the back of the truck quickly attempted to return fire, but Jason's shots had already done their damage as the truck crashed into a nearby grocery store. Everything seemed to be moving in slow motion as Jason began to feel himself quickly getting locked into a zone. It was as if he wasn't missing anything and was seeing everything, everywhere. His mind truly was working it out for him.

He turned and saw Cyprus firing on another vehicle approaching from the opposite direction. Jason quickly turned around as two armed men that jumped from the vehicle begin approaching his direction while firing automatic weapons. Jason immediately dove and took cover behind a tree that was about ten feet to his right as Cyprus took cover behind another tree on the opposite side of the street. Looking over to Cyprus, he saw him checking his ammo as the gun fire was heavy in their direction. Through the gunfire, Jason heard Raymond's voice over the com. Jason peered around the tree and saw about three gunmen headed in their direction firing automatic weapons. The gunfire got louder as they got closer. Jason peeked from behind the tree and spotted Bradford and Ford firing on the men, laying them out with minimal effort. Jason and Cyprus immediately sprinted in their direction to join them. Jason glanced over as Bradford motioned towards Jason, instructing him and Cyprus to fall back while they lay down suppressive fire on the impending threat. Jason nodded in compliance.

Jason stood up and began firing in the direction of the approaching gunmen as he quickly retreated toward the SUV parked around the corner. He motioned for Cyprus to do that same. His aim was immaculate and deadly as his MP5 overpowered their automatic weapons.

The darkness of the night made excellent cover for them, but the sun was slowly starting to rise. The sounds of police sirens could be heard in the faint distance as

Jason and Cyprus made their way towards the truck. Still no sign of Miller, Bradford, Ford, or the package, but they continued to retreat towards the truck as Cyprus covered their six with effective suppressive fire. Miller's voice over the radio com was a bit muffled over the loud gunfire. Jason and Cyprus gazed at one another in confusion as they couldn't really make out what Miller was trying to communicate.

"...... Bradford.......... follow him........."
Jason hit his radio com to respond to Miller.

"Didn't get that Miller, repeat that, I do not copy. I repeat, I do NOT copy"

There was silence for a few seconds, but Miller eventually responded.

"I repeat—Bradford has the package in tow and was separated from us, he is in a blue pickup truck with the package and headed west toward the mountains with heavy threat on his six, follow him, do you copy?!!"

Jason looked around at Cyprus who had a look of confusion on his face.

"We got to move!" Jason barked, as he grabbed his radio com to respond to Miller. "Copy, on our way." Cyprus and Jason hopped into the SUV and begin heading west towards Bradford's reported location. Miller and Raymond sprinted from behind the house ducking a

barrage of gunfire but managed to hop onto the sides of the SUV as Jason floored it while Raymond continued laying down the suppressive fire to clear their rear. The impending sunrise was clear and was quickly making its way up as they sped westward.

Bradford held on to Chasity as she couldn't stop crying. He raced franticly down the road in the truck as his right arm ached in severe pain from the bullet he took. He grimaced in pain as he gripped the steering wheel with his left hand. They were doing speeds upwards of seventy miles per hour headed down a dark wooded road. The bullets coming from the car behind were missing him. They struggled in trying to shoot and chase after him, simultaneously. The closer they got to him, the more the bullets started to hit the back of the truck, and the more the bullets hit, the louder Chasity cried.

"It's ok baby, it's ok."
Bradford cried out to her as he instinctively reached out to comfort her while he steered. He pulled his injured arm back and cried out in pain. He had her strapped and

secured in the seat, but that didn't stop her from being extremely frightened. The truck sped over a hill as Bradford noticed they were rapidly approaching what appeared to be a small neighborhood. Doing almost seventy-five miles per hours at this point, Bradford turned around to gauge just how close they were on his tail. Their lights could be seen in the close distance, he figured they were right on top of him.

Turning his attention back to the road, Bradford attempted to quickly maneuver the truck, but it was too late as the truck crashed headfirst into a steel dumpster on the side of the road, bringing the truck to an immediate halt. Bradford yelled out in pain as the whiplash hit him. The car behind Bradford eventually caught up to him as they immediately noticed his truck incapacitated by the steel dumpster. Chasity's cries could be he heard from inside the truck. The gunmen didn't waste any time hopping out of their vehicle while maintaining a bit of safe distance. Without knowing the status of the threat from inside the truck, they approached it, cautiously. The group begin cocking their automatic rifles and reloading them as they gingerly made their way closer to the disabled vehicle as the child cries could be heard coming from inside.

"Llevarlo hacia abajo!!" one of the gunmen yelled out.
The gunfire that followed was loud and overwhelming as it
immediately drowned out Chasity's crying. After about six
seconds of uninterrupted and heavy gunfire, the signal was
given to cease fire from one of the gunmen. The back of
the truck was riddle with bullets—the tires were ripped to
shreds as three of the shredded tires caused the truck to
drop to its rims.

Chasity's cries were no longer heard coming from the
truck. Slowly and hesitantly approaching the truck, one of
the gunmen kept his assault rifle up, ready to continue
firing at the sign of any life as he made his way closer.
They already had orders to eliminate the girl as there was
no need to hold her hostage anymore at this point. One of
the cartel gunmen cautiously made his way towards the
passenger side of the truck. Reaching the door, he aimed
his gun at the door and slowly opened it with one hand.
BANG!!!!"
The shot was loud and sudden as the bullet from
Bradford's semi-automatic weapon entered the front of the
gunman's frontal lobe and exited the back as he
immediately dropped to the ground.
"DISPARAR!!!"
The second gunmen walked rapidly towards the truck
while opening fire. They didn't get a chance to get many

shots off as Jason, Miller and the team sped over the hill in the SUV opening fire on the gunmen who had surrounded Bradford and Chasity. The men immediately scattered and attempted to take cover as the team rapidly came down on top of their position. Jason slammed on the brakes, but the team had already cleared the SUV before it came to a complete stop, wasting no time in opening fire on the gunmen near Bradford's truck. Jason exited the vehicle and dropped to his knee. He aimed the MP5 and dropped the first gunmen he saw near Raymond's truck. The team continued to open fire on the men as the gunmen ran for cover. Carefully making his way towards Raymond's location, Jason didn't see any signs of life coming from the truck. The sounds of gunfire echoed around him as the team went after the gunmen, yet Jason could only focus on the truck. It was as if the world outside of what he was focusing on at that moment didn't exist.

Agent Terrell's distraught face back in the hospital, popped into his head as he made his way closer to the vehicle. He noticed the truck riddled with bullets and knew they were dead. As he approached the truck, agent Terrell's face, full of pain, and inconsolable horror, made it difficult to breathe as he inched closer to the vehicle. Jason cautiously and slowly made his way to the truck and peaked inside, no movement. Jason heard Miller's voice over the com.

"Barrington, threat has been eliminated, status on Bradford and the package?"

"Not sure, but it doesn't look good." Jason quickly replied into his COM.

Jason opened the door but was quickly forced to duck to the side as Bradford let off a round towards his head.

"BRADFORD, IT'S ME GOD DAMMIT! It's Jason!!!"

Jason peeked back into the vehicle, but Bradford didn't respond as he had dropped the gun and was lying face down, blood was everywhere.

"Bradford? You with me?" barked Jason as he moved closer and closer toward the inside of the truck's cab. There was no answer.

From where he was standing, Jason could see that Bradford had taken a lot of "damage," primarily his back as the back of his Kevlar vest was riddled with bullets and quite a few managed to make it through the vest. Jason stared in disbelief and shock as Bradford's lifeless body lay slumped over the seat, his back towards the seat and his front facing the front of the truck.

The image was hard for Jason to accept, but he needed to know if Chasity was ok. Jason slowly extended his hand into the cab but was immediately startled as a small hand appeared from under Bradford's lifeless body. Jason grabbed the hand as Chasity let out a loud cry that startled Jason once more. He carefully pulled her from under Bradford, picked her up into his arms and immediately examined her body. Miraculously, there wasn't a single bullet hole or scratch on her as Bradford appeared to have taken it all, everything. It was now clear that Bradford's last action, was to protect this girl, a girl he didn't even know—a sacrifice. Jason peered deep into Chasity's eyes but was immediately lost within them. The only thing that he could think about were the words shared with him, by the strange man in the interrogation room about sacrifice. It was all so emotionally overwhelming as he fought back the tears. The team quickly sprinted over to regroup with Jason.

"Is he there?" asked Ford. Jason slowly nodded while holding onto Chasity.
He embraced the small child like she was his own.

"We need to make our exit ASAP." Miller uttered over the com. "Where's Bradford?"

Jason glanced at Ford as he closed his eyes and touched his radio com to speak with Miller.

"Bradford is gone, sir." There was a silence from Miller that was as deafening as anything he'd ever heard.

"Get him," Miller finally ordered. "We're bringing him home. Cyprus and I are back at the truck, we need to leave. I'm expecting reinforcements very soon."

Raymond grabbed Bradford's lifeless body as the team headed back to the truck. As Bradford's lifeless body hung over Raymond's shoulder, Jason stared at it and began thinking on "sacrifice" again. He had never seen it firsthand like this before, but this was it. This was the ultimate sacrifice. Jason found himself becoming emotional, overwhelmed with emotions as Chasity cries continued.

"Shhh," Jason softly instructed, as he continued to genuinely embrace her.

"It's ok baby. It's going to be ok."
He gently wiped the tears from her face and held her tight. He closed his eyes as her cries began to settle down, and she eventually drifted off to sleep. He rested his head on her head as he carefully embraced her. The tears began to slowly fall from his eyes as he and the team made their way back to the truck. As he made his way towards the truck, Chasity slowly raised her head, looked him in his eyes, no longer crying. She smiled and rested her head back on his shoulder. The Mexican police sirens could be heard in the distance. Miller's voice quickly snapped Jason out of his emotional state of daydream.

"The bird will rendezvous with us about ten clicks west of here. Let's move!!"

Once inside the vehicle, Bradford's lifeless body was placed in the back and covered with a sheet as the team sped off to the west, over the hills, as the SUV disappeared over the hill towards the morning sunrise and ultimately, back towards home.

"I heard about your family," Ford calmly whispered through constant head nods. "I'm sorry about that."
Jason nodded in return

"It's not over for them just yet." Jason replied as he gazed out towards the sunrise.

"Can I ask you something?"

"Sure."

"Why do this? With all you've been through over the years. With all that you've lost, why do this? Why risk everything for someone that isn't your family? Why are you here and not out looking for your family?"

Jason started to speak but pulled back. The words were there but they were suddenly hiding behind a cloud of emotions that was buried deep within. He sighed and shook his head and he glared deep into Ford's eyes and returned his gaze out onto the sunrise.

"I would want someone to do the same for me. For my family. I needed that. When I needed it, I didn't' have it so the change I search for on this planet, It starts here."

Jason pointed towards his heart as Ford slowly nodded.

"That's not how the world works, brother. But I dig it. I respect it."

Jason sighed again as he shook his head. His eyes fixated on the distance sunrise, his arms tightly embracing Chasity. There was silence. Not even the sound of the vehicle could break past the wall of emotions that now fortified his immediate conscious. He finally peeled his eyes away from the sunrise and back into Ford's eyes which was still fixated on him.

"What would you do?" asked Jason.
Ford immediately snickered and calmly nodded his head. He starts to answer but pulls back and gazes at Chasity. Closing his eyes, he sighed and slowly shook his head as clearly his mind was cooking up his thoughts and preparing them to be served. He gazed up at Jason once more and nods, this time more emphatically as a tear fell down his face.

"Yeah." he whispered calmly as he nodded his head. Fighting through his emotions, Ford continued to nod and stare into Jason eyes.

"Yeah." he whispered once again.

Jason nodded in return as he knew Ford finally saw everything in a way that illuminated Jason's position more clearly. Jason turned and glared aimlessly out onto the rapidly rising sunrise. He had no idea what was next or, how he'd see his family safely to the other side of this. He struggled emotionally, to see past this moment but in this moment, Jessica's face immediately shifted to the forefront of his mind. It was now the only thing his mind was centered on. He calmly gazed down at Chasity as she rested peacefully against his Kevlar. Wherever they were, he knew Jessica would keep them safe until he made his way back to them or they back to him.

Jason's Story—Chapter Nine—Continue

Her back pressed firmly against the antique China cabinet; Jessica firmly gripped the shotgun. Sweat made its way down from her forehead and into her eyes. She had to stop herself from trembling so intensely. She hadn't realized just how hard she was shaking. She peered into the kitchen and immediately noticed someone, a figure walking outside on the back patio as their shadow could be seen through the blinds. Once again, she placed the shotgun around the body with the strap and tightened it as she retrieved her 9-millimeter. She was incredibly nervous. She hadn't seen this kind of action in about four years. Her breathing had become more intense. Slowly, she circled around to get a drop on the shadowy figure outside on the back patio. Her back still against the window adjacent to the patio door, she slowly and carefully crept towards the backdoor, waiting to see or hear any footsteps. The voice in front of the house, whomever it was, still called out to her. She had already tuned them out. She peeked out of the window to see if the shadowy figure on the back porch was still back there. They weren't. She wasn't exactly certain where they had disappeared to, but they were nowhere to be found.

With her back still pressed against the kitchen wall closest to the patio, Jessica closed her eyes. She had no idea how she would get through this. She struggled to see past what she was up against. Jason's face immediately came to the fore front of her mind. She couldn't help but to think of his wellbeing at this point, even though she was the one currently under inescapable duress.

She closed her eyes and slowed her breathing. The noise that derived from outside didn't seem to know how to break through the fortified wall she was suddenly constructing around all that equated to fear deep within her.

Inhale. Exhale. Inhale. Exhale.

Eyes still tightly shut as she gripped the 9-millimeter tighter. There was quite a bit that she didn't know about all that was happening but what she did know, was that the stakes were even higher now.

She carefully placed her hand on her stomach as tears fell. So much duress. So much stress. It wasn't good. She needed to end it someway, somehow.

Inhale. Exhale. Inhale. Exhale.

She knew what to do. She was trained for this. Whatever it was she believed she needed, she knew it already resided deep within her. She just needed to unearth it. She slowly opened her eyes and noticed more than one figure on the back patio crouched under the window as to not be detected but this was her home. She knew the creaks and cranks on the aged, wooded deck. She knew exactly where they were stepping. Too bad for them.

She quickly aimed the Glock at one of the figures creeping on the back porch and fired.

To be Continued